ALSO BY ALEXIS HALL

LONDON CALLING
Boyfriend Material

SPIRES
Glitterland

HUSBAND MATERIAL

ALEXIS HALL

sourcebooks
casablanca

Published by Sourcebooks Casablanca, an imprint of Sourcebooks
P.O. Box 4410, Naperville, Illinois 60567-4410
(630) 961-3900
sourcebooks.com

Cataloging-in-Publication Data is on file with the Library of Congress.

Printed and bound in the United States of America.
LSC 10 9 8 7 6 5

To Mary
Thank you for believing in these books

PART ONE

BRIDGET DAWN WELLES & THOMAS BALLANTYNE
CHAPEL OF ST. JUDE, KENTISH TOWN
22ND OF MAY

CHAPTER 1

I'VE NEVER SEEN THE POINT of hen parties. Though given my experiences of garden parties, dinner parties, and fancy dress parties, it might be that I just don't like parties in general. Which, in retrospect, might explain why I spent so much of my party-boy years being miserable and hating myself. Personal growth. I was nailing it.

I was also nailing Bridge's hen do. Or rather her non-gender-specific bird do, because she was never going to want her big prewedding bash to exclude half her friends. Also, since she'd made me her maid of honour, it would have meant excluding myself, which would have been weird. Even if, on some level, I might secretly have preferred an evening at home with my amazing barrister boyfriend.

My amazing barrister boyfriend who still felt like an amazing barrister boyfriend after two whole years.

My amazing barrister boyfriend who—on account of the amazing barrister part rather than the boyfriend part—was currently running late.

So there I was in the roped-off VIP area of an affordably swanky cocktail bar wearing a crocheted vulva hat. A bespoke crocheted vulva hat I'd commissioned from one of Bridge's friends when I realised that bachelorette-party genital merch skewed strongly in the direction of all penis all the time. And, obviously,

I could have just not had genitalia-themed decor at all, but then it wouldn't have been a proper non-gender-specific bird do and that would have made Bridge sad. And making Bridge sad was something I wanted to avoid both in my capacity as maid of honour and in my capacity as her, y'know, friend.

James Royce-Royce plucked a dong-shaped lolly from the dong-shaped lolly jar. It was the first time I'd seen him, or his husband James Royce-Royce, without their newly adopted son in months. Their newly adopted son who they had, inevitably, named James. Although to avoid confusion, they just called him Baby J. "I must say, Luc," he said. "I'm a little offended that you went with commercially produced phallic sweeties rather than asking for my contribution."

Bernadette May, a relatively famous cookery book writer who Bridge had gone through so many work-related disasters with that they'd become friends out of sheer necessity, smouldered dismissively from across the table. She was one of those people who could smoulder at anything—and usually did. "That's because your contribution would probably be a real horse's penis rolled in saffron and finished with gold leaf."

"Whereas yours," retorted James Royce-Royce, "would be a Victoria sponge topped with marzipan willies."

"Which is why"—I pulled my vulva more tightly over my head—"I asked neither of you. This is our night to celebrate Bridget, not for you two to have a schlong-themed cook-off."

Bridge was sitting beside me, wearing a penis hat and, like all of the guests, a T-shirt that, owing to a miscommunication on the phone with the printers, read *Bridge's Bitches No Oliver I Think It's Fine We're Using It in the Reclaimed Sense and Anyway It's Too Late to Change.*

"Actually," she said, "I think a schlong-themed cook-off would have been pretty cool."

"Nongendered-genitalia-themed cook-off," said Priya. "I'm not going home to my girlfriends and telling them that I went to a phallocentric baking event."

Girlfriends, plural, was a new-enough development in Priya's life that it had messed up Bridge's seating plan. She and Theresa were still making it work, but an experimental threesome over Christmas had turned into a much less experimental set of regular hookups, which had turned into a solid official relationship just as I was helping Bridge address the invitations.

"You know," I told her, "Theresa and Andi would both have been super welcome. I made spare T-shirts for them and everything."

Priya gave a dismissive shrug. "Yeah, but the truly great thing about being in a throuple is that your partners can keep each other company instead of having to come to shit like this where they have to pretend to like your arsehole friends."

I winced. "Can we remember that not everybody here knows everybody else, so calling people arseholes might come across the wrong way?"

"It's fine." That was Jennifer, who was sitting in her husband's lap sipping a cocktail through a perfectly ordinary straw, thank you very much. "Brian talks like that all the time."

"Then again," said Peter from underneath her, "Brian is kind of an arsehole himself."

Bridget spread her arms wide in an effort to encompass the entire group. "How about we accept that I love you arseholes and leave it at that."

"Thinking about it"—James Royce-Royce was still inspecting his untouched phallic lolly—"we should probably have had arsehole-themed decorations as well."

I glowered at him. "How about we definitely shouldn't. My search history is incriminating enough as it is."

"Is it, though?" Priya was giving me an I-think-not look. "You and Oliver practically live together. I bet your search history is nothing but 'how to make vegan jam' and 'scenic walks near Clerkenwell.'"

Scarily, non-gender-specific bird do aside, that was pretty accurate. "You can't possibly know that."

"Last week," said Priya in a devastating monotone, "you emailed me to ask my opinion on a table lamp."

As one, the guests gasped.

"Luc," cried James Royce-Royce. "No. Not a table lamp."

"Shut up," I responded very maturely.

Priya nodded gravely. "Yeah, he and Oliver are getting into raw, hard-core table lamping."

"Shut up," I responded very maturely.

"They're at it," she went on, "nearly every weekend. In every room. On every table."

"It was one table." I waved my hands despairingly. "One time."

Peering archly over his martini glass, James Royce-Royce raised an eyebrow. "That's how it starts. But before you know it, you'll be getting into the really kinky stuff like uplighters."

"No uplighters!" I yelled. Though Oliver had suggested that one would do wonders for the living area in my flat.

"I do hope," said Peter, "that you're at least using surge protection."

I stood in a way that I hoped was decisive, not huffy. "I hate you all. Does anyone want another drink?"

Thankfully, most tails were already cocked, but a couple of Bridge's work friends called for a round of cosmos. Cosmoi? On the way to the bar, I checked my phone to see if my amazing barrister boyfriend was actually going to show up.

I'm so sorry, he'd texted. Snowed under at work. I'll be with you as soon as possible.

I'm so sorry, he'd texted again. I can't get away quite yet.

I'm so sorry, he'd texted again again. I'll be leaving in ten minutes.

And then: Please don't worry. Everything is fine and I'm definitely going to be on my way soon.

Then: I'm sure you've thrown a wonderful party.

Then: I realise this is substandard boyfriending. I'll make it up to you and to Bridget somehow.

Then: Leaving now. With you in twenty minutes.

Then: Traffic worse than expected. Sorry.

This was so typically Oliver. I was mildly annoyed that he wasn't here. But his panicked texting was also weirdly endearing and I was in love with him. So fuck.

I was just in the middle of composing a playfully frustrated yet reassuring reply when I walked straight into the back of a solid wall of couple.

"Shit." My thumb slipped, and I accidentally sent Oliver a string of nonsense. "Sorry. I wasn't—"

And then my fucking ex turned round. The worst part about it was that for a tiny fraction of a second, before my head started to spin and my throat started to fill with imaginary frogs, I was almost pleased to see him. Because we'd been together for five years, and the bit of my brain that had got used to being in love with him hadn't quite caught up with the whole he's-a-traitorous-fuckface angle.

"Oh my God," said the man who I'd once thought ruined my life. "Luc."

"Miles," I yelped. "It's been ages." *Ages since you sold the intimate details of our relationship to a tabloid for fifty grand.* But I smiled anyway because he didn't deserve my emotional authenticity.

He, on the other hand, smiled like he was genuinely happy we'd run into each other. He'd always had a knockout smile, and his new immaculately groomed beard only made it knockoutier. *Prick, prick, total prick.* "Hasn't it?" He turned to the implausibly perfect-looking young man by his side, a vision in glitter and rainbows. "JoJo this is Luc, Luc this is JoJo."

"Hi." JoJo stood on tiptoes to kiss me on both cheeks. "So how do you know Miles?"

Had he not even mentioned me? Then again, how would you? *By the way, darling, you should know that my last relationship ended because I totally fucked the guy over?* "Oh, we...we used to date."

Miles had circled around and was standing very close to me now. And he'd put a hand on the small of my back in a way that was one part friendly, one part possessive. "Crazy times, right, Luc? And we've got so much catching up to do. Do you want to join us for a drink?"

Even if I hadn't needed to get back to Bridge's party, that would have ranked pretty low on my things-I-want-to-do list, somewhere between getting my eyebrows burned off with a chef's blowtorch and spending a weekend in a bath full of dead squid. "I'd love to," I said, "but I'm actually really busy right now. Bridge is getting married and she's made me her maid of honour and my boyfriend is going to show up any minute—" The moment I mentioned Oliver, I realised how pathetic I sounded. I might as well have come straight out and added, *But you wouldn't know him because he goes to a different school.*

"Oh, you're still friends with Bridge?" said Miles. "Cool. I know you two always had that—y'know—that nineties gay-best-friend thing going on."

Was he serious? Was he *fucking* serious? "I'm not sure I'd put it quite..."

"And on the subject of weddings"—JoJo was beaming like a cartoon sun—"can I tell him?"

Miles kissed his boyfriend on the top of his tiny head. "I think you're going to have to now."

"We're getting married!"

I looked down at JoJo's outstretched hand, and sure enough, there was a sparkling band of diamonds, chosen with way more taste than I would ever have had and, honestly, way more taste than I would have expected Miles to have. Maybe he'd bought it with the money he got for selling me out. "Oh," I said, and then, realising that he was probably expecting a slightly bigger reaction, I added, "Congratulations."

For a second nobody said anything, but the awkwardness of the moment very much spoke for itself. Because how was I supposed to react to this? Here was Miles, smiling that shoe-salesman smile at me, flaunting his adorable fiancé like he was one of those puppies you keep in a designer handbag and acting like he hadn't completely fucking betrayed me.

"Anyway," I continued, "I should. I might. Yeah."

I was just disentangling myself when the music changed, and "Tartarus" came on.

"Tartarus." The breakout single from Jon Fleming's multi-platinum album *Pendulum of the World*. As part of the hype for the second season of *The Whole Package*, my dad had given this series of powerful, heartfelt interviews about how his struggle with cancer had made him confront his own mortality and realise what really mattered in life. Somehow the fact that he'd never had cancer in the first place—that nobody had even told him he had cancer or given him any reason to suspect he might have cancer—had got lost in the noise, and he'd become this poster child for survivors everywhere. He was even doing a public awareness campaign for the NHS.

Anyway. *Pendulum of the World* was his album about how fucking wise and brilliant he was now he was a selfish old prick instead of a selfish young prick, and "Tartarus" was this navel-gazing dirge about staring into the abyss and coming back stronger that had won the bastard a Grammy and could entirely fuck off. Especially because the last thing I needed just when I'd had an unexpected run-in with the narcissistic ex who'd sold me out for short-term gain was to be reminded of my narcissistic dad who'd sold me out for short-term gain.

In an effort to distract myself, I looked down at my phone. My text to Oliver had somehow autocorrected from It's okay, see you soon to Its okay see your document, which had prompted a series of replies reading:

> What document?
> Was that text meant for me or somebody else?
> Lucien, is something wrong?
> I'll be there as soon as I can. If something is wrong, tell me.
> I'm sorry I took so long.

And I should probably have replied, but I couldn't quite face it. Fate or the universe or whatever had decided to rub my clearly happy and successful piece-of-shit ex and my clearly happy and successful piece-of-shit dad in my face within thirty seconds of each other. And while I was also *technically* clearly happy and successful, it felt a whole lot less clear with my amazing barrister boyfriend sitting in traffic while I was being introduced to fabulous, perfect look-how-engaged-and-beautiful-I-am JoJo and his Technicolor waistcoats and his sparkly ring.

Especially since, as I suddenly remembered, I was still wearing a crocheted vulva on my head.

Bridget's friends were relying on me for a cosmo top-up, but right then my maid-of-honour duties seemed less important than my get-the-hell-out-of-there duties. The bar was too loud and too hot, and I needed some air. So I tucked my phone into my jeans and slunk off to sit outside and do some good old-fashioned feeling sorry for myself.

Except, as it turned out, even that was easier said than done because we were in fucking London, so sitting outside would have meant plonking my arse down on a pavement that approximately twenty-seven million people were trying to walk along at the same time, all desperately hurrying from wherever they had been to wherever they were going and not inclined to give the benefit of the doubt to someone getting in their way.

Not being quite self-loathing enough to let a whole city trample over me, I went to look for somewhere I could sit down and, because of the previously mentioned London issue, failed to find anywhere that wasn't already occupied and wound up wandering into a badly lit park that, in a better state of mind, I'd have avoided for fear of being murdered and/or arrested.

And that was the point when I realised that my best friend had made me maid of honour for the wedding she'd been dreaming about since she was five, and I'd just bailed on her non-gender-specific bird do.

Fuck.

Fuckity, fuckity, fuck.

In a way it was comforting. People always worry that being in a relationship will change them, so it was good to know that being with Oliver hadn't completely destroyed my ability to be a shitty friend. And a shitty boyfriend. And an all-around shitty person.

Fuck.

At last I found an empty bench and collapsed onto it like a sack of deeply shitty potatoes—the kind that have been left in the kitchen too long and are getting weird knobbly things growing out of them. Because that was me, wasn't it? I was a knobbly-sprouting potato of a person. I'd been given the perfectly simple job of getting a bunch of people who liked each other to have a nice time in a bar full of fruity drinks and penis nibbles, and I'd managed to fuck even that up.

I checked my phone again.

Where are you?

Fuck. I'd fucked that up too.

WHERE RU ??!!?? RUOK???!

That wasn't Oliver, that was Bridge. Which meant she'd noticed I was gone. Which meant I was making her special night— well, I suppose her actual special night was the wedding night, but her slightly less special night—all about me.

I pulled off my crocheted vulva hat and stared at it, and it stared back accusingly like a sexual Eye of Sauron.

Fuck.

I was the worst maid of honour ever.

Fuck.

I was a bad friend and a bad boyfriend, and the reason people kept screwing me over and abandoning me was because I sucked and deserved it.

Fuck.

"Is this seat taken?"

Turning around, I saw Oliver standing behind me. He looked a funny mix of composed and dishevelled, his tie loose around his neck and his formal shirt unbuttoned to reveal his *Bridge's Bitches No Oliver I Think It's Fine We're Using It in the Reclaimed Sense and Anyway It's Too Late to Change* T-shirt beneath. He looked more worried than angry.

"How did you find me?" I asked.

"Bridget said that you'd disappeared, so I asked around to see if anybody had seen a tall man with a vagina on his head running away from a cocktail bar."

"Vulva," I said.

"Pardon?"

"The vagina is internal—the external part is the vulva."

Oliver gave me his warmest, reassuringest smile. "Either way it was a distinctive enough look that you weren't hard to find." He came around the bench, sat down next to me, and put his arm around my shoulders. I leaned in to him without even thinking about it. "Bridget told me she saw Miles. She thought that might have been why you left."

I nodded. "They were playing my dad's song too."

Oliver gave me a little squeeze. "That sounds like quite the perfect storm. I'm sorry I wasn't there."

"So was I. Fuck, sorry, I mean... I mean it would have been great if you were there. I don't mean... I know you had to work."

"I know what you mean."

"It just would have been great to be able to say 'Hi, Miles, fuck you, my life is great.'"

Oliver gave a sort of half laugh. "You could still have said it."

"Yeah, but I'd have had no proof."

"*You're* proof."

One of these days I was going to stop being surprised when Oliver said exactly the right thing. But this wasn't the day. "For fuck's sake, Oliver. Stop being so...so...completely great."

And for a while we just sat there, and I let myself feel safe and held and loved, and he took my hand and didn't say anything because he didn't need to.

"Also," I said, because I'd decided that feeling nice was overrated and I wanted to ruin the moment, "his fiancé is, like, twelve."

"I assume not literally?"

"No, but he's…like…this tiny little pretty boy called *JoJo*. I mean who the hell is called *JoJo*?"

"I assume that's rhetorical?"

"I'll tell you who's called JoJo," I went on. "A prick, that's who."

Oliver was still there and still, despite my decision to insult an innocent stranger, not judging me. "Perhaps. Although personally I think the man who sold you out and made you afraid to ever trust anybody again is a bigger prick."

"Oh yeah. He's a huge prick. Which is ironic because his actual prick is quite tiny."

"Is that true?" Oliver gave me another smile. "Or are you just trying to make me feel special?"

"You know, I can't remember. But he *deserves* to have a tiny prick. And if you could tell all your friends he has a tiny prick, that would be fantastic, thanks."

That made Oliver laugh. "For you, Lucien, anything."

So I kind of had to kiss him.

And then I kind of had to kiss him again. Y'know, just in case.

And then it felt…it felt okay. Because the rest of the world didn't matter. I mean it did because I had, like, friends and a job and things I actually cared about. But *Miles* didn't matter, and JoJo *certainly* didn't matter. "I think…" I said. "I think I can go back now."

So we got up, I put my vulva hat back on my head, and I let Oliver Blackwood—my amazing barrister boyfriend—escort me back to my best friend's non-gender-specific bird party. And I knew, deep in my heart, that everything was going to be fine.

After all, it wasn't like I was ever going to see Miles again.

CHAPTER 2

"OKAY," I TOLD ALEX TWADDLE. I was seriously running low on jokes, but the ritual was so much part of my life now that I wasn't about to give up on it. "Let's try this one. There's a man who works on a bus selling tickets, and he loves his job, but one day he loses his temper with a passenger and throws them off the bus and they fall under a car and die."

"I say"—Alex looked outraged—"that's not on at all. Especially not for a bus conductor."

"No," I agreed, "it's very poor behaviour and, spoiler, you should remember that because it might be relevant later."

"Good to know." For a moment, Alex looked contemplative. "I say, that might help with your jokes in general. Give a chap a bit of a pointer on what a chap's supposed to be paying attention to."

"Duly noted. Anyway, he gets sent to court for throwing this passenger under a car."

Alex nodded. "For being a bad conductor, you mean?"

The Alex-joke-foreboding was beginning to rise up. "Yes, I suppose so. Although I think they'd probably just have called it murder. Anyway, the judge sentences him to the electric chair."

"I say, how ironic."

Abandon joke. Abandon joke now. "Ironic in what way?"

"Well, you know, chap's a bad conductor, gets sentenced to

the electric chair. I say, it'd be rather droll if he was *such* a bad conductor that the chair didn't work, wouldn't it? Be sort of like a play on words."

"Yes." I was trapped. Trapped in an absurdist prison of meta-humour with a posh nitwit who was secretly a genius that delighted in tormenting me. "Yes, that *would* be droll. So anyway, they send him to the...umm...to the electric chair and it...um...it doesn't work."

Alex grinned. "Ah, because he's a bad conductor, you mean?"

"Yes."

"Oh. Actually, old boy, wasn't quite as droll as I'd anticipated. Not in practice."

There should have been some kind of joke-related emergency service you could call to rescue you in situations like this. "Sorry."

"Not your fault. Although in retrospect I think knowing the twist in advance made it less comical."

"You don't say?"

Alex nodded. "Yes, you see the essence of humour is surprise. So if you want to get better at this joke-telling lark, you might want to keep your cards a little closer to your chest."

"Thanks. I'll bear that in mind." Okay, this was it, I was nearly—

"Tell you what, I'll show you how it's done."

There was no possible way this could end well.

"I say, Rhys." Alex stuck his head into the social media office. "Do you have a second?"

Rhys Jones Bowen emerged walking backwards and talking into his phone, which he was holding at a high selfie angle. "Hello, Internet," he was saying, "this is Rhys Jones Bowen from See Arr Ay Pee Pee, the dung beetle charity. I've just finished up my morning coffee, and now Alex from the front office has called me through because he wants something, so I'm just going to see what that is and—"

"Rhys," I asked, "what are you doing?"

He gave me a look like I'd asked a very silly question which, to be fair, I had. "What does it look like I'm doing; I'm live streaming."

"Is that a thing that's happening now?"

"Got to move with the times, Luc."

I treated him to my most sceptical expression. "We really don't. Half our computers are still running Windows 7, and there's a map in the hall that shows two Germanies."

Sadly, Rhys ignored my entreaty to keep the twenty-first century out of our office. "Why don't you say hello to the internet, Luc."

"I refuse to believe that anybody is watching this."

"Excuse me, I'll have you know I've got five hundred and seventy-three viewers."

That seemed at once like not very many, and far more than I expected. "Are you sure?"

He showed me his phone, and I watched as the 573 popped up to a 574, while beneath his video a stream of chat messages spammed variations on Who's this prick? and Where's Rhys?

"Can I tell you my joke now?" asked Alex. "Although, in the spirit of full disclosure, it's really more Luc's joke."

Rotating to bring Alex into frame, Rhys gave a nod. "Go on, then, this'll be great"—he made air quotes with his one free hand—"'con-tent,' as we influencers call it."

Alex smoothed out his hair and did his best to look streamable. "Right, so there's this bus conductor who's rather bad at his job, and a judge sentences him to be executed."

"That seems a bit of an overreaction." Rhys turned his attention back to his phone. "You see, folks, that's the problem with the criminal justice system. The rich and the powerful, well, they can get away with anything. But ordinary people like you and me and this bus conductor, it's different rules for us, isn't it?"

If I'd been smart about it, I could've ducked out while they were distracting each other. I wasn't smart about it. "It's just a joke, Rhys."

"It may be a joke, but it highlights a very real sociopolitical inequality."

He had a point. "In the original version of the joke, he has *legitimately* killed somebody."

"But has he, though?" asked Rhys Jones Bowen, looking grave. "Or was he just in the wrong place at the wrong time? You see it's very easy, Luc, for you to sit there in your comfortable office and judge a man, but stories like this happen every day. An ordinary bus conductor is going about his business, and the years of abuse from an unfeeling public and the exploitative conditions he's been forced into by a privatised system of public transport..."

"Steady on." Alex had suddenly taken an interest. "I know a lot of chaps who did *terribly* well out of privatisation. Picked up some absolute *bargains*, making themselves simply *pots* of money now. And they're all jolly nice fellows."

Oh God, what had I done. A simple pun about a slightly obsolete public-sector job had turned into a debate about the long-term impacts of Thatcherism. "You see it's all right for *them*," Rhys was saying. "But you can't have one without the other, can you? For every one of your friends getting rich off the proceeds of crony capitalism, there's a poor bus conductor out there, just trying to get by, accidentally killing a passenger because he's had to work a triple shift because his daughter needs heart surgery and the NHS doesn't have any free beds and—"

"Should I..." I asked helplessly. "Should I have told the one that goes 'What's brown and sticky?'"

"What *is* brown and sticky?" asked Alex.

I gave him an apologetic smile. "A stick."

"True." Alex gave an approving not. "Yes, you should have told that one. It would have been less likely to get political."

Rhys was giving a no-harm, no-foul grin. "Still, nice to have a good debate now and then, though, isn't it? Next week we'll do religion." He turned his attention back to his phone. "Anyway, folks, that's all from me for now. I've got work to be getting on with. Remember to look up the Cee-Arr-Ay-Pee-Pee website and to follow us on the Twitter, the You Tubes, the Instant Gram, Tick Tocks and Only Fans. Be seeing you."

He closed the stream and slipped his phone back into his pocket.

"Umm, Rhys," I began tentatively, "what was that last platform you mentioned?"

"The Tick Tocks? You've got to be on the Tick Tocks these days, Luc. It's all about video content."

"Got to get with the twentieth century," agreed Alex.

"No, not TikTok," I said. "The one after?"

Rhys beamed. "Oh, Only Fans? Yes, I was reading this article and people were saying that it was getting very popular, and so I thought, as head of social media, I should probably be on that too. It's been doing rather well."

"Has it?"

"Oh yes. People do keep asking me to take my shirt off, though."

I wasn't sure how far down this road I wanted to go. "And do you?"

"Well, not in the last couple of weeks because it's been quite nippy out."

Okay. So I wanted to go exactly this distance and no further. "Great. Good on you. Nice to see that you're taking initiative. Now if you'll excuse me, I've got some very important...fundraising to do."

I didn't exactly bolt, but I didn't exactly not bolt either. The advantage of having your own office was that it always gave you somewhere to hide when you suddenly discovered that one of your coworkers had unwittingly stumbled into the world of soft-core pornography. Which admittedly wasn't a thing that happened often but was within the spectrum of things that happened often enough at CRAPP that having a sanctuary was really, really nice.

My ancient computer had barely finished booting up when my phone buzzed. The text preview read Just for your information, which told me it was Oliver before I even saw his name.

> Just for your information, I think we were photographed
>   walking back to the party.
> I can send you the article if you'd like but it's nothing to
>   worry about.

Two years ago I'd have seen it already because my Google alerts would have told me about it. But the new, sensible shit-together-having me didn't need to stare obsessively at every mention of my name in every scandal sheet. It's cool, I texted back. I trust you.

The door swung open and Alex Twaddle poked his head inside. "Luc, old man, Dr. Fairclough wants to see you about something media-y."

Fuck. Not again.

> Actually do send it to me. I might need it for self-defence.

A couple of seconds later, a link to the offending piece popped up. The headline was *We Always Knew He Was a Tw*t*, which I thought was unfair for two reasons—firstly because they blatantly hadn't always known that, they'd just said it because of the hat, and secondly because it wasn't like I was even doing anything. I was walking across a park with my boyfriend. If I hadn't been wearing a vulva on my head, it would have been quite a sweet picture. Hell, even with the vulva.

But Dr. Fairclough wanted to see me anyway. Which was...it was not okay. Things had been going well for nearly two whole years. The most recent Beetle Drive had been a huge success. We had more donors than ever. What more could I do here? Get a second, even more respectable boyfriend?

Deciding that indignation felt better than dread, I marched up to Dr. Fairclough's office and showed myself in.

"Ah, O'Donnell," she said. "I've just seen this picture." She rotated her screen towards me and there we were: me, Oliver, and the vulva hat.

And this time I wasn't backing down. "Yup. That's me. And that's my boyfriend who I love, and that's a hat shaped like a vulva because I was celebrating a friend's hen night and I thought having only penis hats would be heteronormative and/or transphobic, so yes, I was walking through the park with a set of labia crocheted to my face and I am not ashamed, and if Cee-Arr-Ay-Pee-Pee has a problem with that, then they should remember that this time I'm dating a lawyer and I'll take them to fucking court."

Dr. Fairclough blinked exactly once. "I wanted to make sure you were okay."

"Oh." It's not that I'd been looking for a fight. But I did feel a bit like a matador who'd shown up at the arena only to have the bull politely ask if I needed it to hold my cape.

"After all," she went on, "it's a very mean headline. They call you a twit."

They hadn't, in fact, called me a twit. "I've had worse."

Dr. Fairclough blinked exactly once more. Sometimes I thought she genuinely was part praying mantis. "Well, thank you for this little talk. I hope you consider yourself to be emotionally supported."

In a funny way, I did. Yes, I was pretty sure that Dr. Fairclough believed that human feelings were an evolutionary dead end caused by a misguided lack of exoskeleton, but she was trying, and I could give her points for that. "Thanks, Dr. F."

"Don't call me 'Dr. F.'"

"Sorry. Thank you, Dr. Fairclough."

My life was in a good enough place that not getting told I had to change my entire personality or lose my job felt like relief, rather than elation, but I was still relatively upbeat when I got back to my office and started pinging emails to people who had promised us money at the Beetle Drive.

An hour or so later, there was a knock at my door. This was unusual in itself because CRAPP wasn't a knocking kind of office. It was a poking-your-head-in, wandering-through-without-being-asked, spilling-hot-coffee-on-you kind of office.

"Come in?" I said without really thinking about it.

And there was Miles. Without his fiancé but still looking like a man who knew full well he was engaged to a tiny ball of sparkling wonder and was borderline smug about it. "Hi."

I was too shocked to be angry, too angry to be depressed, and too depressed to be shocked. "Hello?" I tried to make it half greeting, half interrogation.

"I... After we met the other night... I got talking to JoJo and I explained who you were and why things had been awkward—"

"Were things awkward?" I asked in my most casual I-definitely-didn't-have-to-run-away-and-hide voice.

"You know they were. And I know things between us ended badly."

I almost couldn't bring myself to call him out on that. But only almost. "Ended badly? You fucking sold me out to the fucking tabloids. That's not *us ending badly*, that's *you completely shafting me*."

"I was young and stupid and reckless."

"You were young and an arsehole."

"Be fair, Luc." He gave me that knockout smile of his. "You were kind of an arsehole yourself."

"Okay, so we were both arseholes. But only one of our arseholes walked away fifty grand richer."

Somehow, he had the gall to act disappointed. "Don't make this about the money. It wasn't about the money."

"Oh, good. So it was about deliberately hurting me, was it? That makes it so much better."

Without being asked, Miles sat down in my office's one free chair. "That's not what I meant. I...I guess I was feeling trapped and it seemed like a way out."

"And the cash was just a bonus?"

Finally he had the common decency to look ashamed.

"And so," I powered on, "you rock up here and tell me this after all these years and, what, that's supposed to make it okay?"

He hung his head. "Not okay, no. I wanted... JoJo wan— *We* wanted to invite you to the wedding."

"I'm sorry." I glared at him. "For one completely absurd and obviously incorrect minute, I thought you said you wanted to invite me to your wedding."

"Yes."

There was no way I was having this. "Let me think. How about...*no*? How about *no way in fucking hell what are you even talking about you piece of absolute shit*."

"You've got a—"

Fuck. It was happening again. I was Bruce Willis in *Die Hard 2* with the same shit happening to me twice. "And don't say I've got a right to be angry. I *know* I've got a right to be angry. The thing is, until you barged into my office like...like...like Bargey McBargeface...I didn't have to be angry because I didn't have to think about you at all. I could think about ordinary things like my job and my boyfriend and the fact that one of my coworkers doesn't realise he's an amateur porn star."

"An amateur—"

"Don't ask."

Miles stood up, straightening his jacket in a way that said *I am being the only reasonable person in an unreasonable situation.* "Look," he said. "I knew it was a risk coming here."

"What did you think you were risking, exactly? Because it seems to me like you had nothing to lose from this little visit whatsoever."

Apparently he was going to blank that. "It'd mean a lot to JoJo if you came."

"I don't even *know* JoJo. Why does he give a shit? Why should *I* give a shit?"

"You were a big part of my life, so it seems right that you should—"

This was making sense. Bullshit sense. Selfish sense. Very, very *Miles* sense. "Oh, right, so it's an absolution thing. You want me to be there so that you can put the shitty thing you did to me behind you and start a new shiny life with your new shiny husband and say to yourself, *It's okay, no need to feel bad, Luc's fine with it, he came to my wedding and everything.*"

"Think about it." From inside his jacket, Miles retrieved a delicately printed piece of cream-coloured card and laid it on the desk beside me. "Moving on will be best for both of us."

And that was the problem. I *had* moved on. I'd moved on really fucking well. "Just go."

He just went, stopping in the door on the way out to give me an enigmatic "See you around." Then I was left sitting at my desk staring at a wedding invitation, with swirly silver writing saying MR. MILES EDWARD GREENE AND MR. JOHN JOSEPH RYAN REQUEST THE PLEASURE OF YOUR COMPANY AS THEY CELEBRATE THEIR UNION. RSVP.

CHAPTER 3

IT WAS MY TURN TO cook. By which I mean it was the one night a month when my overwhelming sense of guilt at never cooking overrode both my and Oliver's awareness that I was horrendously bad at it. Since Oliver had, after a long email exchange with Bronwyn, come to the conclusion that it was ethically unsupportable to be vegetarian but not vegan if you claimed to care about animal welfare and had therefore cut out animal products entirely, I'd decided to make a sweet potato, chard, and celeriac rainbow-layered pie. Which had seemed like a great idea when I'd Googled *good vegan recipes* a couple of days ago. Then seemed like quite a poor idea when I'd been wandering around Tesco's wondering where the fuck they kept their celeriac. Then turned out to be an unbelievably poor idea once I'd started trying to make it.

For a start, store-bought pastry *wasn't* vegan so I'd had to make it from scratch, and I quickly learned that whipping up your own pastry from coconut milk, flour, and almond oil was really, really hard. Especially when, according to the recipe, you were supposed to do it in the twenty minutes your beetroot was roasting in the oven so everything would be nice and ready when the time came to combine it all.

An hour and ten minutes into the one-hour prep time that the recipe had promised, I was covered in flour to my elbows, juggling three different roasting tins that had to go into the oven at different times, trying to work out whether my pastry needed more coconut milk (I'd bought extra in case) or more flour (I'd bought extra in case) or less of one or the other (in which case how was I meant to take it out), and fast returning to my monthly realisation that I should never, ever be allowed in a kitchen.

Eventually I got the pastry to a sort of play-dough consistency where I could just about squoodge it into a cake tin and start filling it with layers of chard leaves and semolina, which would apparently absorb the juices but which I was beginning to strongly suspect would not in fact absorb anything. I wrestled the whole mess into the oven, set the timer, and made a brief despairing effort to clean up before realising that I had no idea where to start.

Oliver arrived home just as the smoke alarm went off.

"Smells delicious," he yelled from the hall before heading into the front room, grabbing a sheaf of documents he'd been working on, and waving them frantically under the smoke alarm.

"Thanks. It's supposed to be a pie."

"And what's it *actually* going to be?"

"Honestly?" I came through from the kitchen, yoinked the papers gently out of his hand, and took over waving duty. "Probably a takeaway?"

The beeping stopped, and Oliver recovered his documents before giving me a belated honey-I'm-home kiss on the cheek. "I'm sure it'll be fine."

It was never fine. But over the course of our relationship I'd watched Oliver gamely chomp his way through roasted squash that was practically mulch, spinach soup that was practically jam, and more watery stews than I could keep track of.

In the end I served up a kind of vegetable gruel with bits of either burned or raw crust floating in it like incredibly shit dumplings. Oliver seasoned his liberally and tucked in.

"Are you okay?" he asked once he'd managed to swallow a particularly tricky lump of chard. "This is fine, but from the mess"—he indicated the carnage that still filled the kitchen—"it seems like you were more than normally distracted."

I took a deep breath. This wasn't going to be a big deal. I wasn't going to let this be a big deal. "It's Miles."

"I'm sorry. I didn't realise seeing him shook you up that much."

"No, I mean, it's Miles *again*. Like, he came to see me."

Between his training as a professional barrister, a lifetime of nodding and smiling for his judgmental parents, and two years of pretending to like my cooking, Oliver had one hell of a poker face, but I thought I saw a flattering hint of jealousy creep into his eyes. "When?"

"Today. At work."

Oliver frowned. "That seems inappropriate."

"Yeah, Miles has never been big on *appropriate*." To be fair, neither had I.

"What did he want?"

"He wanted to say, 'I made a terrible mistake, run away with me,' and I said, 'Of course I will, big boy.' I'm packing my bags this evening."

Oliver put down his fork and gave me a stern look. "Lucien."

"He wanted to invite me to his wedding."

"Ah." For a moment he was quiet. "Do you want to go?"

I was a bit surprised he'd even asked. "Of course not. It would be fucking weird."

"Well then." He reached across the table and took my hand. I thought it was meant to be affectionate, but he probably also wanted an excuse to stop eating the pie. "That seems to be a problem with a very simple solution."

"It's just..." *Fuck.* He'd done that thing where he was all supportive of my choices to make me confront the fact that I wasn't actually sure about them. "I keep wondering if it might be good for me maybe?"

His thumb traced gently across my knuckles like we had all the time in the world and nothing mattered more than this conversation right now. "Good in what way?"

"I dunno. Sort of...closure-y? Like it might help to be able to stand up and say, 'Hey, you totally destroyed me that one time, but I'm fine now, so I wish you well.' Also, I'd really like to show up at his wedding with my gorgeous, successful boyfriend and rub it in his stupid, smug, beardy face."

Oliver laughed. "Should I feel flattered by that or exploited?"

"Oh, we're too special for a bit of exploitation now, are we?"

"Depends on the situation."

It was nice to be able to have this, just sitting with Oliver being very slightly flirty, even while I was having a mini-crisis. But that didn't make the mini-crisis less crisisey. "I keep going in circles," I told him. "One moment I'll be all *Why are you even considering this, fuck him,* and then I'll be like *But isn't that giving him more power over you,* then I'll be back to *Or maybe that's what he wants you to think,* and—gah."

"You're a complicated man, Lucien O'Donnell."

"Thanks, I try." I sighed. "I guess the whole let-us-reconcile-even-though-I-shafted-you thing is bringing up a lot of stuff, and I'm not sure where I want to...well...put the stuff it brings up."

Oliver gave me a reassuring nod. "That makes sense. But for what it's worth, I don't believe this is as much like your dad as you might be thinking."

That's exactly what I was thinking. Even if I hadn't put it into quite those words. "Isn't it, though? Aren't I just setting myself up to go through life with people shitting on me and then saying,

'Hey, remember that time I shat on you? It'd be great for me if you could put it all behind you and say we're cool now'?"

"I think, or rather I *hope*"—he gave me earnest eyes over the remains of his bowl of non-pie—"that the difference is you're not invested in Miles. He's not trying to be a part of your life; he's only asking you to come to his wedding. And he's probably asking for selfish reasons. I don't doubt that it's about making him and his new husband feel better rather than making *you* feel better. But he's not asking you to commit to anything."

"They'll expect a gift."

Oliver smiled. "Then get them a toast rack and put a note in it asking when he's going to pay back the fifty thousand pounds he owes you."

I enjoyed seeing Oliver's mean side. It didn't come out very often, but when it did, it was usually on point. "I might do that. If I go. Should I go?"

"You know I can't make that decision for you."

"Why not? It would be super convenient. You could just say, 'Sorry Lucien, I'm wildly jealous, and I refuse to let you go to Miles's wedding.'"

"Sorry, Lucien," repeated Oliver obligingly. "I'm *wildly* jealous, and I refuse to let you go to Miles's wedding."

"Oh, that's rubbish." I gave him my best sulky face. "You clearly don't mean it."

Oliver cast me a look of mock contrition. "I know, I'm an inadequate boyfriend and I don't know why you put up with me."

"You must have a preference, though?" I wheedled.

For a moment Oliver thought about it. He was never a man to give a hasty answer to an important question. "Well, I'd be lying if I said that attending the wedding of a total stranger was my idea of a fabulous night out. And you don't owe Miles anything so neither he nor JoJo should be a factor here."

"I feel like you're about to drop a massive 'but' on me."

"I was heading that way, but now I feel you've cut my 'but' off at the pass."

This was a very serious conversation about very serious things, and Oliver was taking time out of his evening to boyfriend at me, but there was no way I was letting that go without comment. "Oliver, I would never cut your 'but' off."

"Lucien"—his eyes had gone all soft while his mouth was trying really hard to be severe—"you're making it very hard for me to finish my sentence."

"Sorry. Sorry." I paused. "'But' me."

"*But*," said Oliver carefully, "just because Miles is behaving selfishly, that doesn't mean that going to his wedding wouldn't be good for you. If going along and drawing a line under the past would make you feel better, you shouldn't not do it just because it might make him feel better too. Does that make sense?"

It did. Kind of. "But what if knowing it'll make him feel better makes me feel worse?"

"Then maybe you need to revisit the does-he-have-power-over-you question."

Oh. Right. My shoulders drooped. I was supposed to be...not like this anymore. "Why do people keep having power over me?"

"Well, one of them was your father, so power is rather a given. And the other is someone you were in love with who betrayed you."

"So I have to go to the wedding to prove—"

I had no idea where I was going with that, but thankfully Oliver interrupted me. "You don't have to do anything to prove anything. To anyone. Not Miles, not me, and not even yourself."

That's what he thought. He wasn't me.

"In any case," he went on, "you have time. You can think about it. And if you want to go, of course I'll be with you. And if you don't, I'll...still be with you. And we'll do something much more interesting than watching your ex-boyfriend and somebody you've met once throw a massive, expensive party in celebration of a relationship that doesn't mean anything to you."

I blinked. "Wow. That's a cynical take on marriage even for me, and my dad was a junkie arsehole who walked out on my mum before I could talk."

"I'm not opposed to marriage in general." Oliver gave a tight little smile. "I'm just not the sort of person who can get invested in the trappings if I'm not invested in the couple."

I didn't think I was either, really. I'd only agreed to help organise Bridge's wedding because she was my best friend and I was pretty sure she'd do all the important planning herself. Of course, part of it was that for most of my life it hadn't looked like marriage was a thing I'd ever be able to do. And in some ways it was nice to think if I was growing up today, I'd be able to be one of those kids spending his days planning his fantasy wedding to the man of his dreams. But in other ways, it felt kind of like I'd missed out. "I get it. And just to be clear, I'm not *invested* in Miles at all. Like not at all. Not even a little tiny bit."

"Good."

There was a firmness in that *good* that felt more definite than his I'll-support-you-no-matter-what demeanour implied. "Oliver," I said, because I wanted this on record, "you are actually just a smidgeon jealous, aren't you?"

"No."

The response was far too quick to be convincing. I grinned triumphantly. "You are. Oh my God, you are. That's amazing because it means you like me so much you don't want anyone else to have me. Or possibly super insulting because it suggests I'm so damaged I'll go back to a guy who sold me out and is marrying someone else."

"Well, obviously I like you, Lucien," muttered Oliver. "In

general. Not necessarily right now. And I know it's irrational. While I have a long history of people leaving me, it's always been for quite banal reasons, not because they decided to run off with their ex at his own wedding."

Once upon a time, this would have been a teasing opportunity and I'd have said something like *I promise when I leave you, it'll be over something trivial*. But Oliver had been dumped a lot, and even though he'd know it was a joke, it would be a joke that hurt. "I promise I'm not going to leave you. Not over Miles. Not over you going vegan. Not even over that time you got really upset at me for leaving my socks in the living room."

That perked him right up. His eyes got a steely glint. "There is a place," he said, "for socks."

And it probably said something weird about my brain or our relationship that Oliver chiding me about my socks was a little bit of a turn-on. "I'm sorry." I made a futile attempt to sound contrite. "I'm just a filthy sock harlot."

"Lucien, are you attempting to turn my irritation at your failure to pick up after yourself into some kind of sex game?"

I shot him a hopeful look. "Is it working?"

"Well, you have made a terrible mess of the kitchen."

"I know. I deserve to be punished."

"You've already been punished," Oliver pointed out. "You had to eat that dreadful pie."

"That is very much not the type of punishment I had in mind."

Standing, Oliver neatly cleared the bowls from the table. "I don't think framing sex with me as a punishment is quite the compliment you think it is."

"Well, I don't think 'Come and do me because you like me so much' has quite the right flirtatious edge."

"But Lucien"—Oliver's voice had gone very low and very soft—"I do like you. I like you very, very much."

Okay, maybe that was working. Except even after two years of relationshipping and self-care and emotional development, it still scared me how vulnerable sex could make me feel. Which meant it was way easier to say *Spank me, Daddy*, which we both knew I didn't mean, than *Hold me, I love you*, which I definitely did. And I was just trying to find a way to articulate this—see above, re: emotional development—when Oliver came back, unbowled, and took me firmly by the wrist.

"What are you—" I started as I found myself manoeuvred onto the table.

"I'm showing you how much I like you."

Argh. Help. My feelings. I made a valiant attempt not to melt everywhere. "I'll feel bad if we damage this table."

"Really?" he asked. "I won't care in the slightest."

And then he kissed me and I stopped caring too. Because whatever else was going on—in spite of Miles and JoJo Ryan, and Bridge's wedding, and the mess of my past and the mess I was probably going to make of my future—Oliver was mine, and I was his, and I was kind of completely, embarrassingly, disgustingly in love with him. Especially when he knew exactly how to touch me, rough and tender and careful and endlessly…Oliver. When he knew how to make me forget my uncertainties and my self-consciousness so that I wasn't afraid to cling to him like I needed to cling and let him cling to me the way he needed to cling back. And tell him how wonderful he was, how happy he made me. All the other things I was just beginning to find words for.

And not even say *I told you so* when we totally wrecked the table.

CHAPTER 4

FOR THE NEXT COUPLE OF days I back-and-forthed on whether I wanted to go to Miles's wedding or not. The con column was looking pretty long because it would be a faff, Oliver would have an unbelievably shitty evening on account of not knowing anybody, and, oh yes, there was that tiny, insignificant detail that showing up at all would be a tacit admission that I was totes chill with that one time Miles completely fucked me over.

But somehow, that didn't stop me secretly wanting to go.

Because things were good. I was—not that I'd ever admit it to anybody at CRAPP—actually enjoying my job. My relationship with Oliver was as strong as it had ever been, although it wasn't like two years in with Miles I'd been thinking to myself, *Wow, this guy's going to hurt me worse than any human being has ever hurt me in my life.* And, God, what was my brain doing? Why was it comparing the selfish prick I'd dated nearly a decade ago with the objectively better man I was seeing right now?

I mean, Oliver was objectively better, wasn't he? Our relationship was objectively better. We were older and more mature and more sensible and... Wait. Were we just boring? Safe and predictable and full of table lamps. Of course, given recent events, we were getting to the point of having more lamps than tables. Which definitely wasn't boring. After all, if we were still breaking the furniture, we were doing something right.

Okay. This was exactly why I needed to go to the wedding. I need to show my ex-boyfriend, my ex-boyfriend's fiancé I'd met once, and a bunch of strangers that I was free and happy and over it and moving on with my new, infinitely better boyfriend. And if I did that well enough, maybe my own brain would believe me.

Until then, though, I needed to get (a) a grip and (b) back in the moment. Especially because Oliver and I were going out this evening on a proper grown-up, we-are-in-a-relationship date. We were doing—and it was kind of hard to say this with a straight face—*dinner and a show*. He'd booked us a table at this place called Stem & Glory, which was apparently one of the best vegan restaurants in London, and I was *slowly* coming to the conclusion that the best vegan restaurants in the city really were nicer places to eat than an average restaurant that would just serve me a piece of dead cow. Then afterwards...well, that had been complicated. Oliver had wanted to see *Death of a Salesman* at the Young Vic, but I'd told him that if I was going to a vegan restaurant for him, he had to go to *Pretty Woman: The Musical* for me. And honestly, I was kind of psyched about it.

Well, psyched-ish. It had been quite a long day all told because the photocopier had jammed and then Alex had insisted on trying to fix it and got his hand stuck somewhere inside, and Barbara Clench had refused to let me get an engineer to come and extract him because she was concerned that if he was seen interfering with the machine, it would invalidate the warranty. Not that there was much chance of our keeping the incident secret anyway, since Rhys Jones Bowen had been livestreaming the whole time and soliciting possible solutions from his ever-growing army of followers. Or *Rhystocrats* as they'd apparently taken to calling themselves.

Anyway, I was just leaving when my phone rang. It was

Bridget's number, but that was the only clue I had that it was actually her because for a long time she had trouble getting words out. Which was the first sign that something was seriously wrong. Because sure, Bridge lived from disaster to disaster, but she dealt with that by loudly declaring how ruined everything was while at the same time calmly fixing the actual problem. It was a slightly peculiar process but seemed to work for her. When she got quiet, though, that meant she was genuinely stuck and was falling back on my preferred strategy: pretending the problem didn't exist in the hope that it would go away.

"Bridge?" I asked into the silence. "Bridge, what's going on?"

"It's…" The voice was her, but she sounded choked up. "It's Tom."

Shit. There were two ways this could go, and neither was good. "Is he okay?"

"Probably." That was her angry voice. So this was a Tom's-done-something call, not a something's-happened-to-Tom call. I wasn't sure which was worse.

My phone buzzed and a text came in from Bridget. It was a photograph. A photograph of Tom looking furtive with his arm around a pretty young woman. A pretty young woman who wasn't Bridget. For which there must have been a million reasonable explanations that a person who hadn't spent most of his adult life developing deep-seated trust issues could have articulated. Unfortunately, Bridget had called me.

"Crap, Bridge," I said finally. The trick here was to walk the line between being supportive and encouraging her to blow up her own wedding. And I could do that. I could do that. I just had to be nice and as noncommittal as possible and ignore the part of my brain that was screaming, *She's doomed, and so are you. Meeting Miles was a sign, and everything you think you can count on is wrong.* "I'm so sorry. Have you…" What would an emotionally mature and undamaged person do? "Have you talked to him about it?"

There was a burbling sound from the other end of the line that eventually resolved into "I can't get hold of him."

On its own, that wasn't unusual. Tom's job often required him to go quiet for a couple of days, sometimes longer. But it wasn't exactly reassuring. Or at least I wasn't reassured, and I didn't think Bridge would be either. I tried to stick with neutral questions. "How did you get the picture?"

"Liz saw them."

If it had been any of Bridge's other friends it might have been less damning, because a lot of them were like, well, me. The type of people who jumped from fearing the worst to deciding that the worst had definitely happened without even needing a run-up. But Liz was a legit vicar, which meant giving people the benefit of the doubt was basically in her job description. And since she was actually officiating at the wedding, it didn't seem likely she'd be maliciously sabotaging it. "Did she say anything else?"

"Just that they were in a café together and they looked... looked close."

There were still, surely, other ways to interpret an about-to-be-married man with his phone switched off carrying on in a café with a mysterious hot lady who wasn't his fiancée. I just couldn't think of any right at that second. "Do you need me to come over?"

"Don't you"—Bridge gave a sort of noble hiccough—"aren't you going out with Oliver tonight?"

Yes. Yes, I was. And it was going to be super romantic and special and all the things that fancy date nights with your long-term partner were supposed to be. "This is more important."

And the worst—or, from another perspective, the best—of it was that I wasn't lying. Bridge would never have asked me to cancel, but she also didn't have to. She'd been there for me through a metric butt load of crises down the years—through Miles, through all the self-destructive shit I'd pulled after, through nearly getting fired, and through everything with Oliver—so I kind of owed her one. Hell, I owed her twenty. And even if I hadn't, I'd still have been there for her because that's what friends were meant to do and I'd spent way too long not doing it. "I'll be right round," I told her.

She made a sad appreciative noise and, after I'd tried to reassure her that everything was going to be okay in six different ways, each slightly less plausible than the last, hung up.

The next bit was going to be awkward. Well, maybe not that awkward. Because Oliver would understand. Even if we did have a table booked and tickets we'd bought months ago. *Oh, shit.* It was going to be awkward, wasn't it?

And thank you, life, for manoeuvring me into a situation where I'd have to let down either my best friend or my boyfriend. It was like whatever I did, no matter how hard I tried, the universe wanted me to know that, on some level, I was a crappy person. On this occasion, my crapness manifested partly in not wanting to tell Oliver to his face—or even to his voice—that I was ditching him to hang out with a sad bride. I was two-thirds of the way through my fourth draft of my first text when I realised that I was living down to the universe's expectations of me. And, more importantly, not living up to Oliver's. Fuck. That was the problem with dating a good person. They got their ethics all over you.

So I gritted my teeth and called Oliver.

"Lucien?" Great. He already sounded concerned. Either because of boyfriend telepathy or because I normally only rang if I'd set the kitchen on the fire. "Is everything okay?"

"Not really," I told him, and then realising that could have meant anything from *I think we should break up* to *My leg's been bitten off by a shark*, followed up quickly with, "I mean I'm fine, but Bridget's in a hell of a state and... Look, I'm sorry but I'm going to have to bail on this evening."

For just long enough that I could hear my relationship gurgling down the plughole, Oliver didn't reply. Then he said, "Oh."

"Oh?"

Another relationship gurgling pause. "Sorry, I–I know you're Bridget's maid of honour, but I don't often get free evenings and we've been planning this for a long time."

"I know. It's just...she's my best friend."

"And she's my friend too." Oliver sounded unhappy. Worse, he sounded like he was trying hard *not* to be unhappy, which would only make him unhappier. "But you know Bridge... She always has some crisis or other."

"She thinks Tom's cheating on her," I blurted.

"Oh," he said again. For someone who talked for a living, Oliver could be very monosyllabic sometimes.

"Yeah."

He was silent a little longer. "And does she... Is he?"

I wished I had an answer to that. "She's got a picture? Of him with another woman. And...honestly it doesn't look good, but this is *me* talking and I'm not exactly the poster boy for healthy trust-based relationships."

"Thank you for that vote of confidence, Lucien."

"Fuck. No, I didn't mean that. I mean, like, I have, you know, issues because of history shit."

"Sorry. Yes. I do understand. I just—" The breath Oliver took next was so deep it became almost crackly over the phone line. "It doesn't matter. You should go and be with Bridget."

I winced. No wonder I hadn't wanted to do this. "I will. I'm really sorry."

"It's fine." He didn't, if I was being completely honest with myself, sound all that fine. "I'm sure I can get our tickets moved to another night."

"We could go see that grown-up play you wanted to see instead?"

"Oh, no"—I loved that he was making an effort to be cool with this, even if he wasn't entirely succeeding—"I'm very keen to see a musical based on a popular movie from the 1990s. My only regret is that it's going to have original songs instead of thinly repurposing popular music from the era."

That struck me as a very specific concern, and one that was a lot easier to talk about than me ditching him on our first date in ages to hold someone else's hand through something that was almost certainly a storm in a teacup. "Is this because I made you watch *Mamma Mia! Here We Go Again?*"

"Actually, I enjoyed that more than I expected to. Which I will admit was a low bar." For some reason, Oliver trying to make me feel better was making me feel significantly worse. "And while I appreciate your willingness to sacrifice yourself on the altar of Arthur Miller, I'd rather rebook our tickets for *Pretty Woman.* It turns out I am, to my mild surprise, disappointed we aren't seeing it this evening."

"Really?" I asked. "Really really?"

"Oh, yes. Big disappointment. Big. Huge."

"I see what you did there." It was my sardonic voice. But I *had* seen what he did there. And that made standing him up even harder. "You could take someone else?" I offered, trying to get in on the self-sacrifice gig.

"Ah, yes," said Oliver, in a manner that suggested this had been my worst idea since the vegan pie. So my worst idea since very, very recently. "I could call up one of my many married friends and say, 'Hello, would you like to abandon your spouse for an evening in order to see a moderately well-reviewed musical in place of the man I love?'"

"I mean, Ben or Sophie'd love a chance to stick the other one with the kids."

"Perhaps, but the stickee would hate me forever and the important part of that sentence was 'the man I love' not 'my married friends.'"

I wrestled with a weird mix of happy-sad cringe. "I'll make it up to you? I promise?"

He gave a soft, not entirely sincere laugh. "I shall hold you to that, Lucien. Now go help Bridget. I don't... I'd rather... It's absolutely the right thing to do."

"And I love you too," I added slightly too late.

"Well recovered."

We hung up. Then I grabbed my coat, shouted a quick good-bye to Alex, who was still stuck in the photocopier, and made a dash for the door. Because I was a good friend. And a good maid of honour. Which I suppose meant that the joke was on me because, despite all that, I felt like a prick.

CHAPTER 5

I WAS JUST DOING AN emergency Tesco's run to get sorry-you're-sad food when my phone buzzed again.

Thankfully, it wasn't a picture of ambiguous infidelity this time. It was a black-and-white illustration of a man in a tricorn hat jumping a stiffly drawn horse over a fence. Underneath it, Oliver had sent: thinking of you.

Dick Turpin? I texted back.

Yes. I'm amazed we hadn't got around to using him yet, but I checked and we definitely haven't.

I paused in front of the freezers with one eye on my phone and one on the ice cream. Choosing the right emotional-support ice cream was important, but some questions demanded answers. What do you mean, you checked? Do you keep a list?

No. It was an unusually short message from Oliver, which suggested he was attempting to use comic timing in text. It's a database.

You have a dick database. A dicktabase?

Now I'm concerned you think I actually have a database.

I bet you have a database, I typed, relieved things between us seemed to be drifting normalwards. I bet you have an intern who updates it for you.

I think making an intern update my database of dick pics would constitute a hostile working environment.

Depends how nice the dicks are.

That certainly wouldn't stand up in court. Was it weird that I always heard Oliver's texts in Oliver's voice? Or was it weirder that Oliver texted exactly the same way he spoke?

Probably for the best. That kind of thing could get you disbarred.

If you think that's true, he sent back, you know very little about the British legal system.

Dashing off some laughing emojis, I turned my attention back to the fridge. Do you think I should get Häagen-Dazs or Ben & Jerry's?

There was a moment of whatever the text version of radio silence is. It's situational, came Oliver's typically overthought response. But in the circumstances, I'd suggest getting both.

Between juggling my shopping and wrangling with the self-checkout, I didn't manage to put my reply together until I was on my way out of Tesco's, swinging a bag of high-calorie edibles from one hand and texting clumsily with the other. Good call. It's clearly a two-tub problem.

I'm sure there's a reasonable explanation.

I hoped there would be, for Bridge's sake as well as for Tom's. He'd never given me cheaty vibes, and I didn't want to think I'd been that wrong about him. I mean, sure, he'd dumped me for my best friend, but he'd been extremely open about it.

Bridge lived in a tiny one-bedroom flat in Plaistow. She was doing well enough at her job that she could have afforded better, or at least bigger, but she'd been resolutely committed to the idea that she was staying in her starter flat until she got her dream home and her dream life—which in her world would inevitably have come with the dream husband and the dream wedding. The worst thing was, she'd been this close to getting all of it.

I buzzed on her buzzer, and she let me up without even checking who I was. Which was partly typical poor security on her part, but she did it with a sad edge.

She opened the door wearing a dressing gown two sizes too large for her, fuzzy slippers with half the fuzz worn off, and a look of profound melancholy.

"I got Caramel Chew Chew," I told her. "Also one of those needlessly huge bars of Dairy Milk and also a Toblerone, but I think that might have been panic."

"Come in." She gave me the weakest effort at a smile I'd ever seen from her.

In some ways, Bridge's flat was as messy as mine had been. It was just that in her case, it was a mess that said, *I love everything so much that I can't possibly bear to be parted from it because my world is full of beautiful memories* and not *I hate everything, and my pants live on the coffee table now.* She sat down on the battered old sofa that she'd been dragging from flat to flat with her since we'd been at university and wrapped herself in an even more battered purple blanket that she'd been dragging with her even longer.

I tucked up next to her. "Just to establish some ground rules," I said, "do we hate him and think he's evil, or do we trust him and think it's a misunderstanding?"

Bridge laugh-cried. "I don't know. Either? Both. How could he do this to me?"

I thought both would be a bad call, so I picked a lane. And with uncharacteristic evenhandedness I picked the lane marked benefit of the doubt. "He might not have. Liz might have made a mistake."

"Liz is pretty smart. Plus, she's a vicar."

"I don't think that makes her infallible."

"No, but it means I feel bad calling her a liar." Bridge snapped off a triangle of Toblerone. "This was a good call, thanks. I don't know why we only buy them at Christmas."

I took a nibble of the Dairy Milk. There was an art to this

kind of supportive binge—one I'd learned mostly from being on the other side of it. You needed to share enough that you weren't just watching the other person eat but not take so much that you actually limited their access to comfort food. "I don't think she's lying, just that there's lots of reasons Tom could be talking to a random woman in a café."

"Name five."

I nearly choked on my chocolate. "That's not fair. Five is loads."

"Okay." Bridge pulled the blanket a little tighter around herself. "Name three."

"Old school friend, sister he's never mentioned—"

"I've met his sister," interrupted Bridge. "Also the woman in the photo was white."

"Adopted sister we've never heard of."

She gave me a disappointed look. "You're only on the second one, and you've already gone to bad sitcom territory."

"Hey, that trope has been in some very good sitcoms."

"I'd ask you to name three but that's how we got into this mess in the first place."

"Fine." I stared at the Toblerone for inspiration and found none forthcoming. "What if he's hiring her to set up a lovely surprise for your wedding, and when he tells you what it is, you'll be so overjoyed that you forget this ever happened?"

Bridge glanced up suspiciously from the Caramel Chew Chew. "What sort of surprise?"

"Maybe he's...he's arranging a flash mob to do 'All You Need Is Love'?"

For about eighteen nanoseconds, Bridge let this idea calm her. "I do love *Love Actually*."

"Hell, maybe he's even arranging for some creeper with a camcorder to take stalkery footage of you all night."

The eighteen nanoseconds were over. "*Or* maybe he's cheating on me like Alan Rickman. What if he bought that woman a necklace? What if he got her *sex and a necklace*? What if—"

"Whoa, whoa, whoa." I put my hands up. "I know I started this, but we can't just go through every subplot in that entire movie. If we do, you'll wind up being worried that he's going to ditch your wedding to get drunk and watch porn with Bill Nighy."

Bridge flopped back on the sofa. "Is everything going to be a little bit worse now?"

If the *Love Actually* gambit had been a plan, I'd have felt bad because it had taken us to a very unhelpful place. As it was, I felt bad because I was shit at this. "No," I tried. "Tom is not Alan Rickman, you are not Emma Thompson, and that woman definitely isn't... Okay, I admit I don't know who plays the secretary."

"Heike Makatsch," said Bridget immediately.

And I briefly wondered if the way to keep her spirits up was giving her plenty of opportunities to correct me on rom-com trivia. "How did you know that?"

"It's my *favourite film*."

"Even though at least half the stories are incredibly problematic?"

"Yes." She gave me a defiant look. "Now pass me the other ice cream."

I passed, and for a while we just sat like that, curled up on the sofa dual-wielding frozen dairy products and watching romantic movies from the early 2000s. Every half hour or so, we paused so Bridge could try unsuccessfully to reach Tom.

"How did it wind up like this, Luc?" she asked as we watched the credits roll on *While You Were Sleeping*. "I thought we'd finally cracked it. You know, life. I mean, we were both with great guys—"

"Instead of both trying to get with the same great guy," I added.

"Exactly. And now here we are again eating Strawberry Cheesecake Häagen-Dazs and watching old Sandra Bullock movies like nothing has changed."

There was a strange back-in-halls feeling to the evening. And that made me uncomfortable on a number of levels. "You mean nothing has changed because you're having a relationship crisis and I'm with somebody who seems great but is inevitably going to fuck me over?" Because that was how it went back in the day.

"No, I mean... Shit, sorry, Luc. I really do believe you and Oliver are endgame."

"I believed you and Tom were endgame too. Then again, I dated him first and my taste in men is legendarily awful so maybe he *is* just a cheating, necklace-buying scumbucket you're better off without."

Bridge balled up the foil from the Toblerone and threw it at me. "Hey, you're supposed to be making me feel better."

Fuck, I was, wasn't I? And I'd been doing a passable job of it up until then too. "Sorry. I let self-hating Luc take over for a moment there. I'm back now."

"It's all right. I'm just... I'd got used to not feeling this way, and now I'm having to feel this way again and I'm not enjoying it."

I put down the Ben & Jerry's and turned to give Bridget my best sincere look. "Okay, since we're having a back-to-our-youth moment"—I put my hand over my heart—"as your token gay friend, it is my duty to say that you are a fierce, sickening, incredible woman and that when you find a man who deserves you, he'll make you feel like a princess every day of your life in a way that somehow manages to avoid reinforcing problematic gender stereotypes. And if it turns out that Tom isn't that guy, then that's his loss, not yours. And you should have the wedding anyway just to celebrate how awesome you are."

Bridget leaned across the sofa and hugged me. Since she *hadn't* put down her ice cream, it was a mixed experience that I was pretty sure got Häagen-Dazs in my hair, but it was good to know I'd done friending right. "Thanks, Luc," she said. And then, in a slightly smaller voice added, "Would you be okay to stay, if I can't get in touch with Tom?"

"Of course. Oliver'll understand." He wouldn't *like* understanding, but he'd understand.

Swivelling around, she lay down with her head on my lap. "I'm honestly sure you two are going to make it."

"Even though I have terrible taste in men?"

"*Because* you have terrible taste in men. You spent so long refusing to go out with Oliver that he's bound to be right for you."

I wasn't totally sure that tracked, but it was a comforting thought. "Fine," I conceded, "but in that case you have to accept that my letting Tom get away proves he's a good guy too." I paused. "Unless he isn't, of course."

Bridge managed half a laugh. "We'll see. I don't want to think about it anymore tonight."

So we didn't. We queued up *Muriel's Wedding* into *27 Dresses* and let ourselves stop thinking about anything at all.

In the break between movies, I slipped into the hall to ring Oliver and tell him the situation.

"I'm really sorry," I said. "I don't think I'm going to make it home tonight. Things are looking bad so I should probably stay with Bridge."

Once more, I could hear Oliver breathing in that I-will-be-calm way that I hated. "Of course. I... That is, if you think it's... Are you sure you're helping?"

"What do you mean, am I sure I'm helping?" This wasn't the tack I'd expected him to take.

"Just that, well, sometimes it's best to let people stand on their own two feet."

I got that I'd let him down. And I got that he was trying to be reasonable. But this was becoming the kind of reasonable that was worse than angry. "She thinks her fiancé might be cheating on her. This isn't an own-feet situation."

"And you're going to drop everything and run to her every time she and Tom are in trouble?"

"Yes. Because she's my best friend and she's always supported me and I'll always support her."

"There's supporting"—Oliver's tone was getting more restrained and less warm by the moment—"and there's being codependent."

"It's not codependent to be there for your friends."

"I just meant—"

"You just meant that you're cross with me for bailing on you, which is fine. But you're taking it out on Bridge, which is *not*. And also you're doing it in a way that makes you sound weirdly like your dad."

"I do *not* sound like my father. He's never used the word 'code-pendent' in his life. He'd think it was psychobabble nonsense."

This was beginning to feel nastily like a hole, and I should have stopped digging. "You know what I mean. All that 'Let people stand on their own feet, stop mollycoddling' stuff is pure David Blackwood."

"I also never said 'mollycoddling.'"

It was true. He hadn't. And maybe I was just projecting. After I'd told the Blackwoods to go fuck themselves two years ago, we'd barely spoken, but occasionally Oliver would need to go do a family thing and then he'd come back and spend a couple of days being distant and irritable before we could get back to normal. "All right, perhaps that was unfair. But our *mutual* friend is really going through something right now, and you *know* being with her is the right thing to do. I'm sorry I let you down. I'm sorry I spoiled our evening, but I had to make a choice and I'm choosing to be a good friend instead of a good boyfriend."

There was a long silence. I could practically hear Oliver's brain clicking at the other end of the line. "I'm sorry. You're right. I'm being selfish. I've just... You've been very distracted recently and I've been very busy, and this has all come out of... Go and look after Bridget. I'll be fine."

"Okay," I said.

Because there was kind of nothing else I could say. And because I needed to get back to Bridge. And most of all because I wanted to believe him.

CHAPTER 6

THERE'D BEEN NO WORD FROM Tom by the following morning. Or, indeed, from Oliver. But then, I hadn't texted him either. And it wasn't because I didn't want to. It was more that I couldn't tell if we'd had a fight or not, and if we had, whose fault it had been. I mean, I had kind of dropped him on extra-special date night. Like a dick. Except I'd only done that because I needed to take care of my friend. Like definitely not a dick. *Fuck*. I was in a grey dick area.

Still, that was way better than wherever Bridge was. Which was a barely slept, woke up crying, increasingly convinced her fiancé was cheating on her area. We both called in sick because she was in no state to work and I wasn't going to leave her in no state to work. And then we took a box of Frosties with us to the sitting room and huddled on the sofa together.

"I just don't understand," Bridge said through a mouthful of oversweetened breakfast cereal. "The wedding is next week. He can't have just vanished. Vanished with a strange woman. Vanished with a strange woman and thrown his phone away."

"And I'm sure he hasn't," I told her, although I wasn't and hadn't ever been and was getting less sure by the minute. "Something has probably come up at work."

"Something that just happens to involve him putting his arms around women who aren't me?"

I'd hoped sleeping on it would make things seem better, but it hadn't. It had made them seem a whole lot worse. "How...how do you want to play this?" I asked. Because Bridge had made me her maid of honour, which meant it was my job help her plan her wedding or to help her burn it down if that was what she needed.

Bridge put down the Frosties and re-huddled into her blanket. "I don't know. I just want to talk to him."

At this point, I couldn't tell if I was being supportive or useless. Honestly, it was a bit of both. "We could... Do you want to... Should we tell...people? I mean, our friends people. Not, like, strangers in the street."

For a long while, Bridge stared at her phone. "Do you think they could help find him?"

I gave a deeply uncertain shrug. The thing about our friendship group—and I very much included myself in this—was that we were always helpful but rarely useful. "It can't hurt."

"I suppose...I suppose it's worth a try."

I didn't send the call out on our usual WhatsApp group—currently going under the situationally unfortunate name of Bi-bi Baby, Baby Bi-bi—because Tom was in it and, however this played out, it was unfair to be having the Tom-might-be-cheating-on-Bridge conversation in a group chat he was technically part of. It had all the worst elements of talking behind his back and to his face.

Instead, I pinged a message around the Bridge's Bitches (In the Reclaimed Sense) list.

Minor wedding emergency, I texted, Tom seems to have vanished, help pls.

A few moments later, Bridge followed up with AND HE IS SEEING ANOTHER WOMAN AND I AM SAD

From there, the conversation got quite complex in the way that multiperson text chains always did. Priya got in first with a

Luc, is this legit and James Royce-Royce crossed that with an Oh what a prize bastard, assuming this isn't all a tremendous misunderstanding. Then Liz came back, probably replying to Priya with It might be legit, I saw him with somebody and it looked suspicious, which she followed up with But I don't know anything for sure but not before Bernadette had stepped in with Whatever you need darling, we're here for you and Priya had shot a Not sure that's helpful probably replying to James Royce-Royce, to which he had replied with Well, excuse me for caring, I'm sure while the other James Royce-Royce had followed up with I think we can locate him if we work systematically from his last known location. All of which Bridget capped off with a YOUR SO LOVELY BUT I DON'T KNOW WHAT TO DO??

Neither did anyone else, so we called an emergency in-person meeting for those who could make it, with those who couldn't keeping up as best they could via text. By noon, Bridge's tiny flat was packed out with me, Liz, Priya, and James Royce-Royce, who'd spent ten minutes manoeuvring an incredibly complicated stroller up a flight of stairs and then another ten minutes painstakingly de-strollering Baby J and strapping him to his chest.

"This is going to involve you lot needing my truck again, isn't it," said Priya, helping herself to what was left of the Toblerone.

Liz—a small, blond woman who was currently not wearing a dog collar, presumably because she was off duty—leaned back against the wall. "I don't think driving around London without a plan is necessarily going to be the most useful thing to do."

"Do you think we should just leave it to God?" asked Priya.

"In my experience," Liz replied, "God really hates being taken for granted."

James Royce-Royce was gently swaying for what I presumed were baby-related reasons. "Come on, Baby J. We have to help Auntie Bridget."

Priya watched this little routine with visible incredulity. "He can't speak or walk. What help is he going to be?"

"He's providing moral support," put in Bridge loyally, "by being adorable."

"What's that, Baby J?" James Royce-Royce made a theatrical listening gesture. "He's wondering, Bridget darling, if you've spoken to Tom's friends? One of them is bound to have seen him."

I think it said everything about Bridge that, even in the middle of a personal crisis, she didn't want Baby J to feel left out of the conversation. "Well, that's a good idea, Baby J. But I don't quite know what I'd say to them. I can't just ring them up and go, 'Can you tell me where Tom is? I think he's cheating on me.'"

"How about," suggested Priya, "'Can you tell me where Tom is? I'm his fucking fiancée.'"

"Maybe just a *schooch*"—James Royce-Royce held his thumb and forefinger together in the universal gesture for *tiny*—"less sweary than that? Also, not in front of the baby."

Priya gave him a cold look. "He's a fucking baby, James. He's not going to be offended."

"Yes, but if it's all the same to you, I don't want my beautiful son's first words to be"—he put his hands gently over Baby J's ears—"*go fuck yourself*."

"Be honest," Priya told him. "It's more interesting than 'dadda.'"

"You know"—once he'd gone full baby, it was hard to recalibrate James Royce-Royce—"I think he almost said 'dadda' the other day. Well, it was more sort of a…bluh, but he's getting there."

Mercifully, my phone buzzed with an update from James Royce-Royce. If Liz saw him in Harrow, the woman probably lives locally. Followed by: That means your best chance of catching them would be around lunchtime or rush hour, in that area. Then: If you want a more solid plan, I'll need more information.

I looked up. "James suggests we check out Harrow around lunchtime, which is kind of now."

Bridget winced. "But what if I find something I don't want to find?"

"Then you'll have all your friends around you," I said, hoping I sounded reassuring as opposed to platitudey. "Well, a lot of your friends."

At that moment the intercom went off and another of the bridesmaids stumbled up. Her name was Melanie, and she'd been working with Bridge for years.

"Sorry I'm late," she said, dropping her handbag onto the floor. "Couldn't get away from work. Huge crisis. We're just about to launch an adorable children's book by a very promising new writer about an adventurous puppy who loses his favourite bone, but somebody on the art team has only this second realised that in the final illustration of the book, where the puppy has recovered his bone and it's framed very nicely against the sunset so it's sort of silhouetted—"

"It looks like he's got an enormous erection?" asked Priya.

"How did you guess?"

"Sixth sense."

Melanie crossed the living room and gave Bridge a lingering hug. "I'm so sorry, babe," she said. "We'll get this sorted out, you'll see."

"I think"—Bridge relaxed into the hug—"I think we have to sort it out by going to Harrow?"

Priya gave a long-suffering sigh. "Fine. Get in my truck. Someday, one of you bastards is going to have to buy a car."

We all dashed outside to the truck and piled in like clowns in reverse, only to immediately have to pile out again because James Royce-Royce needed to fit a car seat. Or at least transform his stroller into a car seat. Because obviously the James Royce-Royces hadn't just bought a stroller. They'd brought a multifunctional infant transportation device that looked like a spaceship. It was a weird folding contraption with wheels and a pod and a kind of padded area that you could tuck a baby into like Superman being blasted off from Krypton. There was a lot of clunking and a lot of moving parts that didn't seem to be moving quite right and a loud yelp as James Royce-Royce closed his finger in something that really wasn't designed to have fingers closed in it.

"Perhaps," Priya suggested, "it'd be easier if you didn't have a baby strapped to your chest?"

"No." James Royce-Royce flapped his injured hand. "No, I can do this. It's just we've never used the car-seat function because we're normally walking or taking the Tube."

Bridge came forward helpfully-slash-hurryingly. "Let me take him."

With the kind of reluctance you only see amongst new parents and people struggling to kick serious addictions, James Royce-Royce unbuckled Baby J from his chest and handed him over to Bridge. "Support the head, support the head."

"Oh, come on, even *I* know that," I said. "And I'm the last person you should ever trust with a baby."

Bridge was already bouncing Baby J in that instinctively calming way that some people have and I definitely didn't. "But Luc, you and Oliver would make such *sweet* parents."

"Would we? He works all the time, and I've never had a goldfish last more than two days."

"Babies aren't goldfish," insisted Bridge.

"I just know I'd, I don't know, forget to feed it or leave it on the bus or something."

James Royce-Royce looked up from the impossibly complex mechanism from which a car seat was meant to emerge. "That's hard to do. They make quite a lot of noise." Something clicked, and a pair of wheels popped down. "Oh, that wasn't supposed to happen. James usually does this."

"Shift over," Priya elbowed James Royce-Royce out the way, pushed down on a button, yanked on a lever, and collapsed the shuttle-racer-pod machine into a little tilted basket that looked unmistakably car-seaty. "How do you even survive?"

James Royce-Royce contrived to look both huffy and smug. "I have a very helpful husband."

Baby J was transferred to the seat, and the seat was transferred to the truck, where it was strapped in securely by people who knew what they were doing. Then we piled in again and were just about to get underway, like we were in a disappointingly middle-aged road movie, when Bridge burst into tears. And I abruptly discovered it was really hard to comfort somebody when they were sitting behind you in a truck.

"Bridge"—Melanie reached over to make the most reassuring physical contact she could make given the whole truck situation— "babe. It'll be okay. We'll sort this out."

Bridge sobbed. "I know. I mean, I don't know. It's just the last time I was jammed in a truck doing something silly we were taking Luc to Durham because he was in love with Oliver, and Tom was with me and everything seemed so wonderful."

"That was not wonderful," Priya and I chorused.

"Because my relationship had fallen apart," I went on.

"And," Priya pushed in, "I had to drive you bunch of ungrateful shits the whole length of the country."

"And Oliver wasn't even there."

"And none of you chipped in for petrol."

"And then you dumped me on his doorstep in the middle of the night."

"Even though you always say you're going to."

At which point, Baby J started crying, which meant James

Royce-Royce had to unstrap him and do parental things to calm him down, and we were still outside Bridge's flat.

"Sugarplums," said James Royce-Royce, "I love you but if you keep shouting, you'll upset Baby J, and if you upset Baby J, he'll cry all afternoon."

"I'm sorry, Baby J." Bridge half turned in an attempt to join in the baby soothing. "It's just we were so young and hopeful then."

"It was two years ago," said Priya. "And I wasn't hopeful. I was pissed off."

"I've never been hopeful," I added.

"Well, *I* was so young and hopeful." Weirdly, Bridge seemed to have stopped crying. Maybe because it was quite hard to cry and bicker at the same.

Liz leaned forward from the very back seat. "How about we get on the road? It might help you feel better. And your youth and hope might come flooding back to you."

"Hang on"—James Royce-Royce started bundling and strapping—"got to get Baby J settled again."

I thunked my head gently against the dashboard. "We are kind of on a clock here, James."

"Fine. I'll just leave my child untethered so he flies through the windscreen the first time we brake suddenly."

"I think it's more," I tried, "that emergency marriage rescue and baby aren't completely compatible?"

I'd mostly meant that we should prioritise helping Bridge because she was the one having a crisis, but now everyone was staring at me like I'd taken the last After Eight mint without even apologising. "Luc," said Bridget, definitely not crying now. "That's an *awful* thing to say."

"It's *your* fiancé we're looking for," I pointed out.

"But not without Baby J." Bridget sat back with her arms folded. "He's part of the group now."

"I just thought it would be more efficient if we—"

James Royce-Royce glared at me. "If we *what*? Left my child alone in an empty flat with a kitchen knife and a box of matches? Or am I not welcome amongst you now that I'm a *father*?"

"Of course you're welcome, James," I tried, "I just… It's only—"

The truck lurched into gear and Priya eased us out into the road. "Drop it, Luc. You sound like a prick."

I dropped it. Because if Priya was telling you that you sounded like a prick, it meant you'd gone way over the prick line.

The magic of everyone being slightly angry at me got us back into an old groove as we bombed—well, not quite bombed, more travelled at a responsible child-transporting speed—along the north circular. And while I freely admitted that it had been insensitive of me to suggest that having a child made James Royce-Royce a bigger liability friend-wise than, say, me, there's no getting away from the fact that if you'd rated our emergency marriage rescuing out of ten, we were pulling somewhere between a four and a two. I mean, Bridge had stopped crying so we probably got a point for that. And if there were points for effort, we got at least one of those. But in terms of what we were actually achieving, we…sort of weren't.

We arrived in Harrow about an hour after we needed to, which meant that even if Tom and his mystery woman had been out getting lunch, they'd have been able to eat, have coffee, tip the waiter, and slink back to their love nest before we'd even parked. This left us sitting outside a random café, with Bridge once again on the verge of tears, not really sure what to do next.

"What should we do next?" I asked, hoping to keep the action ball rolling so no one had to have emotions.

Bridge threw her hands in the air. "I accept that love is for everyone else in the universe except me, so I'm going to die alone surrounded by cats, even though I don't like cats. And I'll only be found when the juices from my lonely, suppurating corpse leak through onto the married couple below me while they're having a beautiful Sunday dinner with their children."

So score zero for the action ball, then.

"That will never happen," said Priya. "Your cats will eat you way before you start leaking."

"I'm so sorry." That was Liz, who had been sinking farther and farther in the back seat. "I feel this is all my fault."

"It's not your fault." Bridge twisted round. "You're not the one cheating on me."

"We don't know he's cheating on you. I should never have sent the picture. Jesus would not have sent the picture."

Melanie glanced up from Baby J's toes, which she'd been leaning over to this-little-piggy. "Saint Paul might have. I bet he'd have sent it straight to the Ephesians."

"That doesn't help," cried Liz. "I'm a vicar. I'm not supposed to gossip. It's just you're my friend and I'm bad at keeping secrets."

Blowing her nose into a tissue, Bridge made a visible effort to pull herself together. "You did the right thing. I don't want to marry a man I can't trust."

"All is not lost, my little chou bun." That was James Royce-Royce, and for a moment, it was genuinely unclear whether he was talking to Bridge or the baby. "My marvellous husband has just texted us a set of instructions. It's a long shot but apparently if we spiral outwards, then we maximise our chances of seeing Tom, if he's here."

"And if he's *not* here?" I asked.

James Royce-Royce looked apologetic. "Then we'll have had a rather long afternoon in a rather hot van."

"Truck," corrected Priya.

But she followed James Royce-Royce's instructions anyway, taking us on a spiralling path out to the edge of Harrow, then back in again, then back out, then back in. Then we stopped at a pub so that James could change Baby J and the rest of us could get something to drink before we got back in the truck and went back to spiralling.

The thing about spending hour after hour trapped in a metal box with six other people, one of them a baby, was that it made you acutely aware of all the times in your life when you'd been doing literally anything else. Like, for example, not not-quite-arguing with the man you'd somehow managed to stay in love with for the last two years. And who, miraculously, had somehow managed to stay in love with you.

Suddenly it didn't seem that all important anymore whose turn it was to text.

I miss you, I sent.

I didn't get anything back, which I knew rationally meant Oliver was in court, but which I felt emotionally meant I'd destroyed my relationship by being insufficiently committed to *Pretty Woman*.

"This is hopeless," said Bridge for the ninth time.

"There's no such thing as hopeless," said James Royce-Royce, also for the ninth time.

Bridge pressed her nose tragically against the window as she scanned a gaggle of passing Harrovians. "There *is* such a thing as hopeless. It is this thing. By which I mean what we're doing right now. And also me. Because I'm doom— Oh my God, it's him."

"What?" I jerked alert. "Are you sure?"

"Yes." Bridge was already unbuckling her seat belt. "He went into that Tesco Express. The *bastard*."

Priya obligingly stopped dead—and absolutely not

suspiciously—in front of the Tesco Express, and Bridge dove out of the passenger-side door. I dove after her, and Mel dove after me. Liz stayed behind with James Royce-Royce because they were all sitting together and diving over a finally sleeping Baby J seemed like an exceptionally bad idea.

We approached the doors of the unsuspecting late-night, reduced-offering supermarketette like we were a crack squad of secret agents. Okay, possibly more like we were a *crap* squad of secret agents, with Bridge yelling at us to cover the doors and Mel pressing herself against the wall and I swear coming this close to holding her hands like a gun, while I—in a fit of either enthusiasm or paranoia—tried to conceal myself behind a sign advertising massive savings on frozen pizzas.

As inconspicuously as, well, as three people who didn't know much about being sneaky trying to sneak into a public building with massive windows, we dashed inside. Bridge grabbed a copy of one of those magazines with stories like *My Husband Murdered My Dog...But Then He Left Me for My Sister* from an end display and held it over her face.

"What are you *doing*?" I asked in the quietest voice I could manage while still making myself heard past the couple buying Diet Coke next to me.

She peered around the corner of the magazine. "Well, I don't want to be *recognised*."

"You're Tom's fiancée, Bridge. I'm pretty sure he knows what you look like."

"Watch out." Mel ducked behind a precariously balanced pile of four-quid tubs of Cadbury Roses. "Somebody's coming."

The somebody turned out to be a man buying one bottle of milk, three teenagers buying nothing, and somebody whose evening plans I didn't want to speculate about, who was carrying a basket of scouring pads, cling film, and chocolate.

"There." Bridge pointed. And she was, in her defence, completely right. It was Tom, looking extremely calm and inconspicuous, swiping a few essential items through the self-checkout.

The three of us moved into flanking positions, but since he was a professional spy and we weren't, by the time we'd got *into* our flanking positions, he'd already vanished again.

We pursued him into the street where Bridge spotted him again, walking up College Road past the Costa Coffee. We almost managed to kid ourselves he hadn't seen us on account of our amazingly effective spying techniques, but then he turned sharply into Harrow-on-the-Hill station with the air of someone who knew exactly how to find a crowd when he had to.

"He's escaping," cried Bridge. "My fiancé's escaping."

She broke into a run, shedding a shoe as she went. I retrieved her shoe and followed. Melanie followed me. And then, annihilating the last remnants of our subtlety, Priya's truck pulled over and began kerb-crawling along beside us.

"What are you doing?" I demanded, only mildly hysterically, as Priya rolled down the window.

"What do you mean what am I doing? We're following Tom."

"Yeah, but"—I was rapidly running out of breath—"discreetly."

"Mate, Bridge is pelting through London with one shoe on, and I'm driving a giant black truck. Discreet was never an option."

"Okay, but we still need to get him."

Priya kept driving. "Fine. I'll just ditch my truck here in this pedestrian crossing."

The door opened and Liz stumbled out, realising slightly too late that slow for a motorised vehicle was unreasonably fast for a human being. "Come on." She made a beckoning noise to James Royce-Royce who was unbuckling Baby J's car seat.

"Be very careful," he admonished us as he scooted across the truck and passed Baby J to Mel, who had joined us in the walk-slowly-next-to-a-truck-a-thon. "James would have kittens if he knew I'd passed our little boy out of a moving vehicle."

After Baby J was safely transferred and then, once James Royce-Royce was on the pavement, safely transferred back, we dashed up the station steps to follow Bridge. Or at least Mel and I dashed. James Royce-Royce followed as quickly as he could, given his embabyment, and Liz kept a vicarly pace beside him.

Inside, we'd just hit rush-hour crowds, and I could barely tell where one face began and another ended. But then I wasn't Bridge and hadn't developed her highly attuned Tom senses. She saw him swiping his way through a ticket barrier and dashed after him, scrambling over the gates rather than stopping to find her card—and drawing the attention of a Transport for London guard who immediately set off after her. Which left me with two choices: either hang back with an air of supportive dignity or kick off a ludicrous Benny Hill chase through a crowded Tube station.

Benny won.

Tom was just ducking behind a pillar, talking urgently into his phone while Bridge—minus both shoes now—was sprinting to catch up with him and the guard was sprinting to catch up with her and the rest of us were, well, honestly, most of us weren't in the mood to sprint but we were at least jogging lightly to keep pace.

"Tom!" said Bridge.

"Bridge?" said Tom.

"Gotcha!" said the Transport for London guard.

Bridget turned around. "You haven't got me. I haven't done anything."

"You jumped the barrier, miss."

She gave him a defiant look. "Yes, but I'm not getting on the train."

"That doesn't make a difference."

Maybe having a barrister boyfriend had gone to my head. "I think it does," I panted. "The crime is fare dodging, but if you don't go anywhere, there's no fare to dodge."

This did not endear me to the Transport for London guard. "Who works here, me or you?"

By now, Bridge's army of wedding guests had arrived and surrounded Tom, wearing expressions of varying betrayal and exhaustion. Except for Baby J who was, y'know, a baby which meant he looked like all babies always look: grumpy and a bit squashed.

Apparently resigned to being caught, Tom put his phone down and said, "Sorry. She's my fiancée—"

"Oh, *am I?*" asked Bridget.

Which, if he'd needed one, was Tom's big clue that maybe not everything was in a perfect state of totally fineness. "And as you can see," he continued, "we've got a lot to talk about, so would it be okay if we just left and pretended none of this ever happened?"

The guard looked uncertain. Then again, he'd been looking uncertain since we showed up. "I'm not sure I can do that. I think I'm supposed to issue an on-the-spot fine."

"I am really sorry," offered Bridge, "and I really wouldn't have jumped the barrier except it was a romantic emergency."

"Wait, what romantic emergency?" Tom's unflappable demeanour flapped very slightly.

"Yeah, what romantic emergency?" asked the Transport for London guard, suddenly getting interested.

Bridge adopted a posture of supreme indignance. "We're getting married in a week, and he's running around with other women."

"I am bloody not," protested Tom.

"I have proof," Bridge told the Transport for London guard.

The Transport for London guard gave Tom a disappointed look. "Mate, if you're running around on your bird, be a man and admit it."

"I'm not," protested Tom again.

"Look at this." Bridge brandished her phone in Transport for London guy's face. "What's that if it's not running around on his bird?"

The guard assessed the evidence dispassionately. "I agree it don't look great. But there could be an explanation."

"I've been trying to get him to explain himself for days," Bridge wailed. "He ghosted me."

Tom's face had gone very, very impassive. "It was *work*, Bridge. You know, *work*."

"What?" The Transport for London visibly scoffed. "You some kind of spy or something?"

Bridge gave the fakest laugh I have ever heard. "No. Of course not." Her voice had lifted by at least an octave. "He's a"—she paused, way longer than any woman should have had to before saying what her fiancé did for a living—"fireman."

There was a long silence.

"Oh, crap." The Transport for London guard's eyes had gone very wide. "Is this a... Is this an MI5 thing? Is that woman some kind of secret agent?"

"Yes," said Tom without missing a beat. "She's a defector from a foreign power, and it's vitally important that my *fiancée*"—he gave the word a verbal air quote—"and I be able to discuss the rest of this in private."

Transport for London Guy nodded and backed right the fuck off. "'Course. Won't say a thing. You can count on me, agent."

The moment he was gone, Bridge rounded on Tom, brandishing her phone in his face. "Look. I know she's not really a spy, so who is she? What were you doing? And why are you leaving me for somebody from Harrow?"

Tom looked more flustered than I'd ever seen him, which, to his credit, was a lot less flustered than I was in most situations.

"I told you, it's work. And she's not from Harrow. That's why we're here."

"That," Bridge said sharply, "makes no sense."

His flusterance intensifying, Tom glanced around the increasingly crowded platform. "Can we go somewhere else?"

"No." Bridge, still brandishing, was now also bristling. "I have been trying to call you since yesterday, Tom. *Since yesterday.* Where have you been?"

Tom took a deep breath and leaned in very closely. The rest of Bridge's Bitches (Used in the Reclaimed Sense) gathered in. "I have been," he whispered, "in a safe house with an informant."

Bridge de-bristled very slightly. "Oh."

"Now maybe," suggested Tom, "we can finish this conversation somewhere that isn't incredibly public."

Trying not to catch the eye of the Transport for London guard on the way out, we all trooped back to the truck and squeezed in.

"Found him, then?" observed Priya.

"Yes," Bridge was sitting on Tom's lap in the front seat and still not looking totally mollified. "And he's going to explain everything, aren't you?"

Tom surveyed the assembled band of demi-strangers. "You realise this is the opposite of operational security?"

"Just tell me." Bridge could be very firm when she wanted to be.

"The woman in the photograph is married to a major drug smuggler we're investigating. I was moving her into a safe house. We now have to move her to a different safe house, and I'm going to take myself off the case because somehow you got a picture of us together."

"Sorry," said Liz, "that was me. The Lord works in mysterious ways and all that."

Behind his eyes, I could see Tom doing some very painful calculations. "And you sent it to Bridge?"

"And I sent it to Luc," Bridge added.

"And," I finished, "I sent it to...sort of the entire WhatsApp group?"

Tom thunked his head against Bridge's shoulder. "Everybody. Delete. The picture. It's important. Sorry, Bridge. I should have taken this week off."

She kissed him on the forehead. "It's okay. I knew you were in Intelligence. I just didn't know you were James Bond."

"You didn't?" Tom risked a smile. "I thought that was why you wanted to marry me."

James Royce-Royce leaned between the seats. "Oh, that would be a very bad call. James Bond only got married once, and she was dead by the end of the film."

"James," said Tom, "stop helping."

"And..." Bridge seemed to be having a lot of feelings. "And she really was an informant? Not, like, an international sex assassin?"

"She's an informant, Bridge. There are no international sex assassins. International assassins are just ordinary-looking blokes who stab you with an umbrella or slip you an exploding cigar."

"And you haven't bought her a necklace?"

It took me a moment to remember what she meant by that, but Tom got there immediately. "I haven't even bought her a Joni Mitchell CD."

"And we're still getting married?"

Tom gazed up at her, with a loving exasperated expression that Oliver sometimes got when he was looking at me. "I fucking hope so. Otherwise you just compromised a major drug bust over nothing."

They kissed, and they kept kissing for long enough that we all had to suddenly get very interested in our phones. Which was convenient because mine chose that exact moment to ring.

And, thank God, it was Oliver.

"Lucien," he said. "I got your text and I just wanted to call to make sure you were okay. I would have texted back but I was in court."

"I definitely knew that," I told him. "And wasn't in any way worried you were going to dump me."

He gave an embarrassed little cough. "I've been behaving badly because I miss you and want to spend time with you. Dumping you in retribution would be extremely counterproductive."

Lovingly logical Oliver was one of my top five favourite Olivers. "I miss you too. But we found Tom. It turned out he wasn't cheating on Bridge, and we actually caused a minor national security incident."

"That does sound on-brand for you."

"*Minor National Security Incident* is the name of my sex tape."

"Well, that's ruined any possible segue I could have come up with, but when are you coming home?"

"Pretty much now unless—" My phone screen flashed ominously. "Shit, the venue's calling. I have to take this."

And so I hung up on the boyfriend I was just patching things up with to do a bit more wedding admin. Five minutes later, I realised I was going to have to do a lot more wedding admin.

"Uh, guys?" I did my best to attract Bridge's attention.

"Yes, Luc?" She was all smiles again. "And thanks for being there for me. You're the best."

"Yeah, about that. You know the church?"

Bridge's face fell. "The church where I'm getting married?"

"That would be the one. That was their vicar on the phone, and it's... Well, it might have, umm, ever so slightly... Well, it might have burned down?"

CHAPTER 7

"OKAY," I SAID. "I UNDERSTAND. Basically what I expected, thanks."

It was the forty-fifth venue I'd called in two days, and it had given me the same answer as the other forty-four. *No, funnily enough, we can't fit in a lavish wedding of your dreams at less than a week's notice. We're kind of booked up.*

I directed a bad-news expression at Bridge. We were back in her flat with Tom, who was taking a couple of days off to be with his fiancée and avoid getting an informant murdered, and Liz, who was working the church angle. "Sorry," I told them.

"No, it's fine." Bridget had a severe case of it's-not-fine face. "We'll keep going. We can keep going, right?"

Liz looked up from her own phone. She'd annexed a corner of the room and had an enormous leather-bound planner, bulging with sticky notes and spare bits of paper, open in front of her. "I think churches are a no-go. I'd have to find one you had a connection to that wasn't already hosting another wedding, then meet up with their vicar at extremely short notice and arrange a lot of complex theology things. And that *also* means I'm ruled out of officiating."

It was the latest item in a long run of bad news, and Bridge gave an involuntary sob. "But we *promised*," she said. "When you first became an ordinand."

"We originally promised that you were going to be my *first* wedding, and that didn't pan out either."

Both of them glared at Tom.

"Hey"—he put his hands in the air—"would you really want me to have proposed before we were ready just so you could keep a promise you made in your early twenties?"

"Yes," cried Bridge. "It would have been romantic and it would have been perfect, and because we waited, we're *cursed* and everything is falling apart."

Liz shifted uncomfortably. "I think as a vicar I should be on the side of taking marriage seriously?"

"Traitor." Bridge wasn't genuinely angry, but given how emotional the last couple of days had turned out to be, she was straying close to it.

"I think a civil ceremony might be out of the question as well," I added. "Every registered venue I've tried has been booked for months."

Staring at his laptop screen, Tom shook his head. "He's right. We're not going to find anywhere."

"I *think*"—Liz stood up and ran her hands through her hair—"that you might have to decide whether you want a *wedding* or a wedding *ceremony*."

"What's the difference?" asked Tom, glancing up.

"A wedding has legal status. A wedding ceremony is just a party, and then you do the legal bit quietly afterwards."

"I don't want my wedding to be *just a party*," wailed Bridget. "This is supposed to be the most important day of my *life*."

"Well," I tried, "I suppose it depends on what you think makes it important."

I must have done a good job with my calming voice because Bridge seemed genuinely calmed. "What do you mean?"

Urgh. That was what happened when you said nebulously

reassuring things you hadn't thought through. You had to back them up. And I had a seriously limited up-backing game. "I guess... if I was marrying Oliver, what I'd really want—what would really matter to me—would be making sure that it was him and me saying how much we loved each other and wanted to be together in front of all the people we cared most about. Our friends, our family. Well, my family. Well, my mum."

I wasn't quite sure why I'd gone to myself as an example because Oliver and I were a long way from the 'til-death-do-us-part conversation. But it was hard not to have weddings on the brain when everyone around you—including your dickhead ex—was getting married. Still, now that I'd put the possibility out there, it didn't seem...entirely terrible? There was a certain *something* to it, wasn't there? The idea of your thing being a thing that you shared with everyone in a way that, like, made it an official thing.

In any case, I'd pressed the right Bridge-distracting button because she leaned across the sofa and hugged me. "Oh, Luc, that's beautiful. And are you?"

"Are I what?"

"Are you and Oliver getting married?"

Ah. That was the other side of the everyone-getting-married stage of life. I guess I was going to have to get used to that question. "We've not really talked about it."

"Bridge"—Tom had closed his laptop—"can we get back to *our* wedding? You know, the one that's meant to be happening in five days?"

She dehugged. "Right. Sorry. I suppose...I suppose if we can get everybody there, and if it's somewhere nice, and"—her phone buzzed—"oh God, the dress is still being adjusted. I was meant to pick it up today, and now I can't. What's wrong with me? Why can't they make a dress fit my weird alien proportions?"

"You don't have weird proportions," said Tom, with a timing

that I suspected came from practice. "But I would love you and find you sexy even if you did."

"Then why won't my dress be ready 'til tomorrow?"

Tom did not look like he had any idea what might make adjusting a dress take longer than average. "It's probably just technical issues at their end."

"Technical issues." Bridge's voice rose. "It's a dress, not a Dyson Airblade."

There was a soft flump as Liz manoeuvred her planner into her bag. "How about we take a walk? Maybe grab a cocktail—"

"It's two in the afternoon," Bridge pointed out.

"You say that like it's a bad thing."

Bridge's lip wobbled. "Right now, everything feels like a bad thing."

Being Bridget's maid of honour had taught me a lot about how weddings worked, and not necessarily in a good way. Because, sure, it was a joyous celebration of your relationship, but it was also a logistical nightmare that you had to be the James Royce-Royces to enjoy. And, to be fair, their wedding had kicked quite a lot of arse. "I agree with Liz," I said. "Why don't you give us a rundown of what you want in your dream venue, and Tom and I will try to swing it for you while you go and...and...have a relax?"

"Maybe two relaxes," Liz added, "if we hit happy hour."

For a moment, Bridge looked mutinous, and then her shoulders slumped. "Thank you, everyone. I suppose I want somewhere...I don't know...beautiful?"

"The nice thing about doing just the ceremony is that you can go outdoors if you want to." Liz was also doing calming voice, and way better than me, partly because it was her literal job and partly because I'd always been quite bad at it.

That seemed to genuinely cheer Bridge up, and fuck knows she needed it right then. "What do you think, Tom? We could have the wedding in some kind of park? Or a garden?"

"Or a field?" I suggested.

"*Not* a field." Bridge was pretty adamant about this.

"I think a garden would be lovely," said Tom. "If we can get one."

Two hours later, it turned out we couldn't. Unlicensed venues were as booked up as licensed ones, and unregulated celebrants were as busy as ministers and registry offices. While Liz and Bridge were sitting in a relax bar, downing relaxes, Tom and I had tried every park, hotel, and stately home that Google would throw at us.

"It's no good," I concluded at last. "I am a shitty maid of honour."

"And I," added Tom, "am a shitty fiancé."

"There's just no way we're getting a venue at such short notice. We'd have to be royalty."

Tom laughed. He'd always had an irritatingly sexy laugh, which I think I could comfortably admit now he was getting married and I was in a stable relationship. "Yeah, that or massive celebrities."

Well, fuck.

"How massive?" I asked, with a sinking feeling.

"I was mostly joking," said Tom.

"Okay, I get that, but how massive?"

I didn't think Tom was quite on board yet, but he went along with it anyway. "I dunno. *Love Island*–runner-up level?"

"Or…eighties-rock-star-who's-just-released-a-multiplatinum-album-and-has-a-hit-reality-TV-show level?"

Tom gave me a suspicious look. "You don't have to do that."

"I know. But… I mean, what's the point of your dad being a dickhead superstar if you can't use it to help your mates?"

"What's the point of having mates if they're just going to use you for your dickhead superstar dad?"

That was also fair, but when it came to my friends, my balance of *sacrifices made* versus *bullshit dumped* was tilted heavily towards *bullshit*. "I can't make any promises," I said. "Because, well, he *is* still a dickhead. But I'm hoping that he'll like the opportunity to flex."

"It's worth a try," Tom agreed. "And...no pressure?"

No pressure was, as always, one of the most pressurising things a person could possibly say, but it sounded like Tom meant it sincerely. "Yeah. I'll... I might take it outside if that's okay with you?"

Tom gave me a nod, and I sloped downstairs with my phone. I wasn't completely sure who I was going to call. The last time I'd reached out to my dad's manager, he'd fobbed me off with a *Pull the other one, Charlie,* and Dad had only got in touch with me because, at the time, he'd thought he was dying of cancer. Since he now definitely wasn't, I didn't think going through official channels was likely to work.

Huddled on the steps outside the converted town house that was now Bridge's block of flats, I texted Oliver. Y'know, that wonderful boyfriend who I hadn't seen for days.

No luck finding a venue. I'm going to try and call my dad.

For a while there was nothing. Then, Is this a support-me text or a talk-me-out-of-it text?

How the hell should I know? Support me, I think?

Another texty silence. It's a very kind gesture.

That was Oliver code for "I will be there for you even though you and I both know this will end poorly." It's a bad idea, isn't it?

There was another ominous silence. Not necessarily. A pause. You need something, he can help you. Another pause. As long as you don't go in with any expectations.

Oh, trust me I'm going in with zero expectations.

For a while I carried on sitting, trying to psych myself up to start making calls.

Take as long as you need, Oliver texted. I'm making sticky miso peppers this evening and they're quick, so they can be ready whenever you're home. Another pause. Assuming you do come home. Pause. Though I understand if you can't.

God, I hoped I could. This had been a lot, and I'd expected it to be a lot, but I hadn't quite been prepared for how much of a lot it was. And while I was slowly letting myself accept that my best friend's wedding wasn't going to kill my relationship, I'd have accepted it much more easily if I actually got spend time with Oliver. Which, if I swung a venue for Bridge, maybe I'd be able to.

I took a deep breath and rang Mum.

She picked up as speedily as ever. "Allô, mon caneton."

"Hi, Mum." I sometimes worried that I wasn't staying in touch as well as I used to but, on balance, it was more that Mum was no longer my go-to panic dial. And, given I was nearly thirty, that was probably healthy. "How are you?"

"Oh, Luc. Some very bad things have happened."

Part of me was instantly worried. Part of me suspected she was talking about something very minor. "What's wrong?"

"Judy and I, we were thinking we may have to break up with the *Drag Race*. There is just too much of it these days. It is like when you buy something on the internet and then the internet, it thinks to itself, *Well, she bought this thing, she must like this thing, so I will show her adverts for this exact same thing that she just bought from now until the day she dies.*"

"I'm sorry you and *Drag Race* are going through a tough time at the moment."

She gave a deep sigh. "It is very sad for us. There is the *Drag Race UK*, there is the *Canada's Drag Race*, the *Drag Race Down*

Under, the *Untucked*, the *All Stars*. And there are queens on the new series of *All Stars* who were on the last series of the main show. That does not make them an all-star. That makes them someone who lost on a reality TV show quite recently. Also"—she paused ominously—"your boyfriend is incorrect and Bimini was robbed."

I'd taken it as a good sign on a number of levels that Oliver was willing to argue quite fiercely with my mum about *Drag Race*. Not only did it show he cared about me enough to regularly watch reality TV with my family, but it also showed he was comfortable enough with them to be himself, instead of the perfect houseguest he'd been raised to be. He'd even stopped eating the special curry. Lucky git. "Mum, I'm not going to get into a proxy debate about whether Lawrence Chaney's consistently strong performance should have counted for as much as Bimini's growing confidence."

"Well, of course it shouldn't," retorted Mum. "She had no arc. The whole point of the show is to have an arc so people can say, 'Oh, I thought this person was rubbish, but now they are great.'"

"You say that, but that's why mediocre dancers keep winning *Strictly*."

"They are entertainment shows, Luc. I am going to vote for who entertains me. If all you wanted to see were people being good at dancing, they would take away the celebrities completely."

She did kind of have a point. Not that I could address it because I'd rung up for a reason. "Um," I said. "Look, there's no good way to raise this, but do you have a private number for Dad?"

The silence at the other end of the line suddenly radiated concern. "Luc, I thought you had decided that your father was a miserable, bald, old piece of shit with a tiny penis you never wanted to speak to again."

She had a point there too. "He *is* a miserable, bald, old piece of shit whose penis I'm not comfortable talking about, but I think I might"—I swallowed a gagging noise—"need him."

"What could you possibly need him for?" There was an edge of hurt in Mum's voice, and I couldn't blame her. She'd given me everything my whole life, and all Dad had ever done was mess me about and screw me over.

"Bridge's wedding venue has fallen through, and I'm hoping Dad can pull some magic celebrity bullshit for her."

I'd tried to keep it light, but Mum still didn't seem happy. "You know, I am a celebrity too, Luc."

Technically that was true. And if Bridge had wanted to get married in an indie recording studio, the name Odile O'Donnell would probably have opened every door in the building. "I do know, but right now Dad's got that...that big I'm-on-TV, give-me-free-stuff energy, and I really need free stuff."

"I understand," she said in a way that implied that understanding didn't stop her resenting. "And Bridget has put up with you for a very long time, so she deserves to get something back."

I nodded, which was unhelpful in a voice-only medium. "Yeah, I wouldn't have asked otherwise. It's just, y'know, maids of honour gotta maid of honour."

"I understand," she said again, and this time she sounded more like she meant it. She gave me the number that Dad reserved only for people whose calls he would actually take, and after rehashing the great Lawrence/Bimini debate one last time, I rang off.

Then, hands shaking slightly, I called my dad.

At first I was relieved when he didn't pick up, but then I felt bad for being relieved because I was doing this to fix Bridge's wedding and I loved Bridge and wanted her to be happy. So I tried again. And again. And again.

Eventually Bridge and Liz came home, several relaxes to the wind.

"Have you and Tom had a fight?" Bridge asked with mock gravity.

I looked up with what I hoped was a not-traumatised expression. "No, I just didn't want him to see me before the wedding."

"Seriously, though, what're you doing on my doorstep?"

"Calling my dad. I thought he might be able to strong-arm a venue into taking us."

Bridge looked at me with the biggest big eyes I'd ever seen. "Oh, Luc, you don't have to."

"I know. But I want to. Think of it as an early wedding present."

She stooped and hugged me. "It's the best present." Then after a moment she added, "But just to be clear, I do want a real present too."

"Of course."

Bridge opened the door, and she and Liz squeezed past me into the house. And I gave my dad one more go. Which was kind of the story of my life.

Once again it rang and once again there was n—

"Hello?" There was no mistaking that voice. As if top-shelf whiskey could speak. If you liked whiskey. And if whiskey was a prick.

Part of me, the part of me that had thought this was a bad idea from the start, wanted to hang up straight away. But I'd come this far, so bottling it at the last second would have been the worst of all possible worlds. "Dad, it's Luc." I felt small and was worried I sounded smaller. "I was wondering if you could help me out."

He gave me that low, narcissistic chuckle that I'd once mistaken for affection. "So you need the old man for something, do you? What can I help you with?"

"I was...I was wondering if you had any contacts who could get us...get us a nice place for a wedding at literally no notice? We were thinking maybe a park or a house with a garden? If you can't, that's fine."

"No, no, that seems like it should be pretty straightforward. After all, what's the point of being famous if you can't help out your own family?"

This was worryingly easy. *Suspiciously* easy. "And we need to know as soon as possible because it's this weekend and we need to work out how to get everybody to the new venue."

"I said I have it covered, Luc." Technically he hadn't said anything of the sort. "Trust me."

And for a moment, against all the odds and against all evidence, I did. "Thanks."

"Leave it to me," he said. "You've got nothing to worry about."

And then he was gone.

Honestly, the whole thing started to feel unreal three seconds after he'd hung up. Partly it was just the image my dad worked so hard to project. That larger-than-life sense of magic and wonder, like he was a grizzled angel from rock heaven who you'd be lucky to have touch your life for an instant before he moved on. And it was partly that I knew from experience that relying on Jon Fleming to do anything for anybody not named Jon Fleming was a complete sucker's game.

I buzzed the buzzer, and Bridge let me up to the flat where I gave her the good news.

"You don't seem very excited," observed Liz.

"I know." I sat down on the sofa. "It's...it's—"

"He has a complicated relationship with his father," explained Bridget. "Which is why it was so sweet to reach out to him for us."

"It'll probably not come to anything," I told them. "He's not exactly reliable."

But that didn't stop me hoping. And hoping didn't stop me being surprised when, three hours later, my phone rang.

Except it wasn't my dad; it was my mum.

"I just wanted to find out how it went with your father," she said.

"About how you'd expect." I tucked the phone against my shoulder and mouthed "It's my mother" to the room before putting it back to my ear.

"The thing is, mon caneton, after you called, I spoke to Judy and she said that if your father couldn't help you or if you—um, well—if you wanted to tell him to go and fuck himself, then you could have the wedding in her garden."

I shouldered her again. "We *do* have a backup, Bridge," I relayed. "Apparently you can have the wedding in Mum's friend's garden."

"I heard that," said Mum from shoulder height, "and I will have you know it is a very nice garden."

"Apparently it's a very nice garden," I clarified.

"Luc, I think you are being very dismissive of Judy's lovely garden."

I scooped the phone back to my ear. "Sorry, Mum, it's been a long day, and a long few days, and while I'm sure Judy's garden is lovely, I really want this to be special for Bridge."

"Just have a look on the internet and see if you would like it."

It was the least I could do. "Tom," I said, "can you grab the laptop and Google something for me?"

Tom obligingly opened up a browser.

"Is she on Facebook or something?" I asked. It seemed improbable, but then again everybody was on some kind of social media these days.

"No, they have a proper website. Well, English Heritage does."

I made an I'm-not-sure-I-heard-that-correctly noise. "English Heritage?"

"Pfaffle Court is a very old building. According to Judy, the hedge maze goes back to the Restoration."

I passed the words *Pfaffle Court, no, Pfaffle, with a P* and *English Heritage* to Tom. "Hang on, so when you said 'in her garden,' did you mean 'in the grounds of her palatial estate'?"

"I *did* say it was a very nice garden."

Bridget was staring over Tom's shoulder with a look of mounting joy. "Oh, Luc," she said, "it's *perfect*."

"Was that Bridget?" asked my mum, who was never one to stay out of other people's conversations. "Does she like the garden?"

"Yes," I told her. "Yes, she likes the garden very much. But why didn't you tell me about this earlier?"

"You never asked. And you seemed so set on talking to your father, I thought maybe it was important to you."

"Mum, he's never going to be important to me. He's a cockweasel."

"With a small penis," she added. "Actually, he doesn't, but I can pretend. So shall I tell Judy you want her help?"

I glanced at Bridge and Tom for confirmation, and they both confirmed enthusiastically. "God, yes, please. Thank you so much. You are the actual best."

"I know. And you should try to remember that instead of running off to your cockweasel father when you need a favour. In any case, Judy will be very pleased. She said she hasn't officiated at a wedding since 1987."

Wait one tiny minute. "Officiated?"

"Of course, it's her garden. She should be involved."

I was about to protest, but this was getting far too complicated, and there was still the massive logistical task of shifting a large, meticulously planned wedding with over a hundred guests from West London to somewhere in Surrey. "You know what," I said. "I'm sure that'll be fine."

After all that, I didn't get to try Oliver's sticky miso peppers. But then, neither did Oliver because he came to Bridge's. Where he helped us reinvite the entire guest list and arrange transportation and accommodation for everybody who'd already arranged transport and accommodation for somewhere else entirely.

By the time we'd got everything sorted, or as sorted as it could possibly be given the circumstances, we were exhausted—the good kind of exhausted you got from doing something hard but rewarding. And I barely even noticed that my dad had never called me back.

CHAPTER 8

AS IT TURNED OUT, I didn't only miss sticky miso peppers, I also missed asparagus and lemon spaghetti with peas, stuffed butternut squash with maple syrup and freekeh, and spicy aubergine with Szechuan sauce. And Oliver didn't make a big deal out of it—what with being a lawyer he wasn't exactly a stranger to things coming up at the last minute—but I felt bad anyway. Yes, we were in a good place, a good enough place that adapting to each other's lives was just a part of being together that we both accepted and were cool with. Except I was beginning to worry I wasn't so much adapting as bailing. It had been nearly a week of staggering home after another evening of intense wedding planning to find Oliver already in bed—and not *in bed* in a sexy "I've been waiting for you, tiger" way. More in an "I've put on my pyjamas and read my book" way.

And it was temporary. I knew it was temporary and Oliver, I'm sure, knew it was temporary too. Or at least I hoped he did because if he didn't, then he was being worryingly calm about being in a relationship where we were never conscious in the same room. It didn't help that since the wedding was in Surrey now, Bridge and all her bridesmaids were going to be spending the night before in Judy's enormous stately home for a kind of non-gendered-person's night, which I assumed would involve braiding each other's hair, drinking champagne, and talking about boys.

Which, honestly, I'd normally have been up for. Only my personal boy would be at home without me, where he'd been every night that week. Still, best-friend code. Maid-of-honour code. And, unless something went catastrophically wrong, I would never have to do this again.

My plan for the evening involved calling a cab to take me to my flat where I'd stashed my suit, then to Oliver's house where I'd somehow managed to stash nearly everything else I owned, and finally back to Bridge's so we could bundle into a hastily rented limousine and get the party started. And, maybe, somewhere in the middle of all this, close my eyes for, like, ten seconds so I wouldn't show up in all the wedding photos looking like Bridget's stoner cousin.

I was just waiting for the cab and definitely had not closed my eyes for any length of time when Bridge sidled over to me with an apologetic look on her face.

"Oh God," I said. "What's happened now?"

She winced. "Nothing. But..." She broke off for a moment. "You know I love you, Luc?"

"You bloody well better after this week."

"And I do. But I was wondering...would you be hurt if I said I wanted this evening to just be the girls?"

I wasn't hurt exactly, but I was a bit confused. "Well, no. Except that doesn't sound like anything you'd ever say in real life. I've been one of the girls for a clear decade."

"Dammit." She curled her hands into fists. "You caught me. I was talking to Liz, and she pointed out that you're knackered and I should give you the night off. But I also knew if I said that, you'd get all defensive and pretend you weren't."

"I'm not getting..." I began, then stopped. "Okay. Yeah. Maybe a bit."

Bridge gazed at me earnestly. "It won't make you a bad friend or a bad maid of honour. In fact, a good maid of honour should be well rested so he doesn't ruin the most important day of my life."

Oh, I wanted to go home so badly. "Really?" I asked, trying to sound like I wasn't begging.

"Really." She gave a decisive nod.

"You know I love you too, right?"

"You rang your dad for me. If I hadn't worked it out before, I'd have worked it out then."

I was too over-weddinged to put up even a token show of resistance. "Bridge. Thank you so much."

She prodded me lightly in the shoulder. "Go home. And I'll see you tomorrow. Which is, in case you've forgotten, the most important day of my life."

So I went home—or rather, I went to Oliver's, which was what *home* meant these days. Although I didn't like to dwell on that because I was scared that if I looked too closely, it would disappear. In any case, I was going to be crap company this evening because I was exhausted, seeing seating plans every time I blinked and still slightly raw from having spoken to my dad who, surprise, surprise, hadn't called me back, despite the fact the wedding was tomorrow. I suppose I was at least consistent when it came to boyfriending. Much like I'd been consistent at sports in school. Which is to say, terrible in every respect.

I got to Clerkenwell about seven, hopped out the cab, and let myself in with the actual key I actually had. I hadn't been in a key-exchanging relationship since Miles, and that hadn't counted because we'd rented the flat together so he hadn't so much given me a key as received a key at the same time I had. Anyway, I'd texted ahead so I'd expected Oliver to be expecting me. What I hadn't expected was for him to be standing in the hall in full black tie holding a blue-velvet jewellery box.

Oh, shit. I'd forgotten something important. It definitely wasn't our anniversary because while we hadn't worked out when it officially was on account of the whole pretending-to-date-before-officially-dating thing, we'd agreed it was before the Beetle Drive, which had already happened. And it wasn't Oliver's birthday because, while I had forgotten when that was exactly, I knew it wasn't in May.

"What's going on?" I asked in the wary voice of a man who felt he should have known but didn't.

Oliver had gone a little pink. "Well, I felt bad that I wasn't more supportive when Bridget needed your help. And I thought since we missed *Pretty Woman: The Musical*, I could, instead, bring *Pretty Woman* to you."

My gaze flicked from the jewellery box to black-tie Oliver and back again. "You'd better not be taking me to the opera. You know I hate opera."

"I'm not taking you to the opera," Oliver said. "I couldn't get tickets and my private jet is being detailed."

Thank God for that. I'd do many things for Oliver, but I drew the line at watching people sing their feelings in languages I didn't understand. Relaxing slightly, I gave him a quizzical look. "Do I need to be in a red dress?"

"You can if you want to be, but I'm not sure it's quite your style. Although"—he offered the jewellery box—"there is something missing."

"I'm not sure anything else is going to fit in these…" I peered down at myself. "Jeans?"

"You do wear very tight jeans," agreed Oliver. He flipped open the box to reveal a necklace of Love Hearts—the weird chalky sweets with little messages on them—threaded on elastic. "You mustn't get too excited," he went on, "because they're on loan."

I gaped at him. "From whom?"

"Well, I can't say, 'Don't get too excited, I bought these for one pound thirty from a sweet shop.'"

"You could say, 'Don't get too excited, these are disgusting.' Which would be true. My rule is never buy a sweet that's more famous for how it looks than how it tastes."

Oliver's brows dipped scowlishly. "Just take the fucking necklace, Lucien."

I reached out, then hesitated. "You're going to snap the box on my fingers, aren't you?"

There was the slightest of pauses. Then Oliver smiled. "For verisimilitude."

So I reached out, and he snapped, and I tried to look as adorable as Julia Roberts, but I think I mostly looked like someone who'd had a jewellery box closed on his fingers.

"Oh, come on," said Oliver, "that did not hurt. I was very careful."

"It's not the pain. It's the shock."

"You knew it was coming. You literally told me you knew it was coming."

I glared in a not-really sort of way. "Then you try it."

We swapped roles and I tried to offer him the necklace like I was a multimillionaire with daddy issues instead of a completely normal bloke with daddy issues. He reached and I snapped.

"Ow," protested Oliver, shaking his hand.

"Sorry. That happened much faster than I thought it would."

"You have to control it on the way down"—Oliver massaged the red line that was forming across his fingertips—"or gravity takes over."

"I'm sorry," I said again. "You clearly have more jewellery-box-snapping practice than I do. Why do you have jewellery-box-snapping practice?"

He gave a little cough. "I might have rehearsed in the mirror a couple of times. I didn't want to hurt you."

"Oh no." I took his hand and gently kissed it better. "I'm the worst."

"I should have known better than to trust you with a dangerous jewellery box."

"Not going to lie." I kissed him again. "That was a bad call. We both should have known better."

The kissing drifted from hands to mouths and ended with Oliver pressed against the wall and me pressed against Oliver as seconds…minutes…slipped past in a haze of heat and homecoming and the pleasure of being together again.

Eventually Oliver—looking nicely dishevelled in an otherwise pristine tux—drew back. "Under normal circumstances, I'd be delighted to take this to its logical conclusion—"

"By *logical conclusion*," I asked, "do you mean *sex in the hall*?"

"Maybe. But, unfortunately, I left some candles burning upstairs and it's probably best not to leave them unattended for too long."

I stared at him. "You did candles as well?"

"It's been a very long week without you."

This was not making sex in the hallway any less appealing. On the other hand, Oliver had gone to a lot of trouble, and burning his house down would have been a crappy way to thank him. I gestured at the jewellery box. "I think you're maybe supposed to put it on me?"

In the movie, Richard Gere had stood behind Julia Roberts, gazing passionately into a mirror as he fastened the delicate chain around her equally delicate neck. Oliver had to kind of…stretch a piece of elastic over my face, nearly dragging one of my ears off.

"I feel very sexy and desirable right now," I said.

Oliver squinted anxiously at me. "Can you breathe? I think it was designed for children."

"Yeah"—I clawed at my throat—"it's digging, but it's not choking."

"Oh, good. Because unnegotiated choking was not what I had planned for this evening."

"I'd be relieved to hear that," I told him, "but now I want to know when we're going to do the negotiated choking."

"Perhaps after the movie."

"Wait. You got the movie as well?"

He took my hand and started drawing me upstairs. "Yes, and I moved the television upstairs. In my head, it was all very romantic."

"It is very romantic," I admitted. "It's probably one of the most romantic things anyone has ever done for me. But you know, like, feelings make me self-conscious. And being self-conscious makes me defensive. And when I'm defensive, I'm sarcastic."

"And I love you anyway, Lucien."

"Yeah, yeah," I muttered. "I love you too."

Despite my best efforts with my socks and sex toys, Oliver kept the bedroom immaculate. And it was still immaculate. Only now it was immaculate with the downstairs TV balanced on the chest of drawers, candles arranged artfully on every spare surface and—with typically Oliverian attention to detail—new bed linen in shades of red and gold. And the worst thing was, I couldn't even find anything glib to say.

"The thing," Oliver began, "about *Pretty Woman* is that when people first watch it, they either love it or hate it. If they love it, they will always—"

"Oh, shut up, Oliver."

I pushed him down on the bed and straddled him. For a moment, I could only look at this ridiculous, kind, and beautiful man who made ridiculous, kind, and beautiful gestures and was ridiculously, beautifully mine. And he was looking right back at me, his eyes grey velvet in the soft light, the severe lines of his face that couldn't—in moments like these—quite hide how vulnerable he got when he knew he'd been, frankly, extra and was expecting to be rejected or laughed at for it. Leaning down, I kissed him again, the way you only kiss someone when they've filled the room with candles for you.

We were definitely, definitely going to watch *Pretty Woman*. But maybe not for a while.

CHAPTER 9

"AS A LEGAL PROFESSIONAL," SAID Oliver as we set off for Surrey at unspeakable o'clock in the morning in the car Oliver had hired for the occasion, "I feel I should point out that Edward actually has a fiduciary responsibility to his company and his investors, which means dropping a billion-dollar deal in favour of a ship-building contract is somewhat unethical."

I fished the final piece of homemade French toast from the Tupperware box on my lap. "Very much the point of that movie, Oliver."

"I'm aware it's not part of the central romantic fantasy, but it *is* made explicit earlier that he doesn't work with his own money. So by deciding at the last minute to make boats with a surrogate father figure, instead of doing what he told people he was going to do, he's technically committing massive fraud."

"Isn't"—I licked cinnamon from my fingertips—"the implication that he'll make more money from the ships long term?"

"It's a billion-dollar deal. The contract with the navy is only for a few million dollars. That's still over nine hundred million dollars unaccounted for. No wonder Stuckey is incandescent. Not, I hasten to add," Oliver hastily added, "that this justifies his sexually assaulting anyone."

"Are you going to be like this when we go and see the musical?" I asked.

He slid me a mischievous look. "Only if there's a song about business ethics."

"I'm kind of assuming it'll be songs about...shopping? And maybe, I don't know, sex work?"

"Ah," said Oliver, "so you think it'll open with Vivian climbing out of a window in her thigh-high boots, singing,"—he sang— "*The laws that are supposed to protect me make things worse in practice. And well-intended regulations can have negative con-*"—he tapped the steering wheel—"*se-quen-ces. If my profession was decriminalised, it wouldn't be unfairly stigmatised. And I wouldn't have to worry about the sexual offences...*" He paused and finished in his normal voice, "Act, 2003."

I was sitting in a car with a man who would and, thinking about it, could improv a mediocre show tune about the complexities of the UK sex industry. And for some reason I was okay with it. "You," I told him, "are a dork who cares too much."

"And it has taken you two years to work this out?"

"I worked out the cares-too-much thing pretty quickly. The dork has been creeping up on me."

Oliver was blushing very slightly. "Yes, I try to keep it close to my chest."

"Oliver, the only dork you need to keep close to your chest is me."

"You do realise that according to some etymologists, *dork* means penis."

"You can keep that close to your chest too, if you like."

"I think that's poor road safety."

"Fine," I said in fake huff, "I'll go to sleep, then."

Oliver's hand briefly left the gearstick to pat my knee. "You should. It's going to be a long day for you."

And how. I was sure it was going to be a worth-it long day, but I was probably going to be in post-someone-else's-wedding recovery for at least a month. Or to put it another way, I was going to be in post-someone-else's-wedding recovery until the next time I needed to go to someone else's wedding. "But how will I entertain and delight you if I'm unconscious?"

"I'll put a podcast on."

I groaned massively. "Not *The Magnus Archives*."

"What's wrong with *The Magnus Archives*?"

"I'm trying to sleep. It'll give me nightmares. About worms." I paused. "Or spiders. Or strangers. Or the sea. Or the sky. Or meat. Or Edinburgh."

"It's *Magnus*," said Oliver firmly, "or *This American Life*."

I groaned massively again. "Fine. Put on *Magnus*."

So Oliver put on *Magnus*, and we either trundled or whooshed—depending on traffic—our way to Surrey. And, fortunately, I was knackered enough that whatever horrendous things were happening to the employees of the Magnus Institute, this time I slept right through it.

When next I stirred, we'd arrived. Or rather, we'd arrived in the car park, which given how English stately homes worked meant that we were still a moderately long walk from the actual house. In a display of unexpected couple efficiency—given that fifty percent of the couple was me—we retrieved what was left of our wedding costumes from the back seat and took turns straightening each other's ties and brushing off each other's lapels. Not that Oliver's lapels needed that much brushing. I just wanted an excuse to cop a feel. Because while Oliver wore a suit to work every day, this was a special-occasion suit and Oliver in a special-occasion suit was different from Oliver in a barrister suit in a way that was only noticeable if you'd spent slightly too long looking at him.

He was in pearl grey, which brought out the silvers in his eyes, and he'd gone with one of his I'm-secretly-more-flamboyant-than-I-let-on ties—with a pattern of subtle pewter swirls and dusty-pink roses. As it happened, my tie was pink as well, but that was because midnight blue and rose gold were the wedding colours, and given the choice between blue suit/pink tie or blue tie/pink suit, I'd put my foot very firmly down on the side of not looking like a lost flamingo.

"Is there something wrong with my lapels?" asked Oliver.

I kept stroking. "Oh yeah, they're a mess. Extremely dusty."

"Thrilled as I am for you to dust me in a car park, are there not maid-of-honour duties you need to attend to?"

Leaning in, I nuzzled needily into his neck. "I know. I mean, I think it'll mostly be standing around providing moral support while Bridge gets her hair done or whatever. But...your lapels. What if they get dusty again?"

"Then"—his voice was soft and full of his smile—"I shall seek you out at once."

"Please do. Spending a whole wedding without you would be awful."

"I promise you faithfully, Lucien, you will only have to spend parts of weddings without me."

Duly reassured, I left Oliver's lapels alone and we set off down a long gravel drive towards the speck on the horizon that was apparently Judy's house.

"You know"—Oliver had taken my hand as we walked, a habit we'd honed over a number of slightly embarrassing strolls around the parks of Clerkenwell—"it's occurring to me that one day you might have to admit that you're just a bit posh."

I made a choking sound. "I am not posh. I've only got one surname, and I come from a broken home."

"So does Prince Harry. And generally people who make a big

deal out of being too common for opera can't also get a baroness to lend them her front room at short notice."

"It's not her front room, it's her—"

"Grounds?" finished Oliver.

Okay, that sounded worse. And, worse still, Oliver totally had a point. "Oh, this is nice," I told him. "It reminds me of when we were first going out and I didn't like you."

And it was testament to how far we'd come that I could say something like that and he'd laugh. And Oliver laughing in a special-occasion suit was a very good Oliver indeed.

Eventually we arrived at the court bit of Pfaffle Court. And while I didn't know much about history, it was definitely the kind of place that the kind of person who wanted to get married in that kind place would want to get married in. Which was to say, big and fancy-looking with lots of windows and a dedicated posing staircase between two ornate pillars.

"Oh my," said Oliver. "What a lovely Tudor manor."

And, again, it was testament to how far we'd come that I had only a slight desire to shove him into a ditch. "Stop showing off."

"But I've always felt my passing familiarity with well-known, highly distinctive architectural styles is an essential part of my bad-boy image."

It felt bad to be laughing at the notion of Oliver having a bad-boy image because I knew he could be a bad boy when it counted. "Should I ask how you know it's Tudor, or will I regret it?"

He shrugged. "We do a special house-recognising course in barrister school."

"I know you're joking, but even if you weren't, that would not be the weirdest thing about your job."

"My job," began Oliver with the gravity of a legal professional, "is—"

Before he could insist that his job wasn't weird and I could point out that any career that involved wearing a wig but never lip-synching was weird by definition, Melanie came flying towards us with impressive speed for a woman in a rose-gold frock and matching stilettos.

"Luc," she cried. "Great to see you. Can you tell Bridge I'll be back in two minutes? There's an emergency at work. Don't really have time to talk about it"—she took a deep breath—"but one of our authors is starting a book tour of the States on Monday. And we've accidentally booked him appearances in New York, Los Angeles, and Las Vegas."

This seemed a fairly minor crisis by the standards of Bridge and Melanie's jobs. "Aren't they quite *good* places for a book tour?"

"Not when they're New York, Texas; Los Angeles, Texas; and Las Vegas, New Mexico. This is why we don't normally have the UK office book the U.S. tour dates."

Oliver was doing his interested-in-everyone face. "I take it none of those are big book towns?"

"New York, Texas," replied Melanie, sweeping a stray braid out of her face, "has a population of twenty and Los Angeles, Texas, is less than a mile across, but there's quite a nice library in Las Vegas, New Mexico, so...he might like that. Anyway, I have to go and sort this out. Bridge is in a small guest room in the Lodge—that way."

And with that, she dashed off to disappoint a dozen Texans.

"You should probably commence maid-of-honouring." Oliver gently de-coupled our hands. "I'll see if I can be useful somewhere else. Call me if you need me—or even if you don't."

I certainly wasn't sappy enough to stand and watch as Oliver made his way up to the house. And I certainly wasn't shallow enough to linger on the effect some steps and a well-cut suit had on his arse. So having done neither of those things, I went looking for the Lodge and for Bridget.

I found them both in roughly the direction that Melanie had indicated. The guest room looked kind of like the pyjama party scene from *Grease*, although I was sure nobody had been sing-dissing any of the other bridesmaids. There were clothes literally everywhere, and every spare surface was covered in either cosmetics or mimosas. Bridge, mimosa within reach, was sitting at a dressing table with a huge mirror having arcane things done to her hair by someone I hoped was a professional.

"Luc." Her reflection beamed at me. "Have a mimosa."

On the one hand, I really wanted a mimosa. On the other hand, it was 9:00 a.m. and I was barely conscious as it stood. "Maybe in about six hours?"

"In six hours I'll be married and we'll be starting on the champagne." A look of wonderful yet terrifying realisation crept across her face. "Oh my God, I'll be married in six hours. I'll be Ms. Bridget Welles."

We all stared at her. "Bridge," said Jennifer, emerging from what I assumed was the en suite. "That's already your name."

"Yes, but I'll be Ms. Bridget Welles who's married."

Liz pressed a mimosa into my hand anyway. "I think you're going to need this," she whispered.

I looked round for somewhere to sit and found nowhere that wasn't a lap, and that was one step too gay best friend even for me. Eventually, I propped my coccyx against the corner of a chest of drawers, which was very much a sidegrade from just standing.

"Sooo," began Liz in a tone that seemed far too implication-laden for a woman of the cloth. "How was your evening? Was it lovely?"

For a moment I wasn't sure what she meant. Then I glared at mirror-Bridge. "Oh, so you were in on it, then?"

She gave me a look of winsome triumph. "Oliver said he'd *missed* you. And you'd been so nice to me I thought you deserved a night off."

"It was great," I said, offering the PG/appropriate-for-relative-strangers version of events. "We watched old movies and got a relatively good night's sleep."

"That *does* sound great," agreed Jennifer. "Perhaps it's because I'm in my thirties now, but a good night's sleep is one of my top-five bedroom fantasies."

Bernadette looked around from where she was adjusting the line of her deep-blue bridesmaid's dress. "What are the other four?"

"New bookshelves, a husband who knows how to share a duvet, one of those pillows that are good for your back, and Dwayne 'the Rock' Johnson covered in lemon sorbet."

"Lemon sorbet?" asked the hairdresser, who until that moment had been screening the bridal banter with consummate professionalism.

"I like lemon sorbet."

Liz squinted like someone trying to solve a difficult maths puzzle. "Wouldn't it sting?"

"I don't want him *totally* covered in lemon sorbet," protested Jennifer.

"Oh, right." Bridge's mirror face was also trying to solve a difficult maths puzzle. "Because that would be strange."

"Also," I added, "wouldn't it ruin your nice new pillow?"

Finding the room as seat-deprived as I had, Jennifer slumped against the wall. "Given that I'm married, he's married, we live in different countries, and he's the most electrifying man in all of entertainment, I don't think sorbet logistics are the largest barrier to my having a night of steamy passion with the bloke from *Jumanji*."

"Actually"—Bernadette poured herself another mimosa—"if you are going to use a dessert in a sexual context, sorbet is a really good choice. It's mostly water and sugar so it doesn't stain and it doesn't curdle, and it's not as sticky as you might imagine."

Jennifer made a vindicated gesture. "See. I apparently have incredible sexual instincts. The rest of you would be covering Dwayne 'the Rock' Johnson in completely the wrong kind of condiments."

"Asking for a friend," asked Liz. For a friend. "Bernadette, what other foods is it either good or bad to lick off somebody?"

Bridge's mouth dropped open. "Are you allowed to lick things off people?"

"Not at the moment, no," Liz admitted. "But within the confines of marriage, the Church has no policy for or against licking things off people."

"I can't tell"—that was the moment when Melanie rejoined us—"if I have the best or the worst timing. Who is licking what off whom?"

"Jennifer," said Liz. "Lemon sorbet. The Rock."

The look of confusion on Melanie's face was, in context, understandable. "Johnson? Or Gibraltar?"

"I'm not even going to ask"—Jennifer slid slowly down the wall—"why you think I might want to lick the Rock of Gibraltar."

Melanie shrugged. "I don't know. White people shit?"

"If I had to lick a geographical feature," said Bridge with the air of somebody who had drunk way too many mimosas and was giving this way too much thought, "I'd pick Arthur's Seat."

The ensuing discussion of which parts of the country we'd put which parts of our body on lasted long enough for the hairdresser to be replaced by a makeup artist. And I found myself wondering what the hell this ritual would look like if I was, say, marrying Oliver. Would I sit around in a new suit, drinking cocktails with Priya, Bridge, and the James Royce-Royces while a highly trained professional ran a comb through my hair exactly once? Of course, maybe that said more about my hair than the institution of marriage.

Though I had to admit that when the experts had done their work, Bridge did look fucking fantastic. Not that she ever looked un-fucking fantastic. But she looked fucking fantastic...er? Just all happy and glowy and with her flower-woven hair framing her face in ways I could appreciate but not understand.

"Oh my God." Bridge stood up, wobbling slightly with nerves. "Oh my God. I'm getting married in...less than six hours."

I checked my phone. "In two hours. So unless you want to walk down the aisle in a fluffy bathrobe, you should probably think about getting the dress on."

She gave a little squeak. "Oh my God. The dress. Jennifer, can you grab it for me?"

"Sure." Jennifer climbed gingerly back to her feet. "Where is it?"

There was a silence where you would very much hope there would not be a silence.

Bridge turned slowly round. "Bernadette, where's the dress?"

"I thought," said Bernadette, "Jennifer was taking care of it."

Bridge kept turning. "Melanie, where's the dress?"

"I agree with Bridge," said Melanie. "I thought it was Bernadette's job."

"Oh my God." The tenor of Bridge's *oh my Gods* had changed dramatically. "Liz, tell me you picked up the dress."

Liz put her hands in the air. "Hey, I'm not even a bridesmaid! I'm just a redundant vicar. I'm here for the booze and the sex tips."

"I'm sure," I said, not at all sure, "that it's here somewhere."

"It's a wedding dress," cried Bridge. "It's enormous. It's not going to be under someone's lipstick."

From a mixture of helpfulness and denial, I started looking inside, behind, and beneath anything you could conceivably have hidden a very large frock inside, behind, or beneath.

Bridge sank back into her chair. "I can't believe this is

happening. This is my perfect special day. I can't have a perfect special day without my perfect special dress."

I exchanged horrified looks with the rest of the bridesmaids because it was looking a lot like she was going to have to. And, as maid of honour, it was my job to tell her that.

CHAPTER 10

"DON'T CRY." JENNIFER WAS KNEELING in front of Bridge. "You'll ruin your makeup."

"What does it matter if I ruin my makeup," wept Bridge. "I don't have a dress."

I'd given up the search and was now trying to find literally anything else Bridge could put on her body. "We must be able to pull something together."

Bridge looked up. "Oh, right, I can get married in my hippo pyjamas and Liz's hoodie."

"Hey," said Liz. "I got that hoodie at an ecclesiastical retreat. It's practically sacred."

Pulling out my phone, I checked the time. It was 12:10. "It's fine. There's just enough time to send somebody back to London."

"I'll go," offered Melanie.

"The ceremony starts at two." Bridge was attempting to signal despair without touching her hair or face, which made her look like an emoji. "You won't make it back, and then I'll have to get married in hippo pyjamas and a hoodie while I'm missing a bridesmaid."

Liz was already scurrying towards the door. "It's fine. I can go."

"Um"—Bernadette gave a wary look—"how many mimosas have you had?"

Liz ceased scurrying. "Ah. Enough that it took me a moment to realise why this would be a bad idea."

A buzzing emanated from my phonular region. It was a picture of a smug man with white hair. A second or two later, Oliver sent, Richard Dawkins. A dick, a dawk, and a dork.

My heart sank. Not because Oliver was at peak Oliver but because I was going to have to send him away. I called him.

And, true to form, he answered within two rings. "Lucien?"

Oh God. "I'm...I'm really sorry," I said. "But I might need you to go back to London."

"I'm choosing to believe that if you were breaking up with me, you would have done it in a less bizarre way. Although, knowing you, I'm not sure why I think that."

I wanted to bants back but there wasn't time, and this wasn't about me. "Bridge's dress got left behind. Can you...um, pick it up? While driving fast enough that you have a chance to be back here by two, but not so fast you get arrested or killed."

"I will certainly try." It was his I-don't-think-this-is-a-good-plan-but-I'll-do-it-because-I-love-you voice. Incidentally, he had used the same voice when booking tickets for *Pretty Woman: The Musical*. "But this is going to be a very tight turnaround."

"I'll meet you outside." I hung up, then turned to Bridge. "Keys, please. Oliver's going."

We all knew he wouldn't make it, but the fact that someone was trying made us feel very slightly better—the operative word being *slightly*. Because, when I'd got back from sprinting to the main house and sending Oliver sprinting to the car park, the mood was teetering between sombre and inconsolable.

"I don't want to sound pessimistic," began Melanie. "But I

think we should have a backup plan. Because even if Oliver makes it, you still might not have time to get changed."

Bridge made a noise that was an unholy amalgamation of a hiccough, a wail, and a sob. "Fine. I'll get in my pyjamas."

"There must be something else we can do." Jennifer had a mimosa in each hand. "What if you wore one of our dresses?"

"Then"—Bridge's voice clicked up half an octave—"I'll be dressed as a bridesmaid at my own wedding. I'll be always the bridesmaid, never the bride *at my own wedding.*"

We all paced and drank and thought. Honestly, the drinking wasn't helping with the thinking. But it was helping with the not freaking the fuck out.

Eventually Melanie lifted her head from her hands. "Hang on a sec, we're in a rich old woman's house. She must have something fancy you can wear."

"There's a suit of armour in the main hall," Bridge said. "I'll just slip into that."

The great curse of Bridge's life was that she had a tremendous ability to solve other people's problems. But when it came to her own, she could be—and I say this with love—unhelpful sometimes. "No, no." I gave her an encouraging shoulder pat. "Judy's been married about twenty times. I bet she's got a dozen wedding dresses lying around."

There was a pause as Bridge considered this. "So my choices are naked, pyjamas and hoodies, bridesmaid, or whatever your mum's friend can drag out of her bottom drawer."

"Maybe," I admitted, feeling like the worst maid of honour who had ever made honour. "But I think four might be the least worst option."

"Naked would be a statement," offered Bernadette.

"I'll…" I was edging towards the door. "I'll see what I can dig up."

Bridge's reply was kind of a burble, but it sounded like an appreciative burble, so—hoping that all this dashing backwards and forwards wasn't turning me into too much of an unattractive ball of sweat—I set off back to the main house. Of course I didn't know where Judy was, but I was hoping that if I rang Mum, I'd find Judy not far away.

She picked up somewhat less quickly than Oliver had, not because she cared less but because she had a more relaxed attitude to life in general. Actually, come to think of it, I wasn't sure I could imagine two people more different life-attitude-relaxedness-wise than Mum and Oliver.

"Allô, Luc." I heard the sounds of clinking crockery over the phone.

"Hi, Mum."

"You sound out of breath. Are you getting enough exercise?"

Right now, I definitely was. "There's a lot to sort out."

"I'm sure there is, but you are a young man. A little bit of wedding drama shouldn't be making you so tired."

"I've been running all over the place."

She made a dismissive, Gallic noise. "When I was your age, I ran everywhere. It is your job. That is the problem. You are at a desk the whole day, and you never get any fresh air or sunshine."

"I walk to work."

"That does not count. The air in London, it is not fresh at all."

Getting into a debate about air quality in the capital didn't seem likely to help with my current predicament, so I let it slide. "I don't suppose Judy's with you, is she?"

"She is. She is having a croissant."

"A croissant?"

"We are having breakfast."

"It's noon."

I heard the chink of a knife being set down. "Of course. Who eats breakfast before noon?"

A muffled, posh voice said something at Mum's end of the telephone.

"Apparently Judy does normally because she has to get up to feed the chickens, but I do not think that counts. Chickens get up far too early."

More commentary from just out of hearing.

"They cannot be that sensible, or they would not let themselves be eaten. Anyway, mon caneton"—she seemed to be addressing me again—"what do you need Judy for?"

"There's no dress."

For a moment, Mum was quiet. "What do you mean there is no dress?"

"Somehow the bridal party forgot to bring the dress down from London. We were hoping that Judy might have something?"

I heard Mum explaining the situation and Judy responding and the two of them carrying on for quite some while about— from the little I could gather—what a terrible state the younger generation had got themselves into.

"I am handing you over," Mum said at last, and then there was a phone-passing sound before Judy assumed telephonic control.

"Luc, m'boy. Spot of bother with the old frock, is that right?"

"Yes. In that we don't have one. And we were hoping maybe that you did."

"Bound to. Old place is full of tat like that."

That was reassuring in some ways, but not in others. "I was hoping for something non-tat?"

"Pish posh, just a figure of speech. Tell you what, let me rustle up some bits and bobs and I'll let you know."

I'd have asked to be handed back to Mum, but Judy had

already rung off, so I made my way as quickly as I could up to the main house and hoped they'd come down to meet me.

And they had. The courtyard was already swarming with caterers—who, on the whole, had been very good about the last-minute venue change—and was now also graced with two women of a certain age staggering under the weight of more white silk than any reasonable person could have any reasonable use for.

I rushed forward to help and Mum, at least, gratefully unburdened herself, dumping a half ton of dress into my woefully unprepared arms. Judy, who prided herself on making light of all burdens, just fell into step beside me.

"Can't make any promises," she told me over a cascade of organza ruffles, "but there's a fair bit for her to choose from at least. You know I do *miss* weddings. Perhaps I should get married again." She turned to my mum. "How about it, Odile? It'd make it harder for my bastard relatives to object to your being in my will."

"Please tell me you're joking." I glanced between the two of them. "Mum, you can't just marry your best mate for a laugh."

She gave me a disapproving look. "Don't tell me what I can do, Luc." Then, to my intense relief, she turned to Judy. "But I do think he's right. Besides, being married to you would clearly be awful."

Judy gave a won't-stand-for-this-disparagement huff. "I beg your pardon. Being married to me is a wonderful experience. That's why so many people have wanted to do it."

"I'm with Mum on this one," I said. "Marriages are like court appearances—the fact that you've had a lot of them doesn't necessarily mean you're doing them well."

That didn't seem to help. "You're missing out, Odile."

"Perhaps. But I wouldn't want to ruin our friendship. And anyway, I do not think I enjoyed being married so much the last time."

I could see that, but I wasn't sure I liked the implication. "Do you not think Dad was a bit of an outlier? Like he's basically the worst person you could possibly have been married to."

Mum gave me a reassuring pat. "I am sure that is the case, mon caneton. And I am sure that if you and Oliver want to be married, you will be far happier with each other than I was with your father. But for me—I think it is a boat that has sailed."

There was no melancholy in the way she said it, even if it was in some ways an inherently melancholy sentiment. And Mum was always very adamant that she was proud of the life she'd lived and the choices she'd made. Which was good because I was proud of them too. And I wouldn't *really* have minded if she'd wanted to marry Judy. Although since it might have put me in line to be Baron Pfaffle, I would at that point have had to admit that Oliver was right and I was posher than I thought.

We bustled back into the guest room and laid down our various offerings on top of the discarded articles of clothing that Bridge had decided she *didn't* want to get married in.

"Well," said Judy. "Here they are. Not all of them are mine, technically. That one was my sister's." She pointed at a long, flowing gown in an '80s style. "That one was my aunt's, and *that* one, I think, I wound up with after a particularly heavy night of drinking somewhere in Monaco—don't ask."

Bridge came hesitantly over and took a look. "Oh," she said with a tremor in her voice that should have sent ripples through people's mimosas, "they seem...lovely?"

"No need to be polite," insisted Judy, for whom *No need to be polite* was practically a family motto. "Well aware that half of them are ghastly and the other half are worse, but they are *suitable*. And certainly better than wearing nothing at all—and I speak from experience in that regard."

The bridesmaids gave her a look of collective interrogation.

"It was the sixties, he was American, there was a lot of mud and flowers," she explained. "All very harmonious, I'm sure, but one does get rather *bitten*."

Bridge was holding dresses up to herself and checking the mirror. "I think this one's too short."

"Sixties again," explained Judy. "Fabulous time."

"And this one"—she tried another—"might be too frilly."

"That's the sister. Frilly woman all around."

"And this one..." Bridge held up a full-sleeved, almost fairy-tale gown with a train that stayed on the bed as she took the rest of it across the room. "Luc, talk me out of this because this is exactly the dress I wanted when I was nine years old, and nine-year-olds have no taste."

Judy had a faraway look on her face. "Now *that* is from my 1980s husband. Rich as Croesus, fabulous in bed, otherwise a complete shit."

"Well"—Mum gave a laconic shrug—"that was the eighties for you."

"Yes, I don't know how I'd have got through it if it hadn't been for the cocaine."

I looked at the dress. It was definitely...of its era. From a time when if you wanted to show your friends how much better and happier than them you were, you had to blow a ton of money on something vulgar and expensive, instead of just Instagramming yourself in front of something you didn't really own like we did in our more enlightened age. "It's... It might be the best option?"

Bridge was staring at herself in the mirror with an expression of profoundly mixed emotions. "Is it wrong that I sort of love it?"

"You can do nothing wrong today," said Bernadette. "That's the joy of being a bride."

Jennifer set down her mimosa and moved to a better vantage point. "I think I unironically like it. It's got a Princess Diana vibe."

"Sign of the times," explained Judy. "All wedding dresses had a Princess Diana vibe for a full decade."

"Wasn't precisely a model marriage, though, was it?" Melanie pointed out.

"That wasn't the dress's fault," protested Bridge, suddenly strangely defensive of the honour of a forty-year-old taffeta gown.

Judy clapped her hands. "Well, if you like it, you can absolutely have it. We might need to make one or two *tiny* adjustments, but that's why Matron taught me to sew all those years ago."

So Bridge got changed, and while it wasn't quite what she'd chosen and didn't fit quite perfectly, even after Judy had gone at it with pins, I had to admit Bridge did look remarkable in it. Sure, it was a bit dated, but it really did make her look like a princess. And since she'd always been one, deep down, I thought she deserved to look like one too.

CHAPTER 11

BY THE TIME THE BRIDAL party was lurking outside the walled garden where the ceremony was due to take place, there was still no sign of Oliver, which meant the replacement dress was definitely *the* dress, and I was going to have to maid the honours without my boyfriend. It was barely two, I was already knackered, and all the running around had left its mark. Its sweaty, sweaty mark. So, from a certain perspective, Oliver's absence was a plus because he wouldn't be able to see or, for that matter, smell me.

I was just reflecting on how disgusting I was when the "Wedding March" kicked in. Bridge gave an I've-been-waiting-for-this-all-my-life squeak and, letting her father take her arm, glided triumphantly through the archway and towards where Tom was waiting. And, to give him credit, he looked a lot less shocked than he might that his bride-to-be had shown up in a frock that Cinderella's fairy godmother would have turned down for being a touch OTT.

The music crescendoed and Bridge sailed on, and Bridge's train very much…didn't. We'd been aware there was a lot of it, but between me and the bridesmaids we'd managed to kind of carry it as a bundle without getting a full sense of its terrifying magnificence. Now, however, it was unfolding like a giant snake in an exploitative B movie. And because we hadn't had the foresight to stretch it back in a straight line from the door, it was also corner-ing really badly, meaning it was dragging heavily past the aisle and making aggressive moves at the guests. A hapless second cousin had to snatch her child out of its way.

At last, Bridge was at the altar and the bridesmaids were twenty-five feet away, wrangling a cascade of silk that had already swallowed three chairs.

"Dearly beloved," began Judy in her loudest posh-person voice, which was pretty damn loud. "Oh, I say, that's fun, isn't it? I haven't said that in years. We are gathered here today to cel-ebrate the union of this woman, Bridget Dawn Welles, and this chap, Thomas No Middle Name Ballantyne. Then, once the par-ty's over, they're going to go and do the legal bit at an actual reg-istry office."

I could hardly see because I was miles away, but Bridge seemed happy enough, despite the somewhat unorthodox delivery. And Tom had the same look of slightly dazed contentment that every bridegroom has had on his face since the beginning of time.

Judy, too, seemed to be having the time of her life. "Now, I'm meant to say something about marriage and how jolly seriously you're supposed to take it. But, honestly, I've always thought it works best when it's a bit of a laugh. My most successful by far was my fifth husband. We kept each other in stitches constantly. Then one evening we were out on his yacht and he laughed so hard, he fell overboard and was eaten by a shark. And, as I've told every man I've ever slept with, it doesn't matter how you start or how you finish, it's the bits in the middle that matter. All of which said, I hope this wedding will be a wonderful start to Tom and Bridget's life together." She paused for about half a second. "Now. Vows."

They'd written their own, of course, and they were terribly sweet and terribly sincere and—this probably makes me a horri-ble human being—I forgot them the moment I heard them. Then again, they weren't supposed to be meaningful to me; they were supposed to be meaningful to Tom and Bridge. Oliver arrived about halfway through, got stuck in the entrance with the bridal party because of the mega-train and, being a far better person than me, took the whole situation impeccably and even seemed to find the vows genuinely moving. After the vows came the rings, ably presented by Tom's best-man-slash-brother Mike who, unlike the rest of the male guests, *had* chosen to rock a rose-gold suit and was kind of putting the rest of us to shame.

"And so," concluded Judy, "by the power vested in me by absolutely no bugger, I declare you a legally nonbinding man and wife. You may kiss the bride if you want to be disgustingly American about the whole thing."

To nobody's surprise they did, in fact, want to be disgustingly American about the whole thing. I glanced sideways and saw Oliver wiping a tear from his eye, which was unfair because he wasn't as close to Bridge as I was and had never slept with Tom. At least I assumed he hadn't. And to my shock and happiness, my brain didn't vanish down a rabbit hole of wondering who Oliver *had* slept with before we'd started dating, and instead agreed to carry on being genuinely happy for Tom and Bridge in a really straightforward way. It was almost disorienting to have a positive feeling that didn't dredge up a single insecurity or neurosis, but I suppose all the Tom-vanishing, church-burning, dress-losing chaos had worn that part of my psyche down. Which just left the part that liked Bridge and Tom and was glad they were married now.

The happy couple turned to face their guests and were about to make a joyful procession out of the walled garden when they ran into the train issue. It was taking up the entire aisle, had already made a good attempt at wrapping itself around Bridge's legs as she turned, and was currently dragging through the crowd in quite an ominous way.

"If everyone could stand back," I tried, "I think we're going to have to...gather and swing. Bride's family, please keep your heads down."

It wasn't the most dignified exit in the history of matrimony, especially because a small swarm of overenthusiastic page boys and flower girls insisted on showering us all with confetti while we tried to do the sartorial equivalent of turning an eighteen-wheel van in a residential street.

Everything that followed next was a bit of a blur. I remember Oliver's palm at the small of my back steering me from handshake to handshake and photograph to photograph, where I'm sure my fears of looking like Bridge's stoner cousin were starkly realised. Then he guided me to Judy's surprisingly fancy sixteenth-century tithe barn for the wedding breakfast. And there Oliver sat beside me and did the heavy lifting in six identical conversations with other top-table guests that I hardly knew.

I even managed to start enjoying the food before I remembered that I was soon going to have to make a speech. And actually, I was okay with speeches. I made them fairly often as part of my job. Except this was different because it was Bridge, it was Bridge's special day, and she'd remember what I said to her on it for the rest of her life. So I'd worked hard. I'd worked really hard. Almost embarrassingly hard, in fact, because there was still a part of me that defaulted to the it's-okay-I-got-a-D-because-didn't-study excuse.

And, eventually, I'd got the speech to a state where I liked it. Where it was all written out neatly on paper and everything because I thought scrolling through my phone at my best friend's wedding would look bad, and now it was tucked away safely in my breast pocket.

In the breast pocket of the shirt I had spent the last seven hours sweating through. A fact that I only noticed when Tom got to the end of his own speech and said, "The maid of honour."

I stood. The paper was...fine? A little bit wrinkly. Although I was regretting having made my notes with one of Oliver's fancy fountain pens. It had felt very grown-up at the time, but biro would have stood up to the elements—well, the elements of my stressed-out body—way better. The speech was now mostly little rivulets of blue within which I could just about make out fragments of what I remembered as moving-slash-hilarious testimonies to my long friendship with Bridget. Except now they'd been reduced to "—nce we met at uni—ity" and "—vered in s—wbe—y b—mange."

Bugger.

Taking a deep breath, I briefly flirted with the strategy of continuing to inhale until I had composed a new, even brillianter maid-of-honour speech from scratch, but my lungs gave out far too quickly.

"What...can I say about Bridget?" I asked a room full of glazed-faced guests, and then paused slightly too long in the vain hope one of them would tell me. "What...indeed," I continued. For some reason, nobody was coming forward to help me out.

I felt a light pat on my arm and looked down to see Oliver looking up at me with an expression that, to my surprise, was far closer to saying *You can do this* than *Why are you making a fool of me in public.*

"I suppose...I can say...that she's my best friend." *Brilliant start, Luc. Just keep doing facts, and you'll be done before you know it.* "And, actually, that's...sort of everything? She's...the best. She's always there for me, even when I'm not there for her. She's good in a crisis, even though she thinks she isn't. She's kind and she's generous and she sees the good in people, and I wish I could be more like her." Fuck, was I tearing up? *Bring it back with a joke.* "I was going to tell an embarrassing story," I tried, "but I realised it would sound like I was bitter about that one time she stole my boyfriend. Which would be particularly petty since she's now marrying him." I turned to the groom. "Tom...yeah, right call, mate. You've got great taste."

There. That was a conclusion. I sat down. And was just congratulating myself on a job well done, or at least a job not fucked up too terribly, when I remembered the job had a bit more to it. So, like Chumbawamba, I got back up again.

"Um," I said. "I think I'm also supposed to thank a bunch of people, but as you might have noticed, I've kind of lost my notes which means I've forgotten who I'm supposed to be thanking and for what." I briefly wondered-slash-hoped this was a wedding-themed anxiety dream. But, no, I was definitely here, definitely awake, definitely blowing my maid-of-honour speech. "Whoever you are," I went on with wild optimism, "thank you very much. You're great." I very nearly sat down again when I realised I had to make a toast as well. "To Tom and Bridge. Who are also great."

There was one of those silences you don't ever want to hear during a speech.

"To Tom and Bridget," said Oliver firmly. "Who are also great."

"To Tom and Bridget, who are also great," the room dutifully echoed.

And I sat down faster than I had ever sat down in my life.

"Well done." Oliver leaned in to kiss me on the cheek.

Thank God that was over. Now I could just sit here and clap politely while the next person... *Fuck.* I sprang up again. "Shit. Um, the best man."

Now that I'd actually introduced him, Mike stood up with, I noticed, very un-sweated-on cue cards in his hands. While I was sure his speech would be excellent, I wasn't quite able to stay conscious for it. Instead, I plopped my head onto the table, narrowly missing the remains of my souffle. And then felt Oliver rubbing reassuringly between my shoulder blades.

"I fucked that up," I whispered. "I really wanted Bridge to know how much she means to me, and I fucked it up so hard."

Oliver levered my face gently out of the crockery. "Lucien, you've spent the past three months helping Bridget with everything. You organised her non-gender-specific bird party with the slightly offensive T-shirts. You helped track down her fiancé when he went missing. You found her a venue and, for that matter, a dress. And while your speech was"—he gave a tactful little pause—"unstudied, it was clearly heartfelt."

"Yes but—"

Putting a hand to my jaw, he turned my head towards Bridget, who was gazing across the table, misty-eyed and doing heart-hands at me.

"I love you," I mouthed.

"I love you too," she mouthed back.

And I absolutely did not cry.

After that, things were back to being blurry—not that they'd ever stopped. Once we were done with the speeches and the coffee, the dancing began, and at some point Bridge vanished and came back in the dress she was supposed to have been wearing all day. It was simple to the point of minimalism, which felt totally unlike Bridge until you realised it was exactly like her: just a clean sweep of white satin with a scoop neck and a full skirt. And she did look stunning—even more stunning, I mean—and I did tell her so. At least I think I told her so, but the music was loud at that point and she and Tom had a first dance, and a third dance, and a ninth dance to be getting on with, which wasn't the kind of thing I wanted to interrupt.

Sometime around sunset, as the evening buffet was being laid out, I got something that felt a little bit like a second wind—although given the day I'd had, it was more like a fourth or fifth. Grabbing Oliver by the hand, I dragged him towards the dance floor where my friends were already clustered. And suddenly it was like seeing a decade telescoped in front of me. There were the James Royce-Royces, inseparable as always, except now James Royce-Royce had Baby J strapped firmly to his chest. And there was Priya, still doggedly goth-stomping to a song you couldn't goth-stomp to, except the girl who didn't do relationships was now in a relationship with two other women. And there was Bridge, except she was on the other side of the room, in the arms of the man she was going to spend the rest of her life with. Which felt bad for a moment, then good, then something else that was neither. A sort of soft, nostalgic ache for a time you didn't particularly want to go back to but resented that you couldn't.

Then I noticed Oliver was being slightly resistant. "Lucien, you know I'm a terrible dancer."

"You're good at everything," I shouted over the music. "It's one of the things I like-slash-find-intimidating about you."

"There are many things I am poor at, Lucien, and dancing is one of them."

I kept dragging. "Your dancing can't be anything like as bad as my cooking."

I waited for a reply, but there wasn't one.

"Well?"

"I'm afraid I can't think of a rebuttal. Your cooking really is that bad."

"Then dance with me."

"Lucien..."

"Seriously"—I stopped dragging and stepped in close—"dance with me."

He gave a long-suffering sigh. "If it will make you happy, but be warned I am *not* exaggerating. If I were on *Strictly Come Dancing*, they'd put me with Anton du Beke."

"You know," I told him, "I would legitimately love to see that."

We hit the floor just as the playlist flicked over from "Thinking Out Loud" to "I Wanna Dance with Somebody (Who Loves Me)." And I did. I did want to dance with somebody who loved me. And I was. Which was pretty cool.

Although it turned out that Oliver's dancing was, in fact, as bad as my cooking. All elbows and rocking side to side like a dad at a disco, which, thinking about it, was the age group we were both rapidly entering. And wasn't that a sobering thought.

The soberingness of my thoughts must have leaked onto my face because Oliver abruptly stopped flailing and stood stock-still in the swirl of bodies. "I told you I was terrible at this. If you're embarrassed, it's your own fault."

"You could never embarrass me."

I put my arms around his neck and kissed him. And for just one moment it wasn't Bridget's day—it was mine, and his, and ours.

Then the sleeplessness and the rushing around and the fatigue caught up with me all over again, and I sagged against him, and Oliver, being Oliver, led me to a free table at the side of the room without having to ask what was wrong or what I needed.

I was pretty sure I only put my head on Oliver's shoulder for a moment or two, but when I opened my eyes again, it was full dark, and Tom and Bridge were saying their final round of goodbyes. Which meant that it was no longer a dereliction of duty for me to sneak off as well.

So Oliver guided me around one final time, taking me through all the people I had to hug and wave at and say good night to before he could finally, mercifully, take me back to the car and drive me home.

When we got in, he let me lean on him as I staggered upstairs and helped me undress before I flopped into bed. Then he lay with his arms around me while I murmured whatever came into my head.

"Maybe we shouldn't get married," I suggested to the night in general. "It's sooo much work and it makes you sooo sleepy."

Oliver pressed a kiss to the back of my head. "Whatever you want. But rest. You deserve it."

I wasn't sure I did. But I was too exhausted to protest. I shut my eyes and let the cotton-wool darkness swallow me.

PART TWO

MR. MILES EDWARD GREENE & MR. JOHN JOSEPH RYAN
THE ARCHWAYS, SHOREDITCH
26TH OF JUNE

CHAPTER 12

"WHAT," I ASKED ALEX TWADDLE, "do you call a deer with no eyes?"

Alex blinked. "I don't know," he said gamely. "What do you call a deer with no eyes?"

"No-eye deer."

"Oh." Alex blinked again. "That's disappointing. I thought it was a joke." He opened Bing. "Shall we Google it?"

Fuck me. "No, Alex. It's a joke. The joke is 'no-eye deer.' Because it's a deer with no eyes."

"Yes, I know it's a deer with no eyes, and I know you've no idea what it's called, but you've got me wondering now."

"Alex, it's called a no—"

"I say," cried Alex, with fatal enthusiasm, "Rhys? You wouldn't know what the technical term for a deer with no eyes is, would you?"

Rhys influencer-walked into the office, with his phone at the optimum streaming angle. "Not sure that's really the kind of thing there's a technical term for, Luc."

"I don't want to know what the technical term is," I yelled. "I just said, 'What do you call a deer with no eyes? No idea.'"

He considered this for a moment. And then of all the many ends of the many sticks in front of him he grabbed tightly to the wrong one. "So it's a specific deer, then? Are you adopting a deer?"

"No, Rhys. I'm not adopting a deer. Where would I keep a deer?"

"This is tragic." Alex actually had a slightly teary look. "The poor little deer. With no eyes. Was it pollution? If you can't keep it at your house, Luc, I'm sure we've got room on the estate, though the other deer might bully it."

Just when I thought this had got as out of control as it could possibly get, Rhys Jones Bowen addressed his increasingly vast audience. "Hello, Rhystocrats. Got an exciting new conservation challenge for you. My friend Luc is adopting a deer with no eyes who's going to live on Alex's estate. And we need to find a name for him. Or"—he glanced back at me—"or is it a her or some kind of nonbinary deer?"

I flailed like I was Oliver dancing. "It's not a nonbinary deer. It's a completely hypothetical deer."

"So far," Rhys told me, "the names that are winning are Deerdrie, Deery McDeerface, and Steve."

"I might go with Steve?" I suggested, hoping vainly that a quick surrender would end my suffering.

Rhys was still checking his feed. "Oh, somebody here has suggested you call it No-Eye Deer, which I think is very inappropriate. I mean you can't make the poor thing's disability its whole identity."

I was just about to flee back to my office when Professor Fairclough descended from the upper floors. "I heard a commotion," she said. "Has there been a disturbance?"

"I think this place *is* a disturbance," I replied.

"Ah, Professor"—Alex looked up excitedly—"you'll know. What would you call a deer with no eyes?"

"*Capreolus caecus*, clearly." She shrugged. "Assuming it was a trait endemic to the species. If it was suffering from an unknown disease, I'd call it Subject One."

"You can't call Luc's poor little deer Subject One," protested Alex.

Oh God. Why did I keep doing this to myself? "There. Is. No. Deer."

Everyone stared at me in aggrieved confusion.

"Then"—Alex looked genuinely wounded—"why did you ask me what to call it?"

"You know something?" I threw my hands in the air. "I have no idea."

Before the situation could degenerate any further, I escaped into my office. Of course I say *escaped*, but the moment I sat down, I saw that I had an unread email from Barbara Clench.

Dear Luc,

Unfortunately, your request contravenes CRAPP's new policy regarding the photocopiers. In order to avoid a repeat of last month's incident involving Alex, the feed tray, and the fire engine, it has been agreed by the directors that no changes may be made to the photocopiers under any circumstances without the approval of a qualified engineer. I see no reason to make an exception for you.

Kind regards,
Barbara

It had been a while since I'd been in a back-and-forth like this with Barbara, and in her defence, it *was* generally a good idea to have a nobody-touch-the-machines policy when Alex was around. Although possibly "Alex, don't touch the machines" would have got more to the heart of the issue. But this was getting in the way of my ability to do my job.

Dear Barbara,

While I understand the value of this policy in broad terms, the photocopier is out of paper. If we need to call an engineer every time the copier runs out of paper, it might prove unnecessarily expensive.

Kind regards,
Luc

I didn't expect that to be the end of it, and it wasn't.

Dear Luc,

The current policies have been set by the directors, and I do not have the authority to alter them. The rules are clear: you are not to tamper with the photocopiers in any way.

Kind regards,
Barbara

Dear Barbara,

Then can you please call an engineer. The photocopier is out of paper.

Kind regards,
Luc

Dear Luc,

I have spoken to our reprographics supplier, and they have told me that their engineers can only be dispatched to deal with genuine malfunctions.

Kind regards,
Barbara

Dear Barbara,

Fantastic. Then can I please be permitted to restock the paper?

Kind regards,
Luc

Dear Luc,

You may not. The policy remains clear on this matter, and I do not have the authority to alter it.

Kind regards,
Barbara

Dear Barbara,

Do you not see that this is a problem?

Kind regards,
Luc

Dear Luc,

If you disagree with the policy, you may bring it up at the next directors' meeting in September.

Kind regards,
Barbara

Dear Barbara,

And until September we're just not going to use the photo-copiers at all?

Kind regards,
Luc

Dear Luc,

The average UK office worker prints 10,000 sheets of paper a year, of which 6,800 are wasted. This is equivalent to 4.8 trees per person. As an ecological charity, CRAPP should be doing its best to reduce printing and photocopying, not enabling it.

Kind regards,
Barbara

Dear Barbara,

While I'm sure we all agree we should reduce waste, I can't help but feel that there's a more elegant solution than turning our office photocopier into the world's most boring modern art piece.

> Kind regards,
> Luc

Dear Luc,

The current policies have been set by the directors, and I do not have the authority to alter them.

> Kind regards,
> Barbara

I was just resigning myself to three months of working in a paperless office with none of the technologies that made paperless offices actually work, when the door opened and Alex Twaddle stuck his head in.

"If this is about the deer..." I began.

"No, no. Fully acknowledge that the deer was a cruel hoax."

I made a frustrated noise at the back of my throat. "It wasn't a hoax. It was a joke."

"Luc"—Alex folded his arms—"I don't think it's at all funny to mock a deer with a serious disability."

"There. Was. No. Deer."

"It's the principle of the thing. And if you're going to be insensitive, I'm not going to invite you to my wedding."

The old me would have thought if I ever needed encouragement to be insensitive, this was it. And, frankly, the new me thought the same. "You're getting married?" I asked.

Alex's sleepy eyes flashed shock at me. "How do you know?"

Oh, for fuck's sake. "You just threatened not to invite me to your wedding, and that would be a weird thing to do if you weren't getting married. Also, you've been engaged for at least two years."

"I say. Well deduced. That dashed clever boyfriend of yours must be rubbing off on you."

"Clearly."

"Anyway, Miffy and I thought we should, you know, do the decent thing. Being engaged is smashing and everything, but one is technically supposed to get married at the end of it. Besides, can't keep a girl waiting around forever. And neither of us are getting any younger."

Crap. I'd reached the stage of my life where people who were younger than me were worrying that they were getting too old for stuff. "I mean," I said, "you've still got plenty of time, haven't you? Really?"

And now what was I doing? Why was I trying to talk Alex out of marrying the gorgeous, heiress fiancée he'd probably—although knowing Alex not necessarily—been engaged to for years.

He shrugged. "Well, maybe. But you never know what could happen. You could get trampled by a horse tomorrow."

"In London?"

"No, but back at the house. Happened to my uncle Freddie. Three days before his wedding, wasn't looking where he was going. Wandered into the middle of a polo match. Absolutely flattened. Or my uncle Simon. Two days after his wedding. Celebratory shooting party. Wife mistook him for a pheasant."

"Did she?" I eyed him carefully. "Because that sounds like a murder to me."

"Oh, no," exclaimed Alex. "She was terribly upset, poor thing. So upset that my uncle Timothy had to move into the house to comfort her. And when she wasn't feeling better a year later, they moved to Tokyo."

"Big fan of Japanese culture, was she?"

Alex screwed up his face. "I think it was something they *didn't* have they were more interested in, strangely."

"An extradition treaty?" I suggested.

"That's the blighter. Anyway, fearfully nice lady. I do hope she comes back to see Miffy and me tie the knot."

"I wouldn't pin your hopes on it."

"I suppose it is a long way." He paused. "But you'll come, won't you?"

"Technically you haven't invited me yet."

"The proper invitation will be along in a day or so. So sorry it's such short notice. Dashed thing: it turns out a surprising number of people aren't in Debretts." He gave me a faintly chiding look. "You should get that seen to, old boy."

"I'll get right onto it," I said. "Right after I get my seat in the Lords."

"I wouldn't bother. It's all political now."

I decided to let that one die on the vine. "Thanks for the tip."

Alex beamed. "Anytime. Well, not anytime. Not if I'm asleep for example. Or when I'm in the bath. Chap should never talk politics with another chap in the bath."

"What should"—why was I asking this, what was wrong with me—"another chap talk about with another chap in the bath?"

"Rugger."

"Noted."

Alex gave me one of his vague, amiable looks. "In any case, do save the date, won't you? I mean, when I send you the date. I'd tell you but can't remember it off the top of my top."

"Shall do," I said. "Thanks."

And then Alex drifted away, leaving me with a nebulous sense of unsettlement. Obviously I was happy for him—at least as happy as I could be for a man who, when you thought about it, embodied literally everything that was wrong with the British class system—but I was also... I don't know.

This was a lot of...yeah?

It was kind of like I was at a station and everyone else was getting on trains or like I was at a restaurant and everybody else was on their main course, while I was staring at the departure board... or menu...or...

Fuck.

This made no sense. I was happier than I had ever been in my life. So why did I feel like I was failing?

CHAPTER 13

"WE STILL DON'T HAVE TO do this," said Oliver as we got off the Tube in Shoreditch, on our way to do this.

This being attending the wedding of the man who'd ruined my life. Well, ruined a bit of my life. A bit of my life that had seemed quite important at the time.

I took his hand decisively and definitely not desperately. "We do. I mean, I do. I mean, it's a closure thing. Look, I think I need to, okay?"

And Oliver, being Oliver, just said, "Of course."

The problem was, I wasn't actually sure *why* I needed to. I was calling it closure because that seemed a healthy and usefully vague label I could point other people at. And maybe it *was* closure. Maybe after tonight the little box in my head that had *Miles* written on it would finally be closed, and I'd never have to think about him—or what we'd been to each other or what he'd done to me—ever again.

Besides, if it wasn't closure...what did that mean? What was I trying to prove? Or, if I wasn't trying to prove anything, what was I looking for? Or, if I wasn't looking for anything, what the fuck was I doing here?

Fuck.

It turned out that Miles, true to form, had chosen to get

married in an abandoned railway tunnel lined with artisanal graffiti. It would have been a cool and daring choice except this particular abandoned railway tunnel lined with artisanal graffiti was a fully licenced venue, with its own bar. Right now, the exposed brickwork was splashed with rainbow-coloured lights because it was going to be one of *those* gay weddings.

"We still don't have to do this," said Oliver. And this time I was pretty sure it wasn't for my benefit.

"Sorry," I whispered. "At least twelve people I know have already seen me. And while I think no-showing at your ex's wedding is fine, about-facing it isn't."

Mercifully, Miles and JoJo were far too trendy to do assigned seating—much as I'd enjoyed having a confused usher come up to me at the James Royce-Royces' wedding and ask me "groom or groom"—which meant Oliver and I got to skulk at the back like we hadn't done our homework. I kept hold of Oliver's hand, partially because it was nice and partially just to apologise.

He leaned in slightly. "I bet you fifty pounds they have a drag queen officiating."

Okay, this was going to be way more fun if I'd accidentally brought mean Oliver with me. "I am absolutely not taking that bet," I whispered back.

Then I paused. I'd put off it for as long as I could, but I had eventually cracked and web stalked the guy my ex was marrying. And that led me down a hell of a rabbit hole because he was a fucking YouTuber, with a subscriber count in the millions. He had several channels dedicated to various areas of his life, including a new one just for wedding prep, but his main source of "influence" revolved around videos of him looking fabulous and claiming you could look similarly fabulous if you followed his tips and bought the products his sponsors paid him to recommend. Point was, there was no way he was going to be upstaged by anyone on his big day.

"Actually," I said, "you're on."

And my instincts proved dead right, although to be fair, Oliver's did too. Kind of. To a sudden round of applause, the minister entered and took his place on a stage that had been meticulously designed to look hastily improvised. Of course, I say *minister*. What I meant was "tiny drag king in full leather daddy getup wearing a T-shirt that, from the back of the room, I could just about make out read *Gender Is Over*."

"Shit," I whispered to Oliver, "that's Roger More."

"He's looking good for a dead man in his nineties."

I gave him a look. "Not Roger Moore, as in the fourth best Bond actor—*Roger More*. As in *sexually penetrate with greater frequency*. He used to be one of our best mates back in the day."

Oliver looked like he was about to ask a follow-up question when Roger began his typically bombastic introduction.

"Dearly beloved," he began, "in case you haven't noticed, this isn't going to be a traditional service. We aren't in a church and I'm certainly not a priest, but ladies, if you want to see God, call me after the ceremony." He rode the laughter a bit before he continued. "We are gathered here today to celebrate the love of two totally fucking amazing people—"

And I sort of checked out after that because I was having feels. Complicated feels. Because for all I could snark about the indie venue and the rainbow lights and the drag minister, this had been my world for years until one of the *fucking amazing people* we were here to celebrate had blown it up.

"And here they are," Roger finished with a stagy snap of his fingers.

All eyes turned to the back of the room, where Miles and JoJo entered from opposite sides of the archway, linked arms with a precision I suspected they'd practiced at least a hundred and twelve times, and proceeded down the aisle. A well-hidden speaker system kicked in and "Slip Away" by Perfume Genius played over the procession while two professional cameramen captured the whole thing for what I was willing to bet—and a sneaky check of JoJo's Twitch channel confirmed—was a livestream.

And I did have to admit that they both, in their radically different ways, looked great. Irritatingly great. Miles was dressed in a very traditional suit that made him every inch the perfect groom and even managed to make his hipster beard less risible. JoJo was in full makeup, with rainbow eyeshadow out to the temples, and wearing a silk tailcoat over a denim shirt and a black skirt flowing with organza.

Fuck. The man who'd ruined my life was a spread in gay *Hello*. Which I guess would be *Bona to Vada Your Eek*.

The ceremony that followed was irreverent, joyful, and occasionally vulgar, but it was also depressingly touching. Miles and JoJo were clearly head-over-heels for each other, and the guests—me and my cynical boyfriend aside—were clearly head-over-heels for them and their future happiness.

"JoJo," said Miles, looking legitimately glisteny-eyed as he kicked off the exchange of cloying sincerity that made you really miss *love, honour, and obey*. I mean, sure it was outdated and misogynistic, but at least it was short. He swallowed. "JoJo," he tried again, "when we met, I was in a…in a dark place."

Oh, poor you. If you give me some of your fifty grand, I'll buy you the world's smallest violin.

"But," Miles continued inexorably, "you showed me how to be happy again. You came into my life like a bolt of sunshine. You make me feel safe and loved and seen, and I know that I'm a better person when I'm with you."

Considering the kind of person he'd been when he was with me, that was a pretty low bar.

"You've given me so much: your generous spirit, your dauntless heart. You've filled my days with joy and my nights with a frankly astonishing collection of fancy lube."

Pause for laughter. Eye roll.

Miles continued gazing at his husband-to-be with intense devotion. "I love you, JoJo. I always will."

I stole a look at Oliver. It was his blankest face. And that was oddly reassuring.

"Miles." JoJo gazed back. "You're my rock. You're the best, kindest man I've ever known. Except, of course, for my amazing Patreons—I'm kidding, I'm kidding."

Another pause for laughter. Although I liked to think he wasn't joking. Miles deserved to marry a man with sponsored vows.

"I was lost when we met," JoJo went on, "but you found me. I'd forgotten how to believe in myself, but you remembered how to believe in me."

Mean Oliver leaned over and whispered as softly as he could, "Have I developed spontaneous aphasia or are they just saying words at random?"

"You should object," I told him.

"You know it doesn't work like that." He paused. "Especially because this is a wedding."

"I was lonely," JoJo went on. And on. "And now I'm not. Because I've got you, and I know you'll always be there for me, and you've made me happier than anyone ever has."

Oh God. He was crying and not in an artful gets-me-clicks way. He actually meant every word of this, and as usual, I was being a prick.

He dabbed at his eyes, smearing his rainbows a little, but looking so offensively radiant it didn't matter. "I love you, Miles. And I always will."

Pause for awwws.

For about ninety seconds I felt real bile rising up in my

stomach because people were awwwing for my arsehole ex and his jailbait boyfriend. Sorry, jailbait spouse. I'd sort of convinced myself that the wedding would prove to me that Miles was nothing but a tired hipster chasing a YouTube trophy husband and the ceremony would just be a self-congratulatory wankfest to cover their sham of a marriage. Except, in the end, the ceremony had been a self-congratulatory wankfest that had been...really sweet and meaningful. And rather than being doomed forever, it was clear that Miles and JoJo kind of had something.

And I was, once again, the one left behind with nothing.

Wait. No, I wasn't. I hadn't been that for years, even though I'd believed I was for quite a long time. It had been a pisser of a journey, but I was slowly working out that I was more than the shitty things that had happened to me. And one of the best things that had happened to me was sitting right there, helping me mock the vows at my ex-boyfriend's wedding.

Which—and maybe I was an overcompensating person or just a rubbish person—was some #relationshipgoals shit right there.

I gave Oliver's hand a little squeeze. I could do this. I could totally do this. I was fine.

Well. Fine-ish.

Fineoid.

Definitely heading in a fineular direction.

Maybe.

CHAPTER 14

ONCE THE CEREMONY WAS OVER and the new couple had finished kissing—which took longer than it had to—the celebration jumped straight to no-fucks-given dancing. Food was provided via a buffet along the sides of the room, and speeches were made intermittently by microphone from the main stage. In a lot of ways, had the context been very different, it would have been a great evening. I'd loved Bridge's wedding because I loved Bridge, but sitting around while elderly relatives made corny jokes over a meal that, while exquisite, you'd never have ordered in a restaurant, wasn't exactly the way most people I knew would choose to spend a Saturday. A gigantic party in a train tunnel with live music and speeches largely made by professional cabaret artists, on the other hand, was.

Or rather, it had been. Now I spent my Saturdays doing boy-friendly things like hoovering the living room and going to art galleries and/or IKEA, occasionally fielding calls from the James Royce-Royces because Baby J had done something so unbearably adorable that they had to tell everyone immediately. And it wasn't that I missed my party days—at least not the way they'd ended with me drinking, dancing, and fellating my way into oblivion. But it had been good for a while, and looking back, it didn't feel so much like something I'd grown beyond as something that had been taken from me.

So I looked around the room with this weird mix of nostalgia and... Actually, maybe it was just nostalgia, but in the serious pain-for-something-lost sense. And then I looked at Oliver. And his reaction was very much *not* nostalgia. It was the opposite of nostalgia. Like fuck-this-shit-algia or something. I think he'd have been more comfortable at a bullfight.

"Are you hating this?" I asked.

He had to raise his voice to be heard over the music. "By what metric?"

"Um? Any metric?"

"I believe I can honestly say," he shouted in that nightclub nobody-can-hear-this-because-nobody-can-hear-anything way, "that I cannot imagine a scenario in which I would enjoy watching two people I don't know get married in a disused train tunnel full of repetitive electronica and flashing lights more than I currently am."

I tried to be cool with that. Or even to be flattered by it—after all, it would have been a bit weird if my boyfriend had been super happy at the wedding of my arsehole ex. But the truth was, the arsehole ex wasn't the only issue. This issue was that Oliver was... well.

Okay, this was difficult. Because the reason I'd needed to date someone like him to begin with was that I'd needed to distance myself from the parts of queer culture that looked bad to a certain kind of rich straight person. And while I'd come to realise that Oliver was more than a respectable job and a wholesome jumper, it still weirded me out that he found so little value in what I'd always instinctively thought was *our* community.

"You don't feel, like, connected to any of this?" I asked, even though I already knew the answer.

He winced. "I wish I did and I'm sure I should. But no."

"It can be fun, though," I tried. "I mean, isn't it great to be in a place where you know nobody's judging you for who you are?"

There was whatever passed for silence in a room full of wedding noise. I got that sinking sensation that I hadn't had for a while, where I knew I'd said the wrong thing but I wasn't sure how.

"Lucien"—Oliver had a pained, sincere look about him, and I wished I'd kept my mouth shut—"I love that you feel accepted by this world, and I'd never want to take that away from anyone. But I've never felt any of"—he made a slightly helpless gesture—"this is for me."

"It could be for you." That probably wasn't right. "I mean, it is for you." That probably wasn't right either.

He leaned a little closer to my ear so that he could stop having to yell complex things about his relationship to identity politics over wedding music. "I understand that you're trying to make me feel included, but I'm afraid you're doing the opposite."

Fuck. How was I doing the opposite? "I didn't mean to," I whisper-yelled. "I just mean—you know—you've got a right to be part of this."

"That's not the reassurance you think it is."

Shit, this was turning into *Drag Race* all over again. "Can't you let it be?" I tried. It was the wrong thing to try.

"Lucien." He was using my name *a lot*, which was never a good sign. "I absolutely don't want to denigrate anybody's values. But places like this are... Well, I'm sure for people who like to express themselves in this kind of way that they're very empowering. But for me..." Now he ran a hand through his hair. Also not the best of signs. "It's like this whole event is telling me I'm doing my identity wrong if I'm not draping myself in rainbows at every opportunity. Ironically, it makes me feel judged."

It was nothing he hadn't said before. It was just extra weird for him to be saying it at my ex-boyfriend's wedding while we were surrounded by my ex-friends. Because there was a part of me that still belonged here and hated that he didn't. "I think that's just in your head."

He gave a cool blink. "I'm aware. But I'm also aware that I've told you on more than one occasion that I don't feel especially represented by this kind of thing, and you've consistently failed to believe me. So I sometimes think it might not be quite as much in my head as all that."

Fuck, were we having a fight? Was this a fight? Had I tried to show off my amazing barrister boyfriend to my arsehole ex and wound up having an embarrassing fight in the middle of said ex's fabulous queer wedding? "Oh my God, Oliver," I hugged him in the hope of de-escalating. "I didn't mean to make you feel... Shit, I'm a crappy boyfriend and you're so great for doing this for me and you don't have to like anything you don't want to like and we can go if you—"

"Luc? Luc O'Donnell?" I turned to see a man with an obscenely expensive suit and no sense of timing making his way around the edge of the dance floor towards us.

It took me a moment to recognise him. "Jonathan?"

We didn't hug. Even at university Jonathan had never been the hugging type. Honestly, we hadn't massively got on. On account of him being driven by a passionate desire for success and me being driven by a passionate desire for naps. He was one of those people who had sort of aged laterally, in that he looked almost exactly the same as when he was twenty. He'd somehow picked up a single grey streak in his hair, which gave him a bit of a werewolf vibe—only not in a sexy way—but otherwise he was the same lanky, grumpy git I vaguely remembered.

He stared at me for a long moment. "I have to say, you are the last person I expected to see here."

"Same. You don't even like Miles."

"Since when is *I don't like you* an excuse to get out of a

wedding?" His mouth, which was a sneery kind of mouth, got sneerier. "I mean, you felt obliged to show up and Miles literally sold you out to the *Daily Express*. What chance did I have?"

The thing about Jonathan was that he'd occupied a strange position in our friendship group. Someone told me once that the reason Christmas cracker jokes are so bad is that they're designed to be shared with the whole family and it's way easier to get everyone to agree that a joke is awful than to get them to agree it's funny. Jonathan was a human Christmas-cracker joke. We all hated him, and we were pretty sure he hated us, but somehow that brought us together. Unfortunately, without that context he was just a mildly unpleasant man. Then again, so was I.

"Anyway"—I gave a sickly smile—"this is Oliver Blackwood, my boyfriend. Oliver, this is Jonathan..." Aaaand I couldn't remember his surname. "This is Jonathan, who I knew at university, but we didn't like each other."

"Good to know you're still a cock, Luc," said Jonathan.

Strangely more in his element now I was asking him to be polite to an arsehole in a suit, Oliver offered his hand. "Lovely to meet you. If it helps, Luc didn't like me either."

"I like you now," I protested.

Oliver laughed. "I should bloody well hope so. It's been two years."

"So..." Jonathan had always had the eyebrows of an angry cartoon character, and now they knitted together ominously. "What didn't he like about you?"

"He thought I was boring."

"Me too," said Jonathan.

"Oliver, I didn't," I lied. "I just thought you were...you know, overachieving and a bit serious." And too good for me, but I was fucked if I was admitting that in front of Jonathan.

"Being overachieving and serious are very underrated

qualities." You could never tell if Jonathan was joking. He delivered everything in the same unplaceably accented monotone.

For whatever reason, Oliver had concluded that was both a joke and one he could join in on. "Perhaps we can exchange details. Then we can meet up some day and discuss our favourite shades of beige or compare pension plans."

Jonathan glanced at me. "Keep this one, Luc. He's all right. Anyway, what are you doing these days?"

"I work for a charity that protects bugs that eat shit." Two years ago, I'd have cringed. Now I liked to think I was owning it. Okay, renting it. "You?"

"I run a shop."

I opened my mouth, then closed it again. "You...run a shop."

"Yeah, big building, people come in and buy things. I know your parents are pop stars, but this is basic stuff."

How I'd known this man for ten years and not punched him once, I'd never quite worked out. I suppose the seven-year gap in the middle helped. "I know what a shop is, you utter turd. I just thought you'd be in finance or something. Not selling...groceries?"

"I don't sell groceries. I sell bath and bedroom furniture because people will always need it. I've got three stores, about to open a fourth. And, yeah, I'd probably earn more in the city, but I'd have to work for some prick with a hedge fund."

"From where I'm standing," I said, "you're still working for some prick." In hindsight, we didn't know each other well enough anymore for me to be making that kind of joke, but I was a bit on edge on account of Miles and how Oliver and I hadn't quite got a resolution on doesn't-like-rainbows-gate.

"Fuck off, O'Donnell." He turned back to Oliver. "Nice meeting you."

"And you," returned Oliver because he was a better person than me and didn't randomly insult people at weddings.

"Sorry," I said once Jonathan had vanished into the crowd. "I'd say I don't know what happened, but he was always like that."

Oliver gave me a faintly chiding look, which I'd have found sexy if it had happened in the bedroom. "As, I suspect, were you."

"No, I just act like a wanker. He really is one."

"I would say wankers are in the eye of the beholder, but that raises some disquieting images."

I gave an involuntary blink. "Yeah, I definitely don't want to think about Jonathan wanking, let alone wanking in my eye."

In an effort to be a good boyfriend, I asked Oliver once more if he wanted to go, and he told me he was fine, and not dog-in-a-burning-room fine. And I still wasn't quite ready to draw a line under the evening—still hadn't quite got whatever nebulous thing I was hoping to get and couldn't describe but was increasingly sure I'd know when I saw it. So we stayed, and for a while we bounced around half-forgotten acquaintances, repeating the ritual of how-are-you-what-have-you-been-doing all over again. Over the next couple of hours I caught up with at least half a dozen people I hadn't seen in the best part of a decade and found that they were almost all either city bankers or performing artists, with precious little middle ground. Most of them were also married. And I wasn't sure how I felt about any of that.

We were on our second or third circuit when I almost collided with Roger. Or Heather, I suppose, given she wasn't performing. And since she'd taken off the moustache, I was fairly confident we were back in a she/her pronoun space.

"Fuck, Luc," she said. "I-I did not expect to see you here."

I'd been hearing that a lot, in tones ranging from pleasantly surprised to unpleasantly surprised. Heather, though, sounded genuinely shaken. We'd been close back in the day. But she'd been one of Miles's best friends, and she'd really vocally sided with him at the time. Which, for some reason, hadn't gone down well with me.

I gave a limp shrug. "Yeah but...bygones, I guess?"

Her eyes narrowed. I'd forgotten quite how good her bullshit detector was. "I don't buy that for a second. What Miles did to you was fucked up, and you have every right not to forgive him."

"You forgave him pretty quick," I pointed out. Beside me, Oliver was sliding very quietly into I-am-not-a-part-of-this-conversation space.

She stuffed her hands very firmly into the pockets of her leather jacket, somehow projecting an attitude of apologetic defiance. "I *stuck by* him because I was more his friend than yours and we're all entitled to our mistakes. Even massive mistakes that hurt people. But I'd have completely got it if you never wanted to see him again. Or me, for that matter."

One day, I was going to have someone fuck me over and then not play the you've-got-every-right-to-be-angry card to guilt me out of being angry. "I'm sure that would have made things much easier for you."

"Is that why you're here, then?" The look on her face was still 80/20 between suspicion and regret. "Are you just Banquo's ghosting at us?"

And that stung a little. Because I wasn't quite ready to admit that what went down between me and Miles had affected other people as well. People that, once upon a time, I'd cared about and who'd cared about me. "Honestly," I said, "I'm not great at self-awareness but I think it started as a sincere attempt to be over it."

Oliver was maintaining his tactful silence, but he laid a hand softly on my shoulder.

"And are you?" asked Heather.

I had no way to answer that yet. "Can I get back to you after the wedding?"

"For what it's worth," she told me, "I'm sorry things went down the way they did."

I sighed. "Not your fault."

"No, but it was still a mess and I could have handled it better. Just at the time…I-I don't know. I felt like Miles was getting a lot of shit and—"

"Wait a minute. I'd had my sex life splashed all over the News of Whatever. How was *Miles* getting shit?"

She shot me a withering look. "Oh, come on. You know what Priya is like. You know what Bridget is like. You know what James Royce is like. They might have had good reasons, but they were fucking vicious. Not just to Miles but to everybody who didn't directly take your side as loudly and vocally as they did. So yeah, I stood up for him, and I said a bunch of things that I shouldn't have, and"—she took a deep breath—"I'm sorry."

I'd never looked at it like that before. Not that I'd ever had any obligation to because I was still very much the shaftee in this situation. But while Miles had wound up with custody of most of our associates and acquaintances—the Jonathans of the world—I *had* taken most of our real, close friends with me. As alone as I'd felt, as little as I'd appreciated them for it, I'd always had all the people that mattered in my corner.

Fuck, was I going to have to be nuanced about this? Being nuanced about things sucked. "I-I guess I see how that was tough. And—and probably a lot of us could have behaved better."

"Thanks." Unexpectedly, she hugged me. "This must be really strange for you."

I said, "And how," but I hugged her back in a way that I hoped communicated something more along the lines of *This is weird and complex but ultimately I think positive, and I'm glad we got a chance to reconnect even though it was in less-than-ideal circumstances, and I wish our past had involved less bullshit, even though neither of us was directly responsible for the bullshit in question.*

When we'd parted with the usual promises to definitely stay in touch for real this time, no lie, for serious, Oliver slipped his arm around me. "I hope I wasn't too unhelpful," he whispered as we wandered off. "That seemed quite intense, and I was concerned I'd be intruding."

"Yeah, it was kind of. Intense and..." I gave a nonspecific hand wave. "Blah."

"Ah, yes," Oliver agreed. "The blah will get you every time."

"I guess..." Apparently my mouth had more words to release. "I guess I hadn't really thought about how *big* the whole Miles thing was. How many people it affected who weren't, y'know, me. I was too busy getting wasted and feeling hard done by."

"I understand getting wasted and feeling hard done by are what your early twenties are all about."

I gave him a sceptical look. "I suppose you spent yours studying for the bar and, I don't know, developing a deep sense of altruism."

"Don't talk nonsense, Lucien." His lips twitched. "I've *always* had a deep sense of altruism."

The annoying thing was, he probably had. "Yeah, and I bet if your boyfriend had sold your sex life to a newspaper, you'd have been all 'It's okay; you have hurt me but you are entitled to make mistakes.'"

"I'm not sure any newspapers would want to pay for my sex life."

"Hey"—I poked him in the shoulder—"don't do yourself down. You're a saucy legal stud, and don't let anybody tell you otherwise."

He considered this. "Of course, prior to 1967 I'd have been a saucy illegal stud."

"Very illegal. You'd have been minus twenty."

"I meant for reasons of orientation rather than age."

Well, that was embarrassing. "Oh. Right. Yeah." Pausing our wedding circuit, I tipped up his chin and kissed him lightly on the lips. "Fine. You're a better gay than me."

"It's not a competition, Lucien," he said loftily. "But. Yes. Yes I am."

I kissed him again. "I think you're a better most things than me."

"You know that's not true at all."

"Name…" I was about to say three, but then I remembered the way Bridge had outmanoeuvred me. "Five."

"Only five?" he asked. "Very well. You can eat a dessert without feeling unnecessarily guilty about it."

"Wait." In my head, Oliver had just laughed it off. But in reality he'd gone for it. Of course he'd gone for it. "You don't have—"

"You have a good relationship with your mother. You don't blurt out insulting things at people you like."

"Have you met me? That one doesn't count."

"Fair enough. You don't need a live-in boyfriend to remind you what work-life balance is."

"I think," I said, "you'll find I do. It's just the other way round."

"You were always good at your job, Lucien. You sometimes pretended not to be, but you were."

I grinned. "Are we counting that as one or two?"

"Neither, that was justifying the previous assertion."

"M'lud," I added for him.

"Shush," he told me, getting all stern and exciting. "That's three so far. You're more willing to do things that frighten you. And, as we've established, you can dance."

"Okay." I narrowed my eyes. "Name seven."

He didn't miss a beat. "You're slightly taller and more annoying."

"Oh, for fuck's sake," I muttered. "I completely love you. And thank you for coming today. I know it's, like, the opposite of your scene."

"It's fine." He gazed at me in that sincere, silver-eyed Olivery way. "I'd say I'd do anything for you but, as a lawyer, I'd never use such imprecise language. I am, however, happy to accompany you to an ostentatious wedding for an unpleasant person. Did you get what you needed?"

I sighed. "Honestly, I'm not sure what that would even have been. Unless you count Miles pooing himself on the way to the altar."

"Would that not just have been quite unpleasant for everybody?"

"Well, yes, but then years from now I could look back and say, 'Sure, he fucked me over and turned our whole life into a jagged, broken lie, but he still took a massive dump in his pants at his own wedding.'"

"I suppose that's why there's a popular saying: The best revenge is living well, or watching somebody soil their underwear."

"I mean," I admitted, "I probably don't *actually* need to see him poo himself."

Oliver glanced speculatively towards the happy couple. "Are you sure? It could be arranged."

"How?"

"Laxatives in the champagne. There's a twenty-four-hour chemist up the road."

I'd heard people say the key to a good relationship was still being able to surprise each other. But I think, maybe, it was an unexpected willingness to arrange public defecation. "We...we shouldn't. And, anyway, I'm over Miles. Not, like, in the romantic sense. I mean, definitely in the romantic sense. But also in the what-he-did-no-longer-has-power-over-me sense. And I'm not a therapist but I think trying to make him shit his keks isn't the best way to signal I've moved on and I'm now a more complete human being."

Oliver offered a conspiratorial smile. "What if I did it so we had an excuse to leave?"

"How about," I suggested, "we just leave. Because I'm done with this, and you're clearly hating every minute of it, and I'd rather spend time with, y'know, you than a bunch of people I've not spoken to in a decade."

"I see no flaws in this plan. Although we should give our congratulations to Miles and JoJo before we go."

"Oh my God. You can't even bail on a party impolitely."

"Eight," said Oliver. "You bail on parties better than me too."

Ideally, I would not have given our congratulations to Miles and JoJo. Except no. *Fuck it.* I'd made the choice to come here, and I was—if I said so myself—fucking nailing it. Okay, maybe not nailing it. Perhaps pinning it? Or putting it up with some of those little adhesive Velcro things? Either way, I was being mature and evolved and above it all, and if I was now hurtling towards a space in which tradition demanded that I kiss Miles on his smug, beardy cheeks and tell him that he and JoJo looked amazing and had thrown an amazing party, I could do it. I could do it with a smile on my face. Because none of this mattered anymore.

"Miles," I said as we entered handshaking, cheek-kissing range, "JoJo. *Congratulations.*"

"I'm so glad you could make it." Miles gave me an awkward half embrace.

JoJo nodded. "Yeah, it meant a lot to the both of us."

"Wouldn't have missed it," I lied. "This is my boyfriend, Oliver Blackwood."

Oliver shook both their hands with the disarming formality of a man who was professionally formal and disarming. "Delighted."

"I'm really glad you found somebody," Miles told me. "I know things got pretty rough for you after we broke up."

They had, indeed, got *pretty rough* after we *broke up*. Or to put it more accurately they'd got fucking *hellish* after he'd *completely betrayed me*. But no: calm, centred, rising above. If you looked in the dictionary under *over it*, you'd have found a picture of me. "Yeah, got to admit I was in a bad place for a few years."

"But," Miles went on cheerfully, "it's great to know we can be friends now."

Wait. *What?*

The party was loud, but it felt like everything had come to a crashing halt.

I blinked. Then, when opening my eyes failed to reveal that the last three minutes had just been a dream about unmitigated gall, I blinked again. Since the world was resolutely failing to dissolve into fairy dust and sugar clouds, I figured I was stuck with it.

Reaching out, I patted Miles companionably on the shoulder. "Let's be clear," I told him, trying to match his air of casual mateyness. "I'm glad you're happy. You and JoJo seem like you'll be great together. But we are *never* going to be friends because you will *always* be the guy who sold me out for the price of a Toyota Supra."

Then I leaned in, kissed him on his beardy cheek, turned around, and left the wedding.

CHAPTER 15

AS MATURE AND GROWN-UP AND (mostly) over it as I'd been at Miles's wedding, the drive home was by far the best part of the evening. Now that I was no longer feeling the pressure to be supportive of my dickhead ex and his child bride, I could join in with Oliver in mocking their vows (we get it, you like each other), their choice of venue (we get it, you're unconventional), and the guest list (we get it, you know a lot of artsy people and rich bastards).

Although that did make me feel a bit bad in retrospect when, two days later, JoJo showed up at my office.

"Chap to see you," explained Alex. "I mean, I say 'chap,' but he is wearing rather a lot of makeup and, well, one's supposed to be sensitive about these things, isn't one?"

The list of people it could have been was very short, not that I had any idea what JoJo Ryan was doing at CRAPP. "If it is who I think it is, Alex, then you're good. He's a chap."

"Pleased to hear it. Wouldn't want to call a chap a chap when a chap was actually a chapess. Fearfully bad form to go around mis-chapping chaps, isn't it?"

"Oh, fearfully," I told him and went through to see what the hell was going on.

Unfortunately, Rhys Jones Bowen had got there first.

"Hello," he was saying, directing his phone at himself and JoJo, "don't be alarmed, I'm just making some content for our social media. Perhaps you'd like to tell the Rhystocrats who you are and why you're visiting Cee-Arr-Ay-Pee-Pee today."

JoJo looked a little perplexed but more patient than I think I would have been under the circumstances. "I'm JoJo Ryan." He gave a camera-ready smile. "And I've come to speak to somebody who works here."

"I work here," offered Rhys. "How about speaking to me?"

"No, I mean a specific somebody."

"Ah, how about me?" asked Alex. "I'm pretty specific."

I got the slow, creeping sense that this was going to turn into one of *those* work moments. "Alex, you *know* he's here to see me. He already told you."

"Might have changed his mind," Alex pointed out. "Fellow can, you know."

"Alex, you don't even know who this guy is."

That made Alex do his indignant face. "Yes I do. He's JoJo Ryan."

"Who is?" I prompted.

"Who is here to see somebody who works for CRAPP, and frankly, Luc, I think it's very selfish of you to want to keep our visitor all to yourself."

Rhys looked around from his phone. Apparently, the chat had been updating him. "According to the Rhysocrats, JoJo Ryan is some kind of You Tuber." Grinning, he extended a hand. "Lovely to meet you, JoJo. Always nice to meet a fellow influencer."

I sighed. "You're not an influencer, Rhys."

"Excuse me, I have nine hundred and seventy-four followers." He paused. "Well, nine hundred and seventy-two, really, because one of them is my auntie Margery and another is my auntie Margery's python."

I wasn't going to ask. I wasn't going to ask. I wasn't going to ask. "Why does your auntie Margery have a python, and why does it follow you on YouTube?"

"She's got a python," said Rhys, and I instantly regretted my lack of self-control, "because she's allergic to cats and because she got used to snakes when she was an exotic dancer. And he follows me on You Tube because Auntie Margery thinks he finds my voice calming."

There was so much to process there. "Your aunt was an exotic dancer?"

"Oh yes. Very tasteful, minimal nudity."

I wasn't going to ask. I wasn't going to ask. I wasn't going to ask. "What does minimal nudity look like?"

"Honestly, Luc." Rhys gave me a look of admonition. "Asking a man what his aunt looks like naked is low even for you."

"I wasn't—" But there was no point protesting. I'd only dig myself into a deeper hole.

"Actually"—JoJo finally managed to get a word in—"I *was* here to talk to Luc. About something a bit personal."

Alex gave me an apologetic look. "Ah, as it turns out, he hasn't changed his mind at all. Well played, old boy."

"This was never a game." I made my best welcome-to-CRAPP gesture at JoJo and led him through to the relative privacy of my office.

To be honest, I wasn't thrilled to be leading him through to the relative privacy of my office, but having already made a scene at his wedding, I didn't want to compound it by making a scene at my place of work.

Sitting down at my desk, I tried to psych myself up to apologise. Which was going to be difficult because, in a lot of ways, I wasn't fucking sorry. I'd done more than my fair share of reconciliation bullshit by showing up in the first place. Expecting me to be "yes, we're bros now" was a bridge too far. And not like a little tiny bridge over a brook on a nice walk in the countryside. Like a giant, fucking steel-suspension bridge over a river of fuck right off.

Come on, Luc. Be the bigger man.

"I'm sorry if I spoiled your big day," I tried. I know all the internet rules say you're not supposed to begin an apology with *I'm sorry if*, but it was what he was getting.

JoJo laughed. It seemed like a sincere laugh, which was more than I'd expected. "Sweetheart, I was marrying the man I love in a big party filled with all my friends plus a bunch of other people who aren't my friends but were still telling me how amazing I was. One slightly mean conversation wasn't going to ruin that."

Oh. Okay. "So why are you here?"

"Just to say…" JoJo stared down at his immaculately manicured nails. "Just to say that…I suppose…I suppose I get it?"

Was I offended by that? I thought I was at least a little bit offended by that. Because this guy was twelve and trying to tell me he knew what it was like to get betrayed and abandoned by the fucker he'd just married. Although, now I thought about it, JoJo wasn't that much older than I'd been when I'd dated Miles. Of course, Miles was now substantially older than he'd been when he'd dated me, which was why I felt justified taking the piss. The thing was, though, I hadn't *felt* young at the time. I'd felt pretty grown-up. And here was JoJo, looking at me with the confidence of a young man who didn't quite realise how young he seemed to other people.

See, *this* was the problem with trying to be a better human being to impress your boyfriend. You ended up having to be a better human to everybody.

"Get what, exactly?" I asked warily.

He kept giving me his earnest early-twenties face. "I've been on the internet since I was sixteen. I know you got the whole old-media paparazzi treatment, and I'm sure that was crappy in a slightly different way, but I've had a million strangers telling me what they think of me every day since before I did my GCSEs."

Okay, that did sound awful. Although old Luc would have pointed out that the person who was financially compensated for JoJo's constant harassment was JoJo, not the person who dumped him.

"So," JoJo went on, "I do understand that what Miles did to you was fucking terrible. That's why I wanted you to come to the wedding."

When Miles had told me that he'd invited me to the wedding for JoJo's sake, I'd assumed he was just rightfully ashamed of how selfish it sounded otherwise. "Wait. You *actually* wanted me to come to the wedding?"

"Yeah…" I'd heard more sheepish *yeahs*, but only from actual sheep. "I think I just wanted to see… I don't know. That you were okay, I guess?"

"So you could tell yourself you weren't marrying the King of the Arseholes?" It was probably an unfair comment, but I was trying to ration my enlightenment.

He squirmed in a way that didn't quite fit with the YouTube starlet persona. "So I could tell myself I'd be okay too."

Ah. That was…that was more complicated than I was ready for. "You mean, if he did the same to you?"

It had been kind of the elephant in the room, and now I'd… I dunno. Had I shot the elephant? Had I said, *Hey, is that an elephant?* Was the elephant now rampaging around stomping on things? I didn't think it was a stompy atmosphere. Perhaps we were just staring at an elephant and going, *Yup, that's an elephant all right.*

There was a very, very long silence. At the end of the very, very long silence, JoJo said, "Maybe?"

And there went my last hope of resenting him. Because—and this wasn't a self-esteem issue—JoJo had to be worth more than fifty grand, even accounting for inflation. And in his world everything would happen at the speed of Twitter, instead of the speed of the tabloids.

"And I-I don't think he *will*," he continued. "Obviously I wouldn't have married him if I thought he would."

At this point, I wasn't sure if he was trying to convince me or himself. "I figured."

JoJo picked at one of his perfect nails, leaving a little chip in it. "And we've talked about it—we've talked about it *so much*—and Miles really *is* sorry, even if he's bad at showing it."

"Or saying it," Old Luc pointed out.

Which JoJo completely blanked, either out of politeness, indifference, or the strain of being genuinely upset in the office of a relative stranger. "It almost broke us up when I found out. I wasn't sure I could trust somebody who could do something like that."

"Probably too late to say this," I told him, "on account of that wedding we were both at, but probably you *shouldn't* trust somebody who can do something like that?"

JoJo gave a shrug. "Probably not. But Miles was the first person I'd ever met who really felt like he was interested in me for me, not for who I was."

I sincerely tried to take that at face value and not assume that even if Miles wasn't interested in JoJo's YouTube celebrity, he definitely was interested in being married to a hot young twink.

"And the thing is," JoJo was saying, "if I'd walked away from that, I know I'd have regretted it. So"—he flicked away a flake of glittery nail polish and met my eyes again—"I took a chance."

What did he want, a medal? Congratulations: You Gave an Arsehole a Second Chance. "Better you than me."

"Better me than you," agreed JoJo quietly. "And he... I... It's been a long time. I never expected you to forgive him. I don't think he did either, really. I think he just got caught up in the moment."

That was Miles. Of course, the last time he'd got caught up in the moment, it had been the moment when he was selling... *Oh, for fuck's sake, let it go. It's not about you anymore.* "Good because I-I don't. I know I said I was sorry about your wedding, but I stand by everything I told him."

"And that's fine." JoJo smiled at me. And it was weirdly comforting to be reassured by a man with no sense of irony. "You weren't there for him. You were there for me. And you showed me that even if the worst happens, it'll be...I'll be fine." He paused. And then added in a slightly vulnerable way, "You seem really happy, Luc."

"I *am* really happy," I replied, slightly too aggressively. "And look..." Was I going to let myself say this? Okay, apparently I was. "As much as I hate to admit it, I honestly don't think you've got anything to worry about. Like you said, it's been a long time and Miles is a different person now."

Of course, that person was still a prick. But details.

"Really?" JoJo looked at me with devastating hope in his eyes.

"I wish I could say, 'Once a fuck-you-overer, always a fuck-you-overer' but..." I sighed. Having to see your ex as a person sucked. Having to see the man your ex married as a person double sucked. "For the last couple of years I've been dating a wonderful guy, and he'd want me to say that everybody makes mistakes. And sometimes they make mistakes that hurt other people. But that doesn't mean they should be judged by those mistakes for the rest of their lives." I took a deep breath. This felt almost cleansing. "Then again," I added, "fool me once bitten leopards don't change their spots, so take your pick."

JoJo laughed, and it sounded a bit...sad. And that made me feel bad because somebody that sparkly shouldn't be sad. "I think

I already have," he said. "And I think, when it comes to love, it's worth rolling the dice."

I was about to try and say something wise—or at least come up with something wise I could then decide not to say—but the door opened and Rhys stuck his head in. "I say, JoJo, I was just thinking. You wouldn't want to do a collaboration, would you?"

To his credit, JoJo somehow managed not to tell him to fuck right off. "What sort of collaboration?"

"Well." Rhys had a wild eureka light in his eyes. "I've got a You Tube channel. You've got a You Tube channel. We could do a You Tube together."

"Like what?" asked JoJo, who seemed to be giving this proposal far more time than it probably objectively deserved.

"I don't know. What do you You Tube about?"

JoJo gestured at his face. "Makeup."

"Oh, right. I suppose not everybody is as lucky as me." Rhys indicated his own face. "Would you believe I wake up like this?"

Once again, JoJo demonstrated that he was far more polite than I am by not commenting.

"I believe it," I put in.

"Tell you what," Rhys continued undaunted, "how about we see if we can work on some dung-beetle-themed makeup tips."

"That"—JoJo gave Rhys a surprisingly warm smile—"sounds like an interesting challenge."

To my amazement, JoJo Ryan took Rhys's details and promised to be in touch to talk about the collaboration. Of course *promising* to do something and *actually* doing it were two very different things—just look at my dad and his marriage vows or, for that matter, any other promise he had ever made—but I had a perhaps naive sense that JoJo might make good on the offer.

I left work that day not confused exactly but a bit shaken,

with something JoJo had said buzzing around my head like the tune to an eighties disco classic whose name I couldn't remember.

It's worth rolling the dice.

Which wasn't Oprah. But it was something.

CHAPTER 16

HERE'S THE THING. I LOVED Oliver, I really did. But there was no getting away from the fact we had irreconcilable Saturday differences. In my world, a Saturday was for sleeping until noon, having sex until two—or, y'know, half twelve depending on how close to thirty I was feeling—and then hanging out with friends or visiting my mum, or if I was in a super-domestic mood, curling up on the sofa with a movie. Oliver's ideal Saturday involved "lying in" until nine at the latest, then going for a run or to the gym, following it up with a nutritious breakfast before doing something disgustingly productive. And some days, I could lure him with my wiles into a more Luc-friendly set of activities. Like cuddling and/or blow jobs.

Unfortunately, today was not one of those days. And when I staggered downstairs a little after one, I found Oliver on his knees on the kitchen floor—and not in a fun way. His protein shaker was drying on the rack and his hair was still damp and tousled from his post-run shower, both of which were signs of an Oliver highly committed to productivity. Plus, he was wearing his virtuous grey sweatpants and the no-longer-suitable-for-work-but-I-am-too-ethical-to-throw-clothes-away shirt that he reserved for cleaning. The marigolds were also a giveaway.

I groaned.

"Good afternoon, Lucien," he said cheerfully.

I groaned again. "What are you doing?"

He gave me a look of what I hoped was mock disappointment. But given how seriously he took cleaning, I couldn't be sure. "Are you telling me you've forgotten what day it is?"

"Um, Saturday? And definitely not... Shit, is it your birthday?"

"Yes," he told me. "It's my birthday. This is what I always do on my birthdays."

"You think you're joking. But I wouldn't put it past you."

He huffed out a put-upon sigh. "It's the first Saturday in July."

"And?" I asked.

"So I'm cleaning my cupboards. As I did last year, if you recall."

"Oliver, you have cleaned so many things, I didn't realise I was supposed to be putting them on a calendar."

He set down his bottle of multipurpose surface cleaner with a condemnatory click. "As I thought you'd have learned by now, cleaning is a lot easier when you do it regularly—which is itself easier when you have a routine."

"I don't know what you're talking about." I knelt down beside him. "Clearly, it's much better if you leave it until all your spoons start sticking together and you hate yourself, and then get a nice boyfriend and stealth move into his place."

"And what happens"—he twitched an eyebrow at me—"when my spoons start sticking together?"

"We'll both have to find a new boyfriend and we can move into his place together."

He readjusted his marigolds uncertainly. "I'm not sure that's a sustainable strategy. And while I have no objection to polyamory in theory, I don't think it would suit me in practice."

Leaning in, I kissed him on the nose. "Then I faithfully promise that no matter how sticky your teaspoons get, I will still want to be with you and only you."

"I'm not sure I want to ask..." began Oliver. Apparently, I'd successfully deflected his relationship anxiety by triggering his hygiene anxiety. "But how do teaspoons become sticky?"

"It's not a sex thing," I protested quickly.

"I wasn't assuming it was a sex thing. I'd be less concerned if it was a sex thing."

Oh God. I was disgusting. I was the creature from the disgusting lagoon. "I think," I offered, "it's because most of my cooking involved oil. And then if you don't change your washing-up water properly, you're washing everything in oily water and it comes out with kind of a... You know. Oily film? That dries? And it gets—"

Oliver had gone pale. "I think you should probably stop there."

"Are you going to dump *me* now?"

He thought about it for an unflatteringly long time. "Tragically, Lucien, I will still love you even if you make my spoons sticky." He paused. "Having said which, do not make my spoons sticky."

"It's not a lifestyle choice. It's just...a consequence of other lifestyle choices."

Laughing, Oliver squirted the cupboard again and started to scrub, with a predesignated surface scrubber. I knew it was predesignated because they lived in a separate, subtly different pot from the washing-up sponges, and I'd once made the mistake of trying to clean a plate with one. Embarrassingly, it was one of our worst-ever arguments.

As he scrubbed, his head and shoulders disappeared inside the cupboard, leaving me with ample opportunity to appreciate his arse which—sweatpants or no—was sort of jutting up perkily and moving back and forth in time with his very diligent cleaning.

"Is that what you're doing?" he asked from the interior of the kitchen unit.

"Staring at your arse?"

"Oh, that's what you're doing? But no, I mean...stealth moving."

Honestly, I'd been hoping he wouldn't notice that. "Well, your place is bigger than mine and it's nicer and you wash your sheets and...you're in it."

"I'm glad I merited some mention among the list of utilities."

"To be fair, you can come round to my flat. Your dishwasher can't."

"You should get a dishwasher, Lucien," he said somewhat predictably. "They're actually more ecologically efficient than hand washing."

"I could but I've gone for the even more environmentally friendly strategy of using someone else's dishwasher, thus saving the upfront environmental impact of installation and the long-term environmental impact of us running two separate dishwashers."

Oliver sat back on his heels. "Even before we met, I never ran my dishwasher at half load."

"I did that *one time*. And I said I was sorry." I couldn't tell if this was going really off track or really on track. "But it does sort of make my point. If I had a dishwasher in my flat, I'd run it at half load all the time. I'd have to—I've only got two plates."

"You could always buy more plates?" Oliver suggested.

"True. Or I could just stay here and use yours."

Swapping the designated scrubber for a carefully rationed piece of paper towel, Oliver returned to the cupboard. "I suppose that *is* the best strategy from a strict carbon-footprint perspective." The scrubbing continued. "And, well, since as you observe you've rather stumbled into living here anyway, if you wanted to... Well, there's a certain logic in making it an official arrangement."

The part of me that was terrified of commitment, betrayal, and finding myself ten years down the line telling Oliver to fuck off at his wedding gave a little yelp. The part of me that was terrified of blowing a good thing gave a different yelp. I let them yelp at each other for a bit and tried to distract myself by turning my attention to Oliver's arse.

"That is," Oliver went on, "if you're not... If it isn't too... And, of course, you wouldn't have to give up your flat if you didn't want to. It's just, I don't think you like your flat very much."

"Since I originally got it with Miles, no, I really don't." My brain was still in crisis mode, which meant all it could think of were endless variations of worst-case scenarios. "But that could happen to you as well. What if something goes wrong with us and then you start to hate this house, which you love and clean all the time, because you used to share it with this guy who cheated on you."

Emerging abruptly from the cupboard, Oliver stared at me wide-eyed. "Lucien, are you trying to tell me you're cheating on me?"

"What?" I cried. "No. It's the kind of thing I would do. I mean, it's not the kind of thing I would do. It's the kind of thing the kind of person I am would do if they were going to fuck up their relationship with the kind of person you are."

Oliver took a deep breath. "You are not that kind of person. You just worry you might be every time somebody likes you."

That was at once reassuring and embarrassing. "Stop knowing me," I whined.

"It's a little late for that. I have, as you've observed, actually been living with you for at least a year and a half." He paused. "And as for the house, if it came to it, I'd get a new one. And I'd have more money for the deposit because you'd have been paying half the mortgage."

I stared at him helplessly. "Oh God, you really mean it, don't you? You want me to, like, move in and shit and keep stuff here and—"

"You already keep quite a lot of stuff here."

"No," I said decisively, "I've *left* stuff here. It's a different vibe."

"You've left stuff here, in increasing quantities, for nearly two years."

"That's not emotionally significant. I left a pair of formal shoes at Priya's after my graduation, and she's still got them."

Oliver's mouth was doing that thing where he tried to pretend he wasn't smiling. "I find that very easy to believe. But I don't think you have an entire drawer of variously salacious underwear at any of your friends' houses."

He was right. I didn't. This was unintentional, but it was real. It was very real and it had always been very real. You couldn't get realer than a drawer of pants. "And you...trust me to..." I made a gesture that, frankly, could have encompassed anything.

"Of course I trust you, Lucien. For a start, as I've said many times, you've already been..." He imitated my gesture.

I made a noise. Because all my internal yelping had decided to come out of my brain through my throat.

Drawing off his marigolds with deliberate care, like he was satisfying a really specific but highly mundane fetish, Oliver took my hands in his. "I know this seems frightening and it seems like a lot. But it is not a lot. It is exactly what we're already doing."

I made another noise.

"It's no different," he went on in his gentlest voice, "than when we were first dating. Nothing actually changed. We just agreed to start calling it something different."

My handholding was veering into clutching. "That's...that's true."

"You still make me happy, Lucien. You are still everything I want and a lot of things I couldn't have imagined wanting—"

"Thanks."

"In a good way. We don't have to do this. We can move at whatever pace you like. But you should know that I am yours, more truly than I have ever been anyone's. Because when I'm with you, I'm me. Not someone I think I should be. And I'll be with you, however you want, for as long as you'll have me."

Only Oliver would say something like that in the middle of scrubbing his kitchen cabinets. And maybe that was why I could listen to him, when I sometimes couldn't even listen to myself. Why he made me feel safe and hopeful and worth something when I had a bunch of reasons not to.

Not going to lie, it was kind of annoying.

Because he was right again.

I could do this. We could do this. We were already doing this. We had something strong and right and special, and I'd be more of a bellend than usual if I didn't accept that. Cherish it. Hold on to it.

I opened my mouth to tell him yes, of course I'd move in with him, I couldn't imagine anything better.

Except then, somewhere at the back of my mind, a tiny glitter bomb of a boy in internet-friendly makeup said, *It's worth rolling the dice.*

And so instead, what came out of my mouth was, "We should get married."

CHAPTER 17

I'D AGREED TO MEET JAMES Royce-Royce—the other James Royce-Royce—during my lunch hour outside an embarrassingly middle-end jewellers in central London. He turned up exactly on time with Baby J strapped to his chest, making him look like the world's most wholesome kidnapper.

"Do you two ever put him down?" I asked.

He blinked at me exactly once. "Yes. Just not in the middle of London."

That was fair. The last thing you wanted to do was put your kid down for five minutes and then come back to find he'd been detonated by the bomb squad. "So how's…" I found myself pointing at Baby J.

I didn't know how to talk to or about children at the best of times, and mostly I got away with it because I usually encountered them as part of large groups of less crap people who did all the cooing for me. But today it was just me and Baby J. Worse, Baby J was a particularly difficult child to talk about because when the James Royce-Royces had first brought him home, he'd looked ever so slightly like something Jim Henson had built out of foam and ping-pong balls. And, needless to say, James Royce-Royce would keep saying things like *Isn't he darling? Isn't he the most darling thing you've ever seen?* And I would say things like *Well, he's quite wet. Are they all this wet?*

"He's fine," said James Royce-Royce who, where babies were concerned, was definitely my favourite of the James Royce-Royces.

I redirected my awkward glance from the child to the jewellers. "Um, thanks for coming."

"No problem."

It had been a little over a week since I'd, y'know, accidentally proposed to Oliver in a fit of whatever the hell that had been a fit of. Of course he'd said yes, correctly discerning that if he'd said no, I'd have changed my name, moved to Pluto, and joined the French Foreign Legion. Since then, we'd had one or two short conversations, mostly led by Oliver and mostly focused on what a sensible choice it was to get married because of next-of-kin benefits and mild tax breaks. Which was what happened when, instead of proposing on one knee at the Eiffel Tower, you did it in a kitchen while your partner had his head in a cupboard. And probably meant I owed Oliver...not a do-over exactly, I was never doing that again, but at least a decent ring.

Well. The decentish ring I could get on my budget.

The decentish ring I could get on my budget given about eighty percent of engagement rings were total shit.

"Shall we go in?" asked James Royce-Royce.

Yes. The answer was yes. I couldn't get a ring if I didn't go in. "Maybe?"

"If you don't like this shop, there are three others within eight minutes' walk, two of them within the same price range."

"It's not the shop. I'm just, I don't know, nervous I think?"

"That's because you're a commitment-phobe."

"With good reason."

"Not with good reason," James Royce-Royce told me firmly. "Dogs aren't more likely to bite people who are scared of dogs."

"What? I'm getting married, not a pet."

He looked down at Baby J, who was currently distracted by all the sparkly things in the window. "You had a bad experience once, and you're afraid it'll happen again. But past performance is no guarantee of future results."

I think that was meant to be reassuring. And if I'd been investing in a stock portfolio, it might have been. Or maybe I was unreassurable right now. After all, part of the reason I'd asked James Royce-Royce to come with me, instead of anyone else I could have asked, is that I knew I could rely on him to give me an opinion that wasn't overbearingly romantic (like Bridget or James Royce-Royce) or crushingly cynical (like Priya or, well, me).

"Come on, then," I said with about as much conviction as I could summon. "Let's put a ring on it. By which I mean buy a ring that I can give to Oliver, which he can wear if he wants. Maybe. If it doesn't need resizing, which it probably will."

Pushing open the door, we stepped into that churchy hush that all jewellers seemed to cultivate, as if they were trying to instil a sense of inadequacy that could be dispelled only by spending more than you could afford.

I was instilled with a sense of inadequacy.

And my credit was nowhere near good enough to dispel it.

To quell my rising panic, I peered into one of the counters, as if I knew what the fuck I was doing. Except I didn't. I wasn't even looking at rings.

"Can I help you, sir?"

I looked up to see a slender, ashen-faced man in a three-piece suit who somehow looked like he had a pencil moustache, while also being completely clean-shaven. "Um," I said. "Um."

The unaccountably intimidating shop assistant folded his hands behind his back. "And what might sir be looking for?"

Somehow, he made *sir* sound like an insult.

"I guess," I tried. "Um. A ring?"

"Estate? Eternity? Wedding? Puzzle? Promise? Semi-mount? Signet? Cocktail? Cluster? Claddagh?"

Oh my God, I'd walked into the lair of the riddling jeweller. Any second now he was going to say, *My first is in diamond, but isn't in heart.* "Engagement," I squeaked.

"Ah." In one syllable, he managed to express more disappointment than any of my schoolteachers or university lecturers had ever managed.

I visibly cringed. "Is that okay?"

Without another word, he bent at the waist and drew forth a velvet tray that he laid in front of me very much with the air of someone casting pearls before swine.

Which, as it turned out, he definitely was. Because, looking at the price tags, I couldn't afford anything.

"Do you," I asked, with a disproportionate amount of shame for someone who, at the end of the day, was still about to shell out about five hundred quid in his guy's shop, "by any chance have anything...cheaper?"

The man cleared his throat and took way too long replacing the tray of shit I couldn't afford with a tray of twenty-five-pound cubic-zirconia tat.

"Oh, come on." I made a gestural *Oh, come on* to underscore my verbal *Oh, come on* in the hopes of articulating quite how much of an *Oh, come on* situation this was. "Something in the middle."

"The first tray was in the middle, sir."

I tried to remember that working in customer service was unrewarding and people had to take their entertainment where they could. "Okay, something just under the middle, then. Something below average. Because I am a below-average person, as you have so clearly implied."

"I beg your pardon, sir?" said the gaslighting fuck on the other side of the counter.

James Royce-Royce stepped forward. "We want to see a selection of men's engagement rings in the five-to-eight-hundred-pound range."

I don't know how James Royce-Royce, despite having a still faintly Muppet-esque baby strapped to his chest, managed to have more gravitas than me, but he did. And approximately forty seconds later, we were poring over a tray of exactly the type of rings I'd been looking for in exactly the range of prices I'd been expecting to pay for them. They were, in a lot of ways, quite similar. Because this was one of those areas where men's fashions followed some pretty strict rules, though fortunately those rules more or less matched what I knew of Oliver's taste. Which was to say classic, masculine, and non-ostentatious.

I turned to James Royce-Royce. "How did you…"—I gave a nonspecific hand wave—"for James?"

He shrugged. "It was easy. Got the biggest, shiniest thing I could. Had it custom made."

"Oh, right. Because you're incredibly rich."

He shrugged again. "Not my fault you didn't do a maths degree, Luc."

Welp, he had me there. Once again, I leaned over to inspect the rings in front of me. Between my budget and Oliver's aesthetic, I was able to narrow it down quickly to a gold band, a brushed-gold band, a white-gold band, a subtly different white-gold band, and a white-gold band with a thin strip of rose gold running round the middle. There'd also been one with a diamond set in it, one with three diamonds set in it, and one with a faux Celtic motif, but I'd discounted those immediately on the grounds that Oliver would have fucking hated them. After a moment of thought, I also discounted the plain and the brushed gold because they'd looked too weddingy and Oliver was kind of traditional in some regards, so I wasn't sure he'd like a gold engagement ring.

"Okay." I turned to James Royce-Royce. "Which of these identical rings is least crap?"

"Excuse me, sir," protested the unaccountably intimidating shop assistant. "I can assure you our goods are all of the highest quality."

I glowered at him. "Leave it out, this isn't Tiffany's. You've made it very clear that I'm a middle-of-the road guy, but let's be honest: this is a middle-of-the-road shop."

"Sir appears to have taken offence at my manner," the assistant sneered. "I beg sir's forgiveness."

Obviously he was banking on *sir* being too lazy to walk eight minutes down the road to a shop where sir might be treated less rudely. And he had sir bang to rights. Sir would take a lot more abuse than this if it meant dodging a short walk or a long queue.

Having been momentarily distracted by wiping the dribble from Baby J's chin, James Royce-Royce took a shufty at the merchandise. "I think that one"—he pointed at the ring with the rose-gold detailing—"is the most Oliver. Then again, you know him better than I do."

I did, but he was completely right. Of course, the competition was two completely boring rings with no decoration whatsoever, but Oliver was definitely a subtle seam of rose gold kind of guy. "I'll take it," I said. "And if my boyfri—fiancé needs to come in to get it resized, I want you to be nicer to him."

Despite being quite a lot shorter than I was, the assistant somehow managed to look down his nose at me. "I shall endeavour to accede to sir's wishes."

Although now I thought about it, Oliver had nothing to fear from this guy. Because he very much came across as white-suit, nice-hat Julia Roberts whereas I was more thigh-high-boots-with-a-safety-pin Julia Roberts. In any case, I forked over my seven hundred quid, pocketed the ominous velvet box, and got the fuck out of there.

The velvet box was still ominousing in my pocket at the point our evening reached the me on the sofa watching old seasons of *American Horror Story* and Oliver on the floor with his laptop and his case notes, being all hot and diligent stage.

"Oliver," I said at the same time he said, "Lucien." And then I said, "No, you," and he said, "After you," and we went back and forth like that for a bit until Oliver managed to squeeze in an "I think we should talk about the wedding" and I squeezed back a "Me too."

Then we sat there in silence for about a million years.

"Can I—" I tried at the same time Oliver said, "Do you—" And this time I followed up quickly with, "Okay, I'll go."

I did not go.

Eventually Oliver cleared his throat. "You know that...anything you need to say we'll...we can. It'll be fine."

"I guess..." Why was I so bad at this? "I guess, I just think I... didn't really think it through."

Oliver closed his laptop in a we-are-now-having-a-serious-conversation way. "It's all right, Lucien. I understand."

"I'm sure you do. But that doesn't mean...it was right for me to ask you to marry me when you had your head in a cupboard."

"I confess," he confessed, "I was caught a little off guard."

"Yeah. So. Um." I fumbled in my pocket for the ominous box, couldn't find it, fumbled in a different pocket, dropped to one knee a bit too hastily so it just looked like I'd fallen off the sofa, which had happened more than once, and then finished up with, "Ow. I mean—"

"Are you all right?" A very concerned Oliver got to his feet to help me up and then stared, with a non-flattering amount of confusion, at the velvet box of doom I was shakily holding out to him.

"Well, I banged my leg but, um, Oliver David Blackwood, now that you're not in a cupboard, will you marry me?"

Oliver went through a range of expressions, none of which I could readily identify and at least some of which I was pretty sure were positive. "I thought I'd already agreed to that when I *was* in the cupboard. I assumed you were trying to call it off."

"What? No." I gazed at him in mounting horror, with the moderately affordable ring hovering between us. "Why did you think that?"

"Several reasons, Lucien. It was quite an impulsive thing to do in the first place, we've barely spoken about it since, and you literally just said you'd made a mistake."

I cringed. "Okay, I can retrospectively see how that might have given you the wrong impression. But"—I took a deep breath—"when I said I made a mistake, I meant that I didn't propose in a very romantic way or in a way that expressed how...how great you are and how...like...feelings you make me."

Looking only a little bit as if I'd offered him a live snake, Oliver took the box and opened it. For a moment he stared at the distinctly average ring. Then, "It's beautiful," he said. "Thank you." And then slipped it on his finger and—

"Oh my God," I cried. "It fits."

Oliver looked down at his hand, half-rapt, as though he almost didn't recognise it. "Yes, yes it does."

"And," I added, "it doesn't look awful."

He gave a little blink. "No. No, it looks wonderful."

It did kind of look...wonderful, and he looked wonderful wearing it. Because it was like this little piece of Oliver Blackwood was very visibly mine.

Eventually we noticed that I was still on one knee, and Oliver was still standing, and it created a weird dynamic. So Oliver sat down on the sofa and I sat down beside him, my eyes flicking every now and again to—

"Nice ring," I said.

He normally didn't descend to my level, but tonight, he smirked. "I've had no complaints." Then he grew quiet. "About the...the"—he cleared his throat—"wedding. I spoke to my parents today."

Oh dear. For some reason, Oliver's parents had never liked me. I wasn't sure if it was because of the way I dressed or the fact that my own parents were rock stars or if it possibly had something to do with that one time I told them to go fuck themselves at their ruby anniversary. I'd met them a couple of times since and I'd been marginally better behaved, but the cloud of go-fuck-yourself had trailed behind me like a fart on the way out of a lift. For the first year they'd clearly been biding their time on the assumption that Oliver would come to his senses and dump me—much, to be fair, as I had. But when it had become clear I wasn't going away anytime soon, they'd come to accept me the way one might accept a piece of spinach between a dinner guest's teeth. They knew I was there but, for the sake of their continued happiness, pretended I wasn't.

"And," I asked nervously, "how did that go?"

"They said they'd support me in whatever decision I made."

I winced. "Bad as that, huh?"

"I'm afraid so."

"I mean..." I didn't even know what I was trying to say. I wanted to be supportive of Oliver, but I didn't really want to spend the next however-many months tiptoeing around David and Miriam while they by—infuriatingly—either their presence or their absence made me marrying Oliver all about them. "We can... I mean... Do they..."

To my relief, Oliver cut me off. "Let's just not think about it for now."

Except I wasn't sure that made it better. Especially because Oliver was terrible at just not thinking about things. And my ability to just not think about things scaled proportionately with how important that thing was to think about. Meaning, I was great at ignoring bills and hopelessly unable to ignore mean things people said on the internet. "You know I am always onside with hiding from problems in the hope they'll go away—"

"That's not what I'm doing, Lucien," said Oliver sharply.

It was a bit like what he was doing. But Oliver had been seeing a trained professional for nearly two years because of his parents so I did my best to be sensitive and not poke anything that might be the emotional equivalent of a bear or a mine—or a bear-mine, which would be a bear that would maul you and then explode. I held my hands up in a don't-maul-me-or-explode way. "All right. Just…this is supposed to be about our happiness. And so you need to think about…that. Instead of, you know, what your mum and dad will say."

Some of the tension faded from Oliver's jaw. "I will. Thank you."

Well, that was super convincing. But I knew it was all I was going to get.

"In any case," he went on, making a visible effort to smile, "I presume Odile was far more enthusiastic."

Oh, fuck me with a rusty coat hanger. I'd somehow managed to not tell her. She was going to kill me. Oliver was going… Okay, he wouldn't kill me. But he might take it as a bad sign, ring or no ring, that I'd forgotten to mention the most important thing in my life to the most important person in my life. Joint most important person. Second most important person?

"Yeah," I overcompensated. "She was really excited."

For whatever reason—presumably because he still had a head full of disapproval—Oliver didn't notice that I was talking like I was reading cue cards. "I'm glad. I assume we'll be seeing her tomorrow?"

Oh, fuck me with a rusty coat hanger covered in sriracha sauce. We saw Mum and Judy a couple of times a month, so I should probably have thought of that before pretending to Oliver that I'd told them something I hadn't told them, and needed to tell them in person, and wouldn't see them in person until I next saw them with Oliver.

And all I needed to have said was, *Actually, I was waiting until we next went to visit so we could tell her together.*

But instead I was starting my engagement drowning in lies.

CHAPTER 18

THE NEXT DAY WE WERE standing in Pucklethroop-in-the-Wold waiting for my mum to let us in, and I still hadn't worked out what to do about the fact that I'd lied to Oliver.

The door opened. "'Allô, Luc, mon—" was as far as Mum managed to get before I threw my arms around her.

"Mum!" I cried, then whispered, "Oliver and I are getting married, and he thinks I've already told you," desperately into her ear.

She made an *ah, I understand* noise and, letting go of me, immediately embraced Oliver with a loud, "Congratulations on the wedding. I was so pleased to hear about it when Luc told me that it was happening, which he did several days ago."

"Thank you, Odile," said Oliver.

"Oh, you will have to stop calling me that now you are getting married. You will have to call me *Maman*."

This was going to be a long evening. "Mum, *I* don't even call you Maman."

"That," she glowered at me Gallically, "is because you have no respect for your heritage."

I was about to deliver a fantastically clever and witty reply when the sound of barking echoed from inside and four ecstatic spaniels burst from the hallway. I say ecstatic, but they were, of course, ecstatic to see Oliver, who was great with dogs, and not at all interested in seeing me, who they'd known their entire lives.

On the plus side, Oliver did look incredibly cute kneeling down to receive an armful of fur and puppy-dog eyes.

"Charles," he said, bestowing scratches, pets, and scruffles, "Camilla, Michael of Kent. Hello, Eugenie, old girl; who's a good girl, you are, yes you are." I never worked out how Oliver or, for that matter, anyone else, was able to tell the dogs apart.

Once Oliver had finished greeting the woofles as he occasionally and embarrassingly called them, all seven of us went through to the front room.

"Judy," Mum announced, "look who is here. It is Luc and his fiancé, Oliver, who, as you know, he has told us he is engaged to."

I sort of liked that Mum was bad at deception. Judy, however, as a result of…of…a great many aspects of her tumultuous life history, had no problem with it at all. "Ah, of course." She beamed. "Congratulations, old boys. Meant to bring you a gift, but it's fattening up in the lower pasture."

"You know," said Oliver incredibly gently, "I *am* still a vegan." It wasn't much of a protest, but it was more than he would have managed two years ago.

"Not to worry." Judy seldom let go of an idea once it was in her head. "Keep it in the garden. Good for the grass."

I wasn't sure why I was getting into the details of this given that the nonspecific animal in question was almost certainly fictional, but I couldn't quite help myself. "You realise I live in a top-floor flat, and Oliver's garden is about eight feet across."

"Well, that changes things." Sitting back, Judy stroked her chin thoughtfully. "I'll have to give you a goat instead."

I was beginning to feel like I was in one of those improv games where you had to keep saying "yes and" to whatever your partner came up with. "I don't think we've got room for a goat either."

"Don't be silly," Judy told me, undaunted. "Everyone's got room for a goat. They're tiny. Practically stackable."

Thankfully—and I use this word advisedly—Mum came to my rescue. "Judy, stop talking about the marvellous wedding present you are getting them for the wedding you definitely knew about. We are here to eat the extra-special vegan special curry—"

"Mum," I interrupted. "Have you remembered Gruyère is still not vegan?"

She shrugged. "I found the vegan cheese. You can buy vegan everything these days. You can even buy the vegan bacon. I said to Judy, I said I thought vegans did not like bacon. Why make bacon for people who do not like bacon?"

"It's not about liking or not liking." I was hoping my unfailing support of my boyfriend's dietary choices balanced out my entirely failing to tell my mum we were engaged. "It's about ethics. Like when you were protesting against nuclear weapons in the eighties."

A look of worrying comprehension crossed Mum's face. "Oh. So, he does it to get laid?"

"Yes," said Oliver, as he de-spanielled the sofa. "My refusal to drink milkshake brings all the boys to the yard."

"Well," returned Mum, "since, as I already knew, you are engaged now, you need to have only one boy in your yard."

It was at about this point that Oliver's inability to contradict authority figures clashed terminally with Mum's inability to lie. He turned to me. "Would I be completely out of line in thinking you hadn't actually told your mother we were getting married at all?"

"What?" cried Mum valiantly. "No. That is outrageous. Why would I have said so many times that Luc had told me you were getting married if he had not told me you were getting married? How could I possibly have known?"

Oliver was looking unconvinced. But also, and this was the important bit, unfurious.

"And what about the goat?" Mum had clearly decided she was going down with the ship. "How could Judy have arranged a goat for the wedding if she had not already heard about the wedding?"

Having created a small oasis in a sea of dog, Oliver sat down and was immediately re-dogged. "Call me a cynic, but it has crossed my mind that the goat might be imaginary."

"Don't be silly, Oliver. How can you give somebody an imaginary goat?"

I folded myself onto the floor next to Oliver and put my head in my hands. "Mum, it's fine. Thanks for covering for me, but you need to stop helping now."

Mum's attitude shifted in a nanosecond. "In which case, Luc, I need you to know that I am very offended."

"I'm sorry I didn't tell you," I mumbled. "I meant to, but it was kind of a sudden thing, and I wanted to do it in person, but then I accidentally told Oliver I already had...."

"Yes"—that was Oliver—"why did you do that, Lucien?"

My head was staying in my hands. It seemed the best place for it. "Well, you'd told your parents so I was worried that you'd think if I hadn't told Mum it would mean, I don't know, something."

"It means," Mum said, "that Oliver is a better son than you are."

I looked up. "Then that's fine. Because you've got him now."

Mum considered this. "That is a fair point." She sat down on the sofa and put her arm around Oliver. "Luc, this is Oliver, he is my son. He is a very nice boy, he has a good job and always calls his mother. Oliver"—she gestured contemptuously at me with her free hand—"this is some ungrateful shit who sometimes comes to my house and eats my curry and complains about it."

"Mum," I protested, definitely not sounding like a teenager. "I'm really sorry. There's been a lot going on recently—"

She tossed her head. "How would I know? You never talk to me."

"I talk to you all the time. I just didn't mention this one thing."

"To be fair," put in Judy, "it is quite a significant thing. I told my parents about most of my marriages."

"You see," exclaimed Mum. "And Judy was a terrible daughter. She gave her father three heart attacks."

I sighed. "Fine. I'm a terrible son."

"You *were* a terrible son," Mum corrected me. "Oliver is my son now."

Oliver had a faintly panicked look in his eyes, a look that was slowly spreading to the rest of his face. What he still didn't quite get about my relationship with Mum was that we sort of upset each other all the time, sometimes over huge things like, um, me not telling her I was getting married, sometimes over tiny things like whether the guy who used to live next door to us when I was twelve was called Jim or John. It was just that it didn't mean anything because she was my mum and, despite what she was saying right now, I was her son and we loved each other and always would.

"I don't think it's a trade," he said. "I think it's more a jointly and severally liable kind of deal."

Mum smiled beatifically. "Oh, it is so nice having a son who is a barrister. He always says intelligent things instead of insisting the guy next door used to be called John."

"Hang on"—I actually jumped to my feet in a moment of strong emotion—"I never said he was called John. *You* said he was called John."

"I did not say he was called John," Mum insisted. "I said he was called Jim because that was his name. But you never listen to me as well as never telling me anything."

"No, you didn't. You said his name was John, and you remembered specifically because of the Beatles."

Mum shook her head. "No, that was our other neighbour Mr. Starkey. In any case"—she rose majestically from the sofa—"I should serve up the extra-special vegan special curry before the artichoke goes soggy."

This was Oliver's cue to go through to the kitchen and help, Eugenie's cue to follow him, and my cue to sit in the living room having a bizarre conversation with Judy.

"So," I began. "How's…things?"

She absently lifted a spaniel out of the fireplace. "Not bad. Can't complain. Went to see a chap the other day to see if I could have the use of his cock."

"And…how did that go?"

"Very disappointing. He'd sent me a picture of it, but it turns out that wasn't his cock at all. Belonged to another fellow. And you could tell immediately—much smaller, head a completely different shape, and it was bobbing up and down quite erratically."

"It happens," I said.

Judy gave an indignant snort. "Not to me it doesn't. Why is it when you get to a certain age, chaps think you'll take any cock they offer you? I mean, I said to him, 'Sir, I have handled many cocks in my time, and that is by far the scrawniest, scraggiest, least satisfying specimen I've ever—'"

It was at that moment that—to my mild relief—Mum poked her head round the door. "Oh, by the way, mon caneton, though I am still very angry with you, I should also say that I am over the moon for you and Oliver. Obviously, my own wedding was a cocaine-fuelled rager and my husband was a piece of shit who fucked three of the bridesmaids, but I am sure things will be different for you."

"I suppose," I said. "There'll be less cocaine, and I'm pretty sure Oliver won't want to have sex with any of the bridesmaids…"

Mum nodded sagely. "It is one of the advantages of being a gay."

I let that one slide. "I think it's also an advantage of marrying somebody who isn't a complete arsehole."

"I suppose that might also be part of it. But are you *absolutely sure* about the cocaine? Because if you did want some, I am certain I could arrange it."

There were few things of which I was absolutely surer. "No cocaine. Also, you don't have to arrange anything."

For a moment I was worried I'd offended Mum again. "But of course I will arrange things. You are my son, you are supposed to plan your son's wedding. You are also supposed to pay for your son's wedding."

"Technically, that's daughters," pointed out Judy. "Which was a bit rough on my old man what with my having so many. Still the bugger owned half the Home Counties so he could afford it."

"I don't *have* any daughters," Mum replied. "And anyway Luc is a gay so—"

"Can we *please* not have the gay-as-a-noun conversation again?" I asked.

Mum shook her head. "Not now, Luc, this is very important."

It took me a moment to realise that the very important thing that she was discussing was why it was okay for her to take over my and Oliver's wedding. "Slow down a minute. It's generous of you, Mum, but we really don't need you to pay for anything."

"Well, I was just speaking to Oliver, and he said it was very kind of me."

"Yes, but that's because in his world 'It's very kind of you' is code for 'I'm too polite to say no.'"

Bearing four bowls of extra-special vegan special curry with a dexterity that should have been impossible for anybody who hadn't been a professional waiter, Oliver emerged from the kitchen. "Did I hear my name?"

"I was just explaining to Luc," said Mum before I could get a word in edgeways, "that you were very happy for me to pay for your wedding."

"Actually"—he started handing out curry—"I'm afraid Lucien's right. What I said was that it was very kind of you, which is true. But doesn't technically signal approval. You see, there are also downsides to having a son who's a lawyer."

Mum sighed. "So I am seeing. Bon. I have swapped you back."

"Still not a swapping situation," I reminded her.

She ignored me. "Stop trying to change the subject. Why do you not want me to pay for the wedding? I am old, I am rich, and I want to be part of your special day."

"You will be part of my special day," I told her. "You can walk me down the aisle or something. But I wouldn't feel comfortable taking your money, and you're not buying me cocaine."

She folded her arms stubbornly. "Luc, if anyone is going to buy you cocaine, it should be your mother. I know the best kinds, I know the best people. Of course, a lot of them are dead because... well. Cocaine dealers, they often have very unhealthy lifestyles. Long hours, bad diet. And it's a very stressful business."

"We have some savings." That was Oliver, poking nervously at the extra-special vegan special curry. "At least, I have some savings. Lucien made the mistake of going into the charitable sector."

"Well, that is even worse," cried Mum. "That means Oliver is paying for the whole thing like you are one of those brides that you order through the mail."

I scrutinised this analogy from every angle to try and find one that was flattering. "It's not like that at all. It's just Oliver's got slightly more money than me and—" Okay, it was sounding a tiny bit like that. "And anyway," I finished, trying to steer us in a different direction, "it's going to be a small ceremony. Just friends and family, and I don't have that many friends or like half my family."

Thinking about it, we hadn't actually discussed the size of the ceremony. Or the date of the ceremony. The location of the ceremony. Or anything about the ceremony at all.

"Then," Mum went on relentlessly, "if it is going to be so very small, it does not matter if I pay for it."

Putting aside the extra-special vegan special curry, which always managed to be worse than the regular special curry because Mum took it as licence to indulge her creative side, I tried to have an intense debate with Oliver about whether we should let this happen. Except, since I couldn't talk, I was forced to rely entirely on my eyebrows and nose. Unsurprisingly, we failed to reach a firm conclusion.

"Can we," I asked, "think about it?"

"Well, of course you can think about it," said Mum. "I'm not a monster. To be honest, I only brought it up now so that I could tell Oliver before I told you so you would know how it feels." She paused. "It does not feel good, does it, Luc?"

I sighed. "No, it doesn't feel good. I'm really sorry."

"You are forgiven." She took her place on the sofa next to Oliver. "But the man next door, he was definitely called John."

PART
THREE

ALEXANDER ANTONY FITZROVIA JAMES TWADDLE &
CLARA ISABELLA FORTESCUE-LETTICE
COOMBECAMDEN CATHEDRAL, COOMBECAMDEN
4TH OF SEPTEMBER

CHAPTER 19

WHEN ALEX HAD INVITED ME to his wedding, I'd been...not pleased exactly, because weddings were a faff, but at least mildly cheered. It was, after all, nice in abstract to know that a coworker thought well enough of you to add you to the list of people he wanted around him on the happiest day of his life. Although given the circles Alex and Miffy moved in, I suspected that the list wasn't exactly short.

And a couple of months later, when Rhys Jones Bowen had suggested that since the entire office was invited, it would make sense to rent a minibus and drive everyone up together, I'd found that mildly cheering too. Then when he'd added that his friend had given us the use of his house to stay in the night before so we didn't have to get up stupidly early to be on time for the ceremony, I was relieved. Because it was always good when somebody else took care of the logistics for you. It seemed like the lowest-stress big-event wedding I could possibly imagine. All I had to do was show up with Oliver at the end of work, and then we could all pile into a bus like we were going on a school trip. It felt, as Alex himself might have put it, jolly.

Except once we were half an hour into the journey, I remembered that I *hated* school trips. They involved putting a bunch of people who only knew each other in a very specific context into a very different context and expecting everything to work. And it never did.

We started out okay, with everybody upbeat and pally and helping each other load their luggage, but things quickly cooled off after we realised that most of us had brought somebody we knew better than we knew the rest of the group, meaning there was no real reason for us to interact *as* a group. Then they cooled off even more as each pair realised that most of the things they'd normally talk to each other about were things they didn't particularly want to be airing in a crowded vehicle full of people who were strangers to one half of the couple and professional acquaintances to the other.

Even that would have been bearable. But then Rhys Jones Bowen insisted on starting a sing-along.

"Come on, you lot," he tried with the kind of valour that led brigades of soldiers into valleys full of cannon. "You're being a right bunch of gloomy Gusses. Everybody join in after me: 'The wheels on the bus go round and round, round and round, round and round…'"

"Isn't that a children's song?" I asked.

"Well, yes, but I don't see why that's causing you problems." Rhys kept his eyes on the road but gave me a very expressive look with his shoulders. "Unless you've forgotten the words."

Was I letting myself get sucked into a conversation I couldn't get out of again? "I think it's more just a bit embarrassing."

"And *I* think that says more about you than it does about the song," Rhys insisted.

From the back seat, Barbara Clench briefly stopped making out with Gabriel, her unfeasibly attractive, much younger husband. "I agree with Luc. We're adults, we shouldn't be singing nursery rhymes; it's inappropriate."

"Only if you sing them to lure children into your van," said

Rhys's date. Her name was Ana with one *n*, and he said he'd met her "on the social media." Given that like many of Rhys's dates she was bizarrely hot and carried herself in a way that suggested she had incredible body confidence, I suspected he'd met her on one social medium in particular. "Otherwise, it's just singing."

Beside me, Oliver had that gleam in his eye he sometimes got when he switched into good-at-joining-in mode. "What if you're singing, but a child hears you and gets lured accidentally?"

"You're the lawyer," Rhys Jones Bowen pointed out. "You tell us."

"Well, I think it would be hard to establish mens rea, but you still might have to answer some very awkward questions."

"No children's songs," Barbara Clench repeated.

"What if we do the dirty version?" asked Rhys. "Wouldn't be a children's song, then."

I was getting sucked in. One more question and I'd be trapped in a vortex of inanity I couldn't escape. "*Is* there a dirty version?"

"There's *always* a dirty version." Rhys was speaking with the certainty of a man who knew most of them.

Schlooop went the vortex. "But…wheels on the bus? What is it? Like, the penis on the bus goes flip, flip, flop?"

Rhys shoulder-nodded. "Something like that, yeah."

"I am *certainly* not singing the *dirty* versions of any children's songs." Barbara Clench had a bit between her teeth, and normally in this kind of situation I would get rapidly out of her way. Except I couldn't because we were stuck in a moving vehicle.

Professor Fairclough had been staring out of the window, largely ignoring us—or at least processing everything we were saying on a higher level. Now she praying-mantised her head back towards the rest of us. "I'm not sure I do know the words, actually."

"How can you not know the words to the wheels-on-the-bus song?" I asked.

"How can you not know the Latin name of the common fruit fly?" returned Dr. Fairclough.

Oliver leaned over to me and whispered, "*Drosophila melanogaster,*" in my ear.

"Drops Ophelia Melanie Jaster?" I tried, which earned a sharp *hmmph* from the professor.

"To be *fair,*" said Ana with one *n*, "the lyrics are a bit controversial."

"Why?" I wondered aloud. "Is there some hidden meaning to 'The wipers on the bus go swish, swish, swish' that I've been missing my whole life?"

She laughed. Honestly, she probably laughed more than the joke deserved, but she was clearly on wedding date behaviour. "No, it's just that a lot of kids these days learn their nursery rhymes from YouTube videos, so they get the American version."

I wasn't sure I wanted to know. "What's the American version?"

"Instead of the bits of the bus doing their things 'all day long' they do them 'all through the town,'" she explained.

For a moment, that helped because while we couldn't agree on what to talk about, what to sing, or if singing was even a good idea, we were completely agreed that putting the words *all through the town* in the wheels-on-the-bus song was absolute fucking blasphemy.

"How do you know so much about it?" enquired Barbara Clench in a moment of rare humanity.

Ana with one *n* craned her neck back to look at the rest of us. "I used to be a primary school teacher."

"Used to be?" Coming from Barbara Clench, that question had a not-going-to-end-well quality.

"Yeah, now I take my clothes off on the internet."

For a woman who, by the looks of her husband, had a full

and active sex life, Barbara Clench could be difficult about this kind of thing. Her lips got very thin. "Don't you find that rather degrading?"

"Sort of," Ana with one *n* admitted. "I mean when you think about it, there's something pretty degrading about the fact that I went to university, did two degrees and a professional qualification, spent three years working seventy-hour weeks with disadvantaged children, and at the end had nothing to show for it but crushing debts and a few nice thank-you cards." She took a deep breath. It sounded like she did this rant a lot. "So I decided that if the choice was getting wanked over by strangers or fucked over by the Department for Education, I'd pick the one that paid better."

There was complete silence in the bus while Barbara radiated the kind of stifling disapproval that you could radiate only after a lifetime of never bothering to examine a single preconception. A silence that persisted until Oliver, in his best peacemaker's voice, said, "What if we try 'London Bridge Is Falling Down' instead?"

Two hours into a four-hour journey we stopped at a service station so that Rhys could have, in his own words "a slash and a sarnie." I took the opportunity to stretch my legs and grabbed one of the family-sized bags of Skittles that they were, for some unfathomable reason, selling at a discount in W.H. Smith. Once we'd taken our welcome break at the Welcome Break, we piled back into the minibus for the second and, as it turned out, more complicated part of the journey.

Coombecamden, the technically-a-city-because-it-had-a-cathedral-even-though-it-was-actually-tiny of which Miffy's father was apparently Earl, was situated a little way south of Liverpool, right by the Welsh border, but Rhys's mate's house was a little way west of *that* and a fair distance into the countryside. Which meant that we spent the next very long time on narrow, windy roads occasionally blocked by sheep, trying to navigate by a bickering consensus of low-resolution satnav, poorly understood maps, and guesswork.

The rain didn't help. It had started drizzling as we passed Birmingham. By the time we hit Stoke-on-Trent, that had upgraded to pissing down. And, once we left the M40 and were into the bit of the country where there were hedges instead of pavements and everywhere was called something like Muclestone or Wetwood, it was raining so hard that the windscreen wipers were just making ripples on a pond.

Eventually, Rhys pulled over on a stretch of grass that I wasn't totally sure he should have been pulling over on, but was too much of a city boy to challenge, and announced, "Here we are," with thoroughly unearned cheerfulness.

"Where is here, exactly?" I asked.

"Charlie's house."

I peered out of the window, but between the rain and the fact that the sun had set an hour ago, I couldn't make out anything except wet and bush. "Are you absolutely certain?"

Rhys tapped his phone, which was showing a little blue circle inside a big blue circle. "Google Maps never lies."

"No," I admitted, "but it's sometimes *very* economical with the truth."

Oliver patted me gently on the leg. "Perhaps one of us should get out and take a look?"

One of us, we all knew, meant Oliver. I certainly wasn't about to go, and Rhys didn't seem to be up for it either. Besides, getting your bearings after a long minibus journey seemed far more like Oliver's skill set than mine in that it was a useful life skill, rather than the brand of occasionally helpful bullshit that I preferred to trade in.

Clambering past me and out through the front of the bus,

Oliver vanished into the night, only to return a few moments later with his hair plastered to his head, his jacket wet through, and his trousers damp to the shins. "There *is* a house there," he confirmed. "But it's on the other side of a rather large field."

"Ah, that'll be it." Rhys's aura of cheeriness had never really gone away, but it had ebbed slightly when it had looked like we might be stuck in the dark and houseless. Now it was flowing back with a vengeance. "The Google Maps do that sometimes in the countryside. They put you in the right general place, but they can't work out where the roads go. I suppose it's because they're hard to see from space."

Ana with one *n* reached out an affectionate hand. "I'm not sure that's quite how satnav works, sweetheart."

"Either way, it seems to be our best option," said Oliver. "So I suppose we should all grab our things and get going."

At the back of the bus, Barbara Clench glowered. "This was *not* a well-planned excursion."

Rhys was still grinning. "No, but it's been an adventure, hasn't it?"

"I'm not sure 'got wet walking across a field' counts as an adventure," I pointed out.

"You know the difference between you and me, Luc?" asked Rhys. And before I could reply, he said, "Attitude. If I want to have an adventure, I'll bloody well have an adventure."

While everyone was disembarking and Rhys was locking up the minibus, I checked our surroundings. We'd pulled into a sort of dip in the hedgerow next to a gate that was *very* firmly chained shut. Up and down the road I could see precisely nothing except water and darkness. On the other side of the gate I could see... I mean, I assumed it was a field. But the way the moonlight was gleaming off the surface made it look almost like a lake. A big, square lake with a cottage on the other side of it.

"The plan," I yelled over the increasingly insistent sound of the rain, "absolutely can't be to wade across *that*"—I pointed at the aqua field—"to get to *that*." I pointed at the cottage.

"I agree with Luc," said Barbara Clench. She'd agree with me on something about once a year. I think she just did it to throw me off. "We'd be better off in the bus."

Ana with one *n* shrugged. "The absolute *worst* plan is to stand here debating. Come on." With her jacket over her head and her overnight bag under one arm, she clambered over the fence and set off. To my relief, she wasn't immediately swallowed by a hidden bog—the water actually only seemed to come up to her ankles—but I wasn't particularly keen to follow her. Rhys, of course, was, which I suspected was only partly because they were dating and mostly because he was the kind of person who genuinely enjoyed doing this kind of thing.

I gave Oliver a pleading look. "Is it too late to go home?"

"Significantly, I'm afraid." Taking me by the hand, Oliver climbed elegantly over the fence and then waited for me to do the same. Well, to do the same in that I also climbed, but I was way less elegant about it.

Squelching down on the other side, I let Oliver wrap his free arm around me, leaned my head against him, and tried to believe that Rhys was right and that this was an adventure. Not just a gigantic pain in the arse.

CHAPTER 20

RHYS HAD NOT BEEN RIGHT. This was not an adventure. My feet were wet. I was trying really hard not to think about what happened when you partially flooded a field full of cowpats, and like most bits of the countryside in the dark, the house was much farther away than it seemed. Or I walked much slower than I thought. One of the two. Probably the second one. I was both tired and unfit.

Rhys found the key under the mat because apparently we were in a part of the world where you could still do that without having your TV stolen, and we all hurried very gratefully inside. Well, nearly all.

"I'll join you soon," said Professor Fairclough. She was at least as drenched as any of us, but it didn't seem to faze her at all. Hell, it made her look like the heroine at the end of a romantic comedy, waiting for some jerk to show up and do a big apology scene at her. "Large areas of stagnant water attract mosquitoes, and I'm interested in observing how the weather affects their behaviour."

"Have a nice time, then," said Rhys, who seemed to have decided that since this was his friend's house he was host by proxy. "Everybody else, who fancies a cuppa?"

Cuppas were duly provided. A dubious advantage of having worked with the same pack of misfits for more than five years was that everybody knew how everybody else liked their tea. Of course none of us ever actually bothered to put that knowledge into practice, but I preferred to think it was sort of an unspoken pact we had, like the opposite of buying a round at the bar. I won't complain if you put too much milk in if you don't complain that I let it stew too long.

We dumped our coats in the hall and our bags under the stairs, then settled down in the sitting room to dry off. Whoever Rhys's friend was, he'd done well for himself because he'd wound up with a cosy little cottage in the borders, with an inglenook fireplace, exposed beams, and tastefully chosen furniture. I flopped down in an armchair with Oliver sitting in front of me, his back resting against my knees.

"I admit," I said, "it was tough getting here but this is pretty okay."

"You've got to realise"—Rhys turned to Ana with one *n*—"that 'pretty okay' is about the closest Luc ever gets to being nice about anything."

Ana with one *n* made an oh-that-makes-sense kind of noise that I'd have been offended by if it hadn't been totally fair.

"What does this Charlie guy do, anyway?" I asked.

"He's *in* something," explained Rhys, in a not-very-explanatory sort of way.

"Broadmoor?" suggested Barbara Clench, who was occupied with Gabriel. As far as I could tell, Gabriel's role in their marriage basically involved standing around, looking decorative, being disproportionately into Barbara, and letting her do most of the talking.

Rhys shook his head. "Consulting, I think."

I sipped my tea and did my best to enjoy the atmosphere. We were, after all, in a nice house, and listening to rain drumming on the windows was always relaxing. "Still," I said, "it's a shame Miffy's dad couldn't have been earl of somewhere more convenient."

Barbara nodded. If she was going to keep being on my side about things, I was going to need to see a doctor because something was clearly wrong with me. "Yes. I hope you'll be more considerate when you're picking a venue for *your* wedding."

"Our wedding?" I asked.

Rhys rolled his eyes. "Oh, not you as well. I thought it was only Alex who forgot he was getting married."

"No, I remember I'm getting married," I began, and then the realisation crept up on me that this conversation was about to go to a very uncomfortable place. "I just wasn't sure what you meant about a considerate venue."

"Well, you've got to admit, Luc," said Rhys, "it's been a lovely trip but it *was* a bit of a palaver."

Definitely going to an uncomfortable place. "Yes, I–I agree with that. It's just that our wedding isn't necessarily... We're not going to necessarily..."

"You're both local, though, aren't you?" observed Rhys. "To London, I mean, not to here. So I'm assuming you'll be having the ceremony somewhere everybody can get to easily."

"Yeees..." This wasn't going well. "For everybody who's *invited*. It's just..."

"It's just we haven't discussed the guest list in detail," said Oliver, who was always way better at being diplomatic than I was. "And a lot of the venues we're looking at are rather small."

Even though Oliver had been the one to say it—or rather imply it strongly enough that they got the hint—they all turned to me.

"I hope"—there was a genuine tremor in Rhys Jones Bowen's voice—"that you are not suggesting what I think you are suggesting."

I squirmed. "Umm..."

Rhys already had his phone out. "Hello, Rhystocrats," he was saying, "this is a bit of a... Well, I've just had a bit of a shock. As you all know, my friend and colleague Luc O'Donnell is getting married soon—"

"Did you..." I seized on the opportunity to claim the moral high ground. "Did you announce my wedding on social media without consulting me?"

"Don't you try to talk your way out of this. The Rhystocrats are going to want to know why you think we're not good enough for your wedding."

"I don't think we'd put it quite like that..." I tried.

Barbara Clench was glaring at me, which at least felt familiar. "How *would* you put it?"

This one seemed like an easy answer. "Well, in your case, I would probably say, 'We hate each other so I didn't think you'd want to come.'"

A deathly silence fell over the room. There was a tiny, tiny chance that *we both hate each other, right* wasn't the most tactful thing to say when you'd just driven several hours to attend a coworker's wedding.

"I...." For a while Barbara couldn't say anything else. Eventually she managed, "I never thought..."

"I didn't mean it like..."

"I knew"—oh God, she seemed genuinely shaken up—"that we were sometimes a little...a little short, but I'd always felt that we had a friendly rivalry."

Fuck. "I didn't mean it like... Just that I thought you hated *me*, and that I was sort of...riffing on that?"

"It didn't *sound* like that was what you were saying," said Barbara, clinging to Gabriel's hand.

"She's right," agreed Rhys, "it didn't."

They were both right because it wasn't. "Would it help if I said I was really sorry?"

Barbara Clench got to her feet. "I think I need a walk."

Her husband got up and went with her, leaving me and Oliver alone with Rhys and Ana with one *n*.

"She can't have..." I tried. Then. "How did...?"

"Don't look at me," said Rhys. "I always thought you two got on."

That made no sense. "How could you possibly think that?"

"Well, you're very similar."

Was it hypocritical to be offended that somebody had compared you to a woman you'd just vehemently denied hating? "We bloody well aren't."

"You're both rude and think you're better than everybody."

"Hey, that is not..." I stopped. Probably best to rephrase. "I'm *nowhere near* as bad as I was a couple of years ago."

Rhys gave a shrug. "And neither's she, but you're still both awful quite a lot of the time."

Words clearly weren't working for me so I made a *grah* kind of noise. "Oliver? Back me up here. I am not an arsehole."

With a gentleness that people normally reserved for angry children and frightened dogs, Oliver patted my leg. "You're a wonderful human being, and I love you. But you can be a *tiny* bit mean sometimes."

Betrayal. Rank betrayal. "So can you."

"This isn't about him." Rhys was looking as serious as he was capable of, which wasn't hugely serious. "You're the one who isn't inviting us to your wedding."

"It's his wedding too," I pointed out.

"And I never said you couldn't invite your work friends," murmured Oliver, traitorously. "I just thought we agreed we wanted to keep it small."

I wasn't letting Oliver lawyer his way out of this one. "How can we keep it small if I invite my entire office?"

"It's not a very large office," he pointed out.

Exasperated, I turned pleadingly back to Rhys. "Why do you even want to come? You can't actually like weddings. No sensible person *likes* weddings."

"Bridget likes weddings," said Oliver, continuing to jam knives into my spine.

"Bridget isn't sensible. Not where romance is concerned."

Oliver gave me a smile that almost made me forget how cross I was with him. "True, she thought we'd be a good couple."

"You see." I jabbed my finger at him triumphantly. "He's mean as well. We're a mean couple. A couple of mean people who say mean things and are mean to each other."

"If it helps," said Ana with an *n*, "I agree that weddings mostly suck."

I slumped back in my chair with unexpected relief. "*Thank you.* Why is the only person who has my back the one I've never met before?"

"Because..." Oliver shuffled around to kneel facing me. He still had that mischievous look on his face that was making it hard to stay pissed off with him. "She's new, and she's trying to make a good impression."

"And also," Ana with one *n* added, "weddings really do suck."

Rhys was shaking his head. "Oh, no, I love a good wedding, me. Everybody dressing up nice, people being all happy. Only a complete knobhead would have a problem with that."

"And now"—I turned my jabbing finger toward Rhys—"*you've* just called your girlfriend a complete knobhead. Why am I the bad guy?"

With her head in Rhys's lap, Ana with one *n* gave a little shrug. "I suppose because a lot of the time I can be a complete knobhead."

"You see?" Rhys gave a vindicated nod. "A good relationship is based on honesty."

Somehow I was still outnumbered. "Look." I gave up. "If it means that much to you…of course you can come to our wedding."

"And Alex and Miffy and Barbara and Gabriel and the Professor?" asked Rhys.

Alex and Miffy we'd have been pretty much obliged to invite anyway since they'd invited us to theirs. To be honest, I was increasingly convinced that weddings were just an elaborate cycle of vengeance that had got really out of hand. Some pair of selfish bastards had forced their friends to come to a tedious party two thousand years ago, and their selfish bastard friends had decided to pay them back by forcing *them* to come a tedious party, and then some wholly independent group of selfish bastards had built an industry around it and here we were. An eye for an eye leaves the world overpaying for table settings.

"Yes." I shot a quick confirmatory glance at Oliver—although honestly at this stage if we were stuck with a wedding full of CRAPPers it was as much his fault as mine so he'd kind of lost the right to object. "You can all come. It'll be lovely. The more the merrier."

"There you go, Rhystocrats," Rhys said into his phone. "Happy ending all around. For more heartwarming content like this, remember to like, share, and subscribe to my channel and to follow Cee-Arr-Ay-Pee-Pee on all of the social medias."

Ana with one *n* looked up from his lap. "And I'm at not-that-ana-the-other-ana in all the usual places, and I upload content daily when I'm not having arguments with my boyfriend's colleagues."

"And in case you're wondering," Rhys added, "I know it seems weird, my channel telling you how to find pictures of my girlfriend's boobies, but I'm fine with it. She's a lovely girl and it's her job." He paused for a moment and added, "Also they're very nice so if you haven't checked them out, do give them a go."

There wasn't a great deal I could say to that, but fortunately a knock at the door meant I didn't have to.

"That'll be the professor," said Rhys.

"Or Barbara," I added apprehensively. "In which case I should go and apologise."

I eased myself reluctantly out of the chair, and when the banging on the door intensified, I tried not to tell myself that it probably *was* Barbara because it would be characteristically impatient of her. Still, it wasn't worth putting off any longer, so I quickened my step a little.

It wasn't Barbara. It was a man and a woman I didn't recognise, both in their midforties. They had a uniformed police officer with them.

"Sorry to interrupt," she said, "but this couple have just called my station, and they tell me you've broken into their house."

CHAPTER 21

"ONE MORE TIME, MR. O'DONNELL," said the police officer after they'd brought us all in, which had taken a while because there'd been one of her and seven of us, of whom three were out in the garden, either being sad or examining insects. "How did you and your friends come to be in Mr. and Mrs. Plastowe's house?"

I told her again. I was sure that everybody else had told her as well, and I was sure our stories would be relatively consistent, but I also didn't quite trust my colleagues to be able to talk to the police without going off on long tangents about mosquitoes, their social media followers, or, in several cases, what an absolute prick I was.

"So then you"—she looked down—"had a cup of tea and argued with your coworkers about why you weren't inviting them to your wedding?"

I nodded. "Yes."

"Why aren't you inviting them to your wedding?"

"Is that part of the investigation?" I asked.

The police officer shrugged. "No. But they seem like nice people. One of them invited you to *his* wedding."

"Did you invite the entire police station to your wedding?"

"Of course."

They probably did things differently in the countryside. "Look, it's nice to get to know you and everything, but is it possible that we could maybe go now? It's been several hours and we have to be up early in the morning."

"I'd love to," said the police officer, with a slightly apologetic tone to her voice. "But the problem is that not only did you break into somebody's house—"

"We didn't break in. There was a key under the mat."

"Still counts as breaking in. But then you also said that you were in the area because you were guests at one of the most exclusive society events the northwest has seen in years, and that means your whole case has been kicked up the chain."

That didn't sound good. "Kicked up the chain?"

She made an afraid-so face. "The Twaddle-Fortescue-Lettice wedding is a big deal. Security alone is dragging in Coombe Valley police, Merseyside Police, and the Northwest Motorway Police... It's a big job."

"Which means?"

"Which means we need to make sure you and your friends aren't planning something...disruptive."

"Disruptive?"

"People do all kinds of funny things at society weddings."

I let my head fall forward onto the desk. "Can you not just call Alex or Miffy? They'll tell you who we are." Probably. Although Alex was never completely reliable when it came to remembering little things like who people were, what day it was, or what was going on.

"Sorry," she said. "Out of my hands."

I went back to...it wasn't a cell exactly because we weren't strictly under arrest. It was more a kind of waiting room. There Oliver was busy having an in-depth conversation with somebody who looked like they were important, and since he was an actual proper lawyer, I figured he knew what he was doing, so I went and sat with the rest of the party. More specifically, I went and sat with Barbara Clench.

"Hi," I said.

She looked at me. "Hello."

"I…" That was as far as I got.

"You don't have to like me, Luc," she said.

I wasn't sure how to respond to that. My initial instinct was *good because I don't*, but that sounded dickish even to me. "It's not…" I tried, but that seemed insincere. "I mean, I don't not… You didn't invite me to your wedding."

Barbara Clench gave me a look. "I was married when we met."

"Okay, but you wouldn't have invited me."

For a moment she didn't reply. Then she laughed. She had quite a nice laugh, just cold enough to sound like she meant it. "You're right, I wouldn't." She looked around the room, then leaned in conspiratorially. "I wouldn't invite any of this lot, to tell you the truth."

"I know, right?"

"And if I'm being really honest," she added, "I don't think I'd want to go to your wedding either."

I breathed one of the deepest sighs of relief I had in a long time. "Oh, thank God. No offence, it's just…"

"We're not friends," she said with an at-last-somebody-gets-it expression. "I've got friends. I assume you've got friends. I don't see why we can't just accept that the only thing we have in common with each other is that our inadequate paycheques are signed by the same people."

"Exactly." This was actually turning into one of my better work conversations. "Tell you what, how about we make a deal. I won't invite you to my wedding, and in return, you don't have to tell me anything about your life or give a single shit about mine."

She held out a hand. "Done."

I shook it and did my best to smile at her.

"But I don't hate you," she added.

"I don't hate you either."

She let go of my hand. "And...let's leave it at that."

Oliver had finished talking to whoever he was talking to, but from the look of very mild frustration on his face—he'd gone into professional mode, so very mild frustration was the worst he was going to show—he hadn't got anywhere. "They're being stubborn," he explained.

"Are we going to prison?" I asked. "Are we going to prison for breaking and entering? Did we break and enter on the way to a wedding?"

Oliver pulled up a blue plastic chair and sat down next to me. "How much detail do you want on this?"

Damn, he was sexy when he was doing the lawyer bit. "All the detail."

"If you insist." He smiled, and everybody else—mistaking my request for interrogation rather than flirtation—gathered round. Well, everybody except for Professor Fairclough, who was looking at a spider, even though, as I was embarrassingly proud to remember, it wasn't technically an insect.

"For a start," Oliver continued, somewhat surprised to suddenly have an audience. "We're not going to prison for breaking and entering because that's not a distinct crime under UK law. Burglary is a crime, and trespassing is a civil infraction. We *did* trespass, but it only becomes burglary if the Crown can show that we trespassed with the intent to either steal or commit grievous bodily harm or unlawful damage."

"We stole tea," Barbara Clench pointed out, with the pedantic attention to detail that made her frustratingly good at her job.

"Technically we didn't," said Oliver. "We drank tea that didn't belong to us, but stealing is when you dishonestly appropriate property belonging to another person with the intent to permanently deprive them of it. Of those five elements—"

"How do you get five elements out of one sentence?" I asked, partly because I liked playing my part in the law-is-cool-and-you're-cool-for-knowing-it game we sometimes played and partly because I was genuinely confused.

"Dishonesty"—Oliver counted on his fingers—"property, appropriation, belonging to another person, and intent to permanently deprive." He held up his open hand. "Five."

"Also," added Rhys, who was lounging across two chairs on the other side of the circle with his head in Ana with one *n*'s lap, "it's only tea."

Oliver gave him an I-wish-it-was-that-simple kind of look. "Sadly, the it's-only-tea defence isn't recognised in court. Our defence is specifically dishonesty."

"Because," I tried, "we thought we had the tea owner's permission to drink the tea?"

Turning back to me—Oliver had been Wimbledoning between us—he gave a sort of half nod. "Interestingly, consent by itself wouldn't be enough either."

"What?" Ana with one *n* sat forward, displacing Rhys's head. "I could get done for theft even if somebody has given me permission to take something?"

"If you came by that permission dishonestly." Oliver had gone into a law rhapsody. I liked law-rhapsody Oliver even at two in the morning at a random police station on the Welsh borders. "The law specifically says 'appropriates,' not 'misappropriates,' and the precedent was set in 1971 when a taxi driver who took money from a tourist's wallet was found guilty of theft because while the tourist had permitted them to take the money, the amount of money taken had been far in excess of any reasonable fare."

Ana with one *n*'s eyes narrowed. "Why do you know so much about theft?"

Feeling a sudden swell of pride, I gave Oliver a possessive hug. "Because he's a lawyer."

"Barrister," Oliver gently corrected me. I knew the difference, I just thought lawyer sounded cooler and less like he made flat whites for a living. "And more specifically I'm the very *unsexy* kind of criminal barrister who deals with exactly this kind of law. I'm afraid I spend a lot less of my time saying, 'My client couldn't possibly have been guilty of this murder because the pings from this cell-phone tower prove he was ten miles away' and a lot more of it saying, 'My client is not technically guilty of theft because although she did leave the restaurant without paying, she formed the intent to do so only after she had already eaten the meal, and therefore at the time the dishonest appropriation took place, the food in question was not in the restaurant's possession.'"

She blinked. "Do you say that a lot?"

"Quite a lot, yes. As I say, I'm not the glamourous sort of barrister. Young people who have skipped out on a bill are quite a large part of my client base, and 'it's only stealing if you decided not to pay before you ate' is a well-known technicality."

Rhys gave the kind of broad grin that suggested he thought he'd had the most brilliant idea. It was a grin he got far more often than he should. "That's not a technicality," he said, "that's a bloody life hack. We never have to pay to go to a restaurant again."

"Bit unethical?" I pointed out.

"True, but think of all the free chips you could eat." Rhys's expression told me that he was thinking of exactly that. One day, I wanted somebody to look at me the way Rhys looked at hypothetical free chips. Although to be fair, Oliver sometimes did.

"I mean," said Oliver in the tones of a man who was determined to at least *try* to put the genie back in the bottle, "you'd probably still have to go to court, and even if you won, the time, effort, and lawyer's fees would cost far more than the chips in the long run."

Rhys, genie that he was, remained unperturbed. "You say that, but I can eat a hell of a lot of chips."

"If you ate enough chips to cover the costs of a legal battle," Oliver observed, "that might just count as evidence you formed the intent to withhold payment before consuming the meal."

"It still seems like a weird loophole to me." Ana with one *n* slipped off a trainer and wiggled her toes distractedly. "Have you ever actually got somebody off with that argument?"

"A couple of times."

She winced. "Isn't that a bit...dodgy?"

Oliver was used to this—so used to it that he'd brought it up unprompted on our first fake date. These days it made me get slightly prickly-defensive on his behalf, but I knew he could field it perfectly well himself.

"I appreciate it might seem that way," he said, "but...well... to take a recent example, a little while ago I 'got somebody off' for exactly this reason. I can't go into details, but the case I made was that my client and her boyfriend only formed the intent to leave without paying because they grew frustrated at the staff consistently misgendering her. She admitted it wasn't the right thing to do, but she was very upset at the time and she found the whole process of going through a court case deeply traumatic. I don't think that being convicted of theft would have made her a better person. I don't think locking her up or fining her would have protected anybody. So, no, I don't think it was dodgy at all."

Ana with one *n* seemed unconvinced. People usually did. "But then shouldn't the defence be that 'she had a good reason,' not 'she happened to eat the food before she decided not to pay for it'?"

"Maybe." Oliver gave a little shrug. "But then we'd live in a world where the law says you're allowed to commit crimes if you think you've got a good reason. And who decides what a good reason is? It's like the it's-only-tea defence. If the law said that stealing only counted as stealing if you took something of significant monetary value, that would mean the law saw stealing a cup of tea from a poor person as a less serious crime than stealing a bottle of expensive wine from a rich person, and that doesn't seem very just." He sighed. "I'm under no illusions about our legal system, I assure you. It has vast structural flaws, and miscarriages of justice absolutely do happen, in both directions. But it's the best system we've got, and its problems generally aren't what people think they are."

"And"—I reached out and touched him on the shoulder, partly out of affection and partly out of a need for reassurance—"*we're* okay, aren't we? We're not going to become, like, the Cup of Tea Seven or something?"

Oliver shook his head. "Fortunately for us, one of the vast structural flaws in our legal system is that being a group of white middle-class people on the way to an exclusive society wedding at which I suspect at least one guest will be an actual high court judge, the establishment is very much working in our favour."

Well, that was a relief. In a checking-your-privilege kind of way. Of course they didn't have to *charge* us with anything to hold us for long enough to make us unfashionably late for Alex and Miffy's wedding, although given that it was going to be this massive posh bonanza full of aristos and arseholes, maybe that would be a blessing.

For a while we sat quietly, contemplating our fate. Then Rhys said, "You know what I don't get?"

"What don't you get?" asked Ana with one *n* so that I didn't have to.

The perplexed look on Rhys's face would have been comical if it wasn't so sincere. "I don't get why Charlie gave us directions to somebody else's house."

CHAPTER 22

THEY COULD HOLD US, OLIVER said, for twenty-four hours pretty much no questions asked. And I was beginning to think they were going to use all of it when I heard a titanic commotion coming from elsewhere in the police station.

"Completely unacceptable," one voice was saying—not a voice I recognised.

"What do you expect in this part of the country," another voice was saying, and this one I thought I recognised but couldn't tell from where. "Bloody Welsh and Irish everywhere."

"I say, steady on, Randy." And that *was* a voice I recognised. That was Alex Twaddle. "There's a Welsh chappy I work with and he's *fearfully* pleasant."

Shit. The randomly insulting guy in the middle was Justice Mayhew. We'd had a run-in at Alex's club a couple of years ago and he'd always struck me as exactly the kind of incompetent, bigoted bully you really hoped *didn't* wield vast judicial power. Still, I suppose if there was ever a time to meet a friendly—well, not friendly, but inclined to be on your side in this situation— judge with a habit of browbeating people, it was when you were in a police station with pending charges of criminal trespass and Grand Theft Darjeeling. The three men made their way through to our little holding area, where Alex beamed an oblivious hello while Justice Mayhew bore down at once on the officer on duty and began yelling.

"Well, *hello*, chaps and girl chaps," Alex said, while in the background an irate jurist well past retirement age spat a stream of invective at a hapless public servant. "Heard you had a spot of bother with the local constabulary. Beastly thing, but we'll soon have it sorted."

"And if this country hasn't *completely* gone to the dogs," Justice Mayhew was saying, "neither you nor anybody *like* you will work in law enforcement again—"

"Incidentally," Alex continued as if nothing loud and distracting was going on, "have you met my—"

"Never seen such a sorry excuse for a uniformed officer in all my born—"

"Daddy-in-law-to-be?" He looked around and, when nobody said *Yes, we hang out all the time over foie gras and cribbage*, went on. "Everybody, this is Miffy's father, Douglas Lettice, the Earl of Coombecamden. Daddy-in-law-to-be, this is everybody."

We waved a series of uncertain hi's and strained milord's at the earl, not quite sure how formal we were expected to be, given the circumstances.

"Right this minute, or God as my witness—" continued Justice Mayhew behind us. He hadn't even paused for breath.

"Delighted to meet you all," said the earl. He was a short man, with beetling brows and hair that had long since shaded to grey. From his tone, I couldn't tell if he actually *was* delighted to meet us or not. He had that aristocratic way of speaking that made everything sound at once like he was discharging a grave duty and doing you a massive personal favour. "Once this little unpleasantness—"

"No respect, that's the trouble, no respect at all—"

"Is dealt with, might I suggest you accompany us back to

Lettice Manor where we'll be more than happy to accommodate you."

I leaned back in my chair. "Oh, thank fuck." Then I realised I'd just said *fuck* in front of an earl and felt weird. Then I realised that I'd just had an incredibly I-know-my-place internalised-classist reaction to saying a bad word in front of a man whose only distinction was that one of his distant ancestors had been mates with the king, and felt weirder. "Sorry, I was just thinking we might have to sleep in the bus."

"Wouldn't hear of it." The earl shot a glance across the room to Justice Mayhew. "Are you done, Randy?"

"Almost. Giving this reprobate a piece of my mind."

The Earl of Coombecamden nodded graciously. "If you could wrap it up a tad quicker, old boy?"

"I'll be speaking to your superiors," Justice Mayhew finished.

And that was it. Oliver had, as always, been right. Whatever the limitations of the British criminal justice system were, they definitely didn't include a tendency to be overly harsh on people who hung out with landed gentry.

The bus, as it turned out, had been left at the crime scene. Well, the tort scene. Well, the scene of the incident that there's unlikely to ever be an official record of because we were never formally charged and an angry racist came and told everybody to let us go. But the police were very nice about it and gave Rhys a lift to pick it up, and then we all got back in and followed the earl to Lettice Manor.

Alex insisted on riding with us, on the basis that it would be "a wheeze"—possibly because he'd never been on a bus before—but it... Well. It wasn't. Not that we weren't all pleased and grateful to be out of custody after only a brief stay of several hours, but somehow ending a four-hour drive with half a cup of tea and being arrested hadn't put many of us in a wheezing mood.

"By the way, Luc," said Alex, "got a joke for you."

Really? Was this how my day was going to end? "*You've* got a joke for *me*?"

"Thought it was about time. Turnabout is fair play and all that. And actually I've done fearfully well out of all the corkers you've given me down the years. Told a couple to Miffy when we first met and she absolutely adored them. Told one to the earl when I asked his permission to marry the filly too."

I wasn't going to ask which. I wasn't going to ask which. "Which?"

"The one about the pieces of tarmac."

I wasn't going to ask why. I wasn't going to ask why. "Why that one?"

"Well, he likes cycling, so he liked that it was about a cycle path. Had to explain the play on words to him, mind, and he agreed with me that it didn't work terribly well joke-wise but that no harm had been done and we shouldn't hold it against you."

"Oh," I said. "Thanks?"

"Anyway." Alex clapped his hands and beamed. "Here's my joke." He cleared his throat. "What does a Roman pirate say?"

"I don't know, Alex." I thought it only fair that I go through the full joke-recipient routine. "What *does* a Roman pirate say?"

"*Summus.*"

Everybody laughed except me. Because I went to a state school. The annoying thing was I could probably work out why it was *supposed* to be funny from context. I mean it was a pirate joke. There's only two endings to a pirate joke, and one of them is just an attempt to subvert the original ending. Even more annoying was that I was about sixty percent sure that at least one other person in the bus was in the same boat I was but had cruelly abandoned me to be the only one sitting here not laughing like some kind of uneducated, humourless joke pleb. "Rhys," I asked, "why is that joke funny?"

Still keeping his eyes firmly on the road, Rhys gave another one of those expressive shrugs that let me imagine his face with perfect clarity. "I don't know, but everybody else was laughing and I thought it'd be nice to join in. Besides, *summus* is a funny word. Sounds a bit sexual."

"It does *not* sound sexual," I protested. "You can't say, 'Baby, I want to summus you. I want to summus you all night long.'"

Ana with one *n* twisted around to look at me. "You'd be surprised. I get all kinds of weird stuff in my DMs."

"You know," I told her, "I don't think I *would* be surprised."

Alex was beginning to look crestfallen. "You didn't tell me what you thought of my joke."

I wasn't sure what to say. "I think I'm not the target audience."

"Really?" Alex looked perplexed. "It's very simple. You see *summus* is the first-person plural of the verb *to be*—"

"Which means it's Latin for *are*," I replied. "Yeah, I worked that much out for myself.."

"Then why didn't you laugh?"

Why hadn't I? I suppose on a meta level I had *got* the joke. Fuck, why did every conversation with Alex end with me feeling like *I* was the one with the problem? "I think...I think to laugh, you need to understand it sort of...sort of instinctively?"

"Ah." Alex nodded. "Makes sense. Moral of that story is to pay more attention to your Latin master."

"I didn't have a Latin master."

For a moment Alex said nothing, then he laughed more authentically than I'd ever heard him respond to any joke I'd ever told him. "Ah, because the chap was English, you mean. Good one."

"No, I mean because I didn't learn... Tell you what, I've got a joke for you too."

Alex sat upright. "Good-oh. Let's hear it."

"What's a pirate's favourite cheese?"

"I don't know," replied Alex dutifully. "What *is* a pirate's favourite cheese?"

"*Yarrr*lsberg."

Aaaand there it was. Dead silence.

"*Yaaaarrrrrrrrr*lsberg," I repeated.

"Why do pirates like Jarlsberg?" asked Alex with near-biblical innocence.

I buried my head in my hands. "Alex, you have *just told me* a joke in which the implicit association between pirates and the syllable *arr* is the basis of the whole punch line."

"Yes, but Jarlsberg doesn't begin with *arr*, it begins with *yar*."

"*Yar* is a valid substitute," I insisted.

"He's right," agreed Rhys. "I often say *yar* when I'm doing a pirate."

For a moment, Alex seemed to be processing, but then he nodded. "Ah, well in that case I consider the joke excellent, and you may attribute my lack of laughter to my failure to understand it instinctively."

Ana with one *n* turned back around in her seat. "What type of cheese do you use to lure a bear out of a cave?" she asked.

Barbara Clench poked her head around the seat in front. "I don't know," she said, "what kind of cheese *do* you use to lure a bear out of a cave?"

"Come-on-bear," replied Ana with one *n*, doing a surprisingly effective impression of somebody waving a piece of camembert enticingly in front of a large predator.

I laughed at that. I thought it deserved it. And so did everybody else. Well, everybody else except Alex.

"Do bears eat cheese, then?" he asked. "I would have thought they preferred honey. Or maybe...wildebeest?"

"Terribly sorry," said Alex, as he led us down a plush-carpeted corridor lined with portraits of rich, dead wankers. "It's just as Miffy and I need separate rooms—can't see the bride before the wedding and all that—we've taken the two best suites already and obviously there's a bunch of family up for the weekend so we're going to have to stick you somewhere a bit substandard."

Until I met Oliver, being stuck somewhere a bit substandard was very much how I'd lived my life. "Don't worry about it. And thanks for, um, you know. The rescue and everything."

Pushing open a door, Alex waved us through. "Oh, think nothing of it. Always happy to help out a chum. Besides, it gave me something to do. Fearfully excited about tomorrow and all that, but it does weigh on a chap."

The substandard room turned out to be significantly better than sleeping in a bus and, for that matter, a fair sight better than sleeping in most houses I'd ever lived in. It was... Unlike Oliver, I didn't know what era it was. Somethingian where the something was the name of a king and/or queen, but that didn't exactly narrow it down. Edwardian? Elizabethan? Somewhere in the middle. Old and fancy is what I'm getting at. Big windows. Four-poster bed. Actual fireplace.

"I suppose it must." That was Oliver, keeping the conversation going while I was trying very hard not to face-plant on the nearest soft object. "Marriage is a significant step for anybody."

The problem with Oliver being a good person was that where I would have made a noncommittal noise and waited for Alex to leave, he'd taken an interest so now Alex was sitting in a chair with the air of somebody settling in for the evening. Or, in this case, early hours of the morning. "Yes, well. Seemed the thing to do. After all, she's a smashing girl from a smashing family. Can't have Mummy and Daddy wondering if you're a homosexual your whole life." He paused. "No offence."

On the one hand, some offence. On the other hand, it was the night before his wedding and we'd dragged him out of bed to spring us from jail. So if there was ever a time to let it slide, this was it.

"You realise"—Oliver was looking terribly sincere—"that even if you were, that would be okay."

Alex laughed. "Oh, of course it would. After all, it is the twentieth century. One of my father's best friends is a homosexual, and they're all jolly supportive of him, especially his wife."

"Um," I said. "Isn't that a bit weird for her?"

"Can't see why it would be. Plenty of chaps have other interests. Daddy's simply batty about steam locomotives."

I really regretted not face-planting. "Okay, but assuming you mean exclusively homosexual, rather than something under the bi umbrella, I think that's quite different from doing a spot of trainspotting?"

"Clearly you've never been married to a railway enthusiast."

"No," I protested, "but I'd like to be married to someone who is attracted to me."

Frowning, Alex tried to take a sip from a glass of brandy that wasn't there. "That's a very shortsighted view of marriage. Surely if one's going to spend the rest of one's life with somebody, it's more important that they're, you know, the right sort of person."

"What?" I surreptitiously massaged a temple. "Like belong to the right sort of clubs and wear the right sort of hat at Ascot?"

Alex blinked. "Well, obviously."

"And," Oliver put in gently, "you feel Miffy is the right sort of person?"

"Of course I do," exclaimed Alex. "Her father's an earl, for pity's sake, and her people have hardly any history of haemophilia."

"Isn't that a bit...eugenicsey?" I asked.

Alex smiled vaguely at me. "Thank you. We do try. Daddy

picked Mummy because Granddaddy said we needed some height in the line."

"Then I'm sure"—Oliver put a reassuring hand on Alex's shoulder—"you'll be very happy together and everything will work out tomorrow."

The look in Alex's eyes, as he glanced up at Oliver, was not vulnerability exactly, because that had probably been bred out of him along with haemophilia and shortness, but a posh facsimile of it. "Cheers," he said. "Decent of you." Then, filled with a new resolve, he bounced to his feet. "Don't know what I'm fretting about, to be honest. After all, there's simply armies of people we've brought in to make everything go smoothly. We Twaddles may not be able to fix photocopiers, but we've been getting married properly for centuries, and we're not about to start blowing it now." He looked momentarily fretful. "Just, you know, being such a duffer. Very real chance I might duff something up."

"You'll be fine," Oliver told him. "Walk in a straight line, repeat whatever you're told to repeat, and say 'I do' whenever someone asks you a question."

"Unless"—I briefly stopped temple massaging—"the question is *Do you love someone else*."

Alex ambled towards the door. "Well, I hope that won't come up. Seems a rather rum thing to ask a chap at his own wedding."

"You're right." I sighed. "I don't know what I was thinking."

CHAPTER 23

AS SOON AS ALEX HAD gone, I proceeded with my face-planting.

"I can't believe," I said into the soft, enticing mattress, "I have to be up for a wedding in three and a half hours."

Oliver sat down next to me. "Surely this cannot be the first time you've staggered home in the small hours of the morning, had a shower, and then left for work or a lecture or some major society function."

"I was in my twenties then."

"You're barely out of your twenties now."

"I'm thirty. I'm an old man. I can't cope with this wild, thrill-seeking, field-crossing, tea-stealing lifestyle anymore." Burying my head deeper into the bedclothes, I groaned like a zombie donkey. "Also, I've got that thing where you get wet and you dry out but you haven't really dried, and my pants are clinging to my bum in this weird way."

He stroked my hair. "You're very sexy right now."

"I am. I'm wearing sexy pants. That's why they're clinging."

"Then I fear you've made a rod for your own buttocks."

"No spanking," I whined. "Too sleepy."

There was a pause. Then Oliver said, "I appreciate I need a sleazy moustache in order to deliver this line properly, but we probably should get out of our wet clothes."

Trying to imagine Oliver in a sleazy moustache was suffi-
ciently…something that I brain-knotted myself back into wakeful-
ness and began peeling my T-shirt off. "Are you here to deliver a
pizza?" I asked. "Is it twelve inches?"

"Yes." It was Oliver's driest voice, which was pretty fucking
dry. "I'm here with the twelve-inch hot sausage pizza you ordered.
Also, my penis."

My jeans had adhered to my legs in a way that might have
looked enticing in a movie but in real life was just clammy. I tried
to wriggle attractively out of them and ended up thrashing around
in a tangle of denim and sheets instead. "I'm not sure porn is your
calling."

"Are you sure? I think the X-Rated Barrister has a certain ring
to it. I was going to call my debut feature *Habeus Porkus*."

"Not *Men's Rear*?"

"That'll be the sequel." His eyes alighted on my, well, mens rea.
"On the subject of which, those are some impressively tiny pants."

"Thanks. I'd love to tell you I was planning something naughty
for the wedding but, actually, I just haven't done any laundry for
a while."

"I'll admit," he said, "that was my first assumption."

Damn. That was the problem with the relationship lasting.
You got to know each other too well.

"Whether a product of necessity or design"—Oliver was still
looking—"they remain very much appreciated."

He drew me into a hug. Mostly a hug. Sort of a grown-up hug,
one of his hands sliding down to continue his appreciation of my
underwear. Such as it was. He was mostly dressed, having shed
only his jacket, which meant he was business casual and I was
rent-boy chic. So that was a mood. Not necessarily a bad mood,
but a very specific one, and one I'd have been uncomfortable with
had it been anyone but Oliver.

"You are quite cold," he said, giving me a little a rub. Of the your-arms-and-shoulders-are-chilly variety. Not of the fun variety.

Trust Oliver to care more about my well-being than my arse.

I shrugged. "I'll be okay. I mean...you can always warm me up."

Unfortunately, Oliver was still fixated on making sure I didn't die of a chill like a Victorian spinster. "Shall I run you a bath?"

The thing was, I didn't need Oliver to run me a bath. I was perfectly capable of running one for myself. But.... It was nice, wasn't it? To be taken care of. "I guess...that'd be lovely."

He drew the quilt from the bed and wrapped it round me— which shifted the vibe from sexy boy slut to starving urchin rescued by kindly gentleman—before disappearing into the en suite. From within came the sound of Oliver's shoes moving efficiently on tiles, along with the heavy gurgling of early-twentieth-century pipework. Eventually I drifted through, where I was largely unsurprised to discover that even the substandard rooms in Lettice Manor came equipped with the kind of bath that Roman senators would fuck their boyfriends in.

"Wow," I said, peering through the steam at Oliver. "You must really love me."

Oliver peered back, his normally austere hair gone curly in the heat. "Well, I do. But have I done something to make it particularly obvious?"

"Just that you've run this whole bath for me," I told him, "and you haven't once mentioned what a horrible waste of water it is."

"Well... It *is* a horrible waste of water, but in the overall scheme of things I think you can permit yourself one bath. Besides"—he gave me a smile that said Mean Oliver hadn't quite left the building—"I think you're probably owed a few."

"Are you saying I don't wash?" I protested.

"I'm saying that between your unwillingness to do dishes and your *occasional* failure to be arsed with a shower, you've probably shrunk your water footprint enough to be indulgent just this once."

I de-quilted and de-pantsed and descended down the marble steps into the steamy, bubbly, lightly scented water. "I wash. Both myself and dishes." I paused. "Not simultaneously. Although, thinking about it, that would *really* cut my water footprint."

"You're right," Oliver conceded. "I've maligned you unjustly. I suppose I'm still traumatised by that time you left a plate in the living room for a week."

"So did you."

"It was your plate." He folded his arms. "And I was waiting to see if you'd notice."

"It wasn't a messy plate. It'd only had a sandwich on it."

"Even so. Plates belong in the kitchen. In the cupboards. Not in the living room."

I stretched out in the water, floating slightly—which frankly felt weird. Most baths I couldn't even straighten my legs in. "Is this what being married to you is going to be like?"

"It's what *I'm* like." There was an unexpectedly defensive note in his voice. "So it may well be?"

Mostly, I'd been teasing, and I'd thought he was to begin with, but somewhere down the line we'd snagged on the brambles of an old argument. "I'm sorry about the plate," I said. "I'd genuinely kind of...stopped seeing it. But I haven't done it again. And, you know, you can always say: 'Luc, pick up your shit.' Or rather"—I did my best Oliver, which was nowhere near as good as the real thing—"'Lucien, please rationalise your paraphernalia.'"

His lips twitched. "I do not sound like that."

"You sound a bit like that. Also, I'm still upset you said I never shower."

"I didn't say you never showered. I just pointed out that sometimes you skip a day."

"Everybody skips a day," I insisted. "It's healthy. For natural oils and things. And it's not like I smell—oh my God, do I smell? You'd tell me if I smelled, right? Except you didn't tell me about that plate."

He undid the top button of his shirt. "Yes, I'd tell you if you smelled, which you don't. I was trying to make a lighthearted reference to the fact that you're sometimes adorably..." That wasn't good pause. "Uninterested in routine."

"Who's interested in routine? It's routine. The clue is in the name." I splashed water in his direction, which made him dance his shoes out of the way. "Also, are you just going to stand there criticising my personal habits while I have a bath?"

That made him pinken slightly. "Of course not. I'll...I'll leave you to it."

"I more sort of meant you could join me if you want to."

He hesitated, with that anxious, half-hopeful look in his eyes he sometimes got around dessert.

"This thing is huge," I added. "How many huge-bath opportunities are we going to get in our lives?"

"Probably several, if we wanted them?"

"Come on, Oliver. I'm lonely and...y'know...*wet*."

"Lucien, I—"

"It'll save water," I interrupted. "Ethics demand that you get in the bath with me."

"It's just..." He hesitated again. "On the subject of routines, I haven't been to the gym recently and, well, the lighting in here is quite harsh."

Ah. Between this and the plate, I wasn't winning any sensitivity awards this year. The thing was, Oliver had been in therapy for about eighteen months now, and while it had really helped him in some ways, it was a steps-forward, steps-back situation. Like, he'd got to the point where he was no longer obsessively going to the gym every day and treating food like the enemy, but worrying less about his body ninety percent of the time had made him more self-conscious the other ten percent. I mean, he was still far and away the fittest person I'd ever seen in real life, but the problem with giving yourself an eating disorder in pursuit of an impossible beauty standard was that if you got rid of one, you got rid of the other.

"Oliver," I said. "You don't have to do anything you're not comfortable with. But you're the most amazing, gorgeous, sexy man I have ever been allowed to do depraved things to. And I don't think that's ever going to change. Even when we're married and we've both stopped trying and you're, like, seventy-five with nose hair."

He looked faintly appalled. "I will never have nose hair."

"Well, I'd be into you, even if you did. Now come on"—I tried to signal this is a safe, if aquatic space—"get in the bath."

Slipping off his shoes and socks, he padded over and crouched down at the top of the steps. "I do know you're not judging me. I just find it very hard not to judge myself."

I tried to be sensitive to Oliver's body image issues, I really did. But, at the end of the day, he looked like him and I looked like me, and sometimes it was hard to remember that when he was being down on himself, he wasn't being down on me by association. Still—and this was definitely something I couldn't have done even a year ago—sometimes when you wanted someone to trust you, you had to trust them first. So I stood, letting the water stream off me like a shit Venus, waded over and kissed him, a hand catching the collar of his shirt, and my lips hard and urgent on his.

Trying to say things that I didn't know how to say. Asking him to believe that I loved him and I wanted him and that he'd never be anything but beautiful to me.

When I finally let him go, he was tousled and blushing and—"Lucien, now I'm drenched."

"Then," I said, "you might as well be in the bath."

I gave him what I intended to be a playful tug on the arm, but I hadn't quite factored in things like gravity and balance and wet marble. Oliver had just enough time for a flail and a "What the—" before we tumbled backwards into the bath with an enormous splash.

Thankfully, it was deep enough and wide enough that we didn't die.

Oliver resurfaced in a flurry of wet fabric and bubbles. Thankfully he was laughing rather than glowering, complaining, or pointing out quite how close he'd come to cracking his head open. "That was very...very you, Lucien."

"It was an accident."

"Exactly."

I took a moment to appreciate Oliver in a near-transparent white shirt clinging to all the bits of his body that I, coincidentally, liked clinging to. "For the record. This"—I made a kind of rectangle that was meant to encompass all of him—"is really working for me."

"Thank you." He looked flustered. "It's, um. It's actually quite uncomfortable."

"There's a solution to that."

He still looked flustered. "Kiss me again first."

In my head, I mermaided into his arms, full of seduction and mystery. But I was very much a land-based organism. So I sort of half stumbled, half waded forward, nearly knocking him over again, and finally managed to smack my lips onto his.

Thankfully, we'd had some practice at this—the kissing, not the navigating a neoclassical bath in an earl's country house—and after a teeny bit of fumbling and nose orientating, we settled into one of the few routines I saw the point of. The world melting away beneath the familiarity of Oliver's mouth against mine. His taste and the heat of him, and the way he always kissed me so carefully at first—like he wanted me to know I was precious—before he lost himself in urgency. And we got rough and messy and desperate for each other.

Even after two years. When surely it should have stopped feeling this way: all, you know, intense and stuff. Honestly, it still kind of scared me sometimes. And not just because the last time I'd let myself get this close to someone, I'd been really badly hurt, but because I'd *never* let myself get this close to someone. I wasn't sure I'd ever known how.

Until I'd met Oliver. And falling in love with him had left me defenceless.

I took the opportunity to make a midkiss play for his trousers. And, again in my head, this had been seamless and sexy. Except in practice, a wet belt was a pisser to undo and wet buttons did not slide easily through eyeholes. I did, eventually, manage to wrangle him out, but I nearly drowned and lost anything that might have resembled dignity.

"Are you all right?" Oliver ask-laughed, as I spluttered back to the surface.

I spat out half the bath. "Fine. Lungs are overrated."

He was still laughing as he kissed me again, and for a while, we made out like *Love Island* contestants, only without the cameras and the sarcastic Scottish voice-over. The water buoyed us up in this slightly magical way and I was light as champagne bubbles, drifting with Oliver through the foam.

Lying back against the wall of the bath, I let him float in my arms for a while. "I can't believe this is going to be us in a few months," I told him.

"Isn't it us right now?" he asked.

"No, I mean—getting married. Not in a cathedral, of course, and not putting all our guests up in a palace the night before but... yeah."

He was quiet. Too quiet. "It does seem rather unreal, doesn't it?"

Even this late at night, even naked and covered in soap, I could tell when he was tense. "Are you okay?"

"Yes, it's just"—for a while he stopped there, leaving me to speculate about all the various justs it could be—"I think in an ideal world, my parents wouldn't be making such a fuss."

I shrugged. "Fuck 'em."

"That's all very well for you to say." He half swivelled to look at me. "And I know you're *right* on some level, but it doesn't really make things any easier."

Yeah, that was the problem. And chances are it would *always* be the problem. "It'll be okay," I tried. "We're having lunch with them next week, and I *promise* I'll do my best to get back in their good graces."

"Thank you, but...their good graces are not that easy to access."

And that was the problem too. Actually, it was the same problem. "I know. But I'll try. Although if it doesn't work, I *do* reserve the right to go back to the *fuck 'em* strategy."

"That seems a reasonable compromise."

He relaxed back against me, and for a while it seemed like we could stay forever in that warm, magical space where all our troubles seemed as insubstantial as foam. Eventually, though, the water cooled and my toes got unattractively wrinkly. And so we climbed up the now-even-slipperier marble steps in search of towels. In some ways, I was sorry to see Oliver shed his still-on, still-transparent, still-clingy shirt but his body underneath, for all his insecurities, more than made up for it. I stroked lightly over his chest, making him shiver, before wrapping him up. Normally, Oliver was a vigorous and efficient dryer, rubbing himself down like he was sanding a bench, but tonight—or I suppose technically this morning—the time, or the bath, or the kissing had clearly got to him because he seemed happy to snuggle dry as per my preferred practice.

Entoweled, we headed back to the bedroom, where what sounded worryingly like the dawn chorus was beginning to filter through the windows.

"What time is it?" asked Oliver, blinking.

I scooped my phone from the table and had a look. "You don't want to know."

"Is it try-to-sleep o'clock or pull-an-all-nighter o'clock?"

"It's quarter to could-go-either-way."

"Ah." He pushed his damp hair back from his forehead. "I'll admit the all-nighter has never been my go-to strategy."

I wouldn't say it had been a strategy for me so much as how things tended to work out. "The trick is to push through the one hour when you really, really want to go to bed."

"Just out of curiosity"—a wave of fatigue washed over Oliver's face—"is that hour now?"

It wasn't right now for me, but I suspected it could come on any minute. "Kind of. We need to find a way to distract each other."

He laughed. "I could run another bath."

"But think of your water footprint."

"Is your way to distract yourself teasing me?"

"It's working." I grinned.

The other issue with the hour of all-nighter criticality was that it always passed incredibly slowly. I glanced around the room, looking for anything to occupy us. And it couldn't be the bed because that was a one-way ticket to sleeping through Alex's wedding. Unfortunately, while our surroundings were sumptuous in many ways, they were surprisingly short on entertainment. I suppose when you could ring a bell and get a servant to bring you a live peacock and a hand job whenever you felt like it, there wasn't much need to also keep a Snakes and Ladders set handy.

Finally, my gaze settled on the fireplace, which was still crackling merrily and casting orange shadows over what I suspected was a very expensive Persian rug.

"Oliver?" I said.

He gave a little jolt. "Yes, I'm awake. I'm definitely awake."

"Oliver," I said again.

His eyes narrowed warily. "That's your I've-got-an-inappropriate-idea face."

I did. I totally did. "You see that offensively posh rug by that offensively pretty fireplace? That's an actual fireplace with, like, fire in it?"

"I'd do a great many things for you, Lucien, but I draw the line at arson."

Because Oliver kept relentlessly to a very sensible bedtime, I'd never seen him quite this dazed before. It was, honestly, kind of adorable. I stared at him. "Oh my God. How did you get to *arson* from 'We should do something to keep ourselves awake'?"

The slightest pause. "Be gay. Do crimes?"

"I was thinking more...be gay, have sex? You know, on the rug, in front of the fireplace. Because it's here and I think we'll regret it if we didn't."

Another pause. "You want me," he asked slowly, "to make love to you in front of the fireplace?"

"Yes." It came out a little more aggressive than I intended it. "Tenderly. In soft focus. With violins."

"Well, I am quite tired, so I suppose that counts as soft focus. And while I'm sure there's a string quartet somewhere in the building, I don't think that would fall within their job description."

"Fine." I cast off my towel and arranged myself as seductively as I could on the rug. "Just. You know. Romance me, baby. Romance me hard."

And Oliver, looking, I thought, significantly more awake than he had three minutes ago, crossed the room after me. He dropped to his knees and settled his body over mine, and I reached up my arms to embrace him. As it turned out, the whole fireplace thing hadn't been totally oversold. The light painted us in tiger stripes of gold and shadows, and the heat fell over us gently like all the good bits of a blanket.

I can't lie, I felt sexy as hell.

"Oh, Lucien," Oliver murmured.

And I gazed up at him, too tired and too happy to resent to my own sincerity. "I love you."

So. Yeah. That was a thing that happened.

Oliver and a fireplace and a soft rug. It was probably the least me thing I'd ever done, and I was okay with that.

CHAPTER 24

I WASN'T SURE WHAT I'D expected Coombecamden Cathedral to look like. On the one hand, it was a cathedral, and cathedrals are usually pretty bling. On the other hand, Coombecamden was a tiny little postage stamp of a place that was considered a city only because of a weird religious convention from the fifteen-forties.

So I was at once impressed and disappointed when we followed the large and surprisingly boisterous wedding party into town—or what passed for town, since a lot of it was countryside because a surprising number of English cities were—and found ourselves headed towards a towering Gothic structure that, while it wasn't exactly Westminster Abbey, also clearly wasn't your local parish church.

"Okay, architecture boy"—I leaned over to Oliver, who was looking out of the window of the minibus with the kind of genuine interest that I was far too cynical to be capable of—"tell me about this one."

"I think it's probably a mixture," he said. "It looks like a medieval core with additions down the centuries until at least the Victorians."

I gave him a sceptical look. "How do you know that?"

"I don't particularly," he admitted, "but when a small town has a big Anglican cathedral in it, it's usually old. Otherwise, it would have been built somewhere more important. And since it hasn't been downgraded to a church in the intervening centuries, it will have been added to over the years. If we go poking around, we might find some desecrated statues from the Reformation."

Trying not to let my second wind ebb away before lunchtime, I did something against his shoulder that definitely wasn't snuggling. "Are we *going* to go poking around?"

"Might be a bit rude at a wedding."

We pulled up across the road from the cathedral and Rhys ordered us all out onto the pavement. Once we'd disembused ourselves, I realised how utterly incongruous the CRAPPers' green minibus looked in the convoy of wedding vehicles. There it squatted amongst the gleaming column of Rolls-Royces, Bentleys, and Daimlers, like a brick that had crashed through a jeweller's window and was now gleefully displacing diamond rings and strings of pearls.

As the crowds gathered and began flowing into the cathedral, we didn't exactly stop standing out. I'd thought we scrubbed up okay. Rhys had his shabby chic thing going on, Ana with one *n* looked fabulous, and even Barbra Clench had turned out nicely in a rather natty blue dress with floral sleeves. But none of us had outfits that cost as much as a small family home or were wearing a hat wider than our shoulders or those grey pinstripe trousers which were fucking awful but which posh men were apparently obliged to put on for formal occasions.

And actually *obligation* seemed to be the order of the day. I'd been low-key expecting something to go catastrophically wrong with Alex's wedding because something going catastrophically wrong was the background music of his life. But it seemed like I'd reckoned without the vast institutional inertia of the upper classes. Sure, Alex could spill tea over donor lists, double-book our only meeting room, and get his tie caught in a filing cabinet he didn't even have any files in. And sure, his peers and the members of his immediate social circle could preside over the collapse of the country's economy and the accelerating deterioration of its social safety nets. But this was a *society event*, and come hell or high water, it would run smoothly and decorously, or the whole system would be for nothing.

We let the crowd carry us in. We'd been seated miles from the actual service, presumably so we didn't accidentally get middle-classness on the happy couple. And once everyone was in place—which took a while because "everyone" was basically every landowner in the Home Counties, plus us—Alex made his entrance. He looked... Somehow he looked like he always looked. There was something about Alex that meant even dressed as he now was, in a three-piece suit, electric-blue cravat, and silk top hat, his essential Alexness shone through. Or maybe it was the other way around. Maybe on some level Alex was *always* wearing an electric-blue cravat and a silk top hat.

After he'd made the long walk down the aisle—in my mind, Oliver elbowed me and said, *The nave, Lucien. The aisle is the bit down the side*—there was a suitable pause before Miffy made *her* entrance. And it was significantly more entrancey. In retrospect, I wasn't sure why Alex had been so keen to avoid seeing her before the wedding because the gown—and the five others she would be wearing over the course of the weekend—had probably been thoroughly profiled on Instagram and in multiple lifestyle magazines. To be fair, it deserved to be, on account of being a designer masterpiece in silk and lace, modern without being trendy, timeless without being fussy, and with a train that said *Fuck off. I am taking up all the space, and I don't care*, but without running all the way out the door like Bridge's had.

On the earl's arm, Miffy proceeded down the nave like, well, like a princess. Not like a fairy-tale princess or a princess in a movie. Like an actual, real-world princess. Which is to say, like an incredibly rich, incredibly entitled person living out a social role she'd been groomed for her entire life.

When she reached the altar, she put back her exquisite veil and let it trail behind her. And I hoped to God, inappropriately given the context, that it was going to be a short service. Because I was already at my limit for grace and/or favour.

"A wedding," began the vicar, or rather, from the robes, the actual bishop, "is one of life's great moments, a time of solemn commitment as well as good wishes, feasting, and joy. Saint John tells us how Jesus shared in such an occasion at Cana..."

Oh no. We'd been here for fifteen seconds, and we were already getting a story about Jesus and some people who couldn't be bothered to hire decent caterers. I guess I'd kind of forgotten, or let myself forget, just how, like, God-centric a full-on religious ceremony could be. And as much as I'd found the all-the-rainbows-all-the-queer-iconography-all-the-time setup of Miles and JoJo's wedding a bit *extra*, this thing we were doing now was *way* weirder. I mean, we were sitting in a medieval building while a man in a triangular hat read to us out of a two-thousand-year-old book.

"The grace of our Lord Jesus Christ," the bishop was saying, "the love of God, and the fellowship of the Holy Spirit be with you."

"And also with you," chorused literally everybody else.

Fuck. Nobody had told me there was supposed to be audience participation. As a child of two eighties rock legends, my upbringing hadn't involved a huge amount of churchgoing. And, for thirty years, that had been fine. But right now it was making me feel that I was living one of those dreams where you discover you're in a play and everyone knows their part but you. Also, you might be naked.

Fortunately, I was not naked. Unfortunately, the bishop was

still talking. "God is love, and those who live in love live in God and God lives in them."

And then somehow by some bullshit cultural magic, everybody was chanting again. *Something something grace something something send your Holy Spirit something something that we may worship you now something something.* The only bit I was really confident I got right was the *amen* at the end, and even that was pushing it.

"In the presence of God," continued the bishop, "Father, Son, and Holy Spirit, we have come together"—crap, had they only just got to the we-are-gathered-here-today bit—"to witness the marriage of Alexander Antony Fitzrovia James Twaddle and Clara Isabella Fortescue-Lettice, to pray for God's blessing on them, to share their joy, and to celebrate their love."

How was there so much of this? How could there be so much of this? I wouldn't have minded, but I'd never seen the slightest shred of evidence Alex was even remotely religious. So all of this pomp and weirdly specific theology about the union between a man and his wife being in a very real sense the same as the union between Jesus and the Church felt like empty ritual. Except no, it was worse than that. Here in this, well, this *cathedral*, it felt like a ritual celebration of power and establishment and orthodoxy. I'd heard it said that the Church of England was the Tory Party at prayer, but until I'd seen a wealthy nincompoop marrying an earl's daughter in front of an actual bishop, I hadn't quite realised how literal that could be.

Come back, drag vicar, all is forgiven.

By the time we got to the bit where the bishop was like, "First, I am required to ask anyone present who knows a reason why these persons may not lawfully marry to declare it now" I was half-tempted to leap to my feet and yell *He can't marry her. He's already married to me* just to make it stop. But I didn't because despite outward appearances and years of practice, I'm not a *complete* bellend.

Then came the vows. Which at least didn't include the creepy *honour and obey* bit, although I was disappointed to discover that apparently *I do* had been replaced with *I will* and even more disappointed to realise the ceremony ended not with *You may now kiss the bride* like in the movies but with yet more audience participation. The bishop asked the entire population of Sloane Square and a bunch of weirdos who worked for a poo-bug charity if we would support Alexander and Clara in their marriage, now and in the years to come, and we all dutifully chanted that we did. Or rather, that we would.

Honestly, I felt kind of gross. It wasn't the God stuff. It was the way everyone else took it for granted that this was...universal somehow. That we were all united in this single idea of what marriage was and should be.

And then just when I thought it was over, there was yet more Bible. And not the lightweight love-is-cool and Jesus-is-groovy Bible stuff. Proper Saint-Paul-to-the-Ephesians Bible stuff. Proper we-are-Christ's-body-and-women-should-be-subject-to-their-husbands Bible stuff. And nobody seemed to notice or care or realise how totally incompatible it was with the scene in front of them. Because not only was Miffy perfectly capable of looking after her own life and career but Alex was the last person that anybody should be subject to on account of how he was—even by his own accounting—a massive duffer.

At last they let us out and we joined the rest of the guests in milling politely in front of the cathedral, while Mr. and Mrs. Twaddle-Fortescue-Lettice posed for endless photographs. And finally, mercifully, we were permitted to return to our vehicles.

I had never been happier to get in a minibus in my entire life.

Thunking my head against Oliver, I tried not to lapse into immediate unconsciousness. "Thank fuck we're done with that."

"Really?" He glanced down at me. "I thought it was rather nice."

That hadn't been the answer I was expecting. "Nice? It was wall-to-wall Jesus and heteronormativity."

"Well, yes," he conceded. "But that's what most weddings are like. It's traditional."

I wasn't sure *It's traditional* was quite the catch-all excuse Oliver seemed to think it was. "Don't you find those traditions a bit, you know, alienating?"

"Why would I?" He gave a shrug that I found genuinely a bit off-putting. "I'm not religious, but neither are most people who get married in churches."

"No"—I was probably too tired to be having this conversation because my voice got sharper than I wanted—"but you *are* gay."

"I don't see what that's got to do with anything." He did. I was sure he did. He just wouldn't admit it because he was slipping into defensive, overly rhetorical Oliver mode.

And I was letting it go. I was letting it go. I was letting it— "Doesn't it make you uncomfortable, though, listening to a guy standing up and basically saying 'God says marriage is for a man and a woman and always has been and always will be.'"

He gave another infuriating, ambiguous shrug. "I suppose I'm simply accustomed to traditional ceremonies using slightly archaic language. After all, I do go to work in black robes and a powdered wig."

"Yes but—" I began, only I wasn't sure what to *but* because what I'd assumed would be mutual commiseration had, instead, turned very quickly from a conversation into a debate and was now at serious risk of becoming an argument.

An argument I wouldn't want to have at the best of times and was particularly keen to avoid having in a minibus in front of my colleagues.

Ana with one *n* looked over the back of her seat. "I'm with

Luc on this one. All the God-Jesus-subservient-women stuff icks me out even if it is just words to most people."

Oliver seemed to be considering this with his complex-ethics hat on, and I wasn't sure that was the hat I wanted him to be wearing. "I do see where you're both coming from," he offered, "and I recognise that I might simply be overgeneralising from early experiences, but there's something I find comforting about a wedding that looks like the weddings I went to as a child."

Now he'd said it, that made a lot of sense. If there were ever people who embodied the weddings-christenings-funerals-and-nothing-else model of Anglican piety, it was the Blackwoods. Only I sometimes wished I could tell which of Oliver's values were really *his* and which he'd inherited from his parents. "And it doesn't bother you that our wedding literally *can't* be like that?"

I should probably have phrased that more tactfully because Oliver visibly flinched. "Of course it does. But that just means I wish the Church would be more accepting. Wouldn't it be rather nice to know that a gay couple could get married in a traditional ceremony if they wanted to?"

"As a regular churchgoer," put in Barbara Clench from the back—of *course* she was a regular churchgoer, "I'd be perfectly happy with a gay couple getting married in our church. What bothers *me* are the people who want a religious wedding when they don't actually attend services."

"That's a tricky one." Oliver swivelled around to face her, and I realised with a mix of relief and frustration that he'd gone from being mildly prickly that I'd implied he might be a bad gay to vanishing down a rabbit hole of abstract reasoning. "On the one hand, I can see why if I was religious, I'd feel that way. On the other hand, I think a quirk of the fact that we have an established Church is that the trappings of Anglican Christianity are part of our secular culture. I mean the Church even gets its own MP."

I came down on the side of relieved, and by way of an olive branch attempted to get interested in the intricacies of establishmentarianism. "It has its own MP?"

"The Second Crown Estates Commissioner," he said. "Then there are the Lords Spiritual in the Upper House. The Church isn't just religion in this country, it's government."

When you looked at it like that, the whole setup of the country sounded pretty fucked up. "That feels wrong."

"Oh, you've noticed that, have you?" Rhys was carefully following the absurdly expensive car in front of us, but still had the wherewithal to participate in a debate about the British constitution. "Now try living in a country that you English bastards have basically taken over. Tell me how it feels then." His voice got a kind of grinning lilt to it. "No offence."

"The problem," observed Professor Fairclough, who as ever had been staring out of the window the whole time and still was, "is that formulating an equitable system of governance is impossible outside of a eusocial species. And the only eusocial mammals are two subspecies of mole rat."

There was the sort of silence that often followed one of Professor Fairclough's interjections. Then Oliver, taking the opportunity to swap an awkward conversation for an obscure one, asked gamely, "Which species of mole rat?"

"The naked mole rat and the Damaraland mole rat."

Ana with one *n* gave an involuntary shudder. "Mole rats are just the worst animals."

"Well, what do you expect"—that was Barbara Clench—"for an animal named after two different kinds of vermin?"

"By most objective metrics," observed Dr. Fairclough, "humans are by far the worst animals, except perhaps in terms of our ability to survive in diverse environments." She paused. "Although in those terms we are arguably inferior to our own gut flora."

Given the alternative was fighting with Oliver about complex shit I didn't want to fight about, I threw myself into the conversation. "Molerat versus Gutflora sounds like a particularly crap monster movie."

"You know what," Rhys said cheerfully, "I'd watch that."

There was another pause. And then, to everyone's surprise, Dr. Fairclough made a second contribution. "I'm not sure how mole rats could fight their own gut flora, and if they were fighting human gut flora, they would need to get inside humans to do it."

We all contemplated that.

Ana with one *n* was getting the what-have-I-got-myself-into look that I sometimes saw on Rhys's girlfriends shortly after they met the rest of us. "Fuck me. That is genuinely horrific."

"Do you think," asked Rhys, with the air of a man about to combust his relationship, "that they'd gnaw through the belly or crawl up through the arse?"

CHAPTER 25

THE PART OF MY BRAIN that was rapidly falling asleep and therefore making random connections it might not otherwise have made strayed to the all-important question of why they called it a *reception* when it always came *after* the wedding.

There was, at least, the small mercy of the CRAPP crew getting our own table so we were able to ignore everyone else for most of the meal. It also allowed them to ignore us which, given we were still deep in the great mole-rat/belly-arse debate, was for the best.

The food, at least, was excellent and because these were the traditional kind of rich wankers as opposed to the trendy kind of rich wankers, there was at least a decent amount of it. But there *weren't* a great deal of vegan options, so Oliver had to content himself with stealing bits of people's side salads, which at least suited those of us—like me and Rhys—who thought vegetables at an event like this were just a scam to keep you away from the good stuff.

Also to my taste was the father-of-the-bride speech. Because it was short and to the point: doing the family proud, pleasant childhood anecdote, happy to incorporate the vast wealth of the Twaddles into the Fortescue-Lettice estate—the last part admittedly more implied than stated outright. Alex's speech, by contrast, was...not short or to much of a point at all.

"Well," he said, rising slightly unsteadily to his feet, "if it isn't dashed nice to see such a dashed lot of dashed fine people and... Gosh, I'm saying 'dashed' rather a dashed lot, aren't I? Anyway, thank you, Daddy-in-law, for your marvellous, marvellous speech, and thank you, Daddy-and-Mummy-in-law, for raising such a smashing, smashing gal as Miffy—I mean, Clara. We call her Miffy you see, for short. Where was I..."

As alienating as I'd found the service, even I had to admit that there was something endearing about watching Alex bumble his way through his groom's speech. Thankfully, he didn't try to do any jokes, although given the audience, the *summus* gag would probably have gone down like "Who's on First." After Alex was his brother Cornelius, who everybody called Connie, and he *did* do jokes—or at least I assumed they were jokes because people laughed. But they were the kind of jokes that were only funny if you went to Eton or, in extreme cases, one specific polo match ten years ago.

If this had been a normal wedding, the speeches would have been followed by dancing of the school disco variety, music provided by a jobbing DJ with a bad haircut or—increasingly—by somebody's Spotify playlist piped through a laptop. Since this was *not* a normal wedding, there was no dancing, just mingling, and the music was both live and classical. Apparently, Oliver had been right about the string quartet, and in retrospect, I was glad they hadn't watched me fuck. One of them had creepy eyebrows for a start.

As it turned out, an all-nighter followed by a long church service followed by a massive meal was an ideal recipe for unconsciousness. So when I felt myself leaning into Oliver like an amateur stripper who had overestimated their skill with a pole, I made a concerted effort to stiffen my lip, gird my loins, stand up, and be sociable. Reacting slower than he usually did—he was also dead on his feet—Oliver got up to join me and we made a round of the hall saying polite hellos to polite strangers who had no interest in us whatsoever.

As usual, Oliver was way better at this shit than I was, even managing to make a few sentences of small talk with some of the more accessible poshos before we moved on.

"I don't know how you interact with these people," I told him as we walked away from a short conversation with a Tory MP and her investment banker husband. "We have nothing in common with them."

Oliver gave a tired shrug. He was doing that thing that people who were good in crowds did where he was really peppy and extroverted whenever somebody was looking and drooping to conserve energy the moment we got out of sight. "They're just people, Lucien."

I sagged in the shadow of a pillar to shelter from the crowd of aristocrats who I was kinda sorta slagging off. "I know. It's...I don't know. It almost feels like you prefer this sack of arseholes to the crowd at Miles's wedding."

"I'll admit," he said, massaging his temples, "I prefer being in a pleasant stately home at the wedding of an affable but harmless man I've met more than once to being in a tunnel full of loud music and cultural markers I've always found alienating. I don't think that's especially wrong of me."

On one level, it wasn't. On another—and maybe it was the not sleeping and the being soft-arrested and the rain and the field of liquid cowpats, but I was feeling a difficult mix of drained and antsy. "I'm not saying it's *wrong* of you," I began, even though I was about to, a bit, "but those were kind of, y'know, my people?"

"They *used* to be your people," Oliver corrected, and I wasn't sure I was in a mood to be corrected. "Your people are Bridge and Tom, Priya and the James Royce-Royces. And, well, and me."

When he laid it out like that it felt really...really small all of a sudden. Not because I didn't love my friends—I obviously loved my friends—but because I'd always felt my friends represented, somehow, a connection to something larger? "I guess I just... It still kind of confuses me that you're totally down with a ceremony that celebrates a God you don't believe in, gender roles that went out of fashion in the 1950s, and a version of marriage you literally can't be part of"—I took a deep breath; this was getting way more intense than I'd intended—"but you're freaked out by a ceremony that celebrates your actual identity."

"Lucien." Like me, Oliver was standing slightly unsteadily, and like me he was hiding behind a pillar to stop what was now, undeniably, an argument spilling over the rest of the party like the world's most disappointing balloon drop. "I'm not sure what you want from me here. We went to a wedding for somebody you hated, and you clearly wanted me to be harsh about it, so I was harsh about it. We're now at a wedding for somebody you like, so I'm trying to help things go smoothly. And apparently that's upsetting to you."

Oh no, was this a me problem? This was probably a me problem. I mean, let's be honest, most things were me problems.

Except, hang on. On this one occasion, maybe incorrectly because self-awareness was never exactly my best feature, I was pretty certain it *wasn't* a me problem. Yes, if I was being fair—and who wanted to be fair in the middle of a fight—Oliver could play the taking-my-cue-from-you card for some bits of Miles's wedding. But he knew how much I loved dunking on rich people, and if he was really that committed to having my back, he'd have totally joined in.

I took a deep breath. "What's upsetting to me"—this seemed like a good time for I-statements—"is that you just seem like you're naturally drawn to a lifestyle I feel alienated by and naturally alienated from a lifestyle I feel drawn to and...and that's a crappy thing to realise when you're about to marry somebody."

"You're overextrapolating." Oliver wasn't normally this blunt, but then he wasn't normally this tired. "If I misinterpreted the situation, then I'm sorry, but I've only been trying to support you. These have been *your* friends' weddings after all."

Fuck that. He wasn't getting away with that. "Can you please drop the I'm-only-trying-to-please-you thing. Either you're bull-shitting me—"

"I'm not bullshitting you, Luci—"

"Either you're bullshitting me," I pressed on, "which is bad. Or you genuinely have no opinions of your own and are still doing that thing I *really thought you'd stopped doing* where you just try to perform whatever it is you think somebody else is expecting of you."

"I'm not—"

It was no use. I'd gone full dam-break. "And now it seems like you're going to want our wedding to be this mega-traditional bells-and-incense thing with no queer iconography because you're so insecure in yourself that rainbows make you uncomfortable."

I'd gone too far. I'd gone *significantly* too far. "I don't believe," said Oliver way too calmly, in a voice I'd never heard him use before, "that the fact I don't feel personally represented by a set of symbols invented by a very specific group of Americans in the late 1970s and popularised as much by global capitalism as by activists makes me *insecure in myself.*"

Part of me wanted to apologise because I'd obviously hurt him. But also, for all he was doing the I'm-a-lawyer-so-I-talk-good thing, I didn't think I was entirely wrong. And unfortunately, as I knew from experience on both sides of the equation, *I'm sorry but I'm right* never went down well.

"I didn't..." I tried.

"You did," he replied. "Now if you'll excuse me, I might take a short walk in the grounds."

I made a confused noise because what could you say to something like that? *No, stay* sounded either controlling or needy but *fine, go* sounded huffy as fuck. Besides, normally when we fought—which we didn't that much—I was the one shutting it down or needing my space or, in extreme cases, hiding in a bathroom. And I hadn't realised quite how rubbish it felt to be on the other end.

Probably I should have gone after him. Except, no, probably I shouldn't because part of being a grown-up in a grown-up relationship was trusting the other person. And so, although an irrational voice in the back of my head was telling me, *If you don't go and find him immediately, he'll realise you're shit and dump you,* I somehow managed to believe more in the two years we'd spent together than the jagged mess of damage that normally dominated my decision making.

Grabbing one of the many glasses of free champagne, I tried to look like an absolutely fine person who was having a nice time at a wedding and happened, just incidentally, to be standing on his own at the moment. Definitely not someone who'd had no sleep and a massive argument with his boyfri—fuck. Fiancé.

I stuck it out for about an honourable ten minutes before deciding I'd made a big enough sacrifice to the maturity gods and could go be needy again.

Unfortunately, the process of finding Oliver involved looking for him, which involved not quite looking where I was going, which meant narrowly avoiding colliding with a guest and narrowly not avoiding sloshing my champagne over him.

I got as far as "Oh shit, sorr—" before Justice Mayhew turned like a stop-motion Medusa and glared at me.

"What," he roared, "the bloody hell do you think you're doing?"

Of all the high-court judges in all the weddings in all the world, I'd walked into him. "I'm really sor—"

"Not good enough. You're being paid to do a job. Do it properly."

In the one and a half seconds it took me to realise that of *course* he'd assumed I was part of the catering staff, he decided I'd had enough time to reply and carried on.

"Well? Don't just stand there gawping. What do you have to say for yourself?"

"I *said* I was sorry," I protested.

Justice Mayhew was still glaring at me. "And *I* said sorry wasn't good enough. That's the trouble with your generation. Don't listen, don't think, don't care about anything but yourselves."

"I was looking for my boyfriend..." I knew the moment I'd said it that it was *precisely* the wrong thing to say.

"Oh, *I see how it is.*" He folded his arms defiantly. "You think that because you're some sort of *protected minority* that you can't be held accountable for your failure to do your bloody job. Well, I've got *news* for you, sonny lad. That isn't the way it works. I know you people think you're entitled to a free ride because you can just run crying to the Equality and Human Rights Commission and they'll make all your problems go away. Well, I'm afraid in the *real world*—"

"I'm a guest, Justice Mayhew." I was really trying to be polite, but I was also a world of not in the mood for this bullshit. "I'm a friend of Alex's and we've met. We've met several times."

"Nonsense. Fine upstanding chap like Twaddle wouldn't be caught dead in a French sewer with a reprobate like you. Now tell me who your manager is, or I'll—"

Fuck it. "Or you'll what? I don't work here. And the next time we meet, you won't even remember this conversation, so the way I see it, I have no reason to stand around and put up with your bullshit."

Justice Mayhew's face was turning exciting shades of crimson. "In all my days," he said, "I have *never*."

"I'm sure you haven't. Now if you'll excuse me, I don't have time for you right now."

I think I might have broken Justice Mayhew's brain because he just stood there fizzing. It would have been kind of satisfying if exhaustion and misery hadn't been taking up all my feel space. Abandoning my half-empty champagne flute to someone who *did* work in catering, I made my way outside without falling foul of any more malignant toffs.

I wasn't the only guest on the terrace, despite the light drizzle which had just set in to anoint Alex and Miffy's wedding with the spirit of pure, unsullied Britishness. Oliver had wandered into the formal gardens and was now walking aimlessly through one of those shin-high mazes that had apparently been fashionable in the narrow window of history where people had decided that a hedge maze was a bit too much but hadn't worked out you could, for example, not have a maze at all. Half jogging, half ambling, I made my way down to meet him. And although I was still mildly peeved at him, the look of genuine pain in his eyes when I ignored the path through the maze because stepping over the walls was easier was so Olivery that I couldn't quite hang onto the feeling.

For a moment we stared at each other over a pointlessly tiny hedge.

"I'm sorry," I blurted out. "I don't do well with..." I made an expansive gesture. "This."

Oliver's expression was less relenty than I'd have liked it to be. "Yes, I noticed. But, and I'm aware this is oversimplifying a complex issue, you do realise that your parents are both richer than mine and probably than several people in that building?"

Oh, so we were still doing this. Maybe I should have left him a bit longer. "Oliver, I just said sorry. Not *please encourage me to check my privilege.*"

He sighed. "You're right. I apologise. I'm…" He sighed again. *Fuck.* It was a double-sigher. This was going to be bad. "We're at a wedding, we're engaged to be married ourselves, and you've told me you think I have internalised homophobia."

Well, that was worth the double sigh. "I'm not sure I did."

"You did."

"Okay but"—I tried to smile but it came out as a grimace—"I once told you that you had an eating disorder, and you found that very romantic."

He didn't smile back. "They're not the same and you know it."

I nodded, reaching a new peak of feel-awful-ness. "I do know. And, again, I'm sorry."

We were silent a while, Oliver continuing to idly search for the intended path through the maze, while I kept pace with him on the straightforward one.

"I think," he said finally, "what I find most difficult is that I can't tell if you're right or not. Or what it would mean if you were. Or, indeed, if you weren't."

I offered another grimace. "I'm glad you've got that therapist."

Still, he didn't smile back.

"Um," I asked, concluding—as I should have concluded a while ago—that I couldn't joke my way out of this one. "What does this mean? For, like, us?"

Oliver stopped and met my eyes. His had gone all dark grey and sad. *Go me.* I was the worst. "I'm not completely sure. But I don't think it means anything for *us.* I think it just means something for *me.*"

"Okay." I felt bad for being relieved this was an Oliver thing, not an us thing or me thing. But I was relieved. "So…what does it mean for you?"

He sighed for a third time. "That you're right: it's fortunate I've got a therapist."

"And...and...the wedding?" Oh my God, Oliver was having some kind of serious emotional something. And I was all, *but my special day*. I was turning into a groomzilla.

"If anything," Oliver murmured, "it should make things easier. You have your preferences, and I'm...I'm interrogating my own."

"What?" I nearly tripped over an ornamental hedgehog. "No. This is...this is not what I meant to happen. I just wanted... Like, I don't know. Maybe a rainbow balloon arch. Not to make you have a complete crisis of identity."

And at last he smiled. "If it helps, I think the identity crisis was long overdue. Although I will say that a rainbow balloon arch still sounds *dreadful*."

"Mr. & Mr. table confetti?"

"Twee."

"Rose-gold penis straws?"

Oliver laughed. "Tasteless, phallocentric, cisnormative, and the kind of thing you'd have at a bachelor party, not a wedding."

"A customised portrait where it's two angels embracing but the angels have our faces."

That earned me a worried look. "Suspiciously specific."

"I found it on a website. It's *really* cute. In, I should stress, an intentionally kitsch way."

"You know the word *kitsch* comes from—"

I did know, we'd been dating for two years and he'd told me before. "Yes, yes, it comes from *volkitsch* which was a central part of Nazi ideology. I like to think we're reclaiming it. Like *queer* and *bitch*."

"You know"—Oliver folded his arms—"saying you're reclaiming something doesn't actually give you standing to reclaim it or make it reclaimed?"

I deployed a sigh of my own. "Yes. I know." And then, because

I was still a bit shaken by quite how badly this had gone, I heard myself asking needily, "So...are we...are we good?"

"Always," he said.

And then he stepped over the little maze wall to kiss me.

CHAPTER 26

A FEW DAYS LATER, OLIVER tried to wake me gently with "I've made French toast."

But firstly, I wasn't sleeping, I was just lying there in sulky dread. And secondly, it was definitely a bribe. Today was the day we were seeing his parents, and like any sensible person, I did not *want* to see his parents. "There are some things," I said, "that you can't make better with French toast. You're making French toast worse by association."

"Well, I can throw it away if—"

"No." I cast off the covers and made a grab for the plate. "No. I will eat it. But I want you to know that I am eating in the full knowledge that this is a bribe."

Oliver looked faintly guilty. As well he might. "I prefer to think of it as me doing something thoughtful for you because I know you're going to do something thoughtful for me."

"Yeah, that's literally what a bribe is."

"No, a bribe is contingent. A bribe comes with expectation. This came after you'd agreed to do the thing I wanted so it's legally a thank-you gift."

Moodily, I munched through the incredibly delicious French toast, trying not to resent how incredibly delicious it was. But it *was* incredibly delicious. *Dammit.*

Oliver cleared his throat. "While I always enjoy watching you pout and/or enjoy my cooking, we are going to need to hurry a little bit."

I mopped up the remains of the maple syrup with the last corner of the toast and inched it, slowly, towards my mouth. "We've got plenty of time. As long as you're happy to wear the shirt you're wearing and not planning to cycle through sixty-five other identical shirts before we leave."

"Lucien." There was a note of warning in his voice. "You know my relationship with my parents is complicated. And I feel better able to navigate it if I'm confident in my appearance and my punctuality."

He might have felt that way. But I'd never seen any evidence that it actually helped. Nevertheless, I'd agreed to this. This being a trip up to Milton Keynes to convince Miriam and David Blackwood that they should (a) come to their son's wedding and (b) not ruin it. Only in more tactful words so they didn't feel "attacked." Clearly, it was going to be a disaster. But Oliver and I had committed to the mutual fiction that it would work. Or, at the very least, be worth trying.

"I'm going to have apologise, aren't I?" I asked, having show-ered, dressed, and buckled myself into the car we'd hired so often we practically owned it. On the other occasions I'd been unable to avoid David and Miriam, I'd just not mentioned it and let them get back to pretending I didn't exist as quickly as possible. But this was different. This was about *mending fences*, whatever that meant.

"I'm not going to ask you to," replied Oliver, with fatal ambi-guity. "But, in all honesty, they might expect it."

Despite the fact it was twenty past ten and I'd deliberately got an early night, I was already flagging. "I mean, I suppose I did tell them to go fuck themselves at their own wedding anniversary, which was probably a bit aggressive."

"It was a very charming but very unhelpful gesture."

"Well, I'm sorry"—it was a good job Oliver liked me pouting because I was doing it a lot—"but I don't have the lawyer words."

Oliver turned us deftly onto the B502. "Yes, but do you have words that aren't *fuck*?"

"Not fucking many," I said.

And Oliver must have been in his head because I didn't even get a pity laugh.

"Look"—I put a hand gently on his knee—"I get I kind of messed this up right at the beginning. And, retrospectively, I really wish I'd de-fuckified my language. But, like, I love you and it's not okay for people to treat you badly and I'm not going to say I was wrong to stand up for you."

A faint blush was creeping across Oliver's cheeks. "Of course it wasn't wrong."

We tooled along in silence for a bit.

"And," I asked awkwardly, "you're going to be okay if this... I mean, even if I don't fuck it up, it still might get fucked or stay fucked and—"

"I hope"—Oliver cast me a dry smile from the driver's seat— "this is you getting the fucks out of your system."

"I'll be a fuck-free zone, I promise. But actually, I do think we need to be ready for the possibility that today ends with your parents not on side with this."

"I am aware of that possibility," said Oliver, with an air of reluctance. "I would prefer, however, to address it only in the event it arises."

"Okay. Only—" I stopped. Because what I could ask? I knew what I *wanted* to ask, which was for him to promise he'd be fine, no matter how this went, and I definitely wasn't going to wake up tomorrow to an empty bed and a fully dressed Oliver saying, *I'm sorry, I can't do this.* But that wasn't fair.

Oliver's eyes flicked to mine in the rearview mirror. "Only what?"

"Sorry. Nothing."

And while that wasn't usually the sort of thing Oliver let slide, today I guess we were both trying to trust each other.

I guess we both needed to.

"Podcast?" I offered hopefully—though, what with the proposing and ring buying and parent wrangling, I'd lost track of what Oliver was into at the moment.

He shook his head. "I'd rather not. Is it okay if we just drive quietly?"

"Sure," I said. Because what else could I say? I mean, it kind of wasn't okay. Not because I was desperate to listen to a podcast but because I was incredibly worried that Oliver didn't want to. Listening to documentaries and whimsical radio dramas was the closest he got to vegging out. So I hated to think what he was feeling right now that even *This American Life* couldn't soothe him.

———————

It didn't entirely surprise me that Miriam and David Blackwood had insisted on taking their vegan son to a gastropub with exactly one vegan option on the menu. After Oliver had ordered his superfood salad, and I'd ordered the same out of masochistic solidarity, his parents tortured the waiter for a while—David by demanding a fillet steak with a very specific set of instructions about how it should be prepared and Miriam by politely but unswayably insisting they make her a vegetable risotto that wasn't currently on the menu.

Once that had been resolved to their satisfaction, we all sat in silence until David Blackwood finally said, "So you're still getting married, then?"

"Yes," replied Oliver, sounding calmer than the tension in his jawline showed me he felt. "And we'd like you to be there."

Miriam, who had been checking the cutlery for cleanliness, set down her fork. "Well of course we'll be there, darling. That was never in question. We just want to be sure you're making the right decision."

Given that the Blackwoods seemed determined to talk as if I wasn't in the room, I was beginning to wish I hadn't been.

"I've already told you"—Oliver's voice got calmer and his jaw got tenser—"that I am. And it's not up for debate."

"But marriage," protested Miriam, "when you're still so young."

Oliver cast a longing glance at a bread roll. "I'm older than you were when you got married."

"This isn't about your mother and me," said David predictably. "Things are very different for your generation."

"And," added Miriam, "different for...for..." She waved her hands in a way that was probably intended to communicate *for gay people* without her having to say the words. "Men aren't like women. You have different needs."

I wanted to ask what kind of needs, exactly. But I wasn't here to challenge causal gender-essentialism-slash-homophobia, I was here to support Oliver. So I stayed quiet.

"You wouldn't understand this," Miriam went on heterosplaining, "but women need commitment."

"Whereas men," David chimed in, "are dogs."

Oliver glanced sharply up from his own hands, which he'd spent most of the conversation staring at. "Have you dated a lot of men, Father?"

There was a very nasty silence. The worst thing about David Blackwood—from an extensive collection of bad things—was that he looked a little bit like Oliver. The same slightly square features, the same hard grey eyes that, on him, I'd never seen soften. It was like a glimpse of the future if I accidentally wound up marrying a terrible person. "I suppose you get this attitude from *him*." He didn't even deign to look at me.

I like to think that the fact I didn't respond to this at all, in any way, counts as one of the seven most noble things I've ever done in my life.

"I'm sorry," said Oliver quickly.

Which wasn't quite the rush to my defence I'd hoped for. But then again, we were here for our wedding not my ego, and pissing off David Blackwood before the main course was a bad strategy.

The uncomfortable silence that followed lasted just long enough for our food to arrive. And then Miriam piped up with, "I must admit, I don't really understand why gay people want to get married at all."

"Equality?" I suggested, hoping that this counted as *engaging* and not *talking back*.

She seemed to be genuinely thinking about this. "But isn't that a bit selfish?"

I glanced at Oliver for help but got nothing. He was gazing into his superfood salad like it contained the mysteries of the universe. And maybe it would have been a good idea to let it go, but I hoped if I kept asking open questions, I could at least avoid another excruciating silence. "Why selfish?"

"Well"—Miriam looked faintly pained—"for normal people, marriage has a tradition behind it. And it seems a shame to try and change that for everybody else just because you feel left out."

"For what it's worth," I said, "I don't consider myself abnormal."

That got Oliver off the bench but not for the team I wanted. "She didn't mean it like that."

"I think she probably did," I began. I'd been about to add *But it's okay, I get that a lot of people think that way*, but I never got that far.

David Blackwood surged to his feet. Which was actually pretty intimidating in a cosy gastropub in Milton Keynes. "How dare you. You come up here, you let us pay for your lunch, and that's how you talk to our son?"

It wasn't the most furious anyone had ever got with me, but it certainly had the highest anger-to-provocation ratio. If I'd been in a more charitable mood, I might have said that at least he was protecting Oliver and I could understand the instinct to protect Oliver. Except I wasn't in a charitable mood, I hadn't asked them to buy me anything, and David Blackwood was an arsehole.

I was just psyching myself up to give a deeply insincere apology when there was a tiny clink as Oliver put down his salad fork.

"Father," he said. "You're making a scene."

David snapped round like a rattlesnake. "Making a scene? I'm not the one arguing with your mother and making snide comments."

"I wasn't—"

But Oliver cut me off. "With respect, you've barely met Lucien. You know nothing about our relationship and, frankly, you know nothing about me. If we're going to talk about snide comments, then you have a thirty-year head start on everybody at this table. And as for Mother"—his gaze flicked to Miriam—"I'm sorry, but you were being homophobic. You're both quite homophobic people."

"How can you say that?" She blinked in genuine horror. "We love you."

He sighed. "You know, I think you do. But from everything you've said to me today, and the way you interact with Lucien and with every boyfriend I've ever had, and with me ever since I came out, you will clearly never see any relationship I have as being as valid as Christopher's relationship with Mia."

"Well, it's different," protested Miriam, with an unerring instinct for saying the worst possible thing.

"It is not." Now Oliver was on his feet as well. And raising his voice. "Lucien sees me with all my flaws and makes me feel loved anyway. Something, by the way, that neither of you have ever managed."

A deep hush had fallen, not just over our table but over the whole pub.

David Blackwood was staring at Oliver with something almost like disgust. "I don't know who you think you are. Your mother and I have given you everything. We fed you, we clothed you, we sent you to university, we put you through the bar, and now you've had your head turned by some artsy fairy who can't keep his arse out the papers, and suddenly you think you're better than us."

I wanted to tell them that he was. Not because I was an artsy fairy but because he was a good person—the best person—and he'd got that way despite having parents who were total shits.

"Then how about this," said Oliver, elegantly pulling on his jacket. "I make good money now, so if you really believe that our obligations to each other are based entirely on what you've spent, sit down, add up what you think I owe you, and I will happily cut you a cheque."

Miriam made an imploring gesture. "He doesn't mean that."

"I'm afraid I agree with Lucien on this one." Oliver's eyes were the steeliest I'd ever seen them. "I think we've all meant exactly what we've said today. Now come on"—he looked at me, relenting slightly—"we're leaving."

I got to my feet so quickly I nearly overturned my chair.

Oliver righted it for me, then took my hand. "Oh, and Dad..." He shot one last look at his father. "Go fuck yourself."

PART
FOUR

CHAPTER 27

"OLIVER," I WHINED, "WHY DO we have to do this now?"

He was sitting cross-legged on the floor, shuffling around the colour-coded index cards that constituted our seating plan. "Because it needs doing."

"But it's Sunday afternoon. We could be having sex—"

"Lucien."

"We could be having a lovely walk in the park."

"The caterers need this information." After a moment's contemplation, he delicately swapped the places of two work colleagues whose names I didn't recognise for what I presumed were reasons of office politics. "As does the venue."

"But not six months in advance."

"Five months," Oliver corrected me.

Shit, time went quickly when you were caught in an endless whirlpool of logistics. "Not even five months. Half the RSVPs haven't even R'ed yet even though we said SVP."

"Yes, but we know who should be coming. And it'll be easier to take people out once we've got the basic structure down than to rush everything at the last minute." Picking up one of the cards I'd filled in, Oliver peered at it. "Who on earth is Peloton? Isn't that a company who does something with exercise bikes?"

"Yes," I told him. "I've invited an entire fitness company to our wedding and assigned them two seats between them."

Oliver turned to me with a deeply disappointed expression. "You haven't assigned them two seats. This is a yellow index card. A yellow index card means one seat."

"Doesn't yellow just mean my group, not your group?"

"No."

I pointed at the seating chart. "Why would I have given the James Royce-Royces one seat between them?"

"You mean this guest who is apparently called Jarrow Robertson?"

"That does not say Jarrow Robertson. I don't even know a Jarrow Robertson. You've met literally every single person in my extremely limited social circle. Who the hell would Jarrow Robertson be?"

Oliver gave me an infuriatingly cool shrug. "A friend of your mother's?"

"As you're very well aware, my mother has one friend."

Calmly, Oliver directed my attention to the Peloton card. "So who is this meant to be?"

"Bridge. And Tom."

"That's definitely a *P*," insisted Oliver, squinting at something that was definitely a *B*. A slightly top-heavy *B*, I will admit. A *B* that could in a certain light be misconstrued by an uncharitable person as having *P*-like qualities.

"Fine, give me a pink one. I'll redo it."

"Pink is for immediate family."

I buried my head in my hands. "What if immediate family need two seats?"

"They'll all need two seats, so it doesn't have to be specified."

"What about Mum?"

"I assumed she'd want to sit with Judy," explained Oliver.

"And it seemed allonormative to insist that a person's plus-one had to be a romantic partner. Besides, I'm not sure we want Judy roaming the wedding breakfast unaccompanied."

He was right on both counts. My dad would have gone stag, but I'd bitten the bullet and not invited the fucker. Which meant immediate family was just Christopher and Mia, Mum and Judy, and... "Are we"—this was messy and there was no tactful way to say it—"are we assuming that David and Miriam are still coming?"

There was a slightly too long silence.

"I am operating on the assumption," said Oliver finally, "that they will. Because they are my parents and, despite our recent disagreements, I choose to believe that they do, on some level, want to be part of my life."

That seemed quite an assumption, given that they hadn't spoken in two months. "You could try reaching out?" I suggested without much enthusiasm. Standing up to them had been such a big step forward for Oliver that it seemed counterproductive for me to be encouraging him to back down.

Oliver was putting all the yellow index cards in a separate pile. "I don't think I will. I have spent my entire life trying to live up to their expectations. It's time for them to try to live up to mine."

"And what if they...don't?"

"Then"—his mouth tightened—"I suppose I shall have to deal with it."

I wanted to say something reassuring, but it was hard to know how. In my experience, hoping someone who'd been letting you down for years would suddenly stop letting you down was a recipe for really bad feels. And the best thing you could do was not invite them to your wedding and not a give a fuck.

Or maybe I was projecting.

Besides, Oliver was a congenital fuck giver.

"At least," I said with a smile, "this puts the rainbow balloon arch back on the table."

I'd meant it as a joke, but Oliver seemed genuinely thrown. "In what way?"

"Well, we don't need to worry so much about what your parents will like."

Aaaand now he'd gone from *thrown* to *frozen*. "Firstly, I think it's very probable my parents *are* coming. Secondly, my tastes aren't anything to do with what I think my parents will like."

I should have pedalled way the fuck back. But I was still sort of committed to the idea that I was cheering him up. "Not even a teeny tiny bit?" I made teeny-tiny fingers to show I was being at least slightly flippant.

"No."

"Okay." I went back to shuffling index cards, but that only lasted about four seconds.

"And I resent the implication," Oliver continued.

Fuck, he was back sounding like his dad again. The Blackwoods were massive resenters of implications. "What implication?" I asked, only slightly disingenuously.

"That I'm some kind of poster child for false consciousness."

In my defence, he was the one who'd gone there. And now that he had, it seemed fair to at least talk about it. "I mean"—I drew in an uneasy breath—"if you feel like you *might be*, then doesn't that suggest that it might be worth thinking about?"

"You're not my therapist, Lucien."

"No, but I'm your, like, your fiancé. This stuff matters to me."

I knew he was angry because he'd put the index cards down. And also because the only thing he said was "Why?" in a tone of actual challenge.

"What do you mean, why?"

"I mean *why?*" Yeah, definitely pissed off. And not in a sexy stern way, but in a you've-touched-a-nerve-you-shouldn't-have-touched way. "Why is it so important to you that my distaste for brightly coloured tat be part of some pathology or personal flaw instead of a feature of my personality?"

"Oliver, queer iconography is not *tat*."

"It is when it's printed on merch and sold for four ninety-five on Etsy."

I dug my fingers into my temples. "Oh my *God*, how is this not trying to please your parents? Sorry, Oliver. Yes, I do actually like things you can buy on Etsy. I do actually like crap that has rainbows randomly painted on it. I even think the MLM flag looks kind of okay, and I'm thinking of buying one to hang in my window because *I love you and I am proud that I love you.*"

There was a right time and a wrong time to tell somebody you loved them. As a weapon in an argument might, just might, have been a wrong time.

"You make it sound," Oliver said in his most have-to-stay-calm voice, "as though who I am and who I love only *count* if I want to put them on a banner or a T-shirt. A banner or a T-shirt that I don't even get to design myself and must, instead, let the 'community' design for me."

"Oh, you did not just air-quotes *community*."

Oliver was on his feet. Why was he on his feet? "We've discussed this, Lucien. I don't choose my friends based on who they want to fuck. My community is people I know and care about."

"You know *me*. You care about *me*."

The expression on Oliver's face as he looked down at me wasn't quite disappointment and it wasn't quite betrayal. How had we even got here from a joke about a balloon arch? "I do. Which is why I accepted your proposal. But what I *don't* want is either to get married surrounded by garish Pride merch or to be made to feel that *unless* I get married surrounded by garish Pride merch, I'm somehow a lesser member of this *community* you're so proud of."

"And I don't want to be made to feel like you don't think my community—*our* community—matters."

He was staring at me like he barely recognised me. "Are you *certain* you want to marry me, Lucien? Because sometimes it—"

Before he could say anything else, his phone rang. It had been sitting beside him on the floor so he could use one of his many organising-things apps for the wedding planning, and that meant we could both see that it was his parents calling.

"I should probably take this," he said. "It might be about the wedding."

"The wedding you just accused me of not wanting."

Sweeping up his phone, Oliver stepped outside into the corridor. I tried not to feel let down that he was still so under his parents' thumbs that he'd taken a call from them in the middle of a fight *about* how under his parents' thumbs he still was. But I didn't quite manage it.

All the same, the time he was outside gave me space to catch my breath. To remind myself that whatever else happened, I loved Oliver and he loved me, and we didn't need flags or banners or, for that matter, rings or weddings to prove it. And that we'd shown over the last two years we were strong and we could come through this, and that was why we were getting married in the first place.

When he came back in, I noticed he was very pale.

"Are you okay?" I asked.

"That was my mother."

"Are they not coming to the wedding?"

"No. It's...it's my father. He's had a heart attack."

"Oh my God." I jerked to my feet. "Is he going to be okay?"

Oliver was concentrating very hard on the pile of index cards. "Actually he's... He didn't make it to the hospital."

"Fuck, I'm sorry."

I tried to hold him, but he wasn't in a mood to be held. And that shouldn't have hurt—he was shocked and grieved, and we'd just had a giant fucking fight about nothing, and different people processed feelings differently—except it did hurt. It hurt quite a lot.

"I need to see my mother," he said. "I should leave."

"Of course." I dithered in a kind of I-want-to-support-you-but-I'm-not-sure-how way. "Shall I come with you?"

"I think"—and, again, I shouldn't have read rejection into his voice but, again, I did—"it would be best if I went alone."

That made sense. Obviously, it made sense. His mother hated me. I was the worst person he could possibly have brought. "Whatever you need. And, like, call. Or don't call. Just…do… do what you have to. I'll be here. I mean, not here. I'll be at home and—"

He gave a nod, cutting me off. Then turned and strode purposefully away.

CHAPTER 28

I WAS SITTING IN MY pants on my sofa, eating kung po chicken direct from the container, when I realised that maybe I wasn't exactly smashing it coping-wise. Oliver had been at his parent's house—well, his mum's house now—for almost a week, dealing with…death logistics. And it wasn't like we hadn't been in contact—there'd been texts and a couple of phone calls—but Oliver had seemed distant. Which I got because, between the administrative faff of arranging a cremation, the emotional sucker punch of your father dropping dead not long after you'd told him to go fuck himself and, oh yes, that enormous fight we'd been in the middle of, he had a lot on his mind. I just wished he'd let me, I don't know, be there? Help? Do something? Feel less useless.

Except I guess that was kind of selfish. The thing was, in all the time we'd been together, there'd never been a point in our relationship when what Oliver had needed from me was absence. Space, occasionally, sure, when work was demanding or when I was being annoying. But this was different. Like, I had no idea what he was thinking, and there was some tiny, messed-up part of my brain that was worried he was hating me. Because if going to bed angry was bad for your relationship, going to organise your father's funeral angry had to be a whole other level of fucked up.

In any case, Oliver was in Milton Keynes, and I was backsliding with alarming rapidity. Which meant I was actually that guy: the one who could only keep it together if he had someone to keep it together for. And, at some point, Oliver was going to come home and find me unconscious in a pile of old socks and pizza boxes, and then be all, "Not only did you destroy my relationship with my family and question the authenticity of my identity over a rainbow balloon arch but you are also a human refuse pile with less self-respect than one of those fish that spends its whole life attached to a larger fish feeding on its leftovers." Except he'd just say *a remora* and assume I knew what it was. And then I'd have to say, "What's a remora?" and he'd say, "It's a fish, Lucien, that spends its whole life attached to a larger fish feeding on its leftovers."

Probably I needed to stop watching *The Blue Planet* while angsty.

Tipping what was left of my rice into what was left of my kung po sauce, I made a glum and futile pact with myself to stop being so shit. Because nobody who had recently celebrated his thirtieth birthday—and by celebrated I mean panicked about—should be going to pieces after less than a week of having to make his own French toast. Not that I made my own French toast. Even if I'd been able to make it as well as Oliver, it wouldn't have tasted the same without him.

Fuck, I had to do something. So I pulled out my phone and messaged the WhatsApp group—currently called Stand by Your Pan.

Help, I typed. Oliver has gone away for, like, five seconds and I am eating takeaway in my pants.

Bridge responded immediately: HOW IS OLIVER??? I EHARD ABOUT HIS DAD :(:(

Trying to talk about someone's dead parents in all caps created tonal issues that even I was sensitive to. I think he's okay. He's not really talking to me.

Why, asked Priya, is there takeaway in your pants?

I'm in my pants. The takeaway is in my mouth.

If I come round to be supportive and shit, will you at least put trousers on?

HES SAD HE DOESN'T HAVE TO WAER TORUSERS IF HE'S SAD

Sorry—that was James Royce-Royce—James can't make it because he's at the restaurant and I can't make it because I have to look after Baby J.

BRING JBABY J IT'LL BE CUTE. LUC CAN'T BE SAD IF THERE'S A BABY1!!!!

For someone who knew me better than anyone, sometimes Bridge didn't know me at all.

Nobody is taking my baby boy to Luc's flat—that was James Royce-Royce somehow texting from a professional kitchen—he'll crawl into a pile of laundry and die.

My flat is clean these days, I protested.

An incredulous digital silence followed. Then a message popped up from Priya: Only because you don't live there.

That was depressingly close to the truth. Keeping the flat clean by the cunning strategy of staying full-time at Oliver's had worked remarkably well, but I'd been back for four days now and it was four days in which I had done approximately zero washing up.

HES SAD YOU ALWAYS LET THINGS SLIDE WHEN YOUR SAD

Luc must have been sad a lot.

Well, I'm sad now, I typed. Come and comfort me.

Fine. Should I bring chocolate or bleach?

I winced. Maybe both?

I'M ON MY WAY RIGH TNOW. DON'T START WITHOUT ME.

Don't start what? I asked.

ANYTHING!!!

I made the executive decision that "anything" in this context didn't include putting on my trousers. So I did and made a desultory start on the washing up. Except washing up reminded me of Oliver, which probably said all kinds of weird things about my habits, both in the relationship and outside of it. I just missed him. And his three different types of sponges for washing specific types of things. And the way I'd hug him from behind instead of doing the drying, and we'd both pretend it was a hundred percent affection, instead of eighty percent affection and twenty percent laziness.

Definitely not crying, I threw away my takeaway container and realised I'd thrown the fork away with it. In retrospect, that might have explained why I had so few forks.

What if I was never going to wash up with Oliver again? What if he dumped me because every time he looked at me, he saw his dead dad? And then what if every time I looked at a bottle of Fairy Liquid I saw the guy who'd dumped me for yelling at him for caring too much about what his parents thought at the exact moment one of those parents was dying of a heart attack.

The buzzer went—and, somewhat predictably, Priya stomped in.

"Where's Bridge?" she asked.

I shrugged. "She said she was on her way right now, which means she'll be here in about an hour."

Slipping her army kit bag from her shoulder, Priya pulled out a bar of Dairy Milk and a bottle of Dettol antibacterial spray. "So." She flopped down on the end of the sofa. "How fucked is your relationship?"

"Wow, I really missed your sunny, supportive disposition."

"Fuck off, Luc. I brought beer."

"What's that saying? Beer, then wine, feeling fine. Beer, then antibacterial spray will ruin your day."

She laughed and rummaged again in her bag, finally producing a four pack of whatever craft IPA she was into this week. "Seriously, though." Flicking open the bottle opener attachment of her Swiss Army knife, she beered us both. "How fucked is it?"

I sighed. "Honestly, I can't tell. Oliver's never been like this with me. But then, his dad's never died so...who knows?"

"In other words," Priya said, "everything's fine and you're just getting in your head like a wanker."

Sitting down next to Priya, I cast her a you-have-failed-to-comfort-me look. "How have you got two girlfriends? Or, indeed, any nonzero number of girlfriends."

"Because they like that I'm creative, low bullshit, and get them off. In my experience, that's what women are after."

"Good to know. Although not super relevant to me right now."

She took a long draught of a beer with a weird name. "And—just to cover the basics—you've tried, like, talking to him and shit."

"I've tried. But he's not really talking to *me*."

"I'll admit that would normally be a sign because you're in one of those annoying, mature relationships where you have to make plans and share your feelings instead of just screaming and fucking. But"—and here Priya, who was being more serious than I was used to, fortified herself with some more beer—"grief's its own thing. He's probably feeling a lot of mixed stuff right now, especially because, from what you've said, his dad was a prick."

"You'd think," I said, "that would make it easier. I mean, not to blow my own trumpet, but I'm kind of an expert on dads who are pricks, and when Jon Fleming finally gets prostate cancer for real, I will give zero shits."

Priya clicked her tongue stud against her teeth. "Speaking as an artist, I don't think anyone gets to be an expert on emotions. Your thing with your dad is your thing with your dad. Oliver's thing with his dad is his thing with his dad, and they aren't going to work the same."

"Oh my God." I stared at her in horror. "When did you start getting nuance?"

"When I stopped being twenty-one. Pay attention." She smirked. "Besides, I'll have you know that the *Guardian* says I have a profound insight into the human condition."

"Doesn't the *Guardian* say that about everybody vaguely left-wing and artsy?" I pointed out.

To which her profound insight into the human condition enabled her to craft the eloquent rebuttal of "Fuck off."

It was about then that the buzzer buzzed again and Bridge staggered up in a flurry of bags and apologies. "I'm really, really sorry," she told us, unloading a bottle of £12.99 wine, another bar of Dairy Milk—there was a sort of unspoken code that comfort chocolate wasn't allowed to have any distracting flavours in it—a bunch of wilted supermarket flowers, and a box of Tesco Rocket Lollies. "Also, I panic shopped. And I would have been here sooner but I was in such a hurry to get here that I jumped on a train without checking which branch it was going down and didn't realise until I hit Bayswater." She tore open the box of rocket lollies, fished one out, and thrust it in my face. "These are great. Try one."

Knowing better than to spurn a rocket lolly offered in the spirit of friendship, I obediently peeled open the slightly sticky plastic wrap and began nibbling. The tip was strawberry flavoured, or rather it was that generic *red* flavour that coded as strawberry by default. There was something so childish about it—brightly coloured, mildly flavoured frozen water served from a slightly soggy box—that it was, in fact, weirdly comforting. It was very hard to have a serious crisis of relationship confidence while you were sucking on a rocket lolly.

"Now tell me everything," Bridge cried. "What happened? What about the wedding?"

Since I still had a face full of rocket lolly, Priya answered for me. "Nothing's happened. Oliver's just gone a bit weird on account of his dad dying, and Luc's freaking out because he can't cope with emotions."

Bridge's eyes were wide. "Oliver's gone weird? What kind of weird? And what about the wedding?"

"The kind of weird," Priya explained, "you go when your dad drops dead of a heart attack a few months after he found out you were marrying a guy you knew he didn't like, and also he was a cock but now he's dead and you're not allowed to think he's a cock anymore."

Bridge's eyes showed no signs of de-widening. "Does this mean the wedding's off?"

"Bridge"—I finally managed to extricate myself from the lolly—"we haven't discussed it." Technically we'd *been* discussing it, and that was part of the problem, but *we were having an argument* seemed such a petty thing compared to a bereavement. "The wedding's not a priority right now. Probably it'll be fine, but if Oliver decides he can't go through with it, I'll support him."

"But you're not meant to support him," Bridge insisted. "Not if he wants to call the wedding off. Then you're supposed to fight for him. You're meant to say, *No, I love you more than anything in the universe, and we're meant to be together forever.* And then he says, *You're right. I've been a fool, a mad, impetuous fool.*"

I divided my attention between a lolly in one hand and a beer in the other. And that was some duality-of-man shit right there. "Firstly, if there's one thing Oliver isn't, it's a mad, impetuous fool. Secondly, he'd never say 'mad, impetuous fool' because he'd be concerned it could be considered ableist. Thirdly, demanding

Oliver put marrying me above dealing with his father's death is a total dick move."

"Not if you really *are* meant to be together forever."

Priya looked up. "No, it's still a dick move. Partly because 'meant to be' is bollocks. And partly because if it wasn't bollocks and you *were* meant to be together forever, you'd be together forever whether you got married or not."

"I know." Bridge subsided sadly. "It's just Luc was going to get married and, well—"

"If he blows this," Priya put in, "he's fucked because no one else will have him."

I would have defended myself but, secretly, I kind of agreed. It wasn't that I was with Oliver because I thought there was no other option. It was just that imagining non-Oliver options made my heart vomit.

"That's not true," Bridge was yelling, "Luc's lovely."

"No he's not. He's a complete wanker."

"Well so are you"—I got back in the game—"and you've got two girlfriends."

Priya shrugged. "As established: cool job, brilliant at sex."

"I'm brilliant at sex," I insisted.

Her eyes met mine and called bullshit on them. "Are you, Luc? Are you really?"

I thought about it. I'd had a lot of sex and, honestly, it had been pretty contextual. In the sense of whether it was good or not had more to do with who, when, where, and how rather than technical prowess of either party. "Solid B+," I said.

"Yeah." Priya opened a second beer. "Figures."

CHAPTER 29

HALF AN HOUR LATER MY flat was looking worse, but I was feeling better. That's the thing about mess—a stack of unwashed dishes says *I hate myself and you should hate me too* but the pile of empty bottles next to a scattering of chocolate wrappers and ice-lolly boxes said *I hate myself but I have people in my life who remind me I shouldn't.*

"And we definitely think," I said, taking what remained of the wine from Bridge's hands and swigging direct from the bottle, "that this is an I'm-grieving situation, not an I'm-taking-the opportunity-to-bail-because-I'm-too-polite-to-dump-you situation."

Having finished the beer, Priya grabbed the wine from me and took a swig of her own. "I know Oliver's repressed, but I think even he would stop short of having his own father killed just to get out of a relationship."

"Maybe his father dying was a coincidence and he made the most of it?" I suggested.

"No," cried Bridge; she'd been crying things all evening. "You and Oliver are perfect for each other and you're perfect together and everything's going to be perfect."

"If we're so perfect," I asked, "why is he in Milton Keynes being sad without me?"

For a moment Bridge didn't have a reply. Then her face lit

up like a Christmas tree which, ironically, it also did anytime she looked at a Christmas tree. "I've got it."

"You're going to say, 'Go to Milton Keynes,' aren't you?" Priya's voice wasn't exactly scornful but had a quality that suggested scorn would be an option.

"Why not?" asked Bridge. "He's there and he's lonely and for whatever silly reason he feels like he can't reach out. His coeur is all cri-ing and he needs you, Luc, he *needs* you."

There was a part of me that wanted her to be right. For this—this thorny mess of grief and antagonism—to be fixable with one big gesture. "What if he *needs* space?"

"Well, which is worse?" Bridge turned her hands into wobbly scales. "If he needs you and you're not there? Or if you're there and he doesn't need you?"

"I think," I said slowly, "it wouldn't be so much *there and he doesn't need me* as *making his father's death all about my insecurities?*"

Priya shot me a sardonic look. "To be fair, you totally are."

"But"—I wagged a crucial point-making finger—"not to his face."

"Wow," said Priya. "You really have grown."

Reclaiming the wine bottle, Bridge leapt somewhat unsteadily to her feet. "I still think that we should go to Milton Keynes right now."

"And who's going to drive you?" asked Priya. "Because I'm quite drunk and also don't want to."

Bridge bounced undeterred. "We'll get an Uber."

"Oliver would hate that," I reminded her. "We'd be intruding on his private grief and the grief of his family who dislike me, while using the services of a company whose business practices he disapproves of."

Deflating slightly, Bridget lowered herself back onto the sofa.

"I want to say, it would be so romantic that it wouldn't matter but...it would matter, wouldn't it?"

"Yeah." I sighed. "It really would."

"Why is everything so complicated?" Bridge wondered piteously. "It wasn't like this when we were younger."

I gave her a drunken pat. "I think it was. I just think we didn't notice. Which"—I cast my mind back a decade—"might explain why we made so many terrible, terrible mistakes."

"Speak for yourself," said Priya. "I stand by every mistake I've ever made."

For a while we passed around the dregs of the wine and commiserated. We didn't have any real answers for each other—not about the Oliver situation or about the wedding situation or about the why-is-everything-so-hard-suddenly situation. But there was a comfort in knowing that, in the tiny space of my flat at least, we were all in the same boat. That we were all in an equally bemused state of making shit up as we went along and then throwing it at the wall to see if it stuck. Which was probably a mixed metaphor, but fuck it, I'd been drinking.

"So how *is* marriage?" I asked Bridge eventually, mostly because once we'd decided that we *weren't* doing a highly irresponsible overnight and over-the-legal-limit drive to Milton Keynes to save a relationship that might not even need saving, she'd started looking almost as down as I felt.

"Oh, it's wonderful," she said. She didn't have wonderful face. "But..."

For a while we waited for her to continue. When it became clear she wasn't, Priya asked, "Wonderful but what?"

"Perhaps she was just bragging that Tom has a wonderful butt?" I suggested in a vain attempt to lighten the mood. "Which to be fair, he does."

Bridge nodded, slightly less glum than ninety seconds ago.

"He does, and it is. I mean, married life, not Tom's arse. I mean, also Tom's arse. It's just…the wedding was so magical and the honeymoon was so *so* magical but then we got back and it was, well, carrying on as normal."

"Aren't you buying a house together?" I asked. "That's pretty fresh-starty."

"In theory, but I work full time and he works full time and the market is a mess and there are chains and things so we can't even put a deposit down until my little flat sells and we've had two buyers drop out already and…" She sighed. "It's so fiddly. Who decided that being happy forever with the person you love most in the universe had to be fiddly?"

Sometimes I thought Bridge's die-hard romanticism in the face of my self-obsession was a deliberate strategy to draw me out of myself, and most of the time it worked. "To be fair," I said, "when you put it that way, it actually sounds like a decent trade."

"Apart from the loving-somebody-more-than-anybody-else-in-the-world part," added Priya. "That bit can go fuck itself."

Bridget's eyes widened. "But what's the *point* if—"

Priya cut her off. "Bridge, I know you're just being sweet and enthusiastic, but you *do* remember I'm with two people right now, yeah? And I don't love either of them more than the other." She upended the wine, found it empty, and tossed it casually into one of my many tossing piles. "Or, for that matter, more than I love my mum or my dad or my sister."

"You've got a sister?" Bridge asked, surprised but weirdly happy. She didn't like other people's families quite as much as she liked other people's romantic partners, but it was a close-run thing.

"Yeah, you'd get on. She's really normal. Works in a bank. Anyway, the point is that I'd appreciate it if you toned down the nobody-can-be-happy-without-that-one-special-person thing just, like, *this much*"—Priya held her fingers so close together they were practically touching. "Because honestly I feel sort of judged."

The only thing in the world that made Bridge sadder than her friends being sad was the idea that she might have had a part in making her friends sad. With a wail of apology, she dropped the tail-end of the Dairy Milk she'd been picking on and threw her arms around Priya. "I'm so sorry. I'm stupid and thoughtless and a bad friend and a bad—"

"Okay, easy, tiger." Priya was giving Bridge the kind of friendly pat on the back that looked a bit like she was tapping out of a submission hold. "I'm a big girl and can look after myself. I just wanted you to be a smidge less…normative is all."

Still a little teary, but finally working out that she'd been aggressively hugging somebody who wasn't super keen on being hugged, Bridge pulled back. "And I suppose *really*," she said, "you're even luckier than Luc and me. Because you've found your special someone *twice*."

Priya leaned around Bridge and gave me a conspiratorial look. "I've made it worse, haven't I?"

"Probably."

Bridge settled back on the sofa. "Made what worse? I just—"

From the hallway, there came the sound of the door opening, and for about eighteen seconds we were convinced it was burglars. Eighteen seconds, it turned out, was exactly enough time for Bridge to take cover behind a chair, me to stand around gawping like one of those sharks with the big mouths, and Priya to vanish into the kitchen, only to return with the largest, sharpest knife I owned.

Three seconds later, it became clear that it wasn't burglars at all. For a start, we could hear them taking their shoes off and hanging up their coat, and it seemed very unlikely that a burglar would bother with those kinds of details. And to clinch it, we also heard a voice call out, "Lucien, are you home?"

Should we leave? mouthed Bridget, to which Priya mouthed back, *Yes, obviously,* while I was busy mouthing, *It's fine.*

"I meant to text on the way," Oliver was saying as he came closer, "but I-I suppose I forgot. I've been rather busy lately." There was still something off in his voice. But of course there was. Like he'd said, he'd been busy lately, and *my actual dad actually died* was one hell of an excuse for being a bit awkward for a couple of weeks.

The sitting room door opened, and the three of us did our best to give Oliver the impression we hadn't been having an intense conversation about what was wrong with him for the last several hours.

"Hi," waved Bridge and Priya, more or less in unison.

Oliver blinked. He looked exhausted. Properly used-up, nothing-left exhausted. "Hello. Lovely to see you. Why are you armed?"

Priya made an apologetic gesture with the carving knife. "Thought you were burglars."

"I suppose"—Oliver ran a hand distractedly through his hair—"this is the wrong time to talk about lethal force in defence of property."

She shrugged. "Up to you. I was sort of thinking you'd want Bridge and me to leave."

"You're welcome to stay," he said at once. I might have been projecting, but I thought exposure to his parents—well, parent now—always set him about three steps backwards on the can't-say-no scale.

"That's code for 'please leave,' isn't it?" observed Priya, passing me the carving knife.

"Not at all," Oliver lied.

"Well, I'm getting tired anyway," declared Bridge slightly too loudly to sound even remotely sincere. "So I should be going home. Good night, Luc." She hugged me, just about managing to let me put the knife down first. "Good night, Oliver." She hugged him, rather tighter and longer. "I was so sorry to hear about your father."

He hugged her back in a way I was trying not to read as *dead inside*. "Thank you, Bridget."

"If you need anything"—she gazed up at him earnestly—"or if Luc needs anything or you want to talk or not talk…"

"Thank you, Bridget," he said again.

"You have to reach out to people," she went on. "You can't lock everything up inside forever, or you'll end up like Luc."

I'd been in the process of returning the knife to the kitchen, but now I swung back. "Oi. I'm doing great these days and it only took me, like, five years."

"I'm not talking to you, Luc. I'm talking to Oliver." Bridge gave him one last squeeze. "We're here for you."

Priya swung her kit bag over her shoulder. "She's here for you. I don't know you that well so I think it would be weird."

"I appreciate it," said Oliver, still incapacitated with politeness.

Eventually, Priya dragged Bridge out the door, leaving me alone with the distant, emotionally distraught boyfriend I wasn't totally sure wanted to see me. And having spent a week wishing Oliver was here so I could do something, I found myself wishing I knew what that something actually was.

We stared at each other like every easy habit we'd built up over the last few years suddenly didn't count.

"Sorry"—Oliver cast a weary glance around my flat—"I think I interrupted…something."

I couldn't work out if telling him I'd had an I Was Sad Without You party would be reassuring or guilt-trippy. "We were just hanging out. I mean…" I gazed at him helplessly. "Like, how are you?"

He was silent for a couple of months. "I'm tired. And I… and I…"

"Do you hate me?" I blurted out. "Did I ruin your relationship with your father? Did we leave everything in a bad place? Are we broken now? And I'm making it all about me?"

"Honestly, you are making it *a little* all about you." I thought he was trying to smile, but I might have just been wanting him to really, really hard.

"Fuck. Shit. Sorry. Do I at least get self-awareness points for realising that?"

"That's making it *slightly more* all about you."

I cringed. "Sorry. I suck."

For the first time in what felt like forever, he almost laughed. "You don't suck, Lucien. I realise I've probably been...worrying recently. And I shouldn't have done that to you."

Oh God, his dad was dead and he was being reassuring. I did not deserve this man in any way. "No, no. You've got to...let yourself...take your time and feel your feels or whatever. And this must be so fucked up."

"Yes." There was something in his voice—something more *there* than when he'd come in. "I suspect I'm still working out quite how fucked up it is."

That had only half been what I meant. "And, well, having a massive fight before you went couldn't have helped."

"It wasn't ideal." He'd stopped smiling, but it didn't seem like he was going to dump me on the spot, which was the closest thing to a win I felt I could reasonably expect.

"I hope," I tried, "it wasn't in your head too much. Like, I know we got kind of heated and it might have felt like I don't... like I'm not...like I'm not on your side. But I am. And I'm totally here for you and stuff, even if we're fighting. You do...you do know that, right?"

For a moment, Oliver looked like he was wrestling with something, but at last he said, "I sometimes let myself forget but, in general, I do."

It wasn't a ringing endorsement, but there was a mild tinkle to it.

"I think," he went on, "we both said some things that we shouldn't have, but perhaps they needed saying anyway."

I couldn't tell if that was ominous or comforting. "Needed saying?"

He gave a sad little shrug. "This may be just another habit of mind I've inherited from my parents, but I tend to believe that the things which feel worst are the things which feel truest. That doesn't mean they always *are*. But...I've been thinking about what you said and..."

"And?" I tried not to sound too hopeful.

"And"—his face got all blank and exhausted again—"I don't have any answers."

"That's okay," I said quickly.

"I confess, it bothers me somewhat. But I'm also aware that now is not the best time for me to be interrogating my values for authenticity. I should probably bury my father first."

I felt beyond bad for him. I mean, we'd had an argument over something that, in retrospect, was completely fucking trivial. So what if I liked rainbows and balloons and he liked podcasts and hanging out with straight people? All that mattered was that we loved each other and his dad was dead, and here was Oliver still steadfastly trying to become a better person because of some bullshit I'd yelled at him a week ago. I gave a kind of can-we-hug-now flail. "I'm really glad you came back."

"I wasn't going to live at my mother's."

"I meant *emotionally*, you doink."

Crossing the room, he pulled me into his arms and we hugged for an embarrassingly long time. "I missed you," he whispered.

"I missed you too," I whispered back. "And I'm so sorry things are shit for you."

He pressed his face against my neck. "I-I can't think about it anymore. At least not right now."

"You don't have to," I told him. "We can do...whatever."

"Would it"—his voice wavered—"resurrect your belief that I'm the most boring man in the universe if I said I wanted to go to bed?"

"Well, I had got us tickets to Alton Towers, but I can move them to another day."

This time he did laugh, although it had an edge of *my dad's still dead* to it. So I took his hand and led him through the bedroom.

"Also," I added. "The advantage of me practically living at your place is that my sheets have barely been slept in."

He shrugged off his jacket and flopped otherwise fully clothed onto the bed. "At the moment, Lucien, all I care about is being with you."

Which was convenient because, while there weren't many things I was confident I could do well, being me was one of them.

I think if I'd let him, Oliver would have passed out where he'd fallen. But because I knew from experience that waking up in your clothes from the night before felt awful, I half coaxed, half bullied him undressed. Then I slid into bed beside him and pulled the duvet over us both.

We lay there for a little while, with me desperately trying to think of something consoling to say that wasn't just...shit. Like *It'll be okay* or *Everything happens for a reason* or *He was a cock anyway*. So, finally, I went with "I love you," because it was true and safe and wouldn't make him think about the thing he didn't want to think about. He murmured my name and pressed in close, his face a sharp-angled shadow in the darkness of the room.

Yeah. Definitely not a words situation.

Carefully I pushed back the tousled waves of his hair, letting my fingers move in long strokes through the strands. He gave another little murmur, half-sad, half-soothed, and tilted his head towards me on the pillow.

Very gently, I kissed him. Not a hello-you kiss or a do-me-now kiss. But the sort of kiss that speaks for you. A kiss to draw us together. To show I was there. To promise I always would be, if he'd let me.

And afterwards, Oliver settled into my arms as if he belonged there, and we stayed that way until morning.

CHAPTER 30

IF THERE WAS EVER EVIDENCE that Oliver was in a bad way, it was that not only was he still asleep when I woke up, but he was still asleep when I got bored of lying in bed—which I thought was basically impossible. Easing myself out from under the duvet as quietly as I could so I wouldn't disturb him, I surreptitiously dressed and sort of, somehow, found myself standing there, looking at him. Like that bit in a country song where the singer is all "Honey, I love you, but something inside me means I gotta go and do a man thing and I hope when I come back you and little Ellie May will be waiting for me." And then I'd die in the second-to-last verse and the last verse would be me going, "Dagnabbit, why did I have to do a man thing instead of staying at home with my wife and little Ellie May."

"Are you staring at me, Lucien?" asked Oliver drowsily. "Are you watching me sleep?"

Oh, fuck. "Only technically. I was mostly thinking, 'Gosh, I wish I could do something to make Oliver feel better.' And you just happened to be in my line of sight. And you just happened to be asleep."

Oliver shifted the pillows into a more ergonomic position. "I don't think there's anything you can do, but thank you for offering."

"I'll...I'll leave you to not be stared at."

He made a vaguely grateful noise and rolled over, and I slipped out, closing the door behind me. Which meant instead of standing by the bed not really knowing what to do with myself, I was standing in my flat not really knowing what to do with myself. So, in the absence of a big green button labelled *Press here to fix boyfriend*, I cleaned.

It didn't bring me quite the same sense of virtuous peace that it brought Oliver, but it was nice to know that when he woke up, he would be in a space that resembled a human dwelling, and not a combination laundry basket/litter bin.

When I was done, he still wasn't up, partly because the job was a lot smaller than it had been last time I'd attempted a major flat tidy and partly because see above re: bad way. It was, however, getting to the point that I thought he might want to eat something, but looking in my fridge, I found there was nothing in it that wasn't six months past its use-by date, an animal product, or in an embarrassingly large number of cases, both.

There was a jar of gherkins—because fridges spontaneously generate gherkins even when nobody buys them—except I didn't think materialising at Oliver's bedside saying, *Hello, darling, I know your father's died and you're having a lot of complicated emotions, but I've brought you a wally* was quite the supportive and/or romantic gesture he needed quite then.

Then I had a genius idea. I would make him French toast. To show that this was a relationship where there was, like, space for each of us to be the French toaster or the French toastee. Then I remembered that there were two tiny flaws in that plan: the first being that I was a godawful cook, and the second being that the main ingredients of French toast were milk and eggs.

But you know what? Fuck it. It was the thought that counted, and there were vegan versions of everything these days. Leaving Oliver a note saying, *Gone shopping, have not run away to be cowboy, back soon*, I headed out into the crisp November noon.

The recipe I'd hastily Googled while heading downstairs to the street required chia seeds, agave nectar, and almond milk, and I had no idea where I'd get any of those. Fortunately, I lived in one of those bits of London where you couldn't walk twenty paces without tripping over a wholefood store or an artisanal cheese stand so I was pretty confident I'd be able to source them without too much trouble. Besides, they sold half this stuff in Tesco. Part of me was a bit concerned that almond milk was supposed to be an ethical no-no, although I couldn't remember why or if I was getting it mixed up with palm oil, but I decided that from Oliver's perspective at least it was preferable to cow.

In the end the ingredient I had most trouble with was "sturdy bread" because I had no idea what that meant and didn't want my French toast to fall apart in the pan. But for some reason when you went up to somebody in a shop and said, "How sturdy is your bread?" they thought you were taking the piss. The internet told me I should be using brioche, but it also told me that brioche wasn't vegan unless you got a specific brand, and that brand only made burger buns. In the end I went for sourdough on the grounds that if a bread that you could use to subdue an intruder in an emergency wasn't "sturdy" enough, nothing was.

Back at the flat, I took the extremely sensible and grown-up precaution of opening all the windows and taking the batteries out of the smoke alarm. And then I got to it. To my joy, the first step of the recipe was basically "stick everything except the bread in a bowl and stick the bowl in the fridge," and I could definitely do that. I mean, yes, I probably put in too much cinnamon because I dropped the spoon, but then cinnamon was one of those ingredients you could never have too much of. Like, y'know, ginger or garlic. Oh God, I'd inherited my mum's cooking genes, hadn't I?

As if this realisation wasn't terrifying enough, it belatedly occurred to me that while getting a nice expensive bread was cool, it meant that it wasn't sliced. And the phrase "the best thing since sliced bread" was a cliché for a reason. In the end I wound up cutting the loaf into roughly a dozen irregularly shaped chunks, none of which could in all honesty be called "slices." There was the end piece, which had the approximate dimensions of a butt plug. Then the next piece was as thick as my thumb at the top and thinner than my bread knife at the bottom. Then there were two bits that were mostly crumbs; one halfway decent slice that somehow got fat in the middle and thin at each end; and the rest was a mixture of wedges, triangles, and lumps that I hoped, perhaps naively, would hold up fine in the pan.

When the requisite fridge-leaving time had passed, I fished out my batter and began soaking my bread. The recipe suggested that twenty to thirty seconds a side would be fine, but I gave it a bit longer because I wanted to be sure. Some of the thinner slices, or the thinner bits of the thicker slices, fell apart almost at once, but I figured I still had enough for an okay breakfast.

One by one, I transferred the slices of vanilla-and-cinnamon-infused bread to the pan and, as instructed, gave them three to four minutes on each side until golden brown. Or, more realistically, until ghost-white in some places and charred almost black in others. In the end I threw two pieces away, ate one myself to make certain I wasn't feeding Oliver something actively poisonous, and piled the rest as attractively as I could on a plate.

It was at about this point that I realised I'd forgotten to buy any toppings, so I grabbed some more of the agave nectar and gave it an artful drizzle. Okay, not artful exactly but presentable. Then, waving my way through the billows of smoke that I'd *mostly* managed to confine to the kitchen area and hoping I didn't smell too badly of charred almond milk, I went through to surprise Oliver with breakfast in bed.

He was where I'd left him, in a crumple of duvet, dozing a kind of doze I recognised: the doze of somebody who didn't really want to be conscious but whose body was all unconsciousnessed out.

"I made French toast," I told him plaintively.

He blinked in a disorientated way. "You did what?"

"Made French toast?" For some reason, it came out like an apology.

"Lucien, that's very sweet of you but you realise it's not vegan."

"Obviously I realised it's not vegan. It's full of cow juice and chicken boxes. But I used substitutes. Because I'm amazing and you're lucky to have me."

"You are and I am, but"—he cast his bleary eyes over my quite literally burnt offering—"that looks ambiguous."

I perched myself on the edge of the bed. "Well, you have to eat. But I understand if you don't want to eat this."

Pushing himself into a sitting position, he selected the least awful piece of French toast and ate it valiantly. "Actually, out of everything you've made me, this is one of the least dreadful. Some bits of it are even quite nice."

I'd take that. "There's also coffee," I said. "Which I've definitely not fucked up."

And for a while we sat in silence, sharing my okay French toast and my genuinely decent coffee. Oliver was looking slightly better than he had last night, which meant he was looking kind of like the zombie version of himself, instead of the ghost version. He was propped against an artful construction of pillows, the duvet drawn to midchest height, picking at his late breakfast/early lunch with visibly increasing energy. At some point in the near future, he might even be standing upright.

"Soooo…" As ways to begin a conversation went, a long *so* was up there with *Hi, have you considered changing your broadband provider?* "Do you want to...talk? Or not talk? Or go for a walk? Or stay in bed? Or have me go away? Or—"

"At the moment, I think I'd mostly like you to stop listing things."

I took a deep breath. "Sorry. How are you?"

"Not so great. My dad died."

Okay, so that was either a good sign because he had the strength to be sarcastic. Or a bad sign because that's the answer I would have given and I was a dick. "Stop channelling me, and be serious. You don't have to confide in me, but this was a big deal and I'm worried about you."

"I'm sorry to worry you, Lucien. And I will be... I'll be... Everything will be fine."

"I know that," I told him. "But it's obviously not fine right now. And I know you don't like feeling..." I tried to express very gently through mime *that you aren't living up to the unrealistic expectations foisted on you by your parents, one of whom is now dead.* "But I love you even when you're..." I'd run out of gentle mimes. "Crap."

He laughed. "Wonderful pep talk, Lucien. Have you considered volunteering as a bereavement counsellor?"

"I just mean it's safe to be crap with me. Like I let myself be crap with you literally all the time."

"You know that's not true." He fixed me with a gaze that seemed to be saying about twelve different things at once. "Some of that French toast was really quite edible. Besides, I'm not with you for your cooking or your ability to wash up, I'm with you because you make me feel better than anyone ever has. And I often wish I could be more like you."

"Well"—flustered by his sincerity, I poked him in the duvet lump where I thought his knee was—"I don't want you to be anyone except yourself. And..." Finally my brain and heart and neuroses caught up with each other. "If that means you need to deal with this on your own, then I get it and I'll be here."

With very Oliverian fastidiousness, he set the plate neatly on the bedside table. "The truth is, I don't think I'm dealing with it very well."

"I'm not sure it's the kind of thing you can deal with well? I think people just feel what they feel and stumble through it?"

"Yes but"—his eyes darkened to a miserable slate—"I think what I'm mostly feeling is angry."

"That seems pretty normal?" I offered.

"I'm sure it is. It is not, however, a helpful state to be in when one's arranging a funeral and trying to be there for one's mother."

"Where's Christopher? Can't he help?"

"Christopher," said Oliver, with an edge of frustration, "is in Afghanistan. He'll be back for the funeral but not before. And I'm trying very hard not to resent him, but at the moment this feels very typical."

I hoiked my feet onto the bed and crossed my legs. "Tell you what. How about we draw a circle around this room and say that in here you can be as bitter, resentful, and straight-up mean as you like. It won't hurt anyone, and no one will find out, and I won't think any less of you because I couldn't—and also because I'm a horrible person anyway."

Oliver didn't say anything for so long I thought even the mystical power of the circle of venting couldn't overcome his fundamental need to give people the benefit of the doubt. Then he sucked in a breath like he was surfacing in the hundred-meter butterfly. "I realise what Christopher does is very important and helps a lot of people, but it's incredibly fucking convenient that it means he's never around whenever anything needs doing. And I'd say if I didn't know better, I'd think he'd chosen his career specifically to keep a thousand miles between him and his family as much and as often as possible. But I can't say that because I don't know better because it's fucking true. He's done this his whole life—from holidays with his friends when he was sixteen to his gap year to studying in Edinburgh to his year abroad to Médecins Sans Fucking Frontières. If they gave a medal to the most selfish altruistic person in the world, Christopher would win it and then not show up at the ceremony."

I think it was air more than complaints that Oliver had run out of. The Christopher Sucks speech had actually left him a little flushed. And I did feel sort of bad for Christopher because, while everything Oliver had said was probably accurate, given the Blackwoods, I'd have signed up with MSF as well. And from what Mia had told me the one time we'd met, they got their own flavour of shit from Oliver's parents.

"Oh God." Oliver pressed his forehead to his knees. "I'm a terrible person."

I moved closer and put a hand on his back. "Okay, I should have made the rules of the Hate Room clearer. Nobody is allowed to judge you here, including *you*."

Oliver's shoulders heaved, and he made a sound like he wanted to cry but couldn't. "It's just too much. He's spent his whole life running away and I've spent my whole life dealing with the things he's running away from, and it's never been good enough, and it'll never be good enough, and now it can't ever be good enough because our father is dead."

For a moment, I just stroked him in what I hoped was a comforting way. "Listen," I said finally. "You know how I said this was a no-judgment zone? Well, I'm going to say some really naff things now, and I need you not to tell anybody or laugh at me."

He turned his face slightly towards me. "I shall make a sincere attempt, but it depends how naff they are."

"Right," I naffed. "I know your parents brought you up a certain way, but you can't—oh, for fuck's sake—live your life trying to be good enough for other people. You have to be good enough for yourself. Although, for the record, you're definitely good enough for me."

"Lucien, Lucien, Lucien." I couldn't tell if he meant it as affection or admonition. "That was exceptionally naff."

I rolled my eyes at him in mock rebuke. "Sometimes true things are naff and naff things are true. It's one of the many ways in which reality is bobbins."

There was a tiny pause. "And," he said, "and…you're sure this is…okay?"

"What's okay?"

"Saying these things. I'm not just convincing you that you're about to marry a whiny prick?"

"You're not being a whiny prick." I went back to my hopefully comforting stroking. "This shit is clearly messing with you. It would mess with anyone."

He gave a hollow laugh. "It would mess with anyone in similar circumstances. But I'm deeply aware 'Oh woe is me, my affluent parents whose cultural and literal capital gave me significant unearned advantages that most people can never access and which I largely took for granted were sometimes a bit emotionally unsupportive' isn't exactly the stuff of tragedy."

I was starting to feel like I'd misplayed noughts and crosses and now Oliver had the centre and two corners and wherever I went next, he was going to win. "Oliver. I understand this is complicated, but you're forcing me to either be naff again or shit on your dead father, and I don't want to do either."

"It's the room of hate, remember." Oliver made a small encircling gesture. "So you can do both."

"Okay, fine. Naff thing: Your pain matters, even if other people have it worse. Shitting-on-your-dead-father thing: Your parents were more than just sometimes a bit emotionally unsupportive.

They're total fuckers who made you feel inadequate your whole life. *And* they're kind of homophobic."

"Well," said Oliver, "at least I only have one of them to deal with now."

My eyes went wide. "Wow, really taking advantage of the safe room, aren't you?"

"As you may have noticed, Lucien"—something like a smile touched his lips—"I seldom do things by halves. Besides, my mother's currently being difficult enough for the both of them."

Curling closer, I waited for Oliver to unleash himself.

"Obviously I sympathise. And it's natural that she's taking Dad's death quite…hard. But as well as expecting me to organise everything, she also seems to blame me for everything. Up to and including the crematorium being busy, Christopher not being in the country, and—of course—the small matter of my father's death. Which"—he scowled into the middle distance—"she hasn't said outright was directly caused by my standing up to him. But she has implied it several times."

I made a nervous squeaky noise. "Um. You know she's, like, wrong, right?"

The pause that followed was longer than I would have preferred. "I do, actually. Although, I can't lie, it's difficult when the last words you said to someone before they passed away were 'Go fuck yourself.'"

That hung there for a little bit, like neither of us knew what to do with it.

"I'm so sorry," I said finally, falling into cliché and platitude.

"Don't be." Oliver shrugged. "While, of course, I regret that we didn't have any kind of reconciliation before…before he… well…before that became impossible, what I mostly regret is that I didn't say it years ago."

That also hung there for a little bit.

"Too much?" he asked.

I shook my head. "Not even close. I mean, I'm just glad you're not feeling guilty."

"Oh, I'm feeling guilty as well. But I'm rather hoping that will pass."

There was ring of finality in his voice. And I suppose that was all you could do with grief: stick it out until you got used to it.

Oliver squared his shoulders in a stiff-upper-lippy, pull-yourself-togethery sort of way. "In any case," he went on, "given how brilliantly our wedding planning is going, I don't suppose you'd also like to help me organise a funeral?"

CHAPTER 31

"DAVID BLACKWOOD," SAID OLIVER, "WAS a loving husband, a devoted father, and an absolute demon on the golf course.
We all remember him as a fair and generous man, even if he didn't
always suffer fools gladly. I remember when I was, perhaps, four-
teen we went to this restaurant somewhere in Berkshire, and the
menu was all in French and"—he adopted a posture of studied
relaxation—"well, anybody who knew my father would know
that languages were *not* his strong point. So when he ordered what
he thought was a fillet steak and the waiter brought him fish, the
poor fellow got quite the earful. Of course, the manager was very
apologetic, and I seem to recall we actually got a free bottle of
wine by way of apology. I remember quite distinctly when we got
home and I looked it up and discovered that *filet de flétan* did
indeed mean *halibut fillet*, he looked me squarely in the eye and
said: *Well, it just goes to show, Oliver. It always pays to stand up
for yourself.*

"And that was...that was a lesson he always tried to pass on
to both of his sons. And that's"—a pause, and I couldn't quite
tell whether he was really choking up or doing a very good job
of faking—"that's how I'll always remember him. How I think
he'd always want to *be* remembered. As a force of nature. A man
who fought for what he believed in, who demanded respect and

always received it. Even if it sometimes came at the expense of an otherwise blameless flatfish." And here there was another of those appropriate laughter pauses. "He was a provider, a caregiver, and a role model, and I can truly say that neither I nor Christopher would be the men we are today without his guidance. And on the subject of Christopher, I shall now surrender the lectern to my brother, who will read David's favourite poem, 'If.'"

There was a pause. "Well?" Oliver stared at me. "What do you think?"

"Fine?" I wasn't sure what else to say.

Oliver frowned. Then started pacing around my flat. He'd done quite a lot of pacing over the past week. "Fine? It's my father's eulogy. It can't just be fine."

"I mean," I tried, "maybe you could tell a different story? That one makes your dad sound like a bit of a cock."

"Not to the people who'll be at the funeral." Oliver slumped in a way that was almost a sigh. "He used to tell it himself all the time. And if I left it out, Uncle Jim would be bound to come up to me afterwards and demand to know why I didn't tell the halibut story."

I tucked my feet under me on the sofa. "Oliver, you don't have to do this."

"I absolutely do. A funeral isn't like a wedding. You can't just say, *Sorry, got cold feet, enjoy the party.*"

"The eulogy, Oliver. There's no reason you have to speak. There's the vicar, there's Uncle Jim, there's Christopher. You dad isn't going away unmemoralised."

"And you don't think"—Oliver was frowning into the middle distance—"if the vicar, Christopher, and Uncle Jim all say something and I pointedly don't that won't seem deeply personal?"

"People will just assume you're too upset." I tried to catch his eye. "If anything, it'll read as a loving tribute."

"My mother would never forgive me, even if she believed me. And Christopher would never believe me, even if he forgave me."

This funeral stuff was hard. Not the logistics. They were pretty straightforward, I guess because it wasn't supposed to be the happiest day of anyone's life. But playing this constant game of emotional politics—where I wanted to support Oliver and Oliver wanted to support his family and Oliver's family wanted him to stand up and lie his arse off about what a great guy David Blackwood had been—was exhausting. Especially because I always felt I was losing. "Okay," I said. "But you're allowed to think about yourself as well."

"It's a three-minute speech." At this point, I wasn't sure if he was trying to convince me or convince himself. "That's three minutes out of my entire life."

I sat on my hands to stop myself from getting all frustrated and gesticulatey. "That's not how negative experiences work. And you're a lawyer. You don't need me to tell you that."

"Your point is well made, but this isn't a trauma, it's an inconvenience. I'm going to say some things I don't entirely mean—although to give myself credit, I don't think anything in the speech is strictly untrue..."

"Yeah," I couldn't help interrupting, "you got a lot of mileage out of 'wouldn't be the men we are today.'"

Oliver gave a sassy little nod. "Thank you. I'm glad you noticed. But nevertheless, all I have to do is to stand up and pretend for a very short period of time that my relationship with my father was less complicated than it actually was. That's what everybody has done at every funeral that has ever happened."

I stared at him in his black suit and his black tie. He'd got that faintly hollowed-out look he got when he'd been at the gym more than was probably psychologically healthy for him. "But don't they also say that funerals are, you know, for the living? And you're...the living."

"Yes"—he nodded—"and so is everyone else."

"Yeah, but there's, like, a..." I pulled my hands out from under my arse and did the balancing scales mime. "Like, you're doing something that hurts you a lot that might help other people a little bit, and that's like giving blood but giving all of your blood. And, yeah, you might save two people's lives but you'd be dead. And if you give a little bit of your blood..." I suddenly realised I'd run up against an analogy that, for most of our lives, neither of us had access to "...whenever you're allowed to—"

"So," said Oliver, "in my case not at all until the guidelines changed?"

"Okay, leaving aside homophobic medical policies and my failure to rhetoric properly, tell me honestly and tell yourself honestly how doing this speech will make you feel."

There was a long silence. Then Oliver came and sat next to me. "Frankly, Lucien, it will make me feel miserable. I'm still very much working through what my relationship with my father was or meant, and so putting it into a neat little box and tying that box with a neat little bow and attaching a neat little label that says 'Beloved husband, devoted father' is..." He broke off and then finished in a resentful rush. "Fucking with my head."

"It would," I told him. "It's a heady-fucky thing to have to do. Which is why I'm telling you, one last time, if you want to nope out, you can."

"But—"

"No buts." I produced the assertive finger and waved it in the air. "Blah blah family blah blah expectation. Even with all that, if this is bad for you, that's the most important thing."

Oliver heaved a sigh packed with so many different emotions that if I'd wanted to, I could have sorted them alphabetically, starting with *angry* and ending with *woeful.* "I'm sorry, Lucien. I wish I could be that brave or that selfish but, ironically, it's not how I was raised. And I'm working on that, but my father was inconsiderate enough to die in the middle of the process rather than at the end of it. So here I am, doing what is expected of me, because right here and now right, I cannot imagine doing anything else."

"And," I said, squeezing his hand tightly, "I support you a hundred percent." I didn't say, *even if you don't support yourself* because that wasn't what he needed to hear. Besides, coming from me, it would have been kind of hypocritical.

"If you supported me a hundred percent"—Oliver's lips twitched—"you wouldn't be wearing the same suit to my father's funeral that you wore to your coworker's wedding."

I did, in fact, have exactly one suit, not counting the blue one I'd rented for Bridge's blue-and-rose-gold marital extravaganza. "It's a multipurpose item. It's both frugal and ethical." Standing, I gave Oliver my most morally superior face. "Do you know how many litres of drinkable water go into producing a pair of formal trousers?"

"No," said Oliver, looking—as I should have predicted— genuinely curious. "How many?"

"Well, I don't know either. But I bet it's a lot." And that was about as far as my cheer-up-Oliver routine could run because if we didn't leave soon, we'd be late.

Or at least not early enough to satisfy the ghost of David Blackwood.

———————

Even if I said so myself, we'd done a good job organisation-wise. Maybe because it had been clear from the outset how many rainbow balloon arches there should be, i.e. zero. Weirdly enough, this was actually going to be my first funeral. My dad's parents hadn't been in the picture, which was fitting since neither was he; my mum's dad likewise; and my mum's mum was still very much alive in the south of France, preserved into her nineties by a diet of olive oil and red wine. In some ways, given how few shits I gave about David Blackwood, it was the least traumatic first funeral I could have been to. Apart from the tiny, tiny detail that there was a good chance it would utterly destroy my boyfriend's mental health.

It was one of those sullen wintery days where it felt like the sky was scowling, too pissed off to even do the decent thing and rain. Various mourners were milling around the gardens and outside the main building, looking like mildly irritable shadow puppets. That was the thing about funerals: you were either distraught because the deceased was someone you were incredibly close to, or you were bored and awkward because they weren't but some indirect tie of blood or friendship meant you were obligated to be there.

Also, crematoria were fucking weird. They were basically a quite nice garden outside a factory for disposing of corpses, with a friendly nondenominational chapel bolted onto the front. And to give them credit, they went to a lot of trouble to disguise the whole corpse-disposal aspect of their business, but the honking great industrial chimney was a giveaway that my eyes kept drifting back to. The other eerily industrial thing about the crematorium experience was that—and I don't mean this in a disrespectful way—they didn't half pack them in. Which meant there was a five-minute window between the last service ending and ours beginning. So while Oliver went inside to, I don't know, greet the vicar, hug his mum, have his shirt criticised for old time's sake, I was left trying to herd a bunch of people who didn't know who I was, or have reason to listen to me, into a building they didn't want to be in for a very tight turnaround.

I didn't think I made any friends, but it would have been weird if I had. And, after a little while, Mia was there to help because this was apparently the partner's job. Or maybe she just wanted to get away from the rest of her husband's family.

On the whole, I was proud that we managed to get everyone in and ourselves into our embarrassingly front-row seats bang on the dot of eleven. One of the artfully reassuring people who worked at the crematorium closed the doors behind us and then... Well. That was showtime.

There was something about the chapel itself that I found oddly calming, probably because it had been designed to oddly calm people. The chairs were relatively comfortable and upholstered in a neutral shade of blue, and everything around us was soothing pine and soft uplighting, making it almost possible to ignore the little curtained door with the coffin in front of it.

Much like a wedding, the vicar kicked us off, although out of deference to the Blackwoods' fairly common brand of C of E secularism, he'd agreed to keep the God stuff to a minimum and focus instead on remembering the life of David Blackwood. Which mostly meant his work, his family, golf, and tireless support of the local Conservative party.

My brain really wanted to maintain a running commentary as a kind of defence mechanism, but given I was sitting one space away from Miriam, who was crying softly and, I thought, sincerely, I wasn't quite that much of a prick.

Beside me, Oliver was growing increasingly tense, his hands white-knuckled against his knees.

"You still don't have to do this," I whispered. "Just tell the vicar you're too upset. He must get that all the time."

Oliver bent his head close to mine. "I–I can't."

"And now," said the vicar in what I'm sure must have been his trained funeral voice, "we hand over to David's eldest son, Oliver, who's going to say a few words."

I made a weird grab for Oliver's hand, like he'd just slipped over a cliff and it was my last chance to catch him. But since this was a funeral, and therefore the force pulling him forward was social convention and not gravity, it didn't.

Taking the vicar's place at the lectern, Oliver took a stack of cue cards from his inside pocket and cleared his throat.

I tried to shoot I-love-you-and-I'm-here-for-you lasers out of my eyes, already terrified of how much this was going to hurt him.

The silence somehow got deeper as it lengthened.

The vicar patted him reassuringly on the arm.

Then Oliver straightened his spine, fixed his gaze squarely at the back of the room, and began to speak.

CHAPTER 32

"DAVID BLACKWOOD," SAID OLIVER, "WAS a loving husband, a devoted father, and an absolute demon on the golf course. We all remember him as...as...."

He looked down at his cards.

"David Blackwood," said Oliver, "was a loving husband, a devoted father, and..."

He looked down again. Then he looked up. And his eyes moved over the crowd, pausing just for a second on me before he fixed his attention back on a neutral point.

"David Blackwood," he said, "was a complicated man, and the last words I said to him were 'go fuck yourself.'"

The nice thing about Oliver's family being incredibly British and middle class was that nobody had any way to react to that, so everyone stayed very still and very silent.

"I wish they had not been," Oliver went on, "and I suppose that might seem obvious. After all, who wants their last words to their father to be 'go fuck yourself'? But I think what's not so obvious is that while I'm sorry he's dead... I hope no one here would think that I'm not sorry he's dead. I'm a vegan criminal defence lawyer, for fuck's sake, neither of which my father approved of, incidentally, but in general I don't believe death ever solves anything. Another thing my father disapproved of... He was a proponent of bringing back hanging, which he apparently thought would fix knife crime; the economy; and, if I recall from at least one conversation, immigration.

"But my point is that although I'm sorry he's dead—and this might be the part that surprises people, and Mother, in particular, I'm sorry if this surprises you—I'm inordinately glad I told him to go fuck himself. As I say, David Blackwood was a complicated man. And, indeed, one of the questions I find myself asking now is whether he, too, had he survived, would have been glad I told him to go fuck himself.

"I believe that if he lived by the principles he espoused, he would. After all, as well as hanging, he was also a great proponent of speaking your mind—when he did it, that is, not so much when other people did. And standing your ground—again, primarily his ground, not necessarily anybody else's. But I hope that the double standard he applied to those virtues when it came to his employees, my schoolteachers, tradesman, waiters, most of his friends, and his sons' various romantic partners might, at least, not apply to his own children. I like to imagine that maybe, one day, after perhaps a year or two had passed, he'd have shaken my hand and said, 'You know what, Oliver, I had that coming.'

"Because I'm afraid from my perspective he did, indeed, have it coming.

"And again I don't want to... I don't want anyone to think that I hated my father. Or that I wanted anything bad to happen to him. When I say he was a complicated man, I mean it. He wasn't good or bad, he wasn't always right or always wrong—although he would personally have disagreed with you on that score—and I should also say that all I can really talk about now is the David Blackwood I knew, who won't be the David Blackwood my mother knew or Uncle Jim knew. He's probably fairly similar to the David Blackwood that Christopher knew, but he won't be exactly the same.

"That's the thing about people. I suppose...I suppose in a way we're all complicated men, or women, or nonbinary people. And, thinking about it, if there's one thing I've done today that would really, truly offend David Blackwood, it's bothering to acknowledge that nonbinary people exist at his funeral. 'Why do you have to be so bloody politically correct, Oliver,' he might have said. 'What about women's bathrooms?'

"Where was I? My original draft of this speech opened with, as you might recall, 'David Blackwood was a loving husband, a devoted husband, and a demon on the golf course,' and all of those things were true. Well, except the thing about golf. He was actually quite bad at it. And so when I say he had it coming, with reference to—in case you've forgotten—my telling him to go fuck himself, I don't think I really mean that. At least, not as it came out. I think what I mean was he needed to hear it and I needed to say it. Because my father provided for me and cared for me and supported me, but he also undermined me, made constant jokes about my sexuality while also being incredibly offended by any suggestion he might be even a little bit homophobic, and wielded his disapproval like—I'm sorry, normally when I'm speaking for work, I'm rather better prepared so I don't have a good simile to hand. But I spent my entire life repulsed by his beliefs, terrified of his scorn, and desperate for him to think well of me.

"Although, strangely—or perhaps not, I can't tell—I never once doubted that he loved us. I think that's what made it so very difficult. Because everything he did, everything he said, every belittling remark about my career, every snide joke about anal sex— and I'm terribly sorry, I've now just said *anal sex* at my father's funeral; I suppose there's no coming back from that, really, is there—all of it came from a place that felt to him like affection.

And because he was proud and stubborn, and those are qualities I recognise in myself and value in myself and in some ways have to thank him for, it would never have occurred to him—could never have occurred to him—that if he'd just listen...for once just listen to a voice that wasn't his own...he'd see that...

"And that's where I run out of words. Because I'm not sure what it was I wanted him to see, not really. I suppose I wanted him to see that he was a complicated man. And that I, too, was a complicated man. That Christopher and I were both complicated men. That being me wasn't just a failure state of being him.

"Of course, maybe he knew all that already. Maybe I just didn't know that he knew it. And he didn't know that I didn't know so we just missed each other for thirty years. Or maybe he just didn't give a fuck. Maybe he went to his grave genuinely disappointed that his eldest son was a fairy.

"The thing is, I have no way of telling. And I suppose that's why I say he had it coming. I suppose what I really mean is *we* had it coming. That we would at some point in our lives have to reconcile ourselves either to gradually and politely becoming strangers, or to me telling him to go fuck himself. Because I'd hoped that—and I'll never know if I was right, and perhaps I'm just projecting this retrospectively onto something I said in the heat of the moment—that there was no looking away from a go-fuck-yourself. David Blackwood was a complicated man, and he was the kind of man who only ever heard what he wanted to hear. But a loud, clear go-fuck-yourself...I thought that would get through to him. Or, if it didn't, then at least I would know.

"Anyone who knew David—that's the kind of thing you say at a funeral isn't it, 'anyone who knew David'—anyone who knew him would know that he was a man of statements. In his world, things were as they were and there was no interrogating that or changing it or denying it. I suppose that explains why he was so threatened by the idea of nonbinary people, even though he never met one. He believed what he believed and, like Thomas Jefferson, he considered those beliefs to be self-evident truths. He was a complicated man, but he was, at heart, a man of certainties.

"Which is why it's so strange to me, strange and more than a little painful, that here, at the end, he has left, for me at least, only questions. Had he not, in his typically contrarian fashion, collapsed of a heart attack a few short weeks after I'd finally taken his advice—advice, Uncle Jim, you will be pleased that I remembered well from the halibut story—and stood up for myself, I might have known if we could perhaps…if he would have…

"But I won't. I'll never know.

"And that's what death is really, isn't it? A lot of things you'll never know.

"Although, the truth is, I can't help but feel that if I'd just told my father to go fuck himself ten years ago, we might have been in a much better place today. And I might have been able to stand here and join all of you in pretending my father was simple. Even though he wasn't. Because none of us is.

"Also, I can't help but notice that I've ended this long and—I freely admit—unfortunately rambling speech about my difficult relationship with David Blackwood by questioning, yet again, whether the problem was me all along.

"I'm like my father, I think, in several ways. But that isn't one of them. He would never once ask that question. It would be straightforward to him: 'Oliver, you need to pull your socks up and stop making excuses.' I suppose that's another irony, that a man so obsessed with personal responsibility was so insistent on everything being somebody else's fault. Even the halibut. But then I suppose he saw no contradiction in that. *Don't do as I do, do as I say* and so on.

"And in a way…didn't it work? Because perhaps the end of

all this is that I like who I am. I like that I am, at last, the sort of person who can tell his father to go fuck himself and also the kind of person who can accept that perhaps I should have said it earlier or not said it at all. My father was a man of certainties, but I think I am happy being a man of questions.

"So often, I think, when a person dies—when a *complicated* person dies, even when an unambiguously *awful* person dies, not that I believe there are any truly unambiguously awful people—it's for those of us left behind to pick over ourselves and ask, 'Am I this way in *spite* of this person or *because* of them?' And so often the answer is simply *yes*.

"I am sorry that my father is dead. I am sorry that we will never get to finish the conversation that began when I told him to go fuck himself. I will miss him, as I know we all will. But for all that I will miss him, for all that I loved him and for all that I believed, without question, that he loved me, I still find myself standing in front of you now and this is the only thing I feel able to say with confidence. The only thing I know to be true and fair about someone who is no longer able to speak for himself: David Blackwood was a complicated man.

"Now, assuming there is still time, I rather mean-spiritly assigned Christopher to read 'If.' It was Dad's favourite poem because of fucking course it was."

Stepping away from the lectern, Oliver walked slightly unsteadily back to his seat. Then he put his head in his hands and, very quietly, started to cry. I wrapped my arms around him and drew him close while Christopher took his place.

"'If you can keep your head,'" he began with palpable resentment, "'when all about you are losing theirs…'"

CHAPTER 33

"MOTHER IS NEVER GOING TO forgive me," said Oliver.

We were sitting on the wall outside the crematorium while the rest of the mourners trickled past on the way to the wake, which was being held at the Blackwoods' house. And I wanted to say something supportive, but he was probably right. "I mean... people surprise you?"

"I think I just surprised her in the worst possible way." Blinking, he wiped his eyes, which were still a little red. "I don't know what I was thinking."

"Well...I suppose it was sort of a combination of grief, frustration, and confusion, which is pretty par for the course for funerals."

"Yes, but I didn't have to *tell* everybody." He dropped his head into his hands. "I mean, who does that? Who goes to his own father's funeral and gives a rather incoherent speech about how he wasn't a very nice person actually?"

"Would you have preferred," I asked, in a vain attempt to lighten the mood, "to have made a coherent speech about how he wasn't a very nice person?"

He glanced up. "Obviously, I'm a lawyer."

"Barrister," I corrected. And that, at least, won a tiny smile.

It didn't last, though. Oliver lowered his head back into his hands. "I feel like such a fool."

"You shouldn't," I told him. "It was really brave of you. I mean, there was me, thinking the options were eulogy or no eulogy. But, dark horse that you are, you went through the door marked *Extemporaneous monologue about fatherhood and loss.*"

Oliver made a mortified groaning noise into his hands. "You're not going to be able to make me laugh about this, Lucien. I've done a terrible thing."

"Okay. One"—I put up a finger—"you know when you say I won't be able to make you laugh, I take that as a challenge, even at a funeral. Two, you haven't done a terrible thing. You've just done…a thing. And, yes, it was a slightly unconventional thing and I don't think it's going to become a Blackwood family tradition. But you needed to say it, and at least some people in that room needed to hear it."

He lifted his head again. "I have a therapist for exactly this reason."

"And," I said, "you can talk to her about it on Tuesday."

"I don't know how I'm going to live with myself. I mean," he went on quickly, "not in a suicidal ideation kind of way. In an I'm-not-sure-how-I-can-continue-to-have-self-respect kind of way."

I put an arm across his shoulders. "Hey, I did without self-respect for ages. It's very overrated."

He gave in and laughed at that.

And because it was his father's funeral and he'd just gone through something intense and traumatic, I didn't shout, *Boom, challenge defeated.* Instead, I went on. "Look, maybe think of it like this. Yes, you could have gone up there and delivered the eulogy your mum wanted, but would that have meant anything? Except that the last thing you said about your father was a lie."

"Is that better or worse than the last thing I said about my father being a string of criticism?"

"You said yourself, he had it coming."

"Yes, but that was a rhetorical device."

I gave him a squeeze. "Well, I suppose we did come to bury David Blackwood, not to praise him."

"Lucien"—he looked unflatteringly surprised—"was that a Shakespeare reference?"

"Hey, I did English A-level. Admittedly because I thought it would be a dossy subject. But I have read *Julius Caesar*. Or rather, I've read that specific speech because I expected it to come up on the exam."

Laughing, he turned my face towards his and kissed me gently with closed lips. "I do love you. I love you very much."

"I love you too," I told him. "And I'm very proud of you. I think you did something that...you had to do. And fuck whatever anyone else thinks." I paused. "But, just to be clear, when I die, I want the full he-was-the-best-person-ever-and-definitely-had-no-faults treatment."

"You're that convinced you'll predecease me?"

"You do all the bullshit stuff you're supposed to do to take care of yourself like flossing and taking exercise and eating vegetables without being forced."

"True." He lifted his brows at me. "On the other hand, I now have a family history of sudden heart failure."

I winced. That was one of those jokes that only close relatives were allowed to make. Especially at the actual funeral. Looking around the courtyard, I noticed that most of the mourners had gone, which meant we should probably be goneing too. "Do you feel..." I started. "Are you okay to go to the wake?"

Before Oliver could reply, I noticed that one of the few people who *hadn't* gone was Christopher, who had just come out of the crematorium and was now bearing down on us with Mia trailing behind him like somebody who really did not want to be trailing.

"What the *fuck*, Oliver?" he asked the moment he was within earshot.

Oliver looked up. In his defence, he did seem at least a little contrite. "I'm sorry, Christopher, it wasn't planned."

Somehow, Christopher didn't seem mollified. "I don't care if it was planned, it was fucking selfish. You get up and do this big 'Ooh, isn't it weird how there's this social convention that we don't shit-talk people at funerals' speech like you're an observational comic from 2006." He wasn't exactly shouting. The Blackwoods hadn't been a shouty family, or rather they'd been a family in which shouting was a monopoly tightly controlled by a man who was now dead. "And then I have to come up and read fucking Kipling like a complete knobhead so we can all get on with pretending that the stupid, selfish thing you just did never happened."

It was pretty much the exact opposite of what Oliver's self-esteem needed right then. He hung his head. "And I'm sorry. I really am."

"It was *one speech*, Ollie. One tiny little speech to give us all a quiet life, and now I've got to go and stop Mum having a total fucking breakdown."

And somewhere, the part of Oliver that had finally been ready to confront his father got off the bench. Literally, in a way, because he stood up, straightened his suit, and said: "I understand that you're upset—"

"Don't give me that—"

"No, Christopher." Oliver was icy calm now in a way I had learned to be either afraid of or turned on by depending on context. This was fifty-fifty. "I'm afraid I'm giving you *exactly* that. Because it wasn't one speech, was it? It was a speech and organising the entire funeral. And staying with Mother for a full week after Father died—much of which, I may add, I spent trying and failing to contact you to *tell* you our father had died because she couldn't. And it was Christmas and the Christmas before and the one before that. It was Mum's sixtieth birthday and Dad's sixtieth and Great-Uncle Benjy's funeral. And everything else that you just couldn't quite make because the first chance you got, you ran away to the other side of the world."

Christopher folded his arms, but—although I admit I was biased—it was the kind of defiance you got from somebody who knows the other person has a point. "Ah, yes, your brilliant theory that I spent five years at medical school, went through junior doctor training, and now work for one of the most prestigious international aid organisations in the world *just to stick you with our parents*."

"I'm not doubting your commitment to what you do"—Oliver's calm was holding up, but barely—"but can you please just *once* admit that the consequence of your rather international lifestyle is that I've borne the brunt of—"

"I'll admit no such fucking thing," snapped Christopher. It didn't seem like either of them were in much of a mood to let the other finish a sentence. "You moved out two years before I did, you were financially independent before I was, you didn't have them micromanaging your wedding *and* your marriage and making your wife feel like shit for—"

"I'm sorry," Oliver gave his brother the politest of smiles. "Were you about to lecture your *gay brother* on how hard it has been for you to put up with our parents' opinions about your romantic relationships?"

For a moment Christopher didn't have a reply, probably because there was no good way to answer. "That was low."

"Oh, was it? Did the impact of our parents' constant low-key homophobia on me somehow inconvenience *you*?"

"Fuck off, Ollie, I never... I always... Just fuck off."

At last, Mia caught up with us. She hadn't actually been that far away, but given the raised voices and intense body language, she hadn't been in a major hurry to join the party. "Cleared the air yet?" she asked.

"Christopher has just told me to fuck off," said Oliver. "So no."

Mia sighed. "Christopher, you promised."

"He played the gay card," Christopher protested.

I winced. "Can we maybe not say 'gay card'? It's kind of a right-wing talking point that needs to die in a fire."

Somehow, it always seemed easier for the Blackwood brothers to be conciliatory with each other's partners than each other, and Christopher continued the tradition. "Sorry, Luc. I meant…let's stop playing the who-had-it-worst game and accept that there's an outside chance growing up was shit for both of us."

"Didn't I just do that," said Oliver, archly.

Christopher scowled. "You just made a whole speech about how crap your childhood was."

"And yours as well," Oliver pointed out with a level of pedantry I didn't think was totally well judged in the circumstances. "I didn't think it was fair to speak on your behalf."

"You could have consulted me?"

"Again, it wasn't planned."

"Or"—for a moment the look in Christopher's eyes was a lot like the one Oliver got when I was being particularly difficult with him—"you could have talked to me at any time in the last *thirty years*?"

"I would have, but you were in…" Oliver began. Then he stopped. Then he tried again. "I'm sorry, I'm trying to be reasonable but"—he took a deep I-am-going-to-articulate-a-complex-thought breath—"it wasn't easy for me when we were younger. Nothing I did was *ever* good enough for our parents, whereas you—"

"Whereas I *what*?" demanded Christopher.

"Come on, you were *always* the golden boy."

At that, Christopher gave a hollow, single-shot laugh, like a bark. "Oh, *was I?*"

"Do you know how long they kept reminding me that you got better A-level grades than I did?"

"Well, I did." Christopher gave a near-defiant near-smirk.

"That's because the A-star grade didn't *exist* when I did mine. I got the best grades I could at the time."

The near-smirk vanished, but the defiance got more defiant. "And I *didn't*. They had a go at me for only getting an A in maths until I was three years into my medical degree."

Mia took half a step forward. She looked like she was about to pull out one of the last six pins in a game of KerPlunk. "Is it *possible*," she asked, "just *possible* that they might have made you both think they liked the other one more?"

"Nonsense," said Christopher and Oliver at once.

"Every time I spoke to them," Oliver went on, slightly faster than his brother, "it was *Christopher* is going to be a doctor, *Christopher* has the loveliest girlfriend, *Christopher* said the most interesting thing to us the last time we spoke to him."

"*Oliver* wouldn't be out so late on a school night," Christopher shot back, "*Oliver* knows how to do what he's told, *Oliver* makes time for us."

"Well, I *did*," Oliver snapped back. "Instead of spending all my time backpacking and sightseeing and running around with my friends. Friends, by the way, who they made very certain to tell me all about." He lapsed back into his *parents* voice. "We don't see *nearly* as much of Christopher as we'd like, but then you *have* to give young boys their freedom and he's so very *popular*."

Mia gave me a look of desperation, and I did my best to intervene. "Guys," I tried, "one of you is a barrister, the other one's a doctor. You are both *way* too smart to still be falling for this shit."

"What shit?" asked Christopher, and to my dismay, he seemed to genuinely mean it. "Ollie here did *everything* they wanted, so when I *didn't*, I got hell."

Oliver sneered. He actually sneered. It was like I was dating the evil one in a costume drama. The one who's determined to steal the hero's tin mine. "You mean you did whatever the hell you liked, and they still thought the sun shone out of your backside, so I had to work twice as hard to get half as much—"

"I can't believe you would even suggest—"

"Mia"—I announced over the top of the Blackwood brothers—"do you want to just run off together? I know I'm gay, but I reckon I can work something out."

Stepping pointedly in between Christopher and Oliver, Mia took my hand. "Yeah, let's go to Paris."

Christopher flung a glance at us. "What are you two doing?"

"We're leaving you for each other," Mia explained, "because you're both awful."

"I mean," I added, "you're both in your late twenties or early thirties, and you've been talking about your fucking A-level results."

There was a little silence. Not a this-man-has-made-a-good-point-and-we're-chill-now kind of silence. More an O.K. Corral kind of silence.

At last, Oliver took one of his trademark I-am-being-calm-and-mature-and-you-are-not breaths. "Perhaps we are being a little heated. Christopher, I understand that what I did today caught you unawares. And in an ideal world I should have said something to you beforehand."

He'd been trying to be conciliatory, but Christopher didn't look conciliated. "'I should have said something to you before-hand'? Is that the best you can do?"

"I shouldn't have asked you to read 'If'?" Normally I loved Oliver's dry half jokes, but this clearly wasn't the time.

"How about if you were going to find the backbone to talk back to our...to our...to our *complete prick* of a father..." The moment the words were out, something lifted from Christopher Blackwood—a small something, admittedly, but something. "You should have done it when he was *alive*. When it could be at least a *tiny* bit of use to either of us."

A similar something, and similarly small, seemed to shift in Oliver too. "I didn't plan for this."

"I know you didn't. Just. Fuck." Christopher pulled at his hair in frustration. "I really, really, really resent having to go here because I in no way want to validate your grandstanding bullshit, but you remember that thing you said about how the worst of it is you'll never know how it would have been different if you'd called him on his bullshit earlier?"

"Unfortunately not," Oliver admitted. "I'm afraid, looking back, it's rather a blur. But it feels like something I remember *wanting* to say."

"Well, how do you think *I* felt listening to that?" And there was the note of challenge in Christopher's voice again. But under that, a note of pleading. "Don't you think I wanted to know what *my* life might have been like if you'd stood up for me just fucking *once* before you were fucking *thirty*."

Oliver went very still in that way he had when he was very angry or very devastated. "I wasn't aware you needed to be stood up for."

"I know you weren't." Christopher's shoulders slumped and, with a stiffness that made him briefly look much older, he sat down where Oliver had just been sitting.

"I..." said Oliver finally. "I fear I may have been a bad brother. I apologise."

Lifting his arm, Christopher dragged his wrist across his eyes, like he wasn't sure whether he was about to cry or not. "I'll be honest, I really thought it would feel better to hear that."

"If it helps," Oliver offered, "I thought it would feel better to tell Dad to go fuck himself."

"Well"—Christopher gave a slightly helpless shrug—"thanks for saying it anyway. And I guess I was kind of a crappy brother too."

Mia cleared her throat. "*Or* you had fucked up parents, and this isn't on either of you."

The seesaw of recrimination and self-recrimination hovered briefly in the middle. And, for a moment, it looked like the Blackwood brothers might get off the ride. Maybe even leave the playground entirely. But, then, there was only so much you could fix with one conversation. Eventually Oliver said, "I'm sorry I ruined the funeral."

Christopher seemed to be deep in a think space so Mia gave a laconic shrug. "I wouldn't say you *ruined* it. It was more interesting than most eulogies. Besides, half the crowd probably weren't paying attention and the other half secretly knew you had a point."

"I think that's overly generous," replied Oliver with reflexive modesty.

"Easy there." Mia put up a hand. "I'm not saying it was the St. Crispin's Day speech. Just that not *everyone* who heard it thought you were a complete wanker."

"That might still be overly generous," observed Christopher, glancing up with a strained smile.

Oliver did something smile-like and tentative back. "Fuck off, Chris."

The sky, which had been making passive-aggressive suggestions about rain all day, finally followed through, and a light drizzle began to descend on the courtyard. And for a while we sat there being wet and cathartically glum, but despite Oliver dropping a kiloton truth-bomb all over his father's funeral, we weren't done with social obligations yet. So I hauled myself to my feet and tried to hustle our little group in the direction of the cars. "Come on," I told them, "we're missing the death party."

"I think they're calling them wakes these days," said Mia, taking Christopher by the hand.

As we walked away from the crematorium, Oliver turned to his brother. "How long are you in town for, by the way?"

Christopher cast him a slightly suspicious look. "A week or so."

"We should...that is, if you'd like to catch up?" It wasn't quite a suggestion, but Oliver's voice sounded faintly hopeful.

After a moment, Christopher nodded. "That'd be nice."

The four of us walked on in comfortable silence through the flower-strewn, not-too-corpse-factory-ish garden of the crematorium where even now David Blackwood's body was being consigned to ashes. If I'd been in a poetic mood, I'd have said the rain made it feel like the sky was doing our crying for us. But this was Britain. Rain was just another fact of life. Like taxes. Or the other thing.

CHAPTER 34

SO WAKES, HUH? THEY SUCKED. If funerals were easier than weddings because no one was expected to enjoy them, then wakes might have sucked harder because you sort of were. I mean, not in a Munchkin Village way, but in an "in the midst of death we are in life; the deceased would want us to be joyful" way. And that was a really specific mood. A really specific mood that was hard enough to achieve at the best of times, and even harder to achieve when the deceased had actually been kind of a dick and everybody knew it.

It was practically impossible to achieve when the deceased had been kind of a dick and everybody knew it, and his eldest son had stood up and said he was a kind of dick and everybody knew it, and now fifty people were united not so much in their shared grief as their shared determination to pretend that one particular thing had never happened. Which meant for Oliver the whole event was like a very low-key but ultimately merciful gaslighting as he went around his parents' house shaking hands with the men, kissing the women lightly on the cheek, and saying, "Yes, a terrible loss, and so unexpected" roughly twelve times a minute.

Eventually he and his mother reached the point in their separate rotations where they couldn't avoid each other without admitting they were trying to avoid each other.

Oliver's hand tightened on mine in a way that at least hinted at panic. "Mother…" he began.

Before she went up on tiptoes to kiss him lightly on the cheek. "Oliver, darling, don't forget to pay the caterers."

He gave the slightest of blinks. "I put through a bank transfer yesterday. It should clear within twenty-four hours."

"Thank you." And with a nod as slight as Oliver's blink, Miriam Blackwood moved on.

"Walk?" I suggested because I could feel Oliver starting to vibrate beside me.

He didn't say yes or no, but he let me lead him outside. The Blackwoods had a really nice garden, although I hadn't had much chance to enjoy it the last time I was here. Not that I was going to have much chance now either, what with the drizzle, the fact I was at a wake, and the distress Oliver was radiating like a rubbish halo. They were also middle class enough to have a gazebo, which seemed as good a place as any to shelter from the one-two punch of rain and social obligation.

"Have I paid the caterers," said Oliver bitterly as we sat down on one of the little benches.

"It could have been worse," I offered. "She could have said, 'You suck, you ruined your father's funeral.'"

"I might have preferred it if she had." He ran a hand through his hair. "As it is, I think she's saving that particular bombshell for a future disagreement."

I rested my head on his shoulder. "If it helps, so am I."

That earned a soft laugh.

"Next time you're like, *Lucien, you've left your mug out again*, I can be like, *Yeah, well, at least I didn't ruin my father's funeral.*"

"Ah." He put an arm around me. "What a joy our life together shall be." There was a slight pause. "Assuming, that is, you still want to."

"Want to what?" I asked. "Leave my mug out?"

"Have a life together." Another of those tense little pauses. "I'm just aware that...this has been a lot. That I've, perhaps, been a lot."

I gave him an unhelpfully angled eye roll. "Oliver. It's not your job to make being with you convenient for me. Just like it's not my job to make being with me convenient for you. Which is good because if it was my job, I'd have been fucking fired ages ago."

"Being with you is...is..." He broke off for what felt like an unflattering long time. "I sometimes don't know what I'd do without you. Again," he followed up hastily, "not in a suicidal ideation way..."

"You know," I said, "I'm getting increasingly worried you feel the need to clarify that."

"I'm a barrister. Clarity is my job. And what I'm saying is obviously I'd cope without you because wonderful as you are, I like to think this isn't a codependent relationship. But I'd rather not have to. My life is more interesting with you in it, and you make me a worse person."

"Um." I sat up. "Thanks?"

"That sounded...more flattering in my head."

"How did it sound in your head?" I asked. "You just told me I make you worse. As in, less good."

"I thought it would be a sort of...witty, Wildean reversal."

"How do you ever win a case? Do you stand in front of the jury and say, *You should send this guy to prison—psyche!*"

"What I meant to say..." Oliver was using his you're-being-mean-to-me-and-I-secretly-like-it voice, which was just different enough from his you're-being-mean-to-me-and-I-very-much-don't-like-it voice that we'd avoided some major misunderstandings. "Is that I've spent a lot of my life living by a set of rules that I never really interrogated and you make me interrogate them. I would never have been able to do what I did today without you, and maybe I shouldn't have, maybe it was a dreadful mistake, but I'm inordinately grateful that I was able to do it."

"Oh," I said, trying to not melt into a pile of squish and then drain away in the drizzle. "So I'm your helpful shoulder demon."

Oliver nodded. "Intermittently helpful."

"I will very much take that."

It was inappropriate to make out at a wake, even if we were technically outside the wake in a damp gazebo, so we had a long hug instead. And I was honestly a bit embarrassed to be a long-hug-having person, but sometimes you just had to long-hug.

We were at about the eighty percent mark on the long hug when to my dismay, I saw Uncle Jim making his way towards us across the garden.

"Really gave the old man what for, eh?" he yell-said from the steps.

Oliver and I dehugged and sort of stared at him. It wasn't so much the intrusion as the shock of somebody admitting that the Inappropriate Eulogy of Doom had actually happened. As ever, Oliver pulled himself together faster than I did. "I'm sorry, Uncle Jim. I know he was your brother and...I'm sorry."

Uncle Jim shrugged. "Probably a bloody silly thing to do, all told."

"Yes," agreed Oliver moodily.

"Still," continued Uncle Jim. "You were right. He had it coming."

That wasn't what I'd expected, and Oliver seemed to be languishing in a similar state of flummoxosity.

Ascending into the gazebo, Uncle Jim pulled up an iron garden chair and sat down opposite us. "Be honest with you," he said, "I wish I'd had the balls to tell him to go fuck himself too. And your granddad, for that matter."

"I wouldn't call it *balls*," Oliver replied. Given the audience, he didn't add that he thought it was inappropriately cis-and-gender-normative to associate one particular set of gonads with emotional strength, but he was clearly thinking it quite loudly. "I'd got to the point where I felt it was... Well, I suppose I explained my reasoning fairly extensively already."

Uncle Jim nodded. "You did. You did. There comes a point, doesn't there? One where you've got to make a choice. Stand up for yourself, or spend your whole life getting walked over." Out of nowhere he heaved a sigh so heavy I thought it was going to shake the roof off our little shelter and leave us all to run back inside or get drizzled on. "Suppose looking back, I think I made the wrong one."

"I always thought you two got on?" The tone in Oliver's voice was careful, like he was sneaking up on a butterfly and didn't want to spook it.

"Oh, we did. Best friends our whole lives. I mean, he was my big brother. How could I *not* think he was the business?"

"You could have met him?" I suggested before I could stop myself.

Uncle Jim laughed. "I like you, Luc. In fact, thinking about it, I suppose all this telling people to go fuck themselves was you from the start, wasn't it?"

There really didn't seem to be a good way to answer that. "I'm not sure I'd put it quite—"

"Told *me* to go fuck *myself* as I recall. As part of the group, I mean."

"I think you might have been collateral damage," I suggested.

With an only-half-listening shrug, Uncle Jim moved on. "But yes, we were close. Thick as thieves. But that's the thing about thieves. They're not especially famous for being nice to each other."

He lapsed into a melancholy silence, and I let myself think

back on what I knew about David and James Blackwood. They'd always struck me as of a type, the kind of bluff, untouchable older man who'd been raised to see no difference between humour and cruelty. They'd had something of a ringleader-sidekick vibe about them, certainly. And perhaps that was all you needed to know. After all, who was more scared of the school bully than the school bully's best friend?

"He was a good man, our dad," Uncle Jim was saying, as much to himself, it seemed, as to anybody else. "Honest, hardworking, wouldn't stand for nonsense. Made sure David and me got good careers that set us up for life, and I'm grateful for that. So was David."

Leaning forward, Oliver did his best to engage. "I suppose I didn't know him that well."

"No. He wasn't the affectionate sort. Approved of grandchildren, but didn't care for them."

"I remember," said Oliver, his own voice growing a little distant now. "He stopped giving us birthday presents the moment we turned sixteen."

"Old enough to earn a living," agreed Uncle Jim. "And David was just like him. Not quite as...as of that generation, of course. But a lot of the same values. Neither of them had any time for layabouts. Or weaklings. Or sissies."

I wasn't quite sure where this was going, but the shape of somewhere it *could* be going was beginning to schloomp together out of the haze of rain and reminiscence in front of me.

"Did Father often make you feel like a sissy?" asked Oliver, who seemed to be seeing the same schloomping possibility that I was. A possibility that made a depressing kind of sense for an unmarried man in his sixties who'd spent his whole life in the shadow of an older brother with no time for anyone he didn't approve of.

"I looked up to him." The fact that Uncle Jim hadn't entirely answered Oliver's question wasn't lost on either of us. "Tried to be like him. Wasn't."

"That might have been for the best," Oliver pointed out. "I'm not sure he was the sort of man it's a good idea to emulate."

Now Uncle Jim was staring fixedly into the middle distance. "You know, they say you can't put old heads on young shoulders, but I'll tell you this. You worked that out far sooner than I did."

"Shoulders of giants, Uncle Jim," offered Oliver with what I thought might have been unnecessary kindness.

Another longish silence followed. The fine rain on the roof sounded like an endless bag of rice being emptied into a pan that somehow never filled.

At last, Uncle Jim turned back to us. "Caught me once, you know. At school. I remember...I remember he didn't say anything. But the look on his face was... I mean, in the man's defence, it had only been legal a few years at that point... I don't think I ever quite got over it. Then when you... Well, he didn't say anything then either. Not to me."

"To me"—Oliver's voice was almost impossibly gentle, certainly gentler than I'd have managed with a man who had been happily joining in with jokes at Oliver's expense the last time we'd met—"he said, 'As long as you don't start wearing dresses.' Mother said, 'But what about AIDS?'"

Uncle Jim gave another gazebo-shaking sigh. "At least that was something. Still, it's too late now. He's gone and I'm..."

"Not?" Oliver finished for him.

"Old," corrected Uncle Jim. "I'm an old, bald, fat man who left it all too late. From telling his brother to go fuck himself to... to everything else."

Hoping I wasn't treading on too many toes and that this fell under the broader category of LGBTQ+ community rather than the Blackwoods specifically, I stuck my oar in. "I mean," I told him, "I suppose it *is* too late to tell David to go fuck himself unless you wanted to do it to his ashes. But as for the...the everything else bit...there's still time on that."

Uncle Jim gave a snort. "What, should I buy myself a pair of those leather trousers with the bum cut out and go strolling around St. James's Park?"

Aaaand *there* was the Uncle Jim we knew and loathed.

"For what it's worth," said Oliver with a level of patience that I was at once in awe of and a little worried I took for granted, "I've never worn leather trousers with the bum cut out in my life—meaning no disrespect to people who have. Most people prefer to go cruising on the internet these days. Or Hampstead Heath if you'd rather."

"I still don't..." Uncle Jim began, but apparently he still wasn't sure what he still didn't, so he let the thought trail away into nothing.

Oliver stood and went to crouch by his uncle. "And you don't have to. There's no"—he looked at me—"no right or wrong way to be who you are. If you're happy being..."

"A fat, bald bachelor in his sixties?" suggested Jim.

"If you're happy with your life the way it is," Oliver continued doing his best to ignore Jim's scathing opinion of himself, "you don't have to change it. But if you want to...to explore alternatives, then there *are* alternatives."

Uncle Jim looked down at Oliver. "There aren't, Oliver. Not at my age."

"There are apps," I suggested.

Oliver nodded reassuringly. "And social clubs, if they're more your speed. The world's changing a lot for older men, and often for the better."

"Perhaps." The look in Uncle Jim's eyes was the closest to

thoughtful I'd ever seen him. "Still, change isn't something I'm used to."

"Of course." Oliver's tone was achingly careful. "As long as you realise that it doesn't have to happen overnight and that you don't have to be in a relationship to be—"

"Don't," said Uncle Jim. "Not out loud. I..." He hauled himself to his feet. "Good speech today," he said. "Really gave the old man what for. Had it coming."

Then he turned and walked back to the house.

PART FIVE

OLIVER DAVID BLACKWOOD & LUCIEN O'DONNELL
THE GREEN ROOM, CAMDEN
26TH OF MARCH

CHAPTER 35

"FOR GOD'S SAKE, LUCIEN." OLIVER'S beautifully tidy living room was now—and had been since Christmas—a chaos of increasingly complex index cards, charts, binders, and calendars. At one point I'd tried to tease him about their impact on our carbon footprint, but it hadn't ended well. "I'm not asking you to do much, but you should have booked the band by now."

I wince-cringed. "I know. I meant to do it last week. It's just... Are we totally sure we don't want to go with a DJ? It'd be a lot cheaper, and I don't think anybody especially cares if there's live music."

"We had this conversation." An exasperated tone was creeping into Oliver's voice. He'd been exasperated for a while. "And we agreed—"

For once, I didn't let that slide. "I'm not sure we actually agreed. I think we disagreed and eventually stopped talking about it, and you took that as meaning I'd backed down."

Oliver threw his hands in the air, which was about twelve times more extravagant than any gesture I'd seen him make prewedding and was now the kind of thing he did all the time. "Fine, we'll get a DJ. We can have a fiftysomething failed musician pumping dad-rock over tinny speakers the whole evening."

"Good DJs do exist," I pointed out. "I can get Priya to recommend somebody if you want."

Invoking people who weren't us, I'd learned, was a reasonable way to get Oliver to calm down. It was sort of Pavlovian, the spectre of an audience making his what-will-the-neighbours-think instincts kick in. "I'm very fond of Priya," he said, "but don't her tastes run a little alternative?"

"It's a gay wedding, Oliver," I reminded him for what might have been the hundredth time. "There's no point trying to make it not-alternative because in the eyes of the law and most of society it's alternative *by definition*." Moving a stack of papers that I tried really hard to keep in the right order, I sat on the sofa. "Besides, it's not like Priya has no sense of occasion. She wouldn't send us somebody who'd play lesbian thrash metal over the vows. And also, would there be anything *wrong* with having a DJ playing lesbian thrash metal?"

Oliver looked up sharply from his spot on the rug. "Yes. The fact that it would be *thrash metal*. I am not getting married to thrash metal, lesbian or otherwise. I don't think that's a personality flaw, I think that's a very reasonable preference."

"Fine, I'll book us a string quartet."

"I didn't say *book a string quartet*. You can book whoever you like."

I tried to roll my eyes without Oliver noticing; it didn't work. "What I would *like* is to save a few quid, get a bloke with a laptop, and not have to use my zero musical knowledge to decide which of nine identical-seeming groups of blokes in waistcoats are going to do covers of Ed Sheeran songs at the only wedding we're ever going to have. Especially since neither of us like Ed Sheeran."

"I thought 'Photograph' had its moments."

"'Photograph' does not have its moments," I yelled. "No Ed Sheeran song has moments. I can't believe I'm marrying someone who thought 'Photograph' had moments."

Oliver threw his hands in the air *again*. "You're marrying someone who is occasionally able to resist the hipsterish urge to dislike popular things."

"I like plenty of popular things." My head was starting to hurt. Talking to my boyfriend was actually giving me a headache. "It's just none of them are made by smug ginger men."

"Lucien." Clutching at his forehead like he too was getting a headache, Oliver ticked something decisively off his list. "Hire. A. Band. I don't care which band, but hire a band."

"Fine. Do you want the Shine, Harvest Moon, or Ulysses?"

"What part of *I don't care* am I failing to communicate?" snarled Oliver.

"And do you not think," I asked, "that it is *kind of fucked up* that you don't care what band we hire?"

"There's no *point* caring—the wedding is in three weeks. The choice now is either *band* or *no band*."

"Or DJ," I pointed out.

There was a pause, then Oliver turned around and stared like he didn't recognise me. "Oh my God, this was your plan all along, wasn't it? We agreed on a band—"

"We didn't agree."

"You said that you'd book one—"

"You *told me* to book one."

"And then you just dragged your feet until it was too late so you could get your own way regardless. And that, Lucien, is exactly the kind of thing your father would do."

It was, but that was pretty fucking rich coming from Mr. My-Way-or-the-Highway. "Oh, right, yeah, *I'm* definitely the one acting like his father here. Because this high-handed, controlling, patriarchal *weirdly heteronormative* attitude you're taking doesn't remind me of anybody at all."

One of the many difficult quirks of my relationship with Oliver was that we had diametrically opposed anger reactions. And now Oliver was anger-reacting all over the place, which for him meant getting very tense and calm. "It isn't *weirdly heteronormative*," he said, "not to want to get married in a pub."

That was another old argument, and another one where we'd sort of stopped talking and then Oliver had invented a compromise out of nowhere. "It wasn't a pub, it was a vintage venue space with an attached bar, and I thought it was nice. *You* on the other hand wanted to get married in a Victorian banqueting hall full of pictures of dead white men."

"Firstly"—Oliver began counting on his fingers—"it's Elizabethan. Secondly, it seems a little appropriative and disingenuous to complain about pictures of dead white men when we are ourselves both white men. Thirdly, that venue was at Gray's Inn, which has personal significance for me because it's a body I actually belong to. And fourthly, we didn't go with that venue either, so I don't know what you're complaining about."

Defeated, I slumped backwards, and as I did, my left arm flopped with an uncontrolled floppishness that caught the stack of papers whose order I had so carefully preserved and sent them tumbling to the floor in a mess of sticky tags and handwritten notes.

Oliver grew very still indeed. "Lucien," he said in his most carefully regulated monotone, "I feel like your presence here is becoming unhelpful."

"Oh, I'm sorry." If Oliver's anger instinct was to get super-duper calm, mine was to get super-duper sarcastic, which was probably less mature but also probably healthier in the long run. "Is my involvement in *our* wedding becoming inconvenient?"

"Now you're being—"

"If you dare say I'm being childish, I am getting up and walking out of that door."

Oliver gave me a cold, distant look that I'd seen a couple of times before but had never imagined would be directed at me. "Right at this moment, that might be the most practical thing you can do. Leave this to me, Lucien, I'll have everything finished by the time you're back."

He didn't have to tell me twice. It had been ages since I'd had a good storm-out.

I stormed.

I stormed so extravagantly that I ended up at my mum's house.

"Luc." She opened the door with a look of puzzlement on her face that quickly became one of concern. "Oh no, what has happened? Have you discovered Oliver randomly travels in time and so you have known him your whole life and are only just beginning to realise it?"

"So," I asked, "you've been watching *Doctor Who* or reading *The Time Traveller's Wife*?"

She shrugged. "A bit of both. In different ways, they are very creepy men."

"Doctor Who's a woman now."

"Oh no, Luc, spoilers. I am only up to the one with the big scarf. Anyway"—she stood aside—"you had better come in. I'm afraid I did not know you were visiting so I have not made the special curry."

I followed her into the living room, which always had a faint air of Judy and dogs despite, at the moment, containing neither. "I think I'll live."

"You should eat something, mon caneton. Food is important when you've had a shock."

"Just to clarify," I said, adopting a position of sofaly slumpitide, "I've had a shock because I've had a fight with Oliver about the wedding. Not about him being a time traveller. We're on the same page there, right?"

"You know"—Mum sat down beside me and dragged the coffee table towards us—"I am very happy for you to come here and talk to me about anything you like, even if Oliver is not a time traveller, but you are going to have to make yourself useful for once and help me with my jigsaw."

I stared at the coffee table, which was strewn with little clumps of a partially assembled picture in a sea of pieces, many of them upside down. "What on earth are you doing?"

"Jigsaws are good for people of my age. They stop you getting the Alzheimer's."

"Okay but..." I kept staring, pushing back a rising suspicion that I was very much the Oliver in this room. "Why are you not starting with the edges?"

"Why would I do that?"

Embarrassingly, I had to think about it. "Everybody starts with the edges. It gives you something to—to... It's more efficient." Oh my God, I *was* Oliver. Or maybe it was jigsaws. Were we all, deep down, an Oliver and all it took to bring it out was a disassembled picture of the Moomins?

"No," Mum said firmly. "Efficient is not cutting the picture up in the first place. Doing a jigsaw is not about efficiency, it is about the journey."

I gave her a look. "You mean, the real jigsaw is the friends we make along the way?"

She gave me a look back. "No, Luc. A jigsaw is a jigsaw. Your friends are your friends. You cannot be friends with a jigsaw. What are you even talking about?"

"It's just a thing people say."

A light of what was probably misplaced understanding glimmered in her eyes. "Ah, bon. Then, yes, it is about being, as they say, friends with a jigsaw. One is not efficient when one is being friends with a jigsaw. Now"—her tone grew brisk—"help me be friends with this jigsaw because I am quite stuck." She squinted at her various clusters of Moomin. "I am looking for the last piece of Papa's hat."

"And you don't think it'd be better to—" I let it go. And started combing through the nine hundred and twenty-six pieces that remained in the thousand-piece jigsaw to find the one bit that had a fragment of Moomin top hat on it.

To Mum's credit, it was quite a relaxing process. I mean, I don't think I became friends with the jigsaw. But I did get to know a reasonable amount about it.

"So," asked Mum, holding a piece to the light like she was checking it wasn't a forgery, "what has happened with you and Oliver?"

Obviously, it was complex, and there were two sides to every story, and Mum cared about both of us, and if I wanted her to give me good advice, I'd present the situation in the fairest, most impartial way I could. "He was just a dick," I explained. "He's been a dick for months."

There was a pause, Mum carefully finishing Moomin Mama's bowl of fruit. "Are you sure? Because you know I love you, but between you and Oliver, if I had to guess who was the bigger dick, I would not normally expect it to be him."

"Thanks. And...and...I've been very reasonable. While he's turned into some kind of steamrollery wedding tyrant."

Another pause as Mum either thought about this or got distracted by weird blue-eyed children. "Marriage is complicated, and weddings are complicated, but most importantly weddings are not marriages."

"Are you sure?" I demanded. "Because you know what they say. Steamrollery wedding tyrant me once, shame on you.

Steamrollery wedding tyrant me for the rest of my life, shame on me."

"I do not like that idiom as much as *be friends with a jigsaw.*" Mum sighed. "I can see why you are concerned, but you have been with Oliver for more than two years, and he has never been like this before—"

"Actually," I admitted, "he's quite like this. But I thought I liked it."

"And you don't anymore?"

I tried to wedge a piece of top hat into place, but it turned out to be part of a cat's arse. "It just feels different now. Everything is all...I don't know."

"He's also just lost his father," Mum pointed out. "That can be very hard."

"Yeah, but...but...I felt that made us closer. Like, if anything was going to break us, it should have been that and it didn't. So why is it going to shit now?"

Mum put a consoling arm around me. "It is hard to say without knowing what type of shit it is. There are lots of different types of shit, and they are all shit in different ways."

"It's sort of..." I tried to pin my thoughts down but, thematically enough, it was like trying to nail shit to the wall. "We're arguing kind of...kind of constantly about everything? And we never used to, not like this. And this morning we had the biggest fight we've basically *ever* had, and if you put a gun to my head, I'm not sure what it was really even *about* and just...is that what it's going to be like? Is that what being married will be like?"

With typical sangfroid, Mum shrugged. "Probably not. Probably that is what *organising big, life-changing events with lots of guests and rules and expectations together* will be like. And you don't do that very often."

"We did it fine for the funeral," I pointed out.

"That was not the same. It was his father and so he had the right to be a... What was it? A steamrollery tyrant if he wanted to. But your wedding, that is for both of you."

"Oliver doesn't seem to have got that memo," I told her glumly.

Mum turned to look at me. There was an interrogatey expression on her face I felt quite ambivalent about. "Are you sure you sent it to him?"

"Well, I think so."

"Because the Luc I know, he is not the sort of boy who would get cut out of his own wedding."

That was kind of her. The Luc *I* knew would get cut out of his own funeral. Except if Oliver was cutting me out in order to create the heteronormative marriage of his dreams, you'd think he'd be...happier about it? "I'm not even sure it's that," I said. "I'm involved, we're both involved... It just doesn't feel like us anymore."

"Ah." Mum looked sage. "Perhaps it is too many chefs. They are spoiling the sauce."

"There's not even that many chefs. Like, I know the wedding cliché is everybody else is trying to get you to do their thing. But normally that's the families and my family is you, and Oliver's family isn't even speaking to him, so this is totally on us. We're fucking up our own sauce."

There was a long silence. Mum's sage look had intensified. "Luc." She frowned solemnly. "Why is there a wolf in a wig in this picture?"

"You're the one who bought a Moomin jigsaw. The only Moomins I know are the one in the hat and the other one. Now can we get back to my catastrophically overboiled sauce–wedding?"

"I thought you would appreciate the distraction." Mum slotted a bit of wig-wolf into place. "As for the sauce-wedding, well, have you thought that maybe—maybe not every dish is meant to have a sauce?"

I turned from the jigsaw. "What are you saying?"

"Well, for example, there is a nice Chinese place in the next village, and they do this sort of dry chilli and garlic chicken and it is very good."

"No, I mean, what is this metaphor implying about me and Oliver?"

For a moment, Mum seemed to genuinely resent my pulling her thoughts back from the dry chilli and garlic chicken. "I mean, mon caneton, that you and Oliver may not be the sort who are good at being married."

Inside, I mega-winced. The comparison here was obvious. "Like you and Dad, you mean?"

"No, Luc." Mum looked at me like I was six and had just told her I thought cats were made of marzipan. "Your father and I were not bad at being married, we were bad at him not being a lying, cheating sack of broken penises who only thinks about himself."

"But if we're not good at being married, what can we be good at?"

Another of Mum's trademark shrugs. "Being not married? After all, you don't need to, not really."

I tasted something bitter, a mix of superfood salad and bile. For a moment Miriam Blackwood popped up at the back of my mind saying, *I don't understand why gay people want to get married at all.* Sitting back on the sofa, I shuffled slightly farther away from Mum. Things had got uncomfortable suddenly, and I wasn't used to Pucklethroop-in-the-Wold being uncomfortable. "That's..." My stomach was making wurbling motions, and I didn't like it. "That's not okay to say."

"Why not?" Mum seemed genuinely shocked.

My skin was feeling crawly in a way I didn't want to be associating with my mum's house. "Because that's…that's what people like Oliver's parents say. *Why do you have to get married? It's not like you can have babies.*"

"Oh, Luc." She didn't come any closer—she was usually pretty good at respecting personal space, probably from years of talking people down from bad trips—but her body language got all nonthreatening. "I did not mean it in that way. I only meant that there are some people who are very good together but are not so good at weddings or at being married. Look at Judy. She has had very many boyfriends, all very happily, but her marriages, they never last."

I tried to let myself calm down. "Isn't that mostly because her husbands keep getting murdered or disappearing mysteriously somewhere on Dartmoor?"

"Oh, now be fair, that only happened twice."

Now that I was recovering from my brief was-Mum-a-stealth-homophobe scare, I realised she was trying to comfort me. And then I realised the reason she was trying to comfort me was because I might be too sucky to get married. "But…but…" I flailed. "Everybody is married. My best friend is married. My dickhead ex is married. What does it say about me—about us—if we're the only ones who can't make it work?"

"I know this is not very helpful"—Mum had gone back to the wiggenwolf—"but I think it means what you let it mean."

I vindictively returned a piece of Moomin Papa's top hat to the pile. "You're right, Mum. That isn't very helpful. Because what it means to me right now is that I'm a gigantic failure who can't make it work even with a guy as amazing as Oliver."

Mum sighed. "You know I love Oliver and I think he is very good for you, but he is also—and there is no getting away from this—kind of a messy bitch."

"Mum," I yelped.

"It's okay. I'm using it in the reclaimed sense."

"I should never have taught you that."

"All I am saying is"—she gave a little shrug, then pounced on the piece of top hat I'd tried to hide from her—"you both have your issues. This is not about your failure or his. It's about what's right for both of you."

"Well," I told her, in a voice that was definitely decisive and not at all huffy, "what's best for me at the moment is going to fucking bed."

And, for the second time that day, I treated myself to a storm.

CHAPTER 36

BECAUSE I'D BEEN TOO LAZY to ever take anything down (except that one Rights of Man poster I'd put up and thrown away at least three times), the walls of my old bedroom were kind of a history of things I'd been into my whole life. Starting with the original 151 Pokémon poster from when I'd been about ten, moving up through Cary Grant from the classic movie phase I'd had when I'd been twelve and wanting to feel very grown-up. Then there was the *Brokeback Mountain* poster back from when "two cowboys shag once, then one of them dies" was the best rep you got in mainstream media if you weren't old enough to watch *Queer as Folk*. Also, they weren't even proper cowboys; they spent most of their time looking at sheep. Which, growing up in a place where looking at sheep was about the most exciting thing you could do on a Friday night, wasn't the escapist fantasy I was hoping for.

I scowled moodily at Cary Grant and tried to shake the notion that I might have had a thing for stern-featured clean-cut guys that went back way longer than I thought. And it felt weird to be lying on my childhood bed thinking about adult problems. Because you didn't get much more adult, either in the euphemistic-about-sex way or the realistic-about-bills-and-responsibilities way, than stressing over your wedding.

And, hoo boy, was I stressing. It was just so muddy and

impossible. Because I loved Oliver and I wanted to be with him for, like, ever, but the more I thought about it, the more I got this hard-to-pin-down not-quite-sick, not-quite-scared, not-quite-something feeling that we were doing it wrong. Of course I'd been feeling like I was doing it wrong for...well, not my whole life. When I'd been young and full of unearned confidence, I'd been pretty convinced that I was nailing it and anybody who failed to nail it was suffering from a tragic case of not being me. But then Miles had happened and suddenly I'd realised that the young, confident me was full of shit, and then a whole lot of years had passed and now here I was, slowly getting better but still crushingly aware I was making it up as I went along. Except even by my standards, the wedding had strong doing-it-wrong energy.

I'd proposed almost by accident. I'd nearly been put off buying a ring by a mildly rude man in a mid-range jeweller's. Oliver's parents had been so horrified that they'd made the whole thing feel less like a party than a protest, and then one of them had immediately dropped dead, giving everything a complex set of implications that I was nowhere near getting my head around. And now we were bickering over tiny details that neither of us cared about.

Seriously, though, what was going on with that? How could something that objectively did not matter become the hill you were most determined to die on? Because ultimately, if Oliver wanted a band, fine, we could have a band. We could hire Blue Honey or Felicity or the Corkscrews, and it would make no fucking difference and it would still be the happiest fucking day of our whole fucking lives because it fucking had to be.

Except the more I thought about it, the more I was *determined* to have a DJ. Because I did not want four men in cardigans, or three guys and a surprisingly attractive woman, doing a ska-punk remix of "Thinking Out Loud" over our first dance as a married couple. Especially because Oliver couldn't dance, and it would make a ska-punk remix of "Thinking Out Loud" *our song*. Fuck. We'd been together for nearly three years, and we didn't even have an "our song." Or worse, we did, and it was *This American Life*. We were going to have to have our first dance to Sarah Koenig following a series of small cases through a county courthouse in Cleveland.

To be fair, maybe that was a good argument against a DJ. Because they'd ask, *So what kind of music are you guys into?* and we'd have to say "Well, *my* dad's in a band but I hate his guts, and *he* listens to quirky horror podcasts and spoken-word media about complicated political topics."

Perhaps Mum was right. We just weren't people who were good at being married. Perhaps, given the fact that we—as this wedding was proving—had absolutely nothing in common and had only started dating as a literal hoax, we were the sorts of people who shouldn't be together at all.

My phone rang. It was Oliver, and I—I wasn't in a space to be Olivering right now, so I let it go to voicemail. Which, again, didn't say good things about my relationship. I bet James Royce-Royce never let James Royce-Royce's calls go to voicemail. I bet Bridge never let Tom's calls go to voicemail. I bet Prince Harry never let Meghan Markle's calls go to voicemail. I bet Prince Charles never let Camilla Parker Bowles's calls go to voicemail, although he probably should have, at least in the eighties.

Fuck, we were going to have to break up. We were going to have to tell all the nice people who had RSVP'ed months ago—because Oliver had started sending invitations out before Christmas—that actually, on second thought, we weren't getting married after all and also we were leaving each other because we'd each independently decided the other person sucked and so now we were both available if anyone was interested. Not that anyone should be, on my end at least, because I had a crap job and couldn't make French toast.

Then I'd get drunk, rock up at Miles and JoJo's house, and beg Miles to take me back or at least let me in on a threesome.

Okay, there was a tiny, tiny, very slight possibility I was spiralling.

My phone buzzed. I didn't look at it.

It buzzed again. I didn't look at it again.

The buzzing and the not-looking continued until I ran out of not-looking energy.

Lucien I know you're upset but I'm at your flat. Said the first text.

If you're inside, please let me know. Said the second.

Or if you aren't, please let me know where you are. Said the third.

Not where you are necessarily. It's okay if you want some privacy.

I understand.

But I'm worried something has happened.

Not that I don't think you can take care of yourself.

But well...

Sorry that was probably a bit dramatic, actually texting an ellipsis.

But well I've recently had a poor track record with arguing with people and then having them immediately die.

And I know rationally that hasn't happened.

At least it's very unlikely that it's happened.

But I'm worried it has happened.

Which I know isn't your fault and isn't your problem.

But if you could just text me and let me know that you're okay.

When you're ready.

Sorry I'm being clingy.

Take your time.

I'm just worried.

Lucien?

Are you okay?

Lucien I'm very worried.

Sorry. I didn't mean to get like that. Take as long as you need.

Lucien?

I shouldn't have texted back hello i am a murderer i took lucs phone hes dead now, but I did.

I also shouldn't have followed it up with bet you wish youd got that dj. But I did that too.

Lucien you are not funny.

who is lucien i am a murderer

For a moment I thought I'd gone too far. But eventually Oliver came back with Then how did you know about the DJ?

luc told me, I texted back, while i was murdering him. I hit Send, then immediately followed it up with he said o no if only oliver had let me have a dj i wouldnt have been walking down this dark alley where im getting murdered.

My phone rang. And this time I answered it.

"I'm sorry, I said hurtful things to you." It was a cocktail of three of Oliver's voices: stern poured over a base of secretly amused with a dash of contrite. "But please don't pretend to be murdered."

The words *especially not when my dad just died* hung unspoken between us. And the fact that they remained unspoken was probably a sign that we were in a slightly better space than we had been a few hours ago. "Sorry." I lay back on the bed and shut my eyes. "For that and for, you know, I said some pretty mean things too. I think all the wedding stuff is just getting really…"

"I know." Oliver did his best to beam understanding down the phone at me, and I caught at least some of it. "I assume you're at your mother's."

"Yes," I told him. "I'll...I'll stay here tonight, if that's okay? Because it'd feel a bit shitty to show up on her doorstep and then bail the moment it's convenient." Plus, if I was honest, I wasn't *totally* sure we wouldn't start setting each other off again if I went straight back.

Oliver made a kind of auditory nod. "You're right. It's getting late. I'll miss you, of course."

"I'll miss you too." And it wasn't a lie because I would. I'd miss his warmth and the steady rhythm of his breath in the dark. The way we'd sometimes roll apart naturally in the night and Oliver would always end up rolling back. The special occasions where we'd both wake up horny and work still seemed forever away. Not that there'd been so many of those lately.

But right now? There were also a bunch of things I wouldn't miss. Like the not-quite-arguments and the not-quite compromises and the constant spectres of things not-quite-said. It was almost like one of us was cheating, except it wasn't one of us, it was both of us, and what we were cheating with was our own wedding.

"What are we going to do?" I asked, unintentionally out loud.

Oliver sighed. "Well, having looked into it, I think that you're right, and there's no sense hiring a band if we can't find one that either of us feel strongly about."

It wasn't what I'd meant, but it was the closest we were going to get. "Okay. That's... Thanks."

"But I also think," Oliver went on, "that DJs are a bit—sorry to say this—tacky."

In his defence, they were. It's just I was worried cutting all the tackiness out of our wedding would cut out all the fun. And then fifty years from now I'd be sitting in my old people's home looking back on a day that could have happened to anyone. "So, what? The plan is no music? Everybody standing around talking awkwardly? Or I guess we could get one of those giant games of Twister."

"If you really want a giant Twister, I won't fight you on it."

"Oliver, that was a joke. I don't want to play giant Twister at my wedding."

A teeth-clenching silence echoed down the line. "I'm sorry. I'm genuinely...I'm genuinely trying here. I'm aware I'm probably coming across as—"

"A steamrollery wedding tyrant?" I suggested.

"I'm not sure I'd put it quite like that, but...yes." Another pause. "I think I just...I just want everything to be perfect for us."

Perfect was not a good word for Oliver. In fact, it had nearly ruined our relationship once already. But in some ways hearing him say it was a relief because it meant that...that actually he was the one with the problem here. And it was a problem I kind of knew how to fix. And that was way easier to think about than me or how I felt or if Mum had been right all along. "Okay." I took a deep breath. I could do this. This was doable. We were going to figure this out. "I think you might be getting in your head a bit."

"I am aware," he said a little coolly.

"And I think," I continued, "that where you're getting mixed up is that you're confusing 'perfect for us' with 'perfect.' The *perfect* wedding is in June, in the church you grew up in, and has a live band and centrepieces that match the bridesmaids' dresses. The *perfect-for-us* wedding is you and me and people we care about in a venue that fits a sensible number of people and music we like played by—"

I could hear Oliver relaxing. "A failed musician who says things like 'And now, one for the oldies'?"

"Yeah. Or, I don't know, a laptop. Or if you want, I could ask Rhys to get the male voice choir back."

Oliver's breathing was steadying, which I took as a good sign. "Actually, I was wondering if—and if you think I'm being a steamrollery wedding tyrant do say so—I thought it might be nice to put together a playlist and, perhaps, get every guest to contribute a song."

In practice, I was mildly concerned that this would mean Alex contributing the Eaton boating song and Professor Fairclough contributing a two-hour lecture on Formicidae, but it did sound... "That...that sounds perfect for us."

"Then I'll send out song requests. Thank you for being so... I'm sorry, Lucien, I really am."

"Me too." I thought it best to apologise back, even though we'd now formally diagnosed this as an Oliver issue. And it definitely *was* an Oliver issue. Not one that my years of baggage and self-loathing were in any way exacerbating. "And I'll be back first thing tomorrow to... What's next on the list?"

"Bronwyn wants to finalise the menu."

Oh yes, that was the other big compromise. We were having all-vegan catering. But that one I'd been fine with, even though I'd have secretly loved a burger option. Because unlike the band, it had clearly *mattered*. "I mean, I'm still the opposite of an expert. As long as it's got those spiced-seed things, I'll be happy."

He was smiling now. "She'll be here at noon."

Egh. That meant getting up at a sensible time. "I'll be there," I told him. "Love you."

He love-you-too'ed, and we hung up. Then I lay down on the bed wondering why I didn't feel happier. I mean, we'd fixed the music thing and found a middle ground that *was* a middle ground, instead of something neither of us wanted. And Oliver had apologised, and I'd apologised slightly less than he had which—according to the Disagreeing Couples Act of 1974—meant I'd won.

For fuck's sake, I was getting married. I was getting married to an amazing man I was in love with. As was my hard-won legal right. And, yes, Mum had tried to do that thing that mums do when you're picked last in sports where they tell you not everyone has to be good at everything. But this was my relationship, not a game of rounders. I couldn't just shrug and say, "Well, when am I ever going to need that in real life anyway."

No. This was fucking my wedding. I'd planned it, I deserved it, and I was damn well going to have it.

CHAPTER 37

PICKING A BEST MAN WAS a complicated business. Because you didn't want to be gender normative, but if you got too role-reversey you ended up with something that was gender normative in the other direction. For Oliver, it had been simple. Well, simple-ish because he'd asked Christopher. Which had been obvious in one way (because apparently asking your brother was traditional) but really difficult in another (because post-funeral Oliver and Christopher had only just settled into a place where it was even a reasonable thing to ask). But they'd pushed through it and were now slowly building the kind of relationship where they could actually like each other.

I didn't have the same options. I just had a bunch of friends, all of whom were, in their own special ways, utterly unsuitable. Tom was an ex and technically Bridge's friend rather than mine, both of which made it weird. The James Royce-Royces came as a unit, and it would have felt unfair to ask one but not the other. I refused to ask any of my coworkers, so that left Bridge and Priya. And Bridge *should* have been my go-to choice because she'd made me her maid of honour and I was owed some freaking payback. Only something about Bridge didn't scream *best man* to me.

She was my best *friend*, but when I thought of a best man, I thought of someone who I'd gone on the pull with in a disastrous attempt to get over a failed relationship. Or drunk absinthe with at three in the morning. Or ranted to about how awful it was that all our friends were pairing off like a bunch of squares while we were young, free, single, and totally miserable. And that...that was definitely Priya.

Besides, when I called Bridge to break the good or bad news, she'd been in the middle of a major work crisis because the acclaimed author of *I'm Out of the Office at the Moment. Please Forward Any Translation Work to My Personal Email Address* had vanished overnight somewhere in the vicinity of the Ängelholm UFO-Memorial, leaving only thirty-eight manuscript pages, a cassette recording of Philip Glass's *Akhenaten*, and a note saying *To the Fairest*.

So, yeah, Priya had stepped up. Or at least not told me to fuck off. And was doing a really good job. For a start, she'd totally ignored me when I said I wanted a small, low-key non-gender-specific animal party and instead threw me a massive rager at a friend's gallery. She'd even got me a rainbow balloon arch, although she did tell me we were going to shoot it with BB guns at the end of the evening because—and I quote—"I love you and respect your choices, but balloon arches are twee as fuck."

Whatever. It was my twee-as-fuck balloon arch, and I was going to stand under it for as long as possible. Or at least for a couple of minutes because, it turned out, standing under a balloon arch by yourself wasn't as much fun as I thought it was going to be.

Everything else, however, was kind of amazing. Which shouldn't have been surprising on account of how Priya was also kind of amazing—not that I'd ever tell her to her face, in case she thought I liked her or something. The gallery was one of those old Victorian warehouses that had been repurposed just enough to be usable but not so much that it didn't feel like the owner was elbowing you in the ribs every five minutes, saying *Hey, look at that exposed brickwork and those authentic window fittings. Aren't they funky and incongruous.* It was currently exhibiting a bunch of queer artists who did the type of work that I really liked knowing existed, because it made me feel part of an important cultural thing, but didn't particularly understand because, at the end of the day, queer art was still art. And I was still a total pleb.

Along with the art, there were also drinks, music, lights, and a whole lot of people, approximately half of whom I knew, and the other half Priya knew and had brought along to make me feel cooler than I was. And actually, it was working. I was incredibly cool. I was the sort of person who got to have a super-queer, super-modern non-gender-specific animal party full of exciting people in an exciting venue organised by my exciting lesbian best man. This was, without a doubt, the best part of getting married so far. And the man I was getting married to would have hated it. Well, to be fair, he might have liked the art bit.

For a little while I just floated, drink in hand, basking in reflected relevance, accepting hugs and congratulations from friends, acquaintances, and total strangers. It was like I'd won something, which I suppose from a romantic perspective I kind of had. Eventually I found Priya, tucked in an alcove, next to a mural depicting *The Birth of Venus* as a hot, naked twink. She was with Theresa and Andi and deep in conversation with someone I thought was the gallery owner—a tall woman with a shaved head, who looked like she'd been in the art game long enough to give no fucks.

"Thank you for my party," I said in a rush of un-me-like ebullience.

"Whatever," Priya replied. "You know I think marriage is bollocks. But if it makes you happy, fine."

"Nuanced as ever," observed Theresa, who had put aside her usual academic chic for a little black cocktail dress that still managed to make me feel like I was late for a lecture.

Priya, though, looked like Priya, rainbow-laced Docs and all. "Hey, there's a reason I work in a visual medium."

"And while I *mostly agree* on the patriarchal-bollocks-that-should-have-gone-out-with-the-Dark-Ages front"—this was Andi, an intense woman with bleached-blond swept-back hair wearing one of those tank tops that only a very specific sort of person could get away with—"isn't it an important de jure equality thing? I mean I don't want us to get married"—she made a kind of circular nod indicating her partners—"but I do think we should be allowed to."

The gallery owner flashed a ring. "Married woman over here, fine with it."

"You're all against me." Priya rolled her eyes. "Oh, and Luc, this is Abena. This is her place."

"Thanks," I told her reflexively, "this is a really great venue."

"It's not a venue, mate." She didn't seem offended, more like she wanted to make a point. "It's a gallery. But be honest, would you be here if there wasn't also a party in it?"

My vicarious coolness began leaking out. "No?"

She gave a vindicated nod. "Do the artists a favour. Try to actually look at a couple of pieces. And if you spill a drink on something, you buy it."

I cast a guilty eye at *The Birth of Twink Venus* and tried to think of something appreciative to say. "Well, this is, um...nice?"

And suddenly I wished Oliver was with me. He'd have had something to say about a naked guy on a shell, about how it was, like, a commentary on the constructed nature of...beauty or something.

"It's," I tried, "like, a commentary on the... Like. Constructed nature of beauty."

Priya put a hand on my shoulder. "Luc, we've known each other for ten years, and the most insightful thing you've ever said about a piece of my work was 'Wow, isn't it big.' And that's still more insightful than what you said just now."

"So it's not a…whatever I just said?" I asked.

"Oh, it probably is." That was Theresa, taking a delicate sip from her glass of prosecco. "But it's very gauche to say so."

"It's art," said Priya. "It's not a crossword puzzle. It's not supposed to have *an answer*. It's about what it makes you think and how it makes you feel."

I glared at Twink Venus's tiny penis. "It's making me feel I have inadequate opinions about art."

Andi grinned. "Yeah, that's the other thing art is about. It's about making you feel bad because you didn't go to the right school."

"I went to a fucking comprehensive," put in Priya. "Just like you."

"Yeah." Folding her arms, Andi gave Priya a hard stare. "Then I went and got a job in a pub, while you went to art college."

Priya glowered back in a way that felt more sexual tension than I was really comfortable noticing. "Why am I even dating you?"

"Because I'm amazing in bed," Andi told her.

"Oh, not you as well." I gave a groan. "Do you ever actually have sex, or do you just boast to each other about how great you are?"

Theresa made an I-don't-know-these-people gesture with her free hand. "Ignore it, Luc. It's their thing."

Andi and Priya were still doing their sex glare at each other, and it was heating up the space. I turned to Abena. "Are you beginning to feel like a fourth-slash-fifth wheel?"

"Kind of," she said.

We extricated ourselves from the get-a-room corner, and having taken the measure of me artwise, Abena drifted off. That left me free to scan the gallery for familiar faces. I saw James

Royce-Royce and James Royce-Royce, uncharacteristically unba-
bied, standing with Tom by a grey papier-maché statue of a figure
sitting hunched with its chin on its hands. Its body was covered
in tally marks, and a stack of what looked like cherry stones were
piled at its feet.

"Well," James Royce-Royce was saying, "that's rather melancholy, isn't it?"

I wandered over and exchanged hugs with the three of them.
"Oh, don't. I've just been talking to Priya, and she's made it very
clear that I can't art."

With a smile, James Royce-Royce put a friendly arm around
me. "Don't worry, Luc, my dear. Neither can any of the rest of
us."

"Apparently," I offered, "it's about what it makes you think
and feel."

James thought and felt for a moment. "I'm mostly thinking,
would it go well in the corner of the restaurant?" He turned to his
husband. "You know, by the door to the kitchen."

"Too hot," said James Royce-Royce. "And too humid. The
paper would get soggy."

"It must be…" James Royce-Royce stirred a hand in the air
like he was whipping a soufflé. Assuming you whipped soufflés.
"Lacquered or something. I'm sure it would be fine. And it'd be
nice to have a souvenir of Luc's bachelor party."

"Are the pieces even for sale?" asked Tom, who'd been busy
texting while the James Royce-Royces had been doing compara-
tive art shopping.

Turning, I scanned the room for Abena. "The owner's over
there. You could ask her."

Before anybody could move, Tom looked up from his phone
again. "That was Bridge," he said to none of our surprise. "She'll
be here soon. She got delayed because they sent one of their interns

out to the Ängelholm UFO-Memorial to look for that author who went missing, and now he's gone missing too."

That sounded basically normal once you adjusted for the Bridge's life factor.

"Anyway, pumpkin"—James Royce-Royce gave me a squeeze—"you realise you're officially joining the ranks of the tediously wed."

"How tedious is it going to be?" I asked.

"Well," said Tom with a smile. "I'm still in the honeymoon stage, so not tedious at all."

James Royce-Royce managed to maintain hug contact while turning to face someone else. "You're married to our Bridget. There are a number of problems I can anticipate in your future life, but tedium is not one of them." His expression grew slightly marshmallowy. "In my experience, Luc, married life is rather wonderful. And, of course, now we have Baby J, which means every day is a fresh adventure."

Oh God. We were about to be told a fresh adventure. I was at a party, celebrating the end of my youthful bachelorhood while one of my married friends regaled us with stories about his baby.

"Of course," James Royce-Royce went on, "we should probably be calling him Toddler J now."

James Royce-Royce shook his head. "No, it's fine. We're using *baby* as an affectionate diminutive not as reference to a specific developmental stage."

"There's no need to be so literal, darling. I was just making a funny." Letting me go, James Royce-Royce produced his phone and started scrolling. "Yesterday he made a tower of three blocks, using the blue, the red, and the purple, which I think shows a natural aesthetic sense, but apparently four blocks is what we're shooting for."

We were shown the tower. Then the tower with the blocks in a slightly different order. Then an earlier version of the tower which had only been two blocks. None of which distracted from the fact that Affectionate Diminutive J still looked like a goblin.

"Well," I said, "isn't he...clever."

And, once again, I wished Oliver was with me. Because he could say things like that and he wouldn't sound sarcastic.

"You may scoff, Luc O'Donnell," declared James Royce-Royce. "This will be you in a few years' time."

"Actually," I said, "I don't like to brag but I reckon I could stack three blocks on top of each other right now."

Putting a hand on his hip, James Royce-Royce somehow managed to pout with his eyes. "You know perfectly well what I mean. You and Oliver must have talked about it."

Shitting hell... "Must we?"

"You're about to get married. Of course, you should have. What if one of you does and one of you doesn't?"

Oh no. What if one of us did and one of us didn't? What if *I* did? What if I didn't? We could barely agree on band versus DJ, let alone baby versus not baby. My options were to calmly reflect on the sensible advice my good friend was giving me or get incredibly fucking defensive. "Oh right," I said. "Because I suppose you two knew *everything* about each other's plans and goals and hopes and dreams before you even got engaged."

"Obviously we did." James Royce-Royce was trying really hard not to be aghast but was failing dismally. "Marriage is a serious commitment. It's forever, Luc."

I squirmed. "It's not, though, is it? Divorce is a thing. And also, eventually one of you will die."

"Tell you what," said Tom. "If those are your vows, I will have so much respect."

"They're not my vows." Now I thought about it, I probably needed to finish writing those. "I just mean you can work it out as you go and it's possible to overplan."

The other James Royce-Royce took his husband by the hand and pulled him gently away. "You'll be fine," he said. "Everyone's got their own way of doing things."

"But," James Royce-Royce was protesting, "but...but..."

"Look at Baby J." James Royce-Royce manoeuvred James Royce-Royce's phone to James Royce-Royce's eyeline.

James Royce-Royce visibly melted. "Look at his little face. His darling little face. I miss him so much. Do you not miss him, James?"

"Well"—James Royce-Royce was at his most impassive—"I was with him all day and we've been out for two hours. So. No."

We were interrupted by the tip-tap of heels on the concrete floor and a cry of, "Luuuuuuuc. I'm so sorry I'm la— Oooh, are those new Baby J photos?"

"This is my non-gender-specific animal party, Bridge," I wailed. "We're meant to be celebrating the end of my wild single youth. Not—"

It was too late. James Royce-Royce had his phone under Bridge's nose and she was staring at it, entranced. "Look," he was saying, "here's Baby J—"

Bridge clapped her hands. "Oh my God. He's grown. He's grown so fast."

"He has. He's got so much bigger. I remember when he was only as big as a medium-sized turbot."

"That's very specific," I put in.

But it was ignored. Because baby.

"This is him," James Royce-Royce continued. "Well, actually. I'm not sure what he's doing with those bits of plastic fruit, but it seems advanced. He might be grouping them by size and colour."

James Royce-Royce squinted at the phone. "Honestly, I think he's just licking them."

"That's advanced," insisted James Royce-Royce. "That's using all of his senses to make independent cognitive leaps."

Moving to the baby huddle, Tom put his arms around Bridge. "James, have you been at the parenting books again?"

"It's important to be informed."

Bridge gave another squeal. "What's he doing here?"

"Sitting down," explained James Royce-Royce.

"In a remarkable way," added James Royce-Royce.

I was getting the feeling this would go on for a while. And I took it as a sign of my personal growth that I felt no compelling desire to compete for my friends' attention with an absent two-year-old. Or maybe I just knew I'd lose.

In an effort to look sophisticated and at home, I circled the sculpture, trying to look like I was appreciating it on an emotional and intellectual level.

"So what do you think?" asked a nearby stranger.

While I didn't jump exactly, I gave a busted-not-understanding-art hop. "Ummm..." *Fuck, fuck, fuck.* "The thing about art," I bullshat, "is that it's not supposed to have one interpretation. It's supposed to be, like, about how you think and feel."

He folded his arms, in a calling-my-bluff kind of way. "So what does it make you think and how does it make you feel?"

Since James Royce-Royce was stealing my friends, I decided to steal his criticism. "It's sort of melancholy. And sort of...oh my God, I bet *raw* is a really clichéd thing to say about art. But, like, the choice of materials. And the way the figure is like...barely holding it together."

"It's also pretty angry," said the guy. He was small and slight, with a faint rash of dark stubble across his jaw.

"Is it?" I squinted.

"Well, I was angry when I made it."

"Oh, for fuck's sake." I gave him a dirty look. "That's cheating. It's hard enough having opinions about art without the artist standing there laughing at you."

"I'm not laughing. You were looking at my sculpture. I thought you might be interested."

"Yeah, you have massively misread the situation. I mean," I went on quickly when I realised how rude that sounded, "I'm sure it's great. I just suck at culture. If I was a yoghurt, I–I wouldn't be a yoghurt."

He gave a slow, sly grin. "Wow, you also suck at analogies."

"I suck at many things," I told him.

"And now"—his eyes met mine—"you're just bragging."

I opened my mouth, then closed it again quickly. This was gently circling the outskirts of flirty. And on the one hand that was nice and weirdly affirming, especially because, now I thought about it, I hadn't once thought to ask him if he was planning to sell my story to the newspapers. On the other hand... "Um... I don't mean to... At the risk of making assumptions, I'm engaged."

He laughed. And I flattered myself that he also looked just a tiny bit disappointed. "Oh right, you're Luc. I should have guessed when you had no idea about art."

"Hey, there are at least four other people here who are *exactly* as ignorant as I am."

"I can go flirt with them if you like," he said.

"Nope. All married. So you're stuck with me. Or I suppose you could go talk with literally anyone else."

"Well." His lips quirked back into that devilish smile. "I kind of already know this crowd. So unless you want to go back to your married friends, I'm good."

I gave a hollow groan. "Please don't make me go back to them. They're still looking at baby pictures, and two of them are trying to get a mortgage."

"That's one hell of a stag do."

"Hey." I poked him lightly. "Non-gender-specific animal

do, thank you. And also, I don't know your name, which is rude because you know mine."

"I'm an artist," he told me, "so I'm allowed to be rude."

"Wow, you really are a friend of Priya's."

He laughed. "Sorry. It's Tyler."

"And this…" I gestured hopelessly at the sculpture. "This is an art that you did."

"It is indeed," he confirmed, "an art that I did. A raw, angry, melancholy art that I did."

"What were you raw, angry, and melancholy about?"

He lifted one shoulder in a sort of self-mocking shrug. "The Tavistock Centre."

"Oh," I said, finally getting a piece of art. "Is that why… Are those calendars?"

"Yeah. Honestly, it's a slightly pissy piece of protest art, but having to wait four and a half years for an initial consultation is total shit."

I gave one of those this-is-a-major-problem-that-I-cannot-in-any-way-contribute-to-solving cringes. "I'm sorry. That is… totally shit."

"Don't worry about it. I waited, I got my diagnosis, I waited again, I got referred to an endocrinologist. Finally got on T."

"Yay," I offered.

"And thankfully," Tyler added, "I'm not married so I don't have a spouse who would have a legal right to block my transition. Sorry. Angry statue." He pointed at himself. "Still quite narked."

"If it helps"—I leaned in slightly—"you're hot, free, and single. And if there's one thing I've learned from Priya, it's that making angry art is a great way to pull."

He nodded. "Yeah, I just need to work on not going for the engaged guy at the engagement party."

"For what it's worth," I said, "I absolutely would if I wasn't engaged. Then again, if I wasn't engaged, I'd probably be a self-loathing prick and we'd have a shit time."

"Then I'll take engaged and you not being a self-loathing prick."

I snagged us a couple of glasses of... Actually we'd gone through the prosecco budget and were now into undisclosed fizzy wine. "And a non-shit time."

"A non-shit time," echoed Tyler, raising his glass.

"Of," I added, "an engaged-person-appropriate variety."

He nodded. "I was thinking we could drink, dance, lightly flirt on the understanding nothing would happen, and you could get all the art wrong so I could laugh at you."

"That"—I too lifted my glass—"sounds like my kind of evening."

CHAPTER 38

IT HAD BEEN MY IDEA that we go back to Quo Vadis—the restaurant where we'd had our first, disastrous date—some time before the wedding. And, at the time, the day after our non-gender-specific animal parties had seemed sensible. Besides, scheduling anything at the moment was borderline impossible because it meant planning an event inside planning another event. Our life was logistics all the way down.

Unfortunately, I'd been working on the assumption that our non-gender-specific animal parties would be fairly low-key and wrap up before midnight. And Oliver's had: he'd been for a nice dinner with his nice friends, read a couple of chapters of *Real Life*, and gone to sleep. I, by contrast, had drunk more than I'd drunk in years, partied until dawn with a bunch of artists, had breakfast in—I couldn't remember, been deposited at my flat by kindly strangers, and woken at three in the afternoon with creases on my face from the sofa cushions where I'd apparently passed out.

All of which meant I was hungover and already late for the emotionally significant, relationship-bookending date I had myself arranged when my dad called.

If I'd been thinking clearly, I wouldn't even have picked up, especially since the last time we'd spoken he'd made me yet another empty promise and then fucked off out my life. But see above re late and hungover.

"Have you got cancer?" I asked. "Actually, even if you do, I don't care."

"I'm doing well," he told me as if I'd made a sincere enquiry into his health instead of strongly implying I didn't give a shit whether he lived or died. "Thanks for asking."

"I didn't."

There was the teeniest tiniest of pauses. "I was talking to NME today, and they wanted to know what I was doing for your wedding."

Turning onto Dean Street, I paused because barging into a restaurant late, hungover, and on the phone was the wrong kind of triple threat. "I don't know, Dad. What are you doing for my wedding?"

"Well"—a still teenier, still tinier pause—"that very much depends on you."

I'd say this was Jon Fleming all over, but everything Jon Fleming did was Jon Fleming all over. As far as I could tell, being yourself all over at all times was basically how you got to be his brand of famous. "Sorry, do you want to come to my wedding?"

"I thought you might want me to come."

"Sorry, do you want to come to my wedding but also not want to say you want to come to my wedding because you have the emotional maturity of a...of a...a complete wanker?"

"If you don't want me there, I'll understand. I'm sure you still have a lot of complicated feelings."

Oh, fuck him. He was going down this road again, and while this time I didn't have Oliver with me to call him on his bullshit, that was okay. "Actually," I told him, "my feelings are pretty simple." For a start, I was one hundred percent confident that this was one hundred percent about him thinking it would be good PR to be seen at his gay son's gay wedding and zero percent about anything else.

"I suppose it would be difficult for your mother as well," Jon Fleming mused. It was a *pointed* muse.

And just for a moment, I could see the interview as if I was streaming it there and then: *Obviously I would have loved to go to Luc's wedding, but Odile, she can be so unstable.* I tried to defug my head, which was difficult given how late I'd been out the previous night. "Are you really telling me I have to invite you to my wedding or you'll shit on Mum in the tabloids?"

"Of course not." He sounded offended, the way obnoxious people always sounded offended when you confronted them with their obnoxious behaviour.

Well, this sucked. On one level, I knew my mum could take care of herself. After all, she'd *been* taking care of herself for years, and she'd got spectacularly good at giving no fucks in her old age. On another, less rational level, I always hated it when my crap blew back on her. But I could do this. I was a strong, independent person and I could handle my dad being a bully. "Are you sure," I tried, "because it sounds a lot like that *is* what you're saying and… well…remember that my fiancé is a barrister."

Technically, of course, he wasn't that sort of barrister. I was just hoping that Jon Fleming's inability to pay attention to anything that wasn't himself meant he wouldn't realise.

"I've never had much time for lawyers," Dad replied. And perhaps I was imagining it, but he sounded cagier than he would have if he'd considered it a totally empty threat.

"Yeah, but lawyers are like gravity," I told him. "It doesn't matter if you've got time for them, it matters that they've got time for you. And if you *did* start telling the *Mail* or the *Mirror* anything about Mum that could be considered, y'know, libellous, then I'd actually know who to talk to now. In fact"—I decided to push my luck—"these days I even know a high-court judge or two."

At the other end of the phone, Jon Fleming made a contemplative noise. He didn't seem bothered exactly—it took a lot more than the threat of legal action to bother Jon Fleming—but one of my dad's most useful qualities was a very specific kind of apathy. If fame or money were on the line, he was unstoppable. But for everything else, he'd always take the easiest possible road to get what he wanted, and if something looked like being even the slightest bit difficult, he'd drop it like he had his marriage and his child. "I was just giving you a call," he said at last, "to see if you wanted me at your wedding. But if you don't"—he gave an infuriating pause—"that's your choice. And I respect it."

"It is."

And, with that, I hung up. In some ways, that had gone better than any other conversation I'd ever had with my dad. But you couldn't win with him. You could only make losing feel marginally less shitty. And so I showed up for my very special, emotionally resonant date with my fiancé who I loved, tired, hungover, late, and mentally drained from dealing with an arsehole.

Oliver was already at the table, where he'd probably been for some time. It was the same table we'd sat at nearly three years ago, and he was wearing the same pin-striped suit—including the pocket watch, that I'd since realised was another of his sly nods to a personal style that only masqueraded as conformity.

"Oh God." I half eased, half tripped onto the banquette. "I'm so sorry. Things got out of hand last night."

One of Oliver's eyebrows twitched upwards in a meaner way than I was expecting. "I'm aware."

Fuck, it really was like our first date. I was rubbish and Oliver was annoyed. "And then," I hurried on, "just as I was getting here, my fucking dad rang."

Oliver de-iced immediately. "Are you all right?"

"Yeah. Fine. He wanted to come to the wedding to prove what a big damn ally he is. I told him to piss off."

Normally Oliver championed my taking of no shit from my dad. But normally we had twice as many dads between us. "Lucien," he started. Then broke off. Then tried again. "I…I'm sure you made the right decision. But I'm rather conscious at the moment that—all going well—one only has one wedding. And, indeed, in the majority of cases one father."

He had a point. It's just his point was about him, not about me. And now he needed me to be all sensitive and shit. Poor bastard. Catching the waiter's eye, I requested literally all the water and then turned back to Oliver. "I'm really sorry your dad, y'know, can't. But my dad is not your dad. And my dad definitely shouldn't."

"I do know that," said Oliver, with the air of someone who did not, in fact, know that.

"Look." I slid a hand across the table to take his. "I was there at the funeral. I heard the…the everything. I get that it's a headfuck and a half to have all these questions about who your father was and what he could have been to you and not have any answers."

Oh God. Oliver was biting his lip and his eyes had gone soft in the bad tearsy way, not the good gazing adoringly way. Not only was I late and hungover to our superspecial emotionally resonant date night, I was going to make Oliver cry in a fancy restaurant.

"But the thing is," I added, probably too quickly, "I have those answers about Jon Fleming. You were there when I got them. When someone drops you like a secretly recorded studio album the second they discover they don't have cancer, you know everything you need to know about them. And one of the things you know is that you don't want them at your wedding."

Oliver blinked rapidly. "Of course. I just… It's our wedding and I think it's important that neither of us look back on it with any regrets."

"Believe me, we'd both regret inviting Jon Fleming big time."

"I'm sure we would have. I think I meant more…in general."

"I've also come to terms with not having a DJ."

He gave the sort of smile you gave because it was expected rather than because you really felt like smiling. "And have you also come to terms with…"

"The venue?" I asked. "No balloon arch?"

"It's more everything the balloon arch represents."

Oh no. We were back here again. Did we have to be back here again? "At this point, Oliver, I don't even know *what* the balloon arch represents. Except for trapped air and arguments."

"I've been wondering that myself," he said. "And do you think it might represent, well, this?"

He passed his phone across the table, which was open at Bridge's Instagram feed. And while the three most recent pictures were the book she was currently reading, her brunch, and a house in Knightsbridge with a pink door, there were about twenty shots from my non-gender-specific animal party. A lot of which were me. A fair few of which were me and Tyler.

I glanced from the phone to Oliver to the phone again. Surely he didn't—

Fuck.

A biley panic was rising up my throat. "Listen, that was just a guy I met at the party. And we were having fun and he knew I was engaged and I went home alo—"

"I know, Lucien. And I trust you. I wouldn't be marrying you if I didn't trust you."

Okay. Phew. That was all very reassuring.

What was less reassuring was that he kept speaking. "It's just…you looked happy."

"I...what?"

While I was working on a more substantial reply, the waiter showed with a very large jug of water. "Are you ready to order?" he asked.

Which sent me into a different kind of panic because I hadn't looked at the menu, and I couldn't ever hear "are you ready to order" without wanting to stick "and if not, why not" on the end.

Oliver, of course, had his neuroses in different places. "A few more minutes, thank you."

Clearly, I needed to loop us back to the you-looked-happy thing. But I wasn't sure I wanted to because it could only really mean two things. Either it meant that my boyfriend-soon-to-be-husband straight up resented my happiness, which sucked, or it meant he thought I couldn't be happy with him, which sucked worse. So instead I fluttered my lashes at him in a blatant attempt at distraction and segued into: "Do you want to order for me?"

He twitched an eyebrow. "If you like, although it will include the eel sandwich again, and don't think I haven't noticed you're deflecting."

"How about," I suggested, "I deflect for now and when I've been fortified with an eel sandwich we can, you know, have a serious conversation sort of thing."

"Very well." Oliver disappeared behind his menu with an eagerness that I hoped was about his love of the food, not his desire to avoid talking.

I peeped over the top, trying to get him to look at me. "I'm happy to eat vegan with you."

"You shouldn't have to."

"No, but I can."

"Do you want to?" he asked in a way that I thought had layers.

This was so typical of At-The-Moment Oliver. I'd deflected, he'd accepted the deflect and was now getting around it anyway.

"That's not a fair question. You don't want to either, but you do it because you think it's right. And I think you're usually right about what's right... I just have crappy follow-through."

"You know I don't like imposing my values on other people."

Fuck, this was still a metaphor, wasn't it? I was too hungover for metaphors. "It's not about imposing your values. But we've been together for a long time and people change each other and that's normal. And, unless the people are arseholes, good." I gulped down my third glass of water. "I'm never going to be a vegan the way you're a vegan. But that doesn't mean I'm going to feel I'm missing out if we go to a nice restaurant and I sometimes choose to have the salad."

He seemed, at least, to be thinking about it. And when he asked, "And are you in a salad mood tonight?" I was ninety percent certain he was talking about the food.

"How about"—oh, I was so fucking grown-up—"I compromise. I'd like the eel to start for old time's sake. And I'll join you for a vegan main."

Oliver's lips twitched. "So, I'll order for you, but you'll tell me what to order?"

I grinned at him, getting my own metaphor on. "Kind of the best of both worlds, don't you think?"

This seemed to be going better. It was definitely going better. I'd managed to avoid throwing up in the bread basket, Oliver had nearly smiled, and here we were in our first-date restaurant, not having any awkward conversations about anything.

At least until I popped the last piece of eel sandwich into my mouth.

"Lucien." It was like someone had flicked a switch and put Oliver in serious mode again. "I do need to talk about last night."

"I told you nothing happened."

"And I told you that wasn't the problem."

The biley panic was rising again. "Oliver, there shouldn't *be* a problem. It was one night, I went a bit wild, I overslept, I showed up here with a headache, and I'm sorry."

"But are you sure you…" Oliver began. Then stopped again. "It doesn't have to be one night if you…if you don't want it to."

I reached for my water glass. "Honestly, I'm not sure I could take another one."

"No, but…but you've made it quite clear that you…that you value that way of expressing yourself?"

Oh, for fuck's sake. "A balloon arch is just a balloon arch. It doesn't mean anything except that I like rainbow balloon arches and you don't."

"I don't think that's actually true, and I don't think you do either. And it concerns me that we've had such difficulty designing a wedding that we feel represents us both equally."

This was supposed to be an evening for us. Our special evening. Our last special evening. And all we'd done was talk about my dad and wedding shit. "Oliver, I'm sick of the fucking wedding."

I'd said that way too loudly and way too emphatically.

"And you don't feel," asked Oliver calmly, "that's a rather telling statement to be making a week before you're getting married?"

"It's not about the marriage. It's about the"—I waved my hands about—"the everything else. I just want to be with you like we used to before everything was about place settings and table confetti and never knowing which one of us is being the arsehole."

"What worries me is that it might be neither of us."

I glared at him across the table. "Only you could find that worrying."

"On the contrary"—he was still doing that slightly detached rational thing he did when things were a bit too intense for him— "if one of us is being an arsehole, then everything is simple. That person just needs to stop being an arsehole, and we'll be fine. But if neither of is being an arsehole, then that implies that we might have—and forgive the strong language—fundamental incompatibilities."

In any other context, I'd have found the fact he called the phrase *fundamental incompatibilities* strong language kind of endearing.

This—our special, emotionally resonate date I'd been late for and hungover at—was not any other context.

So I was fucking terrified.

CHAPTER 39

"WHAT KIND OF FUNDAMENTAL INCOMPATIBILITIES?"
I definitely did not screech. "Because it feels like you're blowing
the balloon arch up out of all proportion. Which is, I suppose, at
least appropriate for a balloon-based structure."

"It is not," said Oliver tightly, "the fucking balloon—" He
broke off abruptly as the waiter set down our pea-and-broad-bean
rotolos. "Thank you very much." Then unbroke equally abruptly.
"Arch."

"I know, I know. It's what..." I made the air-quotiest air
quotes that ever air-quoted. "'The balloon arch represents.' Which
doesn't have to be anything, Oliver. It's fucking balloons."

Oliver took a deep breath. I had a sinking feeling this was
going to be logical and wordy. Which was sad because I usually
found Oliver being logical and wordy very hot. "I realise you
would prefer this to be simple, Lucien. But it isn't. Over the past
year, you've said some things to me that have required me to do a
certain amount of self-reflection, and I need to know the conclu-
sions I've reached are acceptable to you, especially if we're going
to spend our lives together."

I briefly put my throbbing head in my hands. "Is this relationship drama or a deposition?"

"I'm not totally convinced you know what a deposition is."

Fair.

"But," he went on, "I'm trying to make this as clear as I can. Because I don't want there to be any misunderstandings or for either of us to make any mistakes."

"You're not a mistake," I told him, less affectionately than the words suggested. "But I'm starting to wonder if you think I am."

"That's not in question. I just want to talk to you about... about how I'm feeling, I suppose."

I sat up and stabbed resentfully at my rotolo. "How you're feeling about rainbow balloon arches?"

"In essence, yes." He gave an anxious little sigh. "Because, in a way, you're correct. I will never truly know if the reason if I am discomforted by the trappings of mainstream LGBTQ culture is because I was raised in an environment where they were viewed negatively. Or because I simply don't feel included by them. Or, indeed, because I have legitimate concerns about their origins and increasing commercialisation. And, honestly, I don't think there's any way to disentangle those things."

This was turning into very much the opposite of the romantic meal I'd envisioned. "Okay? That's good for you, I guess?"

"I just want you to...understand."

He was looking at me kind of the way he had when he first told me he worked in criminal defence. And it made me feel...weird. Mostly good weird. Like, even after three years with Oliver, it still did strange things to my head and my heart that someone could care that much about what I thought. I put my fork down. Because, suddenly, I really did want to y'know... "Understand what?" I asked.

"That I'll never be...that I'll never express my identity in the way you express your identity. And while"—his mouth turned up wryly—"that doesn't come from a wholly uncomplicated place, it isn't a flaw in who I am. It' s just who I am."

I thought I *did* understand that. But then again I'd clearly given Oliver the impression I didn't, and Oliver was way smarter than me. "I–I do get that," I tried. "It's just sometimes hard to get my brain around."

"That's the problem. I'm not sure I want to be something that's hard to get your brain around."

This felt like it was teetering on the edge of a serious place. A potentially relationship-ending, marriage-breaking serious place. So I gambled. "Okay, but I think that ship has already sailed."

"How reassuring." He was giving me an arch look, but he seemed to be listening.

"Not like that. I just… You know you think about things differently from me. About life, about the law. Hell"—I speared a piece of rotolo and waved it at him—"even about food. I don't *want* to be in a relationship with somebody I always agree with."

"I'm not sure that being vegan is the same as processing my identity in a way you can't access."

"Isn't it, though?" I asked, hoping my double or nothing was going to come down double, not nothing. "It's not like being gay—being the kind of gay where you don't wear rainbows or go on marches—"

"I go on marches, Lucien. It's parties I have trouble with, not protests."

"Okay, but I mean, I don't think being gay is more important to you than…" I waved my hands in a tight little circle "…all the rest of it. Like, you actually *care* about shit. Way more shit than I care about. And that doesn't mean you're letting the other side down or anything. It makes you like…like a thousand-piece Moomin jigsaw with a wolf in a wig."

Oliver stared blankly at me. Which I probably deserved.

"Sorry. My mum's randomly got into jigsaws and maybe the Moomins? I should have just said you're complicated, but all the bits make a nice picture."

He thought about this for a long time. Then gave up. "Thank you. I think?"

"Oliver, I'm sorry." I tried again. "I never meant to make you feel that I thought you were, you know, doing gay wrong. Or that you had to be like me. Any more than you think I have to be like you." I paused. "At least, I hope you don't. Because if you do, you're fucked."

"I've never wanted you to be anyone but yourself," said Oliver immediately because he was also way better at being reassuring than me.

"And I don't want you to be anything but that either," I told him. "So we're good."

He wasn't giving me we're-good face. He was giving me we-might-be-good-but face. Which was better than we're-fucked face but not by much. "My lingering concern is that works in theory, but in practice *you* being who *you* are and *me* being who *I* am may not work."

Shit. "Not work how? And if you mention the fucking balloon arch one more time, I swear I'll—"

"You're the one who keeps bringing up the balloon arch. But it *is* an appropriate example. If we get married underneath a rainbow balloon arch, we'll be denying who *I* am, and if we don't, we'll be denying who *you* are. And while that's a relatively trivial matter on its own, these things can add up. Over the long term they can add up catastrophically."

"They haven't so far," I pointed out.

"No, but marriage can change things. That's why the pictures from your bachelor party bothered me so much. You were so happy in them, but it was a happiness I don't think I could ever share with you and, well, I suppose I wanted to make certain you knew that if you wanted to pursue it, I...well, I won't stand in your way."

Oh fucking hell. He was really making this difficult. "Sorry, are you dumping me because I enjoyed going to a party at a queer gallery?"

"I'm not dumping you at all." He picked up his fork, eyed his rotolo, and then put the fork down again. "I think what I'm doing is…is giving you a chance to dump me. If you… Now you…"

"Now I what?" I said, still at very much the wrong volume for this kind of restaurant.

There was a pause. Oliver was breathing in a very, very careful way. And his eyes had gone their flattest, coldest grey. "When we first met," he went on doggedly, "you were, we were both, but you especially were…in rather a bad place. And, sometimes, the person you need to be with when you're in a bad place isn't the person you want to be with when you're…when you're not."

My mouth literally fell open. Fortunately, I'd recently taken a sip of water, so it was empty. "What the fuck? Of all the things I'd expected to go wrong this evening, you going full *I have healed you and now I set you free* was not on the short list."

"I don't mean to…" Oliver broke off, looking embarrassed, as well he bloody well should. "That is…" He squirmed. Again, in a different context, it would have been cute. "I just saw the pictures of you looking happy and in your element, doing the sorts of things that, realistically, you're not likely to do very much of with me. And I–I suppose I got in my head."

"Too fucking right you did." I kicked him under the table, entirely deliberately. "I look happy in those pictures because I'm at a party where I'm celebrating the fact that I'm getting married to the man I love. Who is you. You fool. You numpty. You absolute pillock."

He was blushing now. Really blushing. "Yes. Well. I suppose when you put it like that, it does make sense." Somehow, impossibly, the blush got deeper. "You…you're a very entrancing man, Lucien. And you could be with someone equally entrancing, someone with whom your life could be interesting and glamorous. Instead of, I suppose, whatever I can offer you. Which is, by comparison, rather quiet and ordinary."

My head was throbbing. I laid it momentarily on the table, which might have disrespectful to the restaurant dining experience, but I was having a feel. "For the record, and I can't believe you're making me say this, I've always found you pretty fucking entrancing."

"Are you sure?" He gave a little cough. "Because, right now, I feel like someone you argue about napkins and DJs with."

That was true. But it didn't seem fair to admit it. "Yeah, but… that's temporary. It's a wedding thing. Not an *us* thing." God, I hoped it was a wedding thing, not an us thing. I levered myself back off the table. "Oliver, I'm not going to lie, I had a great time last night. But the reason I had a great time was because when I lived that kind of life before I was miserable and hating myself and trying to prove something to a world that could not conceivably have given less of a fuck." I reached for his hand and he let me take it, the mediocre engagement ring I'd given him gleaming between us. "Basically, that's the first time in a decade I've partied for… for fun. And I enjoyed it, and I maybe even needed it, but I also needed to be coming home to you. I mean, symbolically. Because obviously I went back to the flat and face-planted on my couch."

Oliver's fingers curled tightly around mine. "I don't want to be taking anything away from you. Or turning you into someone you're not supposed to be."

"I don't know who I'm supposed to be," I told him. "I don't think anyone does. And being with you isn't a compromise for me. It's…it's what I want. Otherwise I wouldn't have fucking asked you to marry me."

Oliver gave a little smile. "Yes, that was quite the gesture."

"I know, right?" I risked smiling back. "Didn't think I had it in me. I must really love you or something."

"Yes. Yes, you must." The blush was playing an encore on Oliver's face. "I'm sorry. I've been quite silly tonight."

I rolled my eyes. "I can't believe you tried to get me to dump you at Quo Vadis less than a week before our wedding."

"What can I say? Perhaps this place brings out my insecurities."

"Last time we were here," I reminded him, "I pretended I spoke French to impress you."

"Last time we were here," he replied, "I was entirely convinced you despised me."

I gazed at him in an embarrassingly mushy way. "I've never despised you. And I never will."

"Oh, Lucien"—it was Oliver's driest voice—"you always say the most romantic things."

"Hey, it could be worse. I could have called you a Moomin jigsaw again."

At last, he laughed.

And, figuring I was onto a good thing, I decided to seal the deal romance-wise. "How about we share a lemon posset for dessert?"

"That would be wonderful," replied Oliver, for once letting himself enjoy a thing uncomplicatedly. Or at least he did for about half a second. "Ah, except. I believe it's made with cream?"

I basked for a moment in having, very briefly, not fucked one thing up. "Actually, when I booked, I told them this was our first-date restaurant and that we'd had the lemon posset and you'd gone vegan since but could they do something. And they said they could."

Oliver's eyes got very close to teary again. "Lucien." He swallowed. "That was...that was terribly sweet of you."

If I'd been a lot more grown-up, I'd have said, *It was nothing.* If I'd been slightly more grown-up, I'd have said, *Anything for you, babe*. But wanting to make someone happy as much as I wanted to make Oliver happy was a very naked feeling to be having in a restaurant so, instead, I just gave an embarrassed cringe and said something that came out as "inerenugh?"

By some magic I'd never quite mastered, Oliver caught the waiter's eye, seamlessly volunteered that the meal had been lovely and, from there, segued into a requesting a lemon posset with two spoons to finish. I should have got used to Oliver being good at this shit by now but...I hadn't. Really, all that had changed was that instead making me feel inadequate, it made me feel smug that my boyfriend—fiancé—was polite and considerate and confident and knew how to restaurant.

"You know I'm not letting you use that spoon, right?"

He rolled his eyes in his secretly-into-it way. "When did this become a thing with us?"

"Since we went to this restaurant," I told him, "and you looked at a lemon posset like you wanted to have sex with it. I have to feed you the dessert so it's a threesome, not voyeurism."

"I did not want to have sex with the lemon posset." It was now Oliver's turn to speak slightly too loudly for the restaurant. He lowered his voice. "I wanted to have sex with you, but you were making it very clear there was no possibility of that happening."

"Well"—I grinned at him—"now you get us both."

"Although one of you only temporarily."

My grin froze. "You are talking about the lemon posset, right?"

At this moment the waiter returned with the requested posset, plus two spoons. It was as beautiful as it had been last time, all sunshine yellow and tempting.

"Do you have something you want to tell me?" I asked it, scowling.

It probably said something about our relationship that Oliver had a specific exasperated-fondness sigh. "Mr. Posset, remember that you have a right not to self-incriminate."

"Yeah," I threw back, having seen many police procedurals, "but it may harm its defence if it fails to mention when question-ing something it later relies on in court."

Snatching up both the posset and one of the spoons, Oliver half turned away from me. "Excuse me, I need to confer with my client."

"'By confer with,' do you mean eat? I'm pretty sure you can get disbarred for that."

"I can confidently say"—Oliver dug the spoon into Mr. Posset—"that I know of no barrister who has ever been disbarred for eating their clients."

"But not because it's *allowed*? Because it's never happened."

"I think," said Oliver thoughtfully, "it might be considered a violation of the core duty to act in the best interests of the client. And, for that matter, the requirement not to behave in a manner that diminishes the trust the public places in the profession. But there's never technically been a test case on it."

"Well, it's good a job this lemon posset is your secret lover and not your client."

"Isn't it?"

He reached across the table, offering me a generous spoon of the dessert I was now trying really hard not to think of as Mr. Posset. Thankfully my appetite outweighed my empathy. Which, thinking about it, was why I'd make a crap vegan.

And, anyway, Oliver looked ridiculously handsome just then, his eyes all softly silver, and the stern lines of his face gentled some-how. I leaned forward and, telling myself I was being sexy and ele-gant, and not looking at all like a plastic hippo in a family board game, accepted a mouthful of tart lemony goodness.

Even accounting for the no-cows-were-harmed factor, it was amazing. "Urmgudidfrgurnhwrgrdthsws."

"Pardon?" asked Oliver.

"I said, 'Oh my God, I'd forgotten how good this was.'"

"If I looked anything like that, I can see why you thought I was cheating."

I chased a smudge from the corner of my lips. "Hey, your eating-dessert face is way more cheatingy than my eating-dessert face."

"Logically," he pointed out, "neither of us have any basis on which to make that comparison."

Yoinking the ramekin over to my side of the table, I took control of the situation. "You either get to be pedantic or eat posset. Which is going to be?"

He lowered his lashes is mock contrition. "Posset, please."

While Oliver's eating-dessert face was sexy as fuck, his asking-for-dessert face was sexy as fucker. And for a moment, just for a moment, I half wished this was our first date again. I mean, not literally because it had been a disaster. But I wanted to keep this. This almost fragile feeling of everything being what it was and being for its own sake and not needing to go anywhere or become anything else.

But that was how relationships began. It wasn't how they lasted. You couldn't live forever on lemon posset and French toast. At some point you had to think, really think, about where you were going and what it meant. You had to ask if you were in this forever, and if you were, what were you going to do about it, and if you weren't, what were you even doing.

You were either in or you were out. You either got married or you moved on.

And I never wanted to move on. Oliver was the best thing that had ever happened to me, and I couldn't let him un-happen. If that meant fighting about bands and arguing about venues and making peace with his mother and endlessly rehashing a fucking balloon arch, then...then it was worth it.

It had to be worth it.

Because otherwise, what were we?

CHAPTER 40

THE GOOD THING ABOUT GETTING married—I mean, apart from the whole spending your life with the person you loved bit—was that it gave you a lot to do. Which made it very difficult to have complicated feelings. Or, to put it another way, very easy to avoid having them. And that worked for me right until the night before the wedding.

I'd gone to bed early because I was trying to be responsible, but then I'd had to get out of bed to throw up. Then I'd gone back to bed, but I'd had to get up again to throw up again. And, after throwing up for the third time, I called Bridge. Being Bridge, she answered. Even though it was three in the morning.

"Luc?" she asked—sleepy but doing her best. "Is everything okay?"

I lay down on the bathroom floor. "No. I keep vomiting and I think that probably means something."

Mumbly Tom noises drifted down the phone. Then I heard him getting up and moving into a different room, reasoning correctly that this was going to be a long call. Then Bridge's voice again, "What did you have for dinner?"

"I didn't have dinner. I felt too much like I was going to be sick, and then I was. Loads. And I feel like I'm going to be sick again, except I don't think there's any sick left to be. So I'm just sweating and heaving."

Bridge thought for a moment. "It's all right to be nervous..."

"This isn't nervous, Bridge. This is my body telling me something is profoundly wrong."

"Well." She thought for another moment. "Take some milk of magnesia?"

Another wave of nausea swept over me. "No, I mean profoundly wrong emotionally."

"It'll calm your stomach down," she insisted.

Still feeling wobbly in six different ways for six different reasons, I crawled upright and checked my bathroom cabinet. "I don't have any. I have"—I took another look—"ibuprofen and Bonjela."

"I'll bring you something." I could already hear her getting out of bed.

"You don't have to. Not bring something. I mean, you should stay at home in your home where you live with your husband who you're married to."

The thumping and rustling from the other end of the line suggested she was already getting dressed. "I'll still be married when I get back. You've been my best friend for years. I'm not letting you down now."

"You wouldn't be letting me down," I told her. "You just wouldn't be letting me drag you out of bed at three in the morning when we're both getting up in four hours."

"Well, there you are. I'm rising early, that's all. It's healthy. It's healthy, wealthy, *and wise.*"

Checking the cabinet had taken it out of me, so I lay back down on the floor and tried to enjoy the cool of the tiles. Unfortunately, I couldn't enjoy anything right now. "I'll be fine. It probably *is* just nerves." My stomach churned uneasily. *Oh God.* Was this the universe punishing me for wishing Miles would shit himself on the way down the aisle? "Besides," I went on, "I think I might need to get some air."

"I'll get some air with you," cried Bridge, far too enthusiastically. "We can get air together."

"Why? Do you think I'll need help carrying it?"

Bridge gave a kind of vindicated squeak. "See, you're being sarcastic. That means you're feeling better. Which means I'm helping."

I shouldn't have called her. There was no way she was going to let me spend the few hours before my wedding puking alone into a toilet. Not if I could spend them puking with her. But I'd panicked. Because I was getting married in the morning. And instead of feeling excited or giddy or a little bit anxious, I was feeling like an informer from a seventies mob movie being slowly drowned in cement. And there was no point pretending now that I hadn't known all along that she'd drop everything and come for me.

Married or not she was, after all, my best friend.

"I'm calling a cab," said Bridge from the other end of the phone. "Where shall I meet you?"

I groaned and ground my face against the bathroom floor. "Anywhere but here. The walls are closing in and everything smells of vomit."

In hindsight, *anywhere but here* hadn't been a helpful thing to say. Something that became only more apparent as I half climbed, half fell out of my own taxi and made my way to our agreed rendezvous point in the middle of the Millennium Bridge.

"Why?" I asked as soon as I was in earshot. "Is this because your name is Bridge? So you thought of a bridge?"

Her ash-blond hair was whipping slightly in the wind. "Maybe? I *had* just woken up. Although also the nice thing about being on a bridge is that if you're sick, you can go over the side."

I couldn't tell if that made me feel better or worse. "What if I fall in the Thames?"

"Then wedding nerves will be the least of your worries."

Drawing my coat more tightly around me, I lurched over to the railing. Not because I had any intention of spewing over it, but because we were stuck on a bridge and there wasn't much else to do. It was a weird view because you had the city gleaming on either side, but the sky above and the river below were dull, black, and voidy. Which at least matched my mood. "I don't think this is nerves," I said finally. "I think this is *I've made a terrible mistake.*"

Bridge came and stood beside me. "Oh, it's so pretty at night," she cooed.

"Bridge. What part of *terrible mistake* did you not hear?"

"The part where it makes any sense."

"I didn't say it made sense." Folding my arms on the top of the railing, I sagged. "I said it was how I felt."

For a moment Bridge was silent on the silent bridge. "Are you not in love with him anymore?"

The thought of not being in love with Oliver wasn't even vomit-inducing. It was just…unapproachable from any angle. "Of course I'm in love with him."

"Then everything is going to be fine." Bridge put a comforting hand on my arm. "Love means never having to say 'Oh my god, I've made a terrible mistake.'"

"Except that's not true, is it? You can love someone and still royally fuck up."

"Yes, but because you love each other, you come through it. And that's what marriage is."

I buried my face even farther into the crook of my elbow and made an embarrassing half-sobby noise. "Is it? Is it really?"

"Yes," said Bridge with utter confidence.

"But how do you *know*?" I asked. "What if it's not? What if it's, like, fighting all the time, or one of you walking out in three years, or something you can't do at all because the law says your relationship doesn't count, or constantly trying to keep up with your ex and his twink husband who is going to be way less cute when he gets older and then he'll find out what a prick he's married or—"

Bridge made a confused but gamely sympathetic noise. "Aren't you overcomplicating this just a little?"

"Am I? How can I tell? I've never had to think about marriage before. When was I *meant* to think about it? In the incredibly narrow window between it becoming a legal option and my boyfriend selling me out to a newspaper with a red top?"

"I suppose *ideally*..." Bridge was shuffling uncomfortably, her coat drawn tight around her even though it was quite a mild spring evening. "Absolutely *ideally*, you'd have thought about it at least a little bit before you, you know, proposed?"

I looked up from where I'd been making an unconvincing go of pretending not to cry. "In case you haven't noticed, Bridge, I'm not an *ideally* sort of person. And now I'm stuck because I'm getting married tomorrow, and I don't think I actually want to get married tomorrow. But if I don't, then I've destroyed the only good relationship I've ever had and probably ever will have."

"You must have wanted to get married, though?" Bridge had that hopeful-but-disoriented tone she always got when she butted up against ideas that didn't quite fit her view of the world. "Otherwise, you wouldn't have asked him at all. This is just cold feet."

"My feet aren't the problem," I told her. "The rest of me is. And I guess at the time I wasn't thinking about the future. I just knew I wanted to be with Oliver and I wanted to show him that and I didn't know how."

Bridge was staring at me in a way I never wanted my best friend to stare at me. "What do you mean, you didn't know how?" she asked. "You could have said, 'I love you and want to be with you.' Or..." Inspiration struck her. "Blow jobs. Men like blow jobs."

"Sorry, are you saying my options were propose marriage or suck him off?"

"No," said Bridge firmly. "The first thing I said you should do was tell him how you felt. And I think the fact that you blanked that option might mean something."

"Oh God." I grabbed at my hair. "I...I'm just not very good at expressing myself emotionally. It was right after Miles's wedding and I was in a weird place and it's really hard when you've been with someone a long time and it's working really well but you've got no, like, way of showing or proving or—" I broke off. "And, anyway, he said yes. What kind of arsehole says yes to a proposal from a famously self-destructive person a couple of days after his ex-boyfriend's wedding?"

"I don't know," said Bridge. "I suppose someone who loves you and supports you and wants to be with you no matter what."

I gave another groan. The only thing that was stopping me from crying more was that I'd been sick enough that I was out of fluids. "I know. What a bastard."

She was giving me strong stop-messing-about face. "This is serious, Luc. You're talking about potentially blowing up a wonderful relationship with a wonderful man. Are you sure you don't want to get married and aren't just being, y'know, *you*?"

Fuck. Fuck fuck fuck fuck fuck. "I'm...I think I'm sure, Bridge. Like, we had this really nice evening at Quo Vadis—"

"Oh, your first-date restaurant," cried Bridge, clasping her hands. "That's so romantic."

"Yes." I found I was gripping the rail far too tightly, either for emphasis or security. "That was the problem. It *was* romantic. It was…" Well, actually it had been fraught at the beginning. But then it had been kind of perfect. "It was great. It was the best evening we'd had for ages. And I kept wishing we could just go back to that. Except that's not how relationships work."

There was an expression of deep sorrow in Bridge's eyes, like I was falling into a sad cloud. It was the expression she'd always go to when she was trying not to let me know how badly I'd let her down. "No, Luc. It's not."

"I've fucked everything all the way up, haven't I?"

Bridge was uncharacteristically silent.

"Bridge?" I asked.

"I'm thinking."

"And?"

"I think," she said slowly, "you might have fucked everything all the way up."

If there was ever a time you didn't want someone to agree with you, this had been it. "What do I do?"

She was silent again. And then, "I suppose you've got three options."

"Okay?"

"Get married anyway?" she suggested.

My stomach sloshed in time with the waters below. And my hands got insta-sweaty. "Not wild about that. Next?"

"Leave Oliver at the altar."

"Also not great." My stomach continued to slosh and my hands continued to sweat. "Three had better be a doozy."

"Um…hope really hard that the last few months have all been a dream."

"I'm hoping," I said. "Is it working?"

"I don't know." Bridge's eyes got wide and confused. "I don't feel like I'm in someone else's dream. But how would I tell?"

"Is there a fourth option?" I asked desperately.

"I could try to think of one," offered Bridge, ever supportive. "But since the dream plan was the best I could come up with, it might take a while and be worse."

Oh God. I'd had something wonderful, and I'd ruined it like I always I did. "What if I just ran away?"

"That's still leaving Oliver at the altar, only without having the guts to do it to his face."

"Cool," I said. "Let's do that one."

Bridge subjected me to her sternest stare. "I know you don't mean that, Luc."

"You're right, you're right." I paused. "What if I fake my death?"

"Four months after his father's funeral? Oliver might take that quite badly too."

I turned my back to the river and sat on the ground, head tucked against my knees. "Fuck, the hope-it-was-all-a-dream plan is looking really shiny right now."

Quietly, Bridge lowered herself down beside me. "Well, I could slap you if you like, but I think you might have to accept that this actually *is* reality."

She was right. It sucked, but she was right. "So it's be married when I don't want to be married or tell the man I love, on our wedding day, that I don't want to marry him."

"Yes."

"Fuck."

"Yes."

I looked up, and she looked back. Sometimes I thought Bridge's capacity for compassion was endless, but maybe it just happened to be about the same as my capacity for bullshit. I suppose in many ways that was the same thing. "Leaving somebody at the altar is a pretty shitty thing to do, isn't it?"

Bridge nodded.

"And probably...probably he'll dump me?" That made my stomach move in a whole new and interesting way that I wished I hadn't learned it could move.

"I don't know. I–I think I would." Her nose wrinkled. "I mean, if I was standing there with Tom in front of all our friends and the vicar said, 'Do you take this woman? and Tom said, 'No, but I'd still like to hang out,' I might not respond well."

I sighed. "Guess I really should have taken the blow-job option instead?"

"That *would* have been simpler." She put an arm around me. "If this doesn't seem like a silly question, why *don't* you want to be married to Oliver?"

"I guess," I began, although I wasn't sure how I was going to continue. "I guess because...me and Oliver... It's always been... We shouldn't work."

"Oh, but you *do*," Bridge insisted. "And I always *knew* you would."

"You didn't know, you happened to guess right." I sighed. "The truth is, I don't quite know how we're together. And it's not that we're fragile, it's just that we're...our own thing. And marriage is its own thing. And I'm not sure those things fit."

"You didn't think you and Oliver would fit at all, and you did."

"I know. But this feels wrong, and being with Oliver has never felt wrong."

"Getting married doesn't have to change anything," Bridge offered. "It's just a party and a piece of paper."

"It's not, though, is it?" I said. "It's everything marriage means to everyone who's ever been married ever, or known anybody who's ever been married ever, or everyone who's ever been told they can't get married ever. It's this huge thing that eats things, and I think it's going to eat me and Oliver."

Bridge squidged a bit closer. "Have you thought about telling him this?"

"Yeah, the time to do so would have been literally any time before now."

She made a nervous face. "So that leaves option two?"

"I can't do that either." The thought of how badly that would hurt Oliver was like a knife in my balls.

"It's one or two, Luc," said Bridge with gentle finality.

Which made me realise, well past the eleventh hour, that there wasn't really a choice here. It had to be option one. Because I loved Oliver and, like a prick, I'd asked him to marry me and, supportive of my bullshit as always, he'd said he would. The least I could do was not leave him at the altar.

I had to see this through.

CHAPTER 41

THE HAPPIEST DAY OF MY life was passing in a miserable blur. Bridge got me home at about six and Priya picked me up an hour later, making certain to tell me I looked like crap. Which I did. Oliver was going to be so proud to take this haggard, badly shaven wreck of a human being to be his lawful wedded husband.

And now I'd been deposited in a side room at the Green Room—why had we chosen a venue with multiple rooms that was only named after one of them—where I was managing very diligently not to jump out the window or drown myself in the tall Americano that Priya had bought me in an effort to get me functional.

My brain was blank apart from a scrolling marquee that read *This is a terrible mistake, this a terrible mistake.* But we'd been through this last night: in the vortex of fuckery I'd made of my life, this was the least fucky way to fuck things.

And we'd be fine. We'd be fine. We were a good couple. We worked. We weren't very good at organising weddings, but whatever happened with Oliver, I could be a hundred percent certain I was never doing this again. So that was cool. I had learned a valuable lesson about myself and the world.

Oh God. I was going to throw up.

"Lucien?" I heard Oliver come up behind me as I was crouched over a wastepaper basket in a state of pre-upchuck preparedness. "Are you all right?"

"Totally fine," I told him. "I just dropped some...cuff links."

"You're not wearing cuff links."

"No, because I dropped them."

"Your shirt has buttons on it."

"Obviously." I sat back on my heels. "Because otherwise my chest would be hanging out."

"On the cuffs."

"Oh, right." Clearly the cuff-link jig was up so I switched to a different pretending-everything-was-normal strategy. "Anyway, shouldn't we be not seeing each other before the—" Finally, I glanced Oliver's way and realised that he looked, if anything, worse than I did. I wasn't sure whether to be relieved or insulted. "Actually, are *you* okay?"

Oliver's mouth tightened. Then he stepped inside, closing the door behind him. "Frankly, no."

Fuck, he knew. He fucking knew. I had no idea how he knew, but he fucking knew. "Look," I blurted. "Oliver. Whatever Bridge has told you, it's very out of context."

Walking slowly and a little unsteadily, Oliver pulled a chair over and sank down onto it. It was about the gravest I'd ever seen him. And I'd seen him at his father's funeral.

"Oliver," I began, wanting to go into damage-limitation mode but still not sure what the damage was or how to limit it.

"Lucien."

It wasn't exactly a reply because I'd barely said anything. And it wasn't exactly an interruption because I hadn't been saying anything else. If I was lucky, we'd be able to pass the time until the ceremony just saying each other's names back and forth in tones of increasing concern.

Unfortunately, Oliver thwarted that plan by putting his head in his hands and starting to cry in that quiet, desperate way that people did when they were beyond wrecked.

I was going to kill Bridge. I was going to kill Bridge with a spoon. How had she ever thought this was going to help? Unless this was option four, in which case I had literally asked for it.

"Oliver," I said again, not quite managing to get out of the saying-names space. And since I was kind of already on my knees, I crawled over in what I hoped was consoling rather than flat-out weird way. "It's going to be okay. I love you and I want to be with you and I'm ready to go through with this."

Oliver sobbed. "Please don't."

Oh God. Oh God. Oh God. I'd ruined my boyfriend. I'd ruined my boyfriend on the morning of our fucking wedding. I patted his knee like that was going to be any help at all. "Look, I know I can be flaky sometimes, and I get in my head, but I really am all in. I'm all in *on you.*"

At last, Oliver looked up. His eyes were red and swollen—he apparently hadn't slept any better than I had. Which was weird when you set it against his wedding suit, which was formal to the point of vintage and immaculate in ways that neither of us seemed to be feeling right now. "I mean it, Lucien. I need you to stop."

"But I'm trying to tell you that it's all right. That whatever happens we—"

"I can't marry you."

The words made no sense. Like traffic lights in the rain. Like this blur of colour that took a moment to a moment to resolve into distinct shades of red and amber and green.

I. Can't. Marry. You.

What.

The.

Fuck.

I'd been up all last night worrying about this wanker's

feelings, and here he was doing to me exactly what I had, with great maturity and compassion, decided I couldn't possibly do to him. Lurching to my feet, I grabbed the wastepaper basket and upended it over Oliver's head, showering him in a confetti of old receipts, chocolate wrappers, and those little paper circles from the bottom of hole punches. "You bastard. You utter bastard."

"I'm aware," he said with far too much dignity for a man with a Crunchie wrapper on his shoulder, "that this is selfish and that…" He had to stop because he got all choked up again, for which—given the circumstances—I had zero sympathy. Well, maybe one sympathy. Make it one point five. "And that," he went on, "I'm probably going to lose you."

I was trying to hold on to my anger because the alternative was collapsing on the floor in a pool of broken heart and sad feels. "Yes, Oliver. Leaving me at the altar might just do that."

"I'm sorry," he said, voice breaking. "I'm so so sorry."

Deciding that avoiding the floor was delaying the inevitable, I crumbled down beside him. "Why didn't you say something sooner?" I asked him. And myself as well.

"Because I love you. And, fully acknowledging the irony of this"—with an attempt at composure, he plucked a discarded treasury tag from his collar—"I was afraid of losing you."

It was getting hard to stay angry because my relationship was dissolving, Oliver was falling apart, and I—let's be honest—was kind of being a massive hypocrite. "Well, it's good that you appreciate the irony," I told him, "because you picked a weird strategy."

"And an ineffective one," he agreed.

I got it. I couldn't admit it, but I got it. "I don't suppose it occurred to you to say no when I proposed?"

"How could I?" He gave me this devastated, half-pleading look. "I know what it cost you to ask me, and I know what it meant." For a moment, he seemed unable to go on. He just sat there breathing and looking sad. "I didn't want to hurt you."

"Yeah." I prodded the wastepaper basket with my toe and watched it roll across the floor, then roll a little way back as what was left of the contents settled on the bottom. "Nice of you in theory. Not super great in practice."

"I'm sorry," said Oliver again. "I don't think I understood quite how wrong this would feel."

The last stubborn coffee grounds of my anger vanished down the emotional plughole. Because it *had* felt wrong, and we'd both known it. I just wasn't sure who'd fucked up worse: me by doing nothing or him by doing something at the last possible second. "While I'm not going to say I disagree, I will say dumping me at the altar feels pretty wrong too."

Standing, Oliver collected the wastepaper basket and set it carefully back in its place. Perhaps it was the only thing in the room he knew how to fix. "I know how badly I've hurt you, Lucien. But"—he returned to his seat—"would you truly rather I married you? Even if it would make both of us miserable?"

I imagined the room outside, bristling with our friends, family, and work colleagues I would rather not have invited. How they would all be sitting there, waiting for us to prove our relationship was just as good as theirs. And I remembered last night, standing on the Millennium Bridge with my best friend, trying not to throw up at the thought of letting Oliver down. "Yes." My voice rose, in pitch if not in volume. "Because that's the polite thing to do. I mean, I didn't want to marry you either, but I was going to go through with it because I'm a great person and I didn't want to embarrass you."

A little pause. "Pardon?" said Oliver.

Welp. There went the moral high ground. "Nothing."

"Did you just say," asked Oliver, "that you didn't want to marry me either?"

"That's not the point. The point is I love you so much I was willing to do it anyway."

Twitching out his exquisitely chosen pocket square, Oliver dried his eyes. "Well, that's very flattering. But clearly an abysmal idea."

"Whereas breaking up on our wedding day is a fucking corker."

I drew my knees up to my chest and hid my face against them. This was, like, the worst day of my life. Even worse than the day I passed a newsstand and realised my entire relationship with Miles was now a tell-all story in the tabloids. At least then there'd been a clear villain. Now I was being left at the altar by a genuinely wonderful guy for reasons that were—

Actually...

"Hey," I said. "Hang on. Why *don't* you want to marry me?"

He gave me a challenging look. "Why don't *you* want to marry *me*?"

"Oh, no you don't." I wagged a finger at him. "I'm a *mess*. I'm *obviously* going to have second thoughts about anything that looks even a little bit like commitment. You, though, you fucking *love* responsibility. What's wrong with me?"

"There's nothing wrong with you." He vanished briefly behind his pocket square, emerging again slightly tearstained. "Well, there's quite a lot wrong with you. There's quite a lot wrong with everybody. But my life is infinitely better with you in it."

"And yet." I tried not to sound bitter. I failed hard.

"It's marriage, Lucien." He paused for a long moment. "I know you think I'm very...conventional. You've told me so repeatedly."

"No," I protested. "We discussed this, and we agreed you were a Moomin jigsaw."

"Then consider this part of my Moomin jigsawness."

At that moment, the nice humanist lady we'd got to do our

nondenominational, queer-friendly ceremony stuck her head through the door. "Ten minutes, guys."

Oliver and I stared at each other blankly.

"Great," I told her, giving the least convincing thumbs-up in the history of primates.

Her gaze travelled over the scattering of wastepaper and the two men who were blatantly still crying. "Everything all right?"

"Absolutely." My voice came out like a public service announcement from the thirties. "What could possibly be un-all-right?"

"Okay." The nice humanist lady began a somewhat hasty retreat. "I'm just next door if you need anything."

"Bugger," said Oliver quietly.

I peeled myself off the floor and a made a futile attempt to, in every sense of the word, groom myself. "Well. I guess we'd better head on out there and tell everybody we know that our relationship is a great big joke."

"Lucien." Oliver caught my wrist with unexpected urgency. "Can we... Can I say something first?"

His fingers on my skin were torturously familiar. "I mean... do you have to?"

"Yes."

Part of me wanted to tell him no. That he had no right to ask this of me. But he kind of did. I shrugged. "I guess you've got ten minutes."

He looked briefly flustered, like he'd just taken over the case and the court had denied him recess. "About marriage and the... the Moomin jigsaw."

"Clock's ticking, Oliver."

"I know I don't like rainbows," he said in an incredible rush, "but that doesn't mean I feel represented by the trappings of heterosexuality either. And I know that, technically speaking, marriage is not an inherently straight institution. The thing is, it feels that way to me. It always has. And I'm not sure how to make it...not. And I don't think I want to."

This would have been a lot to take in, even if we weren't on an eight-minute countdown. "You loved Alex and Miffy's wedding. You were in *your element.*"

"Yes, because I wasn't supposed to feel part of it. I was supposed to watch it happen to other people. I enjoy going to the theatre. It doesn't mean I feel an intense desire to be an actor."

I glanced at the door. Then back at Oliver. "Is this going somewhere? Or do you want my last memory of my relationship to be a lecture on the social thingy paradigm of marriage."

"That's what I'm trying to say." Oliver's grip on my wrist tightened so abruptly he nearly pulled me into his lap. "I don't want this to be your last memory of our relationship. I still want to be with you. I want to be with you *desperately.* I want to be with you more than I've ever wanted anything. I just don't want it to be within a framework of...of...the social thingy paradigm of marriage."

This was so typical of Oliver. Not only did he want to dump me at the altar and still go out with me, he wanted me to reassess my entire worldview at the same time. "But...but we were about to get *married.* We can't go from being married back to *dating.* That's...that's not how it works."

"Which is why," declared Oliver, "marriage will always feel straight to me. Because it presumes that a relationship is only valid if it follows a pattern that for most of our lives we were totally excluded from."

Did we have time for this? Was five minutes and counting before we were meant to be getting married the ideal window to debate the role of same-sex marriage within the wider context of queer self-expression? "Okay. Except now we *can* be included. So shouldn't we be, y'know, *trying* to be?"

Oliver shrugged. "For some people, absolutely. But for me, it feels like a framework I didn't create and can't control that I'm expected to impose on my own life."

"And that's why we can't get married?" I asked. Because, oddly enough, I didn't find this very comforting. "You love me and you want to be with me. You just don't want to do it in the way nearly all our friends have done?"

He stood, drawing me close with the lightest tug on my wrist. I don't know why I went—given I still strongly suspected I was angry at him—but I did. "Is that so unthinkable?"

"I–I don't know." I was tired enough and emotional enough that my brain was beginning to turn into an eel sandwich. "And I only have three minutes to work it out."

I'd been staring at the numbers on my phone, but then Oliver gently turned my face to his. "Lucien," he said softly. "You know you are the truest thing I have ever dared choose for myself. And we are the only thing I've ever had that I haven't let other people define for me."

And, suddenly, for the longest-shortest second of my life I didn't feel tired anymore. Or confused or scared. Because Oliver loved me.

Oliver really loved me. And in this way that was just ours.

"And"—my voice was a little shaky—"that's why you're leaving me at the altar? Because you want to be with me so much?"

"It's unconventional, I confess." His eyes glimmered with something that might have been laughter or might have been a few stray tears. "But then you've never been a conventional person. And I'm...perhaps not as conventional as I thought I was."

"You're a mess," I told him.

"Oh, a complete one. But I'm your mess, Lucien. And always will be. If..." He hesitated, his stern mouth softening in that way that felt very particularly mine. "If you still want me."

How could anyone not want Oliver Blackwood? Unlike Bridge, I'd never bothered to imagine what it might be like to be proposed to. But I couldn't imagine it feeling better than this.

"Fine," I told him. "Since you asked so nicely, I'll not marry you."

And I guess the lack of sleep and the wedding-day stress and the whole not getting married after all had finally caught up with Oliver. Because he pulled me tightly into his arms and started laughing. "Lucien O'Donnell, you have made me the happiest of men."

There was a knock on the door, and the nice humanist minister stuck her head briefly back in. "One minute, guys."

"We'll be right out," I called from where my head was buried in the crook of Oliver's neck.

I don't know if we actually waited a minute, but then Oliver gently untangled us, took my hand, and led me through to face all the people who we loved and who loved us and who we'd massively inconvenienced for no reason.

Mum, Judy, and Eugenie were in the front row, two of the three doing an excellent job of not licking the other guests. The Blackwood contingent was on the other side, Mia looking genuinely happy to be there, Miriam looking like social expectation in a cream dress. A couple of rows back, I caught sight of Bridge, wearing an enormous hat and already crying on Tom's shoulder. The James Royce-Royces, of course, were far more interested in Baby J than anything that could possibly be happening around them. And from there it was just a supportive blur of older friends, nearish relations, and the coworkers who'd insisted on coming.

At the front of the room, our best men were waiting for us. Priya, in deference to the occasion, had worn her formal Docs. And the moment she laid eyes on us, she gave me the oddest little smirk, like she knew something was up. Like she'd probably always known.

As we entered—awkwardly in advance of our own music— there was a sudden silence. I didn't realise quite how many people were in my life until they were all in one smallish room staring at me and wondering what the fuck I was doing.

My hand wilted in Oliver's. Making a wedding happen had been bad enough. I had no idea how to make one unhappen.

"Thank you for coming," said Oliver, as if he did this kind of thing all the time. Which, between this and his dad's funeral, he almost did. "I'm afraid Lucien and I have decided that marriage isn't right for either of us, and we'd rather be together on our own terms. Please do enjoy the party and make the most of the open bar."

And then we ran.

Hand in hand.

Up the aisle.

Out the doors.

Through the venue.

And into the sudden storm that had turned a busy London street into... Well, okay, it was still a busy London street. But the pavement was shining silver and the raindrops were playing our tune and I was in Oliver's arms, and we were laughing and kissing, and all around us the passers-by were putting up umbrellas in every colour of the rainbow.

Q&A WITH ALEXIS HALL AND CATHY BERNER

Why did you return to the world of Luc and Oliver and their friends? Was that always the plan?

Err, it definitely wasn't the plan. I've sort of just reached the point in my career that I can sell more than one book at a time, but in general I very much work on the assumption that things will be standalones unless stated otherwise. I think the one exception is probably the Arden St Ives series, which was sold as a complete trilogy.

Plus, there isn't much precedent for direct sequels in the rom-com subgenre. So, y'know, this could be a terrible disaster. Watch this space, I guess?

In general, I try to write romances that feel, to me, like a complete arc—even if I'm leaving the characters in a HFN space rather than an HEA space. With Luc and Oliver, though, I sincerely felt there was more story to tell. We see them grow a lot over the course of the first book but it's clear they have a long way to go both in terms of who they are as people and how they fit into the world.

And, once I started thinking about it, I realised I did have something quite specific I wanted to do with *Husband Material*. So...here we are.

When writing this sequel to *Boyfriend Material,* **how did you decide which characters got "screen time"? Were there any characters you wished you could spend more time with?**

I think part of it is that both *Boyfriend Material* and *Husband Material* are told from Luc's POV, so his friends are necessarily going to be more central. I do wish there'd been a bit more space for Oliver's friends in this book (Jennifer and Peter both get a cameo, and I think Brian gets a mention) but given the focus of the book is on weddings and most of Oliver's friends are quite pointedly already married there wasn't a natural place for them.

Husband Material **followed an interesting structure. Did you have that in mind before you began, or did that develop as the story progressed?**

Nope. I decided going in I was going to blatantly and shamelessly rip off *Four Weddings and a Funeral.* Which is what I'm assuming 'interesting structure' is a polite euphemism for.

Your novels often veer from hilarity to pointed social commentary (a great example is Ana with one N). Do you have those issues in mind when you start writing, or do they just sort of pop up?

This makes it sound like I don't know what I'm doing, but they do just sort of pop up. I mean, I think what Luc and Oliver have going on in terms of their various issues and their relationships to the intersecting branches of their identities is sort of baked into the characters and therefore baked into the premise. But a lot of the rest of the time it's sort of almost circumstantial.

Ana With One N is a good example of this. Like, in a sense, she came about because part of Rhys's deal is that he tends to serial date and so he always brings a different woman to every CRAPP-related event. And, obviously, I didn't want these people to be faceless ciphers, so I needed to get Rhys's date a fairly clear personality, backstory, and worldview.

That's kind of what happened with Tyler as well: I wanted Luc to look at art during his own gender non-specific bird party and to have a healthy, flirty encounter with a guy (to offset all the unhealthy encounters he's had previously). And that just took me down the "what kind of person would know Priya" rabbit hole, which would be someone cool, interesting, arty, and a bit angry. And from there you get Tyler.

What's one thing that both Oliver and Luc might have in the refrigerator at their flats? (Does such an item even exist?)

Margarine. It's a weird crossover point between "random crap that even people who never cook have to put on bread" and "stuff that's actually quite useful and vegan."

Do your fans create some of the best fan art in the world? The correct answer is YES. What are your thoughts on people creating art or stories from your own work?

I am incredibly blessed in terms of the fan art people share with me. It's genuinely humbling to feel you inspire that kind of thing. In general, I'm completely happy for people to create art or stories or whatever they like from my work (although, as always, blah blah legal handwave reserve the right etc.). I am aware that there's some written fanwork out there too, but obviously I don't look at that because it goes to some very complicated places. I don't think there's the same culture of sharing written fanwork as there is with fan art and me seeking it out would just be awkward for everybody. I think the difference is art is a specifically different medium, so the types of work aren't going to compete or conflict or anything like that.

What's your favorite Richard Curtis movie?

It's got to be *Notting Hill*. It's the most coherent out of the three big rom-coms, I think. I mean, *Four Weddings and a Funeral* is iconic but flawed (like Hugh Grant and Andie McDowell meet... three times, I think?) and *Love Actually* is a whole bag of complicated. I will say, I have a soft spot for *About Time*—except the romance in that is a bit of a mess because using your time travel powers to date a girl is never not going to be creepy. It's almost like the rom-com bit is this bolted-on element secondary to the story that the movie actually wants to tell about a guy's quite melancholy relationship with his dad (the dad in question being Bill Nighy which makes everything better).

What are you allowed to tell us about any more books in this world?

Well, I'm not sure what I'm allowed to tell you. But both of them involve side-characters who briefly pop up in *Husband Material*. *The Amnesia Plot* (working title) is Jonathan's story, though he's not the narrator: basically, I've always wanted to do an amnesia book because it's such a trope, so this is my amnesia book. And, also, accidentally my holiday book? Because clearly a holiday book from someone who is at best ambivalent about holidays is going to be great. The next book is Tyler's story, which I haven't quite worked out the POV for yet...and in my head I'm calling it *Himbo de Bergerac* and that's all I'm going to say. I don't think they'll actually let me call it *Himbo de Bergerac*, but I wish they would. (I mean, I don't really. Okay, maybe a little bit).

Cathy Berner, a Congressional staffer turned librarian turned bookseller, works at Blue Willow Bookshop, an independent bookstore on the west side of Houston, Texas. Her colleagues know her fondness for all things romance—when she's talking about a novel she really loves, her voice will rise in both pitch and volume and her hands will start flapping. She's read romance novels since she was a teenager and her love for them has not diminished. Find her on Instagram @catberner or Twitter @bibliopinions.

Blue Willow Bookshop is West Houston's favorite bookshop, serving our wonderful community of readers with opinionated service and fantastic author events since 1996. Find them on social media @bluewillowbooks.

ACKNOWLEDGMENTS

In full, well, acknowledgment of the fact that I always write the same acknowledgments, I would like to extend my gratitude to: my amazing agent, Courtney Miller-Callihan; the fabulous team at Sourcebooks, especially Mary Altman, my very patient editor, and Stefani Sloma, my even more patient marketing type person; my indispensable assistant, Mary (not to be confused with Editor!Mary); Elizabeth Turner Stokes, whose glorious covers are, I'm convinced, responsible for about 90 percent of my sales; and also, y'know, family and friends and stuff.

ABOUT THE AUTHOR

Alexis Hall writes books in the southeast of England, where he lives entirely on a diet of tea and Jaffa Cakes. You can find him at quicunquevult.com, on Twitter @quicunquevult, on Instagram at instagram.com/quicunquevult, and on Facebook at facebook.com /quicunquevult.